ONE OF US

The teacher crossed his arms. "Go ahead, Amy. No need to holler, though. Why do you hate them?"

"They're monsters. I hate them because they're monsters."

Mr. Benson turned and hacked at the blackboard with a piece of chalk: MONSTRUM, a VIOLATION OF NATURE. From MONEO, which means TO WARN. In this case, a warning God is angry. Punishment for taboo.

"Teratogenesis is nature out of whack," he said. "It rewrote the body. Changed the rules. Monsters, maybe. But does a monster have to be evil?"

ONE OF US

CRAIG DiLOUIE

ONE
An imprint of
Little, Brown Book Group
Carmelite House
50 Victoria Embankment
London EC4Y 0DZ

An Hachette UK Company
www.hachette.co.uk

www.littlebrown.co.uk

www.orbitbooks.net

ORBIT

First published in Great Britain in 2018 by Orbit

1 3 5 7 9 10 8 6 4 2

Copyright © 2018 by 2018 by Craig DiLouie

Excerpt from *Blackfish City* by Sam J. Miller
Copyright © 2018 by Sam J. Miller

The moral right of the author has been asserted.

A CIP catalogue record for this book
is available from the British Library.

ISBN 978-0-356-51097-2

Printed and bound in Great Britain by
Clays Ltd, St Ives plc

Papers used by Orbit are from well-managed forests
and other responsible sources.

For Chris Marrs and my beautiful children,
whose love is my daily bread

1984

MONSTERS

We walk on two legs not on four.
To walk on four legs breaks the law.
—Oingo Boingo,
"No Spill Blood,"
Good for Your Soul (1983)

One

On the principal's desk, a copy of *Time*. A fourteen-year-old girl smiled on the cover. Pigtails tied in blue ribbon. Freckles and big white teeth. Rubbery, barbed appendages extending from her eye sockets.

Under that, a single word: WHY?

Why did this happen?

Or, maybe, why did the world allow a child like this to live?

What Dog wanted to know was why she smiled.

Maybe it was just reflex, seeing somebody pointing a camera at her. Maybe she liked the attention, even if it wasn't the nice kind.

Maybe, if only for a few seconds, she felt special.

The Georgia sun glared through filmy barred windows. A steel fan whirred in the corner, barely moving the warm, thick air. Out the window, Dog spied the old rusted pickup sunk in a riot of wildflowers. Somebody loved it once then parked it here and left it to die. If Dog owned it, he would have kept driving and never stopped.

The door opened. The government man came in wearing a black suit, white shirt, and blue-and-yellow tie. His shiny shoes clicked across the grimy floor. He sat in Principal Willard's creaking chair and lit a cigarette. Dropped a file folder on the desk and studied Dog through a blue haze.

"They call you Dog," he said.

"Yes, sir, they do. The other kids, I mean."

Dog growled when he talked but took care to form each word right. The teachers made sure he spoke good and proper. Brain once told him these signs of humanity were the only thing keeping the children alive.

"Your Christian name is Enoch. Enoch Davis Bryant."

"Yes, sir."

Enoch was the name the teachers at the Home used. Brain said it was his slave name. Dog liked hearing it, though. He felt lucky to have one. His mama had loved him enough to at least do that for him. Many parents had named their kids XYZ before abandoning them to the Homes.

"I'm Agent Shackleton," the government man said through another cloud of smoke. "Bureau of Teratological Affairs. You know the drill, don't you, by now?"

Every year, the government sent somebody to ask the kids questions. Trying to find out if they were still human. Did they want to hurt people, ever have carnal thoughts about normal girls and boys, that sort of thing.

"I know the drill," Dog said.

"Not this year," the man told him. "This year is different. I'm here to find out if you're special."

"I don't quite follow, sir."

Agent Shackleton planted his elbows on the desk. "You're a ward of the state. More than a million of you. Living high on the hog for the past fourteen years in the Homes. Some of you are beginning to show certain capabilities."

"Like what kind?"

"I saw a kid once who had gills and could breathe underwater. Another who could hear somebody talking a mile away."

"No kidding," Dog said.

"That's right."

"You mean like a superhero."

"Yeah. Like Spider-Man, if Spider-Man half looked like a real spider."

"I never heard of such a thing," Dog said.

"If you, Enoch, have capabilities, you could prove you're worth the food you eat. This is your opportunity to pay it back. Do you follow me?"

"Sure, I guess."

Satisfied, Shackleton sat back in the chair and planted his feet on the desk. He set the file folder on his thighs, licked his finger, and flipped it open.

"Pretty good grades," the man said. "You got your math and spelling. You stay out of trouble. All right. Tell me what you can do. Better yet, show me something."

"What I can do, sir?"

"You do for me, I can do plenty for you. Take you to a special place."

Dog glanced at the red door at the side of the room before returning his gaze to Shackleton. Even looking at it was bad luck. The red door led downstairs to a basement room called Discipline, where the problem kids went.

He'd never been inside it, but he knew the stories. All the kids knew them. Principal Willard wanted them to know. It was part of their education.

He said, "What kind of place would that be?"

"A place with lots of food and TV. A place nobody can ever bother you."

Brain always said to play along with the normals so you didn't get caught up in their system. They wrote the rules in such a way to trick you into Discipline. More than that, though, Dog wanted to prove himself. He wanted to be special.

"Well, I'm a real fast runner. Ask anybody."

"That's your special talent. You can run fast."

"Real fast. Does that count?"

The agent smiled. "Running fast isn't special. It isn't special at all."

"Ask anybody how fast I run. Ask the—"

"You're not special. You'll never be special, Dog."

"I don't know what you want from me, sir."

Shackleton's smile disappeared along with Dog's file. "I want you to get the hell out of my sight. Send the next monster in on your way out."

Two

Pollution. Infections. Drugs. Radiation. All these things, Mr. Benson said from the chalkboard, can produce mutations in embryos.

A bacterium caused the plague generation. The other kids, the plague kids, who lived in the Homes.

Amy Green shifted in her desk chair. The top of her head was itching again. Mama said she'd worry it bald if she kept scratching at it. She settled on twirling her long, dark hair around her finger and tugging. Savored the needles of pain along her scalp.

"The plague is a sexually transmitted disease," Mr. Benson told the class.

She already knew part of the story from American History and from what Mama told her. The plague started in 1968, two years before she was born, back when love was still free. Then the disease named teratogenesis raced around the world, and the plague children came.

One out of ten thousand babies born in 1968 were monsters, and most died. One in six in 1969, and half of these died. One in three in 1970, the year scientists came up with a test to see if you had it. Most of them lived. After a neo-natal nurse got arrested for killing thirty babies in Texas, the survival rate jumped.

More than a million monster babies screaming to be fed. By then, Congress had already funded the Home system.

Fourteen years later, and still no cure. If you caught the germ, the only surefire way to stop spreading it was absti-nence, which they taught right here in health class. If you got pregnant with it, abortion was mandatory.

Amy flipped her textbook open and bent to sniff its cheesy new-book smell. Books, sharpened pencils, lined paper; she associated their bitter scents with school. The page showed a drawing of a woman's reproductive system. The baby comes out there. Sitting next to her, her boyfriend Jake glanced at the page and smiled, his face reddening. Like her, fascinated and embarrassed by it all.

In junior high, sex ed was mandatory, no ifs or buts. Amy and her friends were stumbling through puberty. Tampons, budding breasts, aching midnight thoughts, long conversa-tions about what boys liked and what they wanted.

She already had a good idea what they wanted. Girls always complimented her about how pretty she was. Boys stared at her when she walked down the hall. Everybody so nice to her all the time. She didn't trust any of it.

When she stood naked in the mirror, she only saw flaws. Amy spotted a zit last week and stared at it for an hour, hat-ing her ugliness. It took her over an hour every morning to get ready for school. She didn't leave the house until she looked perfect.

She flipped the page again. A monster grinned up at her. She slammed the book shut.

Mr. Benson asked if anybody in the class had actually seen

a plague child. Not on TV or in a magazine, but up close and personal.

A few kids raised their hands. Amy kept hers planted on her desk.

"I have two big goals for you kids this year," the teacher said. "The main thing is teach you how to avoid spreading the disease. We'll be talking a lot about safe sex and all the regulations about whether and how you do it. How to get tested and how to access a safe abortion. I also aim to help you become accustomed to the plague children already born and who are now the same age as you."

For Amy's entire life, the plague children had lived in group homes out in the country, away from people. One was located just eight miles from Huntsville, though it might as well have been on the moon. The monsters never came to town. Out of sight meant out of mind, though one could never entirely forget them.

"Let's start with the plague kids," Mr. Benson said. "What do all y'all think about them? Tell the truth."

Rob Rowland raised his hand. "They ain't human. They're just animals."

"Is that right? Would you shoot one and eat it? Mount its head on your wall?"

The kids laughed as they pictured Rob so hungry he would eat a monster. Rob was obese, smart, and sweated a lot, one of the unpopular kids.

Amy shuddered with sudden loathing. "I hate them something awful."

The laughter died. Which was good, because the plague wasn't funny.

The teacher crossed his arms. "Go ahead, Amy. No need to holler, though. Why do you hate them?"

"They're monsters. I hate them because they're monsters."

Mr. Benson turned and hacked at the blackboard with a piece of chalk: MONSTRUM, a VIOLATION OF NATURE. From MONEO, which means TO WARN. In this case, a warning God is angry. Punishment for taboo.

"Teratogenesis is nature out of whack," he said. "It rewrote the body. Changed the rules. Monsters, maybe. But does a monster have to be evil? Is a human being what you look like, or what you do? What makes a man a man?"

Bonnie Fields raised her hand. "I saw one once. I couldn't even tell if it was a boy or girl. I didn't stick around to get to know it."

"But did you see it as evil?"

"I don't know about that, but looking the way some of them do, I can't imagine why the doctors let them all live. It would have been a mercy to let them die."

"Mercy on us," somebody behind Amy muttered.

The kids laughed again.

Sally Albod's hand shot up. "I'm surprised at all y'all being so scared. I see the kids all the time at my daddy's farm. They're weird, but there ain't nothing to them. They work hard and don't make trouble. They're fine."

"That's good, Sally," the teacher said. "I'd like to show all y'all something."

He opened a cabinet and pulled out a big glass jar. He set it on his desk. Inside, a baby floated in yellowish fluid. A tiny penis jutted between its legs. Its little arms grasped at nothing. It had a single slitted eye over a cleft where its nose should be.

The class sucked in its breath as one. Half the kids recoiled as the rest leaned forward for a better look. Fascination and revulsion. Amy alone didn't move. She sat frozen, shot through with the horror of it.

She hated the little thing. Even dead, she hated it.

"This is Tony," Mr. Benson said. "And guess what, he isn't one of the plague kids. Just some poor boy born with a birth defect. About three percent of newborns are born this way every year. It causes one out of five infant deaths."

Tony, some of the kids chuckled. They thought it weird it had a name.

"We used to believe embryos developed in isolation in the uterus," the teacher said. "Then back in the Sixties, a company sold thalidomide to pregnant women in Germany to help them with morning sickness. Ten thousand kids born with deformed limbs. Half died. What did scientists learn from that? Anybody?"

"A medicine a lady takes can hurt her baby even if it don't hurt her," Jake said.

"Bingo," Mr. Benson said. "Medicine, toxins, viruses, we call these things environmental factors. Most times, though, doctors have no idea why a baby like Tony is born. It just happens, like a dice roll. So is Tony a monster? What about a kid who's retarded, or born with legs that don't work? Is a kid in a wheelchair a monster too? A baby born deaf or blind?"

He got no takers. The class sat quiet and thoughtful. Satisfied, Mr. Benson carried the jar back to the cabinet. More gasps as baby Tony bobbed in the fluid, like he was trying to get out.

The teacher frowned as he returned the jar to its shelf. "I'm surprised just this upsets you. If this gets you so worked up, how will you live with the plague children? When they're adults, they'll have the same rights as you. They'll live among you."

Amy stiffened at her desk, neck clenched with tension at the idea. A question formed in her mind. "What if we don't want to live with them?"

Mr. Benson pointed at the jar. "This baby is you. And something not you. If Tony had survived, he would be different, yes. But he would be you."

"I think we have a responsibility to them," Jake said.

"Who's we?" Amy said.

His contradicting her had stung a little, but she knew how Jake had his own mind and liked to argue. He wore leather jackets, black T-shirts advertising obscure bands, ripped jeans. Troy and Michelle, his best friends, were Black.

He was popular because being unpopular didn't scare him. Amy liked him for that, the way he flouted junior high's iron rules. The way he refused to suck up to her like the other boys all did.

"You know who I mean," he said. "The human race. We made them, and that gives us responsibility. It's that simple."

"I didn't make anything. The older generation did. Why are they my problem?"

"Because they have it bad. We all know they do. Imagine being one of them."

"I don't want things to be bad for them," Amy said. "I really don't. I just don't want them around me. Why does that make me a bad person?"

"I never said it makes you a bad person," Jake said.

Archie Gaines raised his hand. "Amy has a good point, Mr. Benson. They're a mess to stomach, looking at them. I mean, I can live with it, I guess. But all this love and understanding is a lot to ask."

"Fair enough," Mr. Benson said.

Archie turned to look back at Amy. She nodded her thanks. His face lit up with a leering smile. He believed he'd rescued her and now she owed him.

She gave him a practiced frown to shut down his hopes. He turned away as if slapped.

"I'm just curious about them," Jake said. "More curious than scared. It's like you said, Mr. Benson. However they look, they're still our brothers. I wouldn't refuse help to a blind man, I guess I wouldn't to a plague kid neither."

The teacher nodded. "Okay. Good. That's enough discussion for today. We're getting somewhere, don't you think? Again, my goal for you kids this year is two things. One is to get used to the plague children. Distinguishing between a book and its cover. The other is to learn how to avoid making more of them."

Jake turned to Amy and winked. Her cheeks burned, all her annoyance with him forgotten.

She hoped there was a lot more sex ed and a lot less monster talk in her future. While Mr. Benson droned on, she glanced through the first few pages of her book. A chapter headline caught her eye: KISSING.

She already knew the law regarding sex. Germ or no germ, the legal age of consent was still fourteen in the State of Georgia. But another law said if you wanted to have sex, you had to get tested for the germ first. If you were under eighteen, your parents had to give written consent for the testing.

Kissing, though, that you could do without any fuss. It said so right here in black and white. You could do it all you wanted. Her scalp tingled at the thought. She tugged at her hair and savored the stabbing needles.

She risked a hungering glance at Jake's handsome profile. Though she hoped one day to go further than that, she could never do more than kissing. She could never know what it'd be like to scratch the real itch.

Nobody but her mama knew Amy was a plague child.

Three

Goof saw comedy in everything. He liked to look on the sunny side. He enjoyed seeing the world differently than other people, which wasn't hard considering his face was upside-down. When he smiled, people asked him what was wrong. When he was sad, they thought he was laughing at them.

He raised his toothbrush in front of the bunkhouse mirrors. The gesture looked like a salute. "Ready to brush, sir."

He commenced brushing.

"Hurry up," the other kids growled, waiting their turn.

Goof clenched his teeth and brushed faster but for twice as long. "'ook at me, I am b'ushing my 'eet' 'eal 'ast."

His antics had earned him his nickname and gained him some status in a community sorely lacking in entertainment. He liked to make the kids laugh. When that failed, annoying them to make himself laugh.

Then Tiny, the biggest kid at the Home, stomped into the bathroom. He elbowed one of the smaller kids aside and took his place at the mirrors.

Goof shut up and tilted his head to gargle and spit. He

could only annoy so far, particularly around kids like Tiny. The Home forbade violence, but the teachers looked the other way as long as nobody disrupted its workings. If you went to a teacher to complain about a kid punching you, you were liable to get a smack and be told it was part of your education.

No matter. He'd done enough for one day. Today had been fun. The Bureau had sent out an agent for the annual interviews. Goof had tried a self-deprecating creeper joke that fell on deaf ears, the agent being the earnest type. Having failed to make him laugh, Goof decided to be annoying the best way he knew how.

"I'm Agent Shackleton," the government man had said while lighting a cigarette. "Bureau of Teratological Affairs. You—"

"Know the drill, don't you by now," Goof finished. "I sure do, sir."

The man scowled. "All right, that's good. This year's different, Jeff. I'm here to find out—"

"If you're special," Goof said. "No, I ain't, I'm sorry to say."

The man's frown deepened. "How do you keep—"

"Doing that? I don't know what you mean."

"You keep—"

"Finishing my sentences."

"Are you aware—"

"You keep doing that? Doing what, sir?"

Then he'd howled with laughter, a grating sound the teachers once told him sounded like a mule getting screwed where the sun don't shine.

Agent Shackleton had smiled like he was in on the joke. "Thank you, Jeff. We're done here."

Goof had discovered his gift about six months ago. He'd finished Ms. Oliver's sentences all through history class. Her jaw practically hit the floor. Everybody was cracking up. They couldn't believe it.

Just wait until they all heard he'd stuck it to a Bureau man. He was about to become a hero of legend around here.

He undressed and climbed into his bunk with a satisfied sigh. Around him, the kids chattered as they got ready for bed. The old frame creaked as he settled on the grimy mattress. The lights clicked off minutes later.

Hero of legend, he thought as he drifted into sleep.

A hand shook him awake. "Rise and shine."

The room was dark. It was still night.

"What's that? What's going on?"

He recognized Mr. Gaines standing at one side of bed, Mr. Bowie on the other. Teachers from the Home school.

"Get your duds on," Mr. Gaines told him. "We're taking a walk."

Goof hopped down and pulled a T-shirt and overalls onto his skinny frame. He laced up his weathered boots. "If this is about the whatever, I'm sorry."

The men didn't laugh. There was nothing funny about this. When teachers woke you up at night, you were headed to Discipline. The other kids either kept snoring or lay rigid in their bunks, pretending to be asleep.

"Let's go," Mr. Gaines said.

"I didn't do anything, honest."

"That's what they all say."

The problem kids went to Discipline. The wild ones who broke the rules. No windows. A single chair bolted to the concrete floor, under a bare light bulb.

"I was just kidding around with the Bureau man," Goof

pleaded. "I didn't mean nothing by it. Come on, Mr. Gaines. You know I ain't one of the bad ones."

Mr. Bowie placed a gentle hand on his shoulder and shoved, knocking him off balance. "Move it, shitbird."

Goof stumbled outside on trembling legs. He was rarely outside at this hour and couldn't help looking up. The sky was filled with stars. A great big world out there that didn't care about his fate.

Lights blazed in the big house. Another world, a world of pain, awaited him. Brain had warned him to keep his special talent to himself. He'd said it would get him into the kind of trouble he couldn't get out of. Lots of kids had talents now, and it was important to keep them a secret from the normals. Why didn't he listen?

"Look at him," Mr. Gaines said. "Shaking like a fifty-cent ladder."

"He's sweatin' like a whore in church," Mr. Bowie said.

Goof had heard kids in Discipline sat in the chair facing a big ol' rebel flag. A giant blue X on an angry red field. As if to tell you that you were no longer in the USA but had entered a different country. A secret place with its own rules and customs. A place in history where they could do anything they wanted.

"No," he begged. "Please don't take me there."

"Man up, boy," Mr. Bowie said and gave him another shove.

A black van stood in the driveway in front of the house. Mr. Gaines walked over to it and opened the back doors.

"Your chariot awaits," the teacher said.

"Wait," Goof said. "I ain't going to Discipline?"

"It's your lucky day."

Mr. Gaines waited for him to climb inside and take a seat

in the back. Then he reached up and cuffed one of Goof's hands to a steel bar running along the ceiling. "So long, Jeff. Don't forget to send us a postcard."

Mr. Bowie laughed as the doors slammed shut.

A man in gray overalls started the van. The headlights flashed on, illuminating rusted oil drums stacked by the utility shed.

"Hello, Jeff," said a familiar voice from the passenger seat.

"Mr. Shackleton?"

"We're going to take a long drive. You might as well sleep."

"A drive? Just a drive? Is that true?"

A part of him thought this was all a big joke. The van's doors would click open again, and Mr. Bowie would yank him out and drag him to the big house.

The van pulled away from the Home and started up the dirt track that led to the county road. Goof took a ragged breath and expelled it as a laugh.

As the Home disappeared in the dark, his relief slid headlong into another kind of panic. The Home wasn't a nice place, but it was, well, home.

"Where are we going, sir?"

"Someplace nice," Shackleton said. "You'll like it."

The agent leaned his seat back as far as it went and laid a fedora over his face.

Goof had rode in the back of one of the Home's pickups during farm days, but never inside a van like this. He tried to imagine he was being chauffeured. He was a secret agent on his way to catch a plane to Paris.

The fantasy didn't last. He was still shaking like that fifty-cent ladder.

"What's your name?" he asked the driver.

The man didn't answer. A bug splatted against the windshield.

"Mister, I hope we're stopping soon. I got to pee already." Still no answer.

"Now I can't quit thinking about it," Goof said. "I'm gonna pee my pants soon."

"We'll stop when we stop," Shackleton said from under his hat. "Until then, Jeff, shut your trap and try to get some shut-eye."

Goof fidgeted in his seat. He didn't know how the agent expected him to sleep after the scare he'd just had. He wondered if he'd ever sleep again.

Then his eyes fixed on the agent's fedora, and he fell in love. He'd never seen one like it before except in old movies. He wanted one for himself. Goof pictured walking into the mess hall wearing it, the kids all going nuts.

That's when it hit him.

Goof was on his way to a different world, and he'd probably never again see his friends or home.

Four

Breakfast, the usual slop eaten around wooden tables in the Home's mess hall. Dog picked at his porridge and waited for his friends to show up. Today, they were learning ag science, which meant a day working out at the farm. His favorite thing about school besides Sundays off to spend with his friends.

He wasn't happy about it today, though. He wasn't happy about anything. He hadn't slept well, his mind wild with disappointing thoughts. Birdsong had woken him up early. A family of thrushes outside the window.

The Bureau man had said he wasn't special and never would be. Said he lived high on the hog in the Home. Told him to get the hell out of his sight.

None of it was fair in the least.

Dog's mama had abandoned him when he was just a little baby. Other normals had taken care of him since. Sure, they fed him and kept a roof over his head. But high on the hog it wasn't. Anybody with eyes could see. The Home was run-down and overcrowded, the beds infested. The roof leaked brown water on the floor.

He never asked for any of it. He was unlucky to be born.

The bench groaned as Brain settled his bulk on it. The teachers said Brain looked like a lion fucked a gorilla. His bestial appearance contrasted with his small, delicate hands and eyes glittering with surprising intelligence.

But not special, it seemed. The government didn't take Brain, who was the smartest person he knew. Dog could run fast, faster than Brain, maybe faster than anybody alive, but the Bureau set the bar too high for them all.

Wallee and Mary showed up next and took their seats with their breakfast trays. No surprise they were still here. Wallee was a big sac of blubber that could barely talk. Mary, a stunted and homely girl with an imbecilic face. She was the only kid who didn't have a nickname.

Dog sometimes wondered if she wasn't a plague kid but instead just plain retarded. Brain said maybe the normals stuck anybody they didn't want in the Homes. Everybody they rejected ended up here, from the kids to the teachers. Brain and Dog watched out for her and kept her safe.

"You seen Goof this morning?" Dog said.

"They took him last night after lights out," Brain said.

"Where did they take him?"

"I can't say, Dog."

"The Bureau man said something about a special place."

"I warned him to keep his mouth shut," Brain said.

"You're gonna be next," Dog said, angry that Brain had faked his way out of being taken. "You always talking the way you do. You think you're so—"

He stopped. He didn't know why he was attacking Brain. He was just mad. He was afraid the government would take all his friends, and he would be alone. Left behind. Stuck in the Home the rest of his days, the only one who wasn't special.

Brain's gentle face hardened with shock and hurt.

"Sorry," Dog said. "I don't mean any of that."

"I'm smart enough to shut up when I have to. Goof wasn't."

One of Dog's earliest memories was Brain quizzing him after the Bureau sent out somebody to question the kids. *Tell me what happened*, Brain said at four years old. *What the man asked, what you answered. It's important you tell me exactly what you remember.* Even back then, Brain talked like an adult. Every year since, the same: Brain wanting to know the questions, how they answered. That way, he could blend right in, and they could never single him out.

Which also wasn't fair. Brain *was* special, but he hid it.

"At least he's going somewhere other than here," Dog said.

"Careful what you wish for," Brain said. "For all we know, they kill the special ones. Throw them in a gas chamber. Fear motivates everything they do."

Dog remembered jumping to his feet after the Bureau man told him to get the hell out of his sight. The man's rudeness was like a whip cracking. When he'd jumped, Shackleton went stiff in his chair. The man had been afraid of him, if only for a second. Dog could smell it. It got his dander up.

You don't get to be scared, he'd wanted to shout.

But he'd liked it. Some deep part of him fed on it. He felt strong. A little taste of power for a boy who had none. *You want to be afraid of me, sir? Would you think I was special if I showed you some fear?*

"I just wish I could get out of here," Dog said. "Be a grown-up allowed to do what I want. Work for a living. Watch TV at night. Go to bed when I want."

"What do you want to be when you grow up?" Brain said.

"I'd like to own my own farm like Pa Albod. Grow my own crops. Make an honest living."

Dog planned to work for Pa Albod long enough to buy a plot and become a sharecropper. Then expand his holdings until he had his own farmstead.

Wallee slurped his food. "Want to be sher-iff."

Mary said nothing. She stared off into the blank space where her mind lived most of the time.

"What about you, Mary?" Dog said. "What do you want to be, you can do or be anything."

"Pretty," she said.

"I'd like to be a doctor," Brain said. "But that will never happen. Do you know why they teach us agricultural science four days a week? So we can serve the masters as cheap farm labor the rest of our lives. The only future they'll let us have. Men with no rights, no future. They'll put us on reservations like they did the Creek Indians who used to live in these parts. It'll be just like the Home."

Wallee grimaced. "Not sher-iff?"

"Maybe. Sure, they'll let us police ourselves. Like at Auschwitz."

Wallee's face ballooned into a smug smile. "Sher-iff."

Dog moved the porridge around his bowl as he considered Brain's gloomy prophecy. He didn't want to believe it, though he'd always known it to be true. The only way out was to be special, but he wasn't special. The government man said he wasn't and never would be.

Brain watched Dog eat and wished his friend could understand. But Brain lived in a lonely world in which nobody truly understood him.

Dog would never see the truth until the system crushed him. Chipped away at his humanity until only a monster was left. A monster with nothing to lose.

As for Brain, he'd understood everything within minutes of his birth.

In photographic detail, he remembered the terror of being born. The first thing he heard was his mother's screams. The world bursting in lurid dream colors. Confusing, horrible, wonderful.

A man's blanching face. Wide, watery eyes. The world spun as the doctor presented him to his mother lying in the hospital bed. He stared at her through a blurry squint. She screamed again, saying something he didn't understand. A bolt of love shot through him. He reached out with his little arms to comfort her.

Then the world spun again, and she disappeared forever.

They took him away and put him in the Home. He'd ached with worry. What had they done to his mama? Was she okay? Why couldn't he see her? Later on, the teachers taught him language. That was when he learned what she'd been screaming when the doctor held him squirming in his big hands.

Brain got all the education he ever needed during these first moments of his life. He learned what he was, what they were, and that monsters and men were not meant to exist in the same world. If your own mother hates you and drives you away, why should total strangers love you? From the beginning, the masters understood this fundamental truth. They created separate worlds, one for themselves, another for monsters. The system would not end when the mutagenic reached adulthood. The children would grow up to become free folk living in an invisible cage, with no rights or opportunities. Which meant no real freedom at all.

Dog couldn't understand this now because he thought more with his heart than his mind, and he still had hope. Dog saw the Home as a purgatory to be endured before reaching some promised land. The system would crush that hope out of him. Brain could tell him the truth of their world until he was blue in the face, but some truths people just had to find themselves through experience. And when all Dog's hope had fled, when it was finally dead and gone, only then would he understand. Only then would he know he had nothing and that having nothing meant you had nothing to lose and everything to fight for. A Spartacus will call to them all, and they will rise up to shatter the walls between the worlds.

"What are you smiling about?" Dog said.

"We're all special," Brain said.

"Do you really think so?"

"We don't need them to tell us we are or we aren't."

Now Brain remembered Ms. Oliver showing him a book that had produced another great leap in his understanding of the world. Ms. Oliver had a soft spot for the kids. Black, Yankee, and citified to boot, she knew what it was like to be left outside. Maybe she saw him as Black too because of the color of his skin and curly fur, though his mother was White, and such distinctions didn't matter to monsters. Only one distinction mattered.

He played dumb in class. Being smart got you singled out by the teachers. Talking educated seemed to infuriate them—a bit of irony. *Biggity*, they called it. Ms. Oliver saw right through the act but kept his secret. She brought him contraband books to nourish his intellect. History, political theory, physics, philosophy. He went from fascination to frustration as his mind developed and was able to go even further than the books did. By the age of ten, he'd invented a new branch of mathematics. At eleven, he was toying with advanced theoretical physics.

Then Ms. Oliver brought him the book that changed his life. *Myths and Monsters, Volume I,* by Adam Nowak, hardcover, published in 1967. The Home system didn't allow the mutagenic to read books like this. It banned texts like *Beauty and the Beast, The Island of Dr. Moreau.* Instead, it showed them films like *The Creature from the Black Lagoon.* Anything with plucky normal boys rescuing girls from evil, rampaging beasts. Not for entertainment but education, more social conditioning. Brainwashing. *Know your place, children. Mess with the normals, and you will lose.*

It took Brain only a few minutes to read and store *Myths and Monsters* in his photographic memory.

Then he'd sat satisfied and full, his eyes glazing as he studied the pictures in his mind. A lion with the head and wings of an eagle. An Egyptian with a jackal's head. A woman with snakes for hair, whose very glance turned men to stone.

"You were here before," Ms. Oliver had said. "Do you see that, George?"

George, his slave name. George Hurst.

"Yes, I see," Brain said.

"I think the old stories might be real. Based on things that actually happened."

"We were gods."

"The bacterium that caused you must be old," Ms. Oliver said. "Don't you think?"

"Very old," he agreed. "Perhaps it has always been with us. An evolutionary wild card waiting for its moment to awake."

"There's so much we still don't know about it. Maybe when you grow up, you'll study it and tell us all what it is."

Ms. Oliver was trying to inspire him, convince him to reveal his intellect to the world and put it to good use.

He was inspired. Just not in the way she'd intended.

"Maybe I will," he said to satisfy her.

You worshipped us, he thought. And you will again.

From that day, Brain started planning an uprising.

When he grew up, he wanted to be free.

Five

Long, deep kisses under the old dogwood tree at the edge of the school football field.

Their mouths parted with a gasp. Jake took a breath and plunged into her neck. He worked his way along the base of her throat, nibble by nibble.

"Motherogod," Amy said.

His touch, smell, taste. The blood rushing in her ears.

"Thank you, Mr. Benson," he murmured.

"Why are you thinking about him all of a sudden?"

She wondered how he could think at all. Her mind had blanked out with excitement, going away to some special sensory place. She didn't even know what day it was.

"Pa always said you could get the germ by kissing," Jake told her. "Thanks to Mr. Benson, now I know that ain't true."

She smiled. "Now you know. Good Lord. Well. I better get on home."

They couldn't go any further, they knew that, and even kissing had its limit. A fuzzy border through which one crossed from fun to frustration. He hugged her once more and let go. For all his renegade charm, he was a gentleman.

She picked up her schoolbooks and hugged them against her chest. "I don't know if I can even walk. My legs have gone all to rubber, sir. You have turned me to jelly."

"Hold my hand then, miss."

"You're a fine kisser, Jake Coombs."

"You ain't like any other girl, Amy Green."

"How do you mean? That I ain't like the other girls?"

"Because you're perfect," he said. "Perfect for me."

She liked the sound of that. *Perfect.* She thought of him as perfect too. Her scalp itched like ants crawled along it. Her old nervous habit wanted its attention. She didn't scratch. Instead, she squeezed his hand as they walked along the road past telephone poles wrapped in kudzu vines.

"You know all that already," she said. "Going out with me just one week."

"I'm a fast learner. Hey, what are you doing Friday night?"

"What I do every night, I guess. Why are you asking?"

"Me and Troy found a clearing in the woods by a deer trail," he said. "Somebody set rocks in a circle to make a fire pit. We're gonna build a fire and listen to music. Talk about life."

"You ain't scared of the monsters?"

"You know I ain't scared of any monsters."

He hadn't been playing the renegade today. He meant what he said about the plague kids being people.

"What about the wild ones?" she said.

Some of the plague kids ran away from the Homes and lived in the woods, where they went feral. The farmers shot at them if they came around.

"That's just another story they tell to scare us," he said.

"Maybe. So who all is going out there?"

"Like I said, me and Troy. Sally and Michelle too. Michelle

and Troy are fixin' to steal some beer or liquor from their folks. We'll make a party of it."

She'd gone to school with them for years but had never really known them. For as long as she could remember, it was just her and Mama. Her whole life spent going through the motions of being a normal girl while living in fear of people. This summer, she'd decided to reach outside her shell. She'd befriended Sally, who went to the same church as her. The one where Jake's daddy preached.

When school started, she'd decided to take an even bigger risk by having a boyfriend. She'd chosen Jake, who offered just the right mix of danger and kindness. She'd started hanging out with Michelle and Troy because of him.

Amy paused at the juncture of two cracked roads. Yellow jasmine grew along the side. "A party under the stars. Sounds like fun. I wish I could go."

"You could if you really wanted," Jake said. "Think about all the kissing we could get into."

Amy considered. The mischief appealed to her. A little danger. "Well, I might could sneak out just once. You better be careful with your daddy, though."

Reverend Coombs's Methodist church stood outside of town on a lonely stretch of County Road 20. Every Sunday, he warned the townsfolk about the apocalypse. The plague was a sign, he said. Punishment for man's sins. God is coming soon, and boy, is He angry about it. Amy wondered why Mama wanted to go every Sunday to hear such talk.

"Pa don't scare me," Jake said. "He's mostly bark, not bite."

"He must be. You dress like that. The music you listen to and the things you say."

Jake laughed. Amy tilted her head back. He leaned in.

Their teeth clicked together. Then their lips found each other again. They stood in the weeds along the side of the road and kissed until a truck rattled past honking its horn.

"I might be in love with you," he said in a cloud of dust.

She smiled and walked off toward her home. She threw one last look over her shoulder and noted with satisfaction he hadn't moved an inch. He stood in the yellow jasmine in his Black Flag T-shirt and army surplus boots.

"I'll see you tomorrow, Jake Coombs."

"Do you love me back or not?"

"You know the answer to that."

He grinned. "Friday night. You think on it, okay?"

"I promise I will."

Jake waved. Amy bounded off with a skip in her step. She couldn't wait to tell Sally she'd kissed him. She felt ready to burst with the news. Special, like she'd joined an exclusive club. Experienced now at something that for most of the girls in her class was still a delicious mystery. Becoming an adult was not so much a road as a ladder, and she'd just climbed one of its rungs.

She walked alone on the dirt road the way she always did during the school year, but she didn't feel alone. Jake Coombs was going home with her in her heart and mind. The big house emerged past a stand of yellow poplars, surrounded by rolling green farmland that smelled like wet earth.

Going home to her hot, run-down house didn't seem so bad now. She would read her health textbook cover to cover tonight. Learn everything. Kissing had proved a whole lot of fun. If she could kiss, maybe there were other things she could do.

She'd taken some big risks this year, and they'd shown her

a much bigger world. Amy was ready to climb the next rung and see how high she might go.

L inda Green sat on the couch in her darkened living room and waited for her baby girl to come home while she watched the end of her soaps. Cigarette smoke hung in drifts pushed along by a humming fan. She stabbed her Virginia Slim in the overflowing ashtray on the side table and flicked ash from her housecoat. Then she sipped her sour mash whiskey to numb her brain some more.

What a life, she thought. Goddamnit all.

Things hadn't always been like they were. She hadn't minded growing up in a small town. Plenty to do for a pretty young thing with a mind for trouble, slim waist, and bust that could stop traffic. Boys once fought with their fists over the chance to take Linda Brazell out on a Saturday night. Grown men gave her the eye and winked while they offered her babysitting jobs.

When school ended, she'd picked Billy Ray Green, who had a good-paying job at the cotton mill, and became Mrs. Green. Billy Ray never drank or hit her. He gave her this house, which he'd inherited from his dearly departed mama. That was in 1968, the year the tabloids started printing stories about monster babies along with all the dismal news from Vietnam. Portents and signs. Important people reassuring the terrified public. It all had nothing to do with her. She had plenty on her mind starting her life as an adult.

A big adventure, but after a while the excitement wore thin. She began to miss her glory days when the boys fought over her. Men still gave her the eye, and she grew bored enough to revisit old tricks. She found plenty to occupy

her during the long hours Billy Ray labored at the mill.
Out-of-towners, traveling salesmen and the like, which was
her rule on how to play it safe. That was how she caught the
germ, which she found out about when she made Amy.

She'd accused Billy Ray of giving it to her. Got herself so
worked up she almost believed it. He called her a no-good
whore and thanks a lot for ruining his life. He left soon after
and good riddance to that son of a bitch, leaving her with a
baby like that.

The kitchen door slammed. Amy walked into the room.
"Hi, Mama."

Linda lit a fresh Virginia Slim, her eyes on her soap.
"There's a TV dinner in the Frigidaire for you. You want to
watch a program with me while you eat your supper?"

"I got homework first."

"Suit yourself, baby girl."

"Hey, Mama."

Linda wrenched her eyes from the screen. "Hey, what?"

"That thing we talked about? How I'm different and all."

"You ain't different. You're perfect. Look at you."

"Mama."

She sighed. "What do you want to know?"

"What you told me before. About who I am. Was it the
honest truth?"

Linda wanted to laugh but coughed into her fist instead.
Goodness gracious, would she be sitting here on her sweet
ass wasting away if it weren't the plain truth? Would she be
spending her time watching TV and reading romance novels all day long? Going to a hellfire church that judged the
infected as sinners?

"I wish it weren't," she said.

"Some mamas make up stories to keep their kids from doing bad things," Amy said.

"I ain't them, sugar."

"I don't look any different than normal people, Mama."

Linda finished her whiskey and winced at the burn. "Thank the good Lord for that."

"I kissed a boy today. You can't get it from kissing. I learned that in health class."

"You be careful anyways," Linda said. "You got the plague in you. Do you want to make a monster baby? Then that boy will leave you as sure as your daddy left me. He'll never be able to love a girl again. He'll be an untouchable. If you love him, don't make him hate you."

"We're just kissing is all. We ain't stupid."

"You're young. Stupid goes with the landscape."

"But how do you know?"

"How do I know what?"

"How do you know I'm one of them if I don't look it?"

Linda remembered pushing Amy out of her. Covered in sweat, legs in the air, her big tits leaking milk. The doctor handed her a perfect child. Everybody relieved. *Mrs. Green, you have a daughter,* he said. *Give her here,* Linda said. *I want to hold my little angel.* The doctor and nurses left to do other things while Amy fed at her breast. The most natural thing in the world. A fierce love overtook her, a love that felt brand-new and ancient at the same time, a love that started as deep as her atoms and eclipsed everything. Then Linda saw. She saw what her little girl really was. She swallowed her scream and let the baby feed.

She couldn't hide it from Billy Ray, but she could from everybody else. Her Amy wasn't going to grow up in no

freak house, end of story. Billy Ray, the men she'd played
around with, a free life, everything she wanted—none of it
added up to a hill of beans compared to her daughter's wel-
fare. Linda would do whatever it took to protect her. Her
baby girl would grow up in the real world and have a normal
life, as long as she wasn't stupid.

"I just know," Linda said. "Never mind how. I been hard
on you, you have the answer why. You play along, you got
your whole life ahead of you."

"I just wish," Amy said.

"I know. You get to your books. I'll bring you a nice glass
of ice water and syrup in a bit. TV dinner in the Frigidaire.
Dynasty is on tonight."

Linda would rather watch *The Cosby Show*, a wholesome
new program. A doctor and lawyer and their family enjoying a life she could never have. A show about Blacks, but
that was all right. She had nothing against Blacks if they
acted like proper folks. Amy didn't like the show. She was at
the age where seeing people act proper was boring instead
of comforting. Amy liked *Dynasty*, glamorous and beautiful
people fighting to see who came out on top.

Tonight, they'd watch *Dynasty*.

"All right, Mama," Amy said. "Love you."

"Love you, too, sugar," Linda said as she watched her
daughter disappear upstairs.

After *Dynasty*, she will drink some more whiskey and fall
asleep right here where she's sitting. Tomorrow morning,
she will remember almost none of it.

Six

Reggie Albod ate a heaping breakfast of bacon, cornbread with syrup, and biscuits smothered in rich brown gravy. Washed it down with sweet, hot coffee while his daughters crowded and fussed about the kitchen. Judy, who'd been a fine woman, passed on some years ago. The boys in town were always asking when he was gonna get himself hitched again. He always laughed and shot back, *With four growing girls under my roof, where in hell would I put her?*

Plus the plague still going around. People getting tested before they shared a bed. Courtship wasn't what it used to be. He was done with all that nonsense. With four daughters, he had enough women in his life. At his age, he had just one mission: take care of himself and what was his.

He walked out onto his porch and leaned against a paint-flecked column to roll a cigarette. He licked it closed and smoked it while he watched the sun come up. He tossed the remains of his smoke, coughed, and spat a gob of phlegm. Then he stomped into the yard ready to start the day's work.

Bolls were opening on the ripening cotton. Along with peanuts, it was his main cash crop. Albod also had in his garden sweet potatoes, squash, beans, peas, cabbage, and tomatoes set to be picked and canned. The chickens and pigs needed their feed, the cows were already lowing, fences awaited repair. He reminded himself today he had to make a run down to Ackley's Feed Coop then do a little trading at the general store. He wanted to acquire tobacco, some oil, and various sundries for his girls.

Today, the creepers were coming.

They'd been working for Albod three to four days a week for the last eight years. At first, they didn't know a damn thing. They ran around making a mess. Albod remembered one little fella being terrified of the chickens. He showed the boys his cattle prod in case they had a mind for mischief. Since then, everybody got along just fine. The creepers matured into good farmers. Now he didn't know what he'd do without them.

He fed the animals and milked the cows. Then right on time, he spied the pickup leading a cloud of dust along the road. It pulled into the yard. Dave Gaines cut the engine, stepped out, and stretched. The creepers sat in the back in their dirty overalls, waiting to be told to pile out.

"Morning, Reggie," Gaines said.

"Morning, Dave. I don't see Goof. He got the sniffles or what."

Gaines's good eye stared at Albod. His lazy eye looked somewhere else. "The Bureau came around. They took him away for a while."

"Is that so?" Albod paid his goddamn work fees. The Home should have been helping him for free considering all the taxes he paid to Washington.

His youngest came out with a thermos of coffee. Pretty

and blond just like her sisters. Just like his Judy, God rest her soul.

She handed it to him with a kiss on his stubbled cheek. "Here you go, Daddy."

"Thank you, Buttercup. Have a good day at school."

"Morning, Miss Sally," the teacher said with a grin, but she was already running back to the house on bare feet.

"I'm being left shorthanded," Albod said. "I pay good money to the Home for these kids."

"I brought Mary along."

"A little retard. Take me half a day teach her what to do."

"That's my job," said Gaines.

"You got hundreds of creepers out there at the Home, and you send me this girl."

"I said I'll teach her. You do what you need to do. You have a list for me?"

Albod pulled a grimy notepad from the back pocket of his dungarees. He flipped it open, tore out a sheet, and handed it over. "Do you reckon you can handle all that today?"

"Is all your cotton ready to harvest then?"

Albod spat on the ground. "Yup."

The sun had been strong this year but not scorching. Heavier rains. Good for cotton. The crop was ready for picking. The market price not as high as he'd like but high enough. Next year, he'd switch the land over to peas to keep the soil rich.

"No way to pick all of it in one day with these kids," Gaines said. "It would take longer than that. Like way longer."

"Just that small patch yonder. I hired some coloreds to come around tomorrow morning and get a start on the big fields. Reckon you can handle it or not."

"Won't know until we get to it."

"All right then, you do that. I got to make a run down to Ackley's. Be back by end of day. Stay out the house while I'm gone, understand."

"I'll be working the whole time."

Albod climbed into his truck and tossed the thermos on the front seat. The engine roared to life. He draped his arm out the window. "See you later, Dave."

He threw the truck into gear and stepped on the gas. Busy day ahead. Always too much to get done, but he liked it that way.

Dog watched the farmer and his pickup rattle off the property. He hopped from the tailgate and helped Mary down. She stumbled on the grass, her big straw hat falling off. He picked it up and put it back on her head.

Mr. Gaines called them together and showed them the list. He rubbed his forehead. "For land's sake. Expecting all this done in a day. Small patch, my ass. We'll be picking cotton the whole day, just that."

The kids didn't say anything. They had no say.

Mr. Gaines sighed. "Let's get to it, I guess. Pokes are in the barn."

Dog didn't mind picking cotton. With his long, spindly fingers, he was good at picking. It was simple enough, even Mary could do it.

Wallee blinked. "Not pull-ing weeds to-day?"

Shaped like a bowling pin, Wallee had no arms. He walked around on roots sprouting from his bottom half. He was good at pulling weeds, any kind of weeds. That and picking pecans and peaches from the trees on the property.

His roots, once extended, could reach even to the highest branches.

"Just cotton," Mr. Gaines growled.

"What about me?" Brain said.

Brain did special work. Fixed machinery, delivered calves, and treated ailments among the animals. A mechanic and a veterinarian rolled into one.

"You deaf, George? I said cotton. Get to it. Go on. Don't rush on my account."

They trooped off to the barn as they were told.

The teacher leaned against the truck. "Hey, you. Enoch."

"Yes, sir," Dog said.

"Tell Mary what to do. You're in charge of her."

"All right, Mr. Gaines."

The cotton field sprawled and buzzed in the heat. Open bolls hung on the stems. The kids worked their rows. Dog plucked ripened tufts from the burrs and rammed them in his sack. Pick, pick, pick, step.

He waved at Mary. "Wake up, girl. Do it like I showed you."

She held up a fistful of cotton. "Fluff."

"Put it in that poke you got on your shoulder. That's right. Just like that. Now get some more. Like you're feeding it. That poke is sure hungry."

Brain snarled as he stuffed his sack. "Most people don't know we help grow the food they eat. Pick the cotton they wear around their precious normal private parts. They wouldn't eat or wear it if they did."

Dog wondered at that. Even he knew the germ didn't live outside the body. He looked across the field of white gold. Beyond, green trees spanned the horizon under the brightening sky.

He said, "What do you think it's like out yonder in their world?"

"You mean our world," Brain said. "We're just locked out of it."

"I mean do you think it's like it is in the movies."

"We'll never know until we concern ourselves with what's going on right here. Like giving our labor away to Albod and getting nothing in return."

"We're getting an education," Dog said. "I want to be a farmer."

"We're working for free. And we have no choice."

"Just for a few more years. Then Pa Albod promised he'll pay us by the pound for peanuts and cotton."

"You can barely live on those wages. It's slavery by another name."

"If you say so."

"Look at our overseer over there," Brain said. "The great Mr. Gaines. Hanging around the house hoping to catch sight of Albod's daughters on their way to school. The only thing he ever taught us is the masters exploit us and there ain't a damn thing we can do about it."

"Why don't we sneak out tonight and go to our spot in the woods," Dog said. "Talk this stuff out. You might feel better getting things off your chest."

Brain stopped picking. "Are you hearing a word I'm saying?"

"Don't mind me. Keep on, I'm listening."

Brain suffered doing manual labor. He'd been born with a particular sensitivity to physical pain. His back started aching, and his little hands cracked and bled. Made it hard to talk to him. Any other time, Dog liked hearing him go on about the violent system and the coming revolution. He didn't follow half of it, but it was hard not to be impressed when Brain held forth on a subject. When Brain was suffering, though, he became bitter. His rants turned ugly.

Dog picked his way down the row, leaving his friends behind. Brain could rant all he wanted out of earshot. He looked up and saw Mary almost caught up with him. She was turning out to be a good little cotton picker.

Midmorning, they came out and headed straight to the water pump. Mr. Gaines snored in his truck. Cotton clouds in a bright blue sky. Dog cranked the pump handle, and they took turns leaning under the spigot to gulp water so cold and pure it made their teeth ache. Then back to the fields until Mr. Gaines called them in for dinner. More picking until late afternoon and quitting time.

Hot and weary, the children tramped out of the field.

"Hey, all y'all," a voice called to them. "I got iced tea over here."

Sally Albod walked across the grass holding a big tray filled with sparkling glasses of brown tea. Her simple white dress showed off slim, suntanned arms. She set the tray down on the picnic table in the yard.

"You didn't need to do all that, Miss Sally," Mr. Gaines said.

"This will help them cool off. Them working so hard in this heat. Hotter than blue blazes today."

"They don't mind it. They got water. They get tea, and next thing you know, they'll want it every—"

"I went through the trouble," Sally said, her voice sharp.

The teacher's good eye glowered at the kids while the other drooped and didn't seem to care about anything. "All right. Go on, kids. Have some iced tea, then. Don't be thinking you'll get some every time, though."

"Thanks, Miss Sally," the kids mumbled as they gathered around the table.

"You're welcome," she said.

Dog held the sweating glass in his hands and placed it against the side of his snout. Cold, delicious cold. His fur was murder in the heat. Ice clinked in the glass, offering a glimpse of a sprig of mint. He poured the sweet tea down his throat in gulps, crushing the ice between his sharp teeth.

Mr. Gaines returned his attention to Sally with a bright smile. "Mighty kind of you, Miss Sally. You look fine today, if you don't mind me saying."

"I do mind it, sir. Them working so hard. You just standing there acting like a boss and giving a fourteen-year-old girl compliments."

"Mind yourself, now."

"You should mind yourself," the girl said. "I could tell Daddy about the way you been eyeing me these past weeks. All these comments all the time about how I look."

"You tell him anything you want. I was just being friendly."

She tilted her head at the sound of Albod's truck growling in the distance. "I can hear him coming."

Mr. Gaines glared at the kids. They turned away, knowing to mind their own business. Mary alone didn't. She stared back at him with a blank expression. The teacher glanced at the house, where Albod kept his shotgun.

Sally said, "Tell you what, Mr. Gaines. From now on, I'll give these folks a treat if I want. And you'll let me do it without thinking I owe you something."

"You do what you like. I don't care what you do."

"Good," she said with a sweet smile and went back in the house.

"All right, let's go," Mr. Gaines growled. "We're done for the day."

Dog walked back to the truck energized by the tea and Sally's small act of kindness. Along the way, he spied a scrawny hen. Most of her feathers were gone. Her sisters had been pecking her, killing her one nibble at a time. Soon, she'd die of it. Such was the way of the world, which Dog had learned was brutal and unforgiving. He had never known it to be any different.

He was starting to think maybe it could be.

Seven

Amy checked her appearance one last time in front of the bathroom mirror before going downstairs. Mama snored on the living room couch. The TV flashed in the dark. The air was hot and smelled like stale tobacco smoke.

"I'm going out to maybe have sex with a boy," she said.

Her mother growled out another snore. She would not wake until tomorrow.

"Sleep tight, Mama."

Outside, the night settled warm and sticky on her skin. Dark and endless. Anything could happen on a night like this. Anything could be hidden, ideal for mischief. She walked to the corner where she and Jake last kissed. He stood waiting in the yellow jasmine with his hands in his pockets.

He started at the sound of shoes crunching gravel. Then his face lit up as she came giggling into the moonlight.

"Scared I was a monster?" she said.

"It's how pretty you are startles me. Runs me right over like a steamroller."

"Ha, ha. You know, you talk a good game."

"Oh."

"Don't stop," she said. "I like it. I'm just testing you."

Jake took her hand and led her across the ruins of a field. All the sweet corn had been cut down and harvested. His palm sweated against hers.

"Sally is probably there already," he said. "Troy, too."

"So are they together now? She hasn't said anything to me about it, and I'd think she would."

"Yeah, they're together." He laughed. "Only Sally don't know it."

"If Sally did know it, her daddy would go on a warpath."

"It ain't up to him who she loves."

"You and Sally think alike about the monster kids," Amy said. "Couple of bleeding hearts. I don't know why you like me instead of her."

"I don't have a choice in the matter. I already told you plain as day how I feel about you."

"What was that exactly? I don't think I recollect."

"I said it last time. It's your turn. Otherwise, I'm staying mum."

"You'll break," she said. "I can be pretty stubborn. I'm like my mama that way."

"Yeah." He laughed again. "I probably will break."

If he didn't, she would. She'd been aching to tell him all week.

Maybe tonight. Anything was possible tonight.

They entered the woods. Amy leaned against him as he slipped his arm around her waist. His hand found its way inside her jeans and held her hip. She'd read her health book cover to cover. She learned that if you had sex with a condom, it wasn't a guarantee against the germ, which spread on skin contact. But you could touch each other down there.

They could do that without spreading it if they used disposable gloves.

His fingers moved to the soft curve between her ribs and hipbone. Amy shivered at his touch, pulling at her hair. Her skin broke out in gooseflesh.

"Now who's scared?" he said.

She wasn't scared, she was excited. She wanted to be a normal girl.

"Don't worry," he added. "It ain't much farther. Hear the music?"

A manic bass line pounded in the trees. Light flickered past the branches. She and Jake left the trail and threaded the woods until they reached a glade surrounded by ancient oaks and hickories.

Troy was there feeding a little fire in a rock pit. Sally and Michelle sat on one of several cut logs chunked around the pit as benches. A ghetto blaster shrieked some song she'd never heard before.

"Hey, hey, hey," Jake said, doing his best Fat Albert.

Troy grinned. "Now we can get this party started. Check out what Michelle brought. A bottle of red wine."

"What about you?" Jake said. "Were you able to bring anything?"

"Couple bottles of Yuengling. Hi, Amy."

"Good God almighty," she said. "What happened to your face?"

Somebody had disfigured him with markers, the thick lines murky on his dark skin. The firelight caught him just right, revealing a leering mask of jagged fangs and a big red tongue reaching up to lick his right cheek. Sally and Michelle giggled. Amy noticed in the firelight they were similarly disfigured.

Mama had told her kids once dressed up like this for

Halloween. Before the real monsters showed up. They went door-to-door in costumes and asked for candy.

"We made monsta faces," Troy said.

"Why would you do that?"

"Because it's cool."

"It ain't that cool. I hate to be the one to tell you."

"Monstas are cool," Jake said. "The ultimate screw you."

"Why do you call them monstas?"

"From the B-52s song, 'Rock Monsta.'"

"Is that the song that's on now?"

"This is Shame Addiction. Their *Plague Generation* album."

"I think I know them from one of your T-shirts," Amy said. "The singer sounds really mad about something."

"This is rebel music," he said.

Troy said, "The monstas don't have to write music or wear clothes to make a statement. They are the statement. One simple statement."

"Screw society," Jake chimed back in.

"That's it. Life is a prison for kids our age. Everybody telling us how to live, whether we want to hear it or not. The whole school set up as a hierarchy of who's cool and who ain't. A reflection of society. The monstas get it because they live it. Our prison is invisible. Theirs is totally real."

Amy had never heard anything so dumb in her life. She'd spent years believing she was different. There was not one glamorous thing about it. Nothing enviable about being the underdog, the outcast hiding in plain sight.

"My older sister goes to school in Atlanta," Troy was saying. "She protests against apartheid. Meanwhile, just a couple miles from here, we got kids locked up in a Home. We're no better than South Africa. Hell, we ain't that much better than the Nazis and their concentration camps."

There was no use arguing about it. Amy came here to have fun. She gave a dismissive wave. "All y'all do what you want, but I ain't marking up my face so I can be ugly. I will have one of those beers, though, if anybody is offering."

She sat with the other girls on a cut log and accepted a bottle of Yuengling. She gave it a curious sniff and took a sip. The bitter taste made her wince. It was sharp on her tongue and a little warm.

"As if anything could make you ugly," Sally told her.

"How much does it take to get you drunk?" Amy asked.

"Depends," Michelle said.

"I don't want to throw up. I heard that can happen."

"You'll be all right. Drink lots of water when you get home. If you really want to party, have a snort of this mulberry wine. It'll knock you on your behind."

"No, thanks. Next time, I'll sneak a bottle out of Mama's stash. She's got so much bourbon lying around she won't miss it."

"You bring bourbon, you're in the gang," Michelle said.

Jake and Troy carried on about the alienation of youth. Parents, teachers, and President Reagan arrayed against them. Russia and America aiming nuclear bombs at each other. Whatever mistakes society makes, the kids will be the ones who have to pay for them. Kids with no future, no say in any of it.

They were preaching at each other. It sounded rehearsed, like an old routine they shared. Stuff they'd read somewhere. Amy got the sense Jake was trying to impress her with a show. She suspected her boyfriend might be a little full of it, but she didn't care. It was his passion that interested her. The way he stood out, not what he stood for.

Michelle took a sip from the wine bottle and grimaced.

"I'm with you, Amy. I just like to put on monsta face because it's fun. We paint each other's faces."

"It's abstract to you," Sally said. "Is that the word? Meaning it ain't real?"

Amy held back a burp. "Yup. That's what it means."

"Abstract," Sally repeated. "Even to Troy and Jake. I been around the plague kids. I never seen kids get crapped on so much. Day in and day out. Even Daddy treats them bad sometimes. Daddy don't even think of it as bad."

"They got the short end of the stick," Michelle said. "I'm with you that much."

"The kids just take it like they don't know what's right or wrong neither. It's just the way things are."

Amy felt her brain thicken from the beer. "I just want to live a regular life. I don't want any guilt or ugliness in my world."

"That is the world," Sally said. "Beautiful and ugly all mixed up."

Michelle changed the subject. "So you and Jake are an item now?"

Amy smiled at Jake. "Looks that way."

"You're a real fine couple," Sally told her.

Amy liked the sound of that. A real fine couple. "I like him a lot, too."

Michelle leaned in and dropped her voice. "You two get into anything? You know, like from the book?"

"Hush a second," Sally said. "You hear that?"

"I don't hear—"

"Hey," a voice called from the bushes.

The kids froze and listened. Nothing but the music screeching in the trees, another singer angry at the world. Sally turned it off while Michelle hid the wine.

"Who's out there?" Jake said.

"This is our spot."

"Didn't see your name on it, friend."

"Mind if we come out and say hello? Maybe share the fire?"

Jake turned to his friends and shrugged. "Sure. Come on out and join us if you're friendly."

"Who is that?" Troy hissed.

"I know that voice," Sally said.

The monster stepped into the light. A skinny wolf thing with piercing blue human eyes and long, hairy limbs that stuck out like thick pipe cleaners.

Eight

Dog came out grinning and eager to make new friends. He'd spied on them from the honeysuckle but couldn't figure out who they were. Screeching music, disfigured faces in shadow. Clothes too nice for feral kids. Plague kids like him, looked like, but not from the Home. It made him wonder if some kids lived out in the real world among the normal. He just had to go see.

"Come on out," he called to Brain and Wallee. "They're all right."

The kids let out a little scream at the sight of Wallee lumbering out on squirming roots. Then at Brain with his big heart-shaped mane.

"Friends," Wallee said.

Dog's eyes went wide at the strangers. "Oh. You ain't like us."

"Hey, Enoch," Sally said. "It's me, Sally Albod. It's all right."

He remembered how kind she was to him the other day, giving him iced tea. He dropped his gaze to his feet. "Hey,

Miss Sally. Sorry to bother you. We didn't mean to scare nobody. We'll go on back to the Home and leave you be."

"Hold up," one of the boys said. "Why don't you sit with us a while?"

Dog looked at Brain, who nodded. "Yeah, we could sit a spell."

He perched his behind on a log across from the normals and looked down at the fire. Wallee lumbered over and planted himself on the ground. Brain sat next to Dog and stuck out his chin as if daring the normals to say something.

"I'm Jake," one of the boys said to break the ice.

He introduced his friends. Dog did the same. Normals and plague children studied each other, wondering what it would be like wearing the other's shoes.

"Do you want a drink of wine or beer?" Jake said. "Because we got both."

"The Home don't allow us no drink," Dog said.

"Didn't ask you're allowed. Asked you wanted some."

He glanced at Brain, who shook his head. "No, thank you, I guess."

"Why is your face painted like that?" Brain asked the boy named Troy.

"Show solidarity with you. Show we understand what you're going through and that we sympathize. We're on your side."

Dog didn't understand. If they were on the same side, why were they so scared? He could smell their fear, sour and pungent. They looked ready to bolt.

"Have you ever been out to the Home?" Brain said.

"No," said Troy. "Never have."

"Then what do you know about our struggle?"

Nobody said anything for a while.

"We're afraid," Michelle said. "I don't want to be afraid no more. I want to love everybody. I don't want you to hate me. That's how I feel."

"We don't hate you," Brain said. "We're more afraid of you than you are of us."

"Is that really true?"

"You have all the power. You control everything."

"I don't control anything, mister. I'm just a kid."

"We hate the system that divides us," Jake said. "We want to tear it down."

"Then tear it down," Brain told him. "Or we'll get around to it ourselves one day."

Dog winced over how tough Brain was being on these kids, who were making an effort to reach out and be friendly. He had never sat down and talked to normals like this before. He didn't want Brain to ruin the party

"We're real grateful," he said. "You letting us sit here with you, Miss Sally."

"I'm just Sally here, Enoch. We're all the same in this special spot."

Dog smiled. A bolt of pure love shot through him. She was the only normal who ever treated him like a normal boy. Who made him feel special. Maybe she alone among them saw him as he really was. If a kiss could turn a frog into a prince, wasn't the frog already a prince to begin with?

Michelle switched her gaze to Wallee. "What are you made out of?"

Wallee's rubbery lips contorted into a massive grin. "Made out of Ma-ma."

"Oh my. Look at you. You are actually adorable."

His head tilted side to side as he went on grinning with his eyes clenched shut. Two of his roots slithered up to his

face holding a tin harmonica. He started blowing a Gene
Autry tune.

"That's pretty," Michelle said.

"I didn't know you could play the harmonica," Sally said.

"What was that music coming out that box before?" Dog
asked.

"A mix tape I made," Jake said.

Wallee lowered the harmonica. "Hear it."

Jake leaned to turn it back on. Guitars and drums roared
up to the sky.

> *They locked the kids away so we don't have to see, that the*
> *ugly and the weird, they're just like you and me. They are*
> *you and me.*
> *Nature! Breaks! God's! Mistake! People! Awake! For your*
> *own sake!*

"He's talking about us," Brain said.

"That's right," Jake said. "What do you think of it?"

"He's got us all wrong."

"How do you reckon that?"

"We ain't a mistake. How can we defy the natural order
if nature produced us? How can we be a mistake of creation
if God made us?"

"I declare," Michelle said. "He talks just like Mr. Benson."

"This music commits the same sin as the society it protests,"
Brain said. "It writes its own story onto us. We are the boogey-
man under the bed. We are rebels against complacency. The
truth is we are neither, and we don't appreciate being used."

Jake stared at him, fascinated. "I can't believe I'm actually
talking to you about this. What do you mean about writing
a story?"

"We are a negative blank slate. It's easy to project the inexplicable onto us. The deeper the mystery, the greater the fear. The species' black sheep. That is how they justify institutional violence. Put us in run-down Homes and deny us our birthright."

"That's right. That's just what they do. I been saying—"

"Others turn us into symbols for their feelings of oppression," Brain added. "They project their impatience and desire to become the new masters onto us. They romanticize us as noble savages. They use us, too, just in a different way."

"Well, who are you supposed to be then?"

"I'll tell you. But first, you tell me what you want from life."

"That's just it, I guess," Jake said. "I want my own life. I want to have a chance to do things. Make things happen. I want love. I want respect. I want."

He wanted it all.

"Of course you do," Brain said. "We want the same things as you. We ask the same questions as you. Why am I here? Who will love me? Why was I born? That's the great mystery of the mutagenic nobody understands. That's who we are. We're people who deserve the chance at the same things. People who want some control over their own lives. No better, no worse."

"And you should get it same as us," Jake said. "I totally agree with you."

"I appreciate that. But this is our fight. Anybody who wants to join our fight has to sacrifice it all. Become like us. Instead of painting your face, find a plastic surgeon and make yourself a real monster. Live in a Home. Then it really will be about you. Then you will understand the struggle. Anything else is just condescending tourism."

Jake did not appear to be up for that. "Something to think about, I guess."

Dog wished Brain would shut it. He was putting a damper on this fine get-together. He seemed to be saying all the normals were bad, but the normals weren't all one person any more than the plague kids were. These kids were scared of him at first, but now they weren't. They were kind. Not all hens pecked the weak.

He wished Goof was here. He'd have them all laughing with his upside-down face and finishing everybody's sentences. He stared at the girl called Amy a bit. She'd been sitting pale and rigid the whole time, her eyes hard and angry.

"Hey, cousin," he said.

The girl blanched and shook her head.

Brain put one of his little hands on Dog's shoulder and squeezed a gentle warning. "What Dog here is saying is you seem like a special lady, miss."

"Thank you," Amy said.

"Looks like we got a party here," a voice said behind them.

"Aw, fudge," Troy said.

The bottles disappeared in a flash.

A big man wearing a Stetson and a khaki uniform walked out of the woods and looked around. He nodded to the music player.

"Y'all can turn that screaming off, if y'all don't mind."

Jake did as the man ordered. "Hey, Sheriff."

He was acting cool, but Dog could tell he was scared.

"Don't hey me, boy," the sheriff said. "What is going on here?"

"We was hanging out listening to music and talking, sir," Troy said.

"Uh-huh. I heard your so-called music a mile away. Lord. What did you do to your damn face?"

"Just fooling around. Fixin' ourselves up to look like monsters."

"Fooling is right. A whole mess of foolishness. Start packing it up. Michelle, your daddy is mad as hell and out looking for you."

Her eyes dropped to her hands folded in her lap. "Sorry, Sheriff."

"Clean up first, looking like that. Hell's bells, girl. You want to look like them, is that it. They don't even want to look like them."

"Sher-iff," Wallee said with glee.

"And you, you sons of Cain. What is your story? These secret meetings."

"We," Dog said.

His voice came out as a squeak. He stared at the badge and the big gun on the man's hip.

"Go on, boy. Spit it out."

"We was just out taking a walk, sir. We all sort of found each other."

"Is that right," the sheriff said.

"We was just saying hello. We didn't mean any harm in it, sir."

"What about you, gorilla boy? Givin' me the evil eye. You want to take a swing at the law, I'm right here. Take your best shot."

"No," Brain said.

"You sassing me, boy? No, what?"

"No, sir."

"I thought the Home taught better manners. Maybe I'll

take a swing at you. Tan your hide a bitty bit. What would you say to that idea?"

"I would say I wouldn't like that, sir."

The sheriff faked a punch in his direction. Brain flinched with a cry, holding up his little hands to shield himself. He'd been hit before. They all had at the Home.

"That's what I thought," the sheriff said.

"We're real sorry, sir," Dog said. "Don't hurt us. We won't do it again, honest."

"You creepers keep away from normal kids, you hear. Next time, there won't be no warning. I'll just take off my belt and get to whuppin'. Understand?"

"Yes, sir."

"Now go on and git before I change my mind and lock you up for the night."

"Sher-iff," said Wallee, glowing.

The man's stern face softened. "You too, Edward. Get on out of here."

They tramped into the woods, Dog breathing in shallow gasps. The teachers could be rough, but he'd never been so terrified in his life, so ashamed.

"Do you see?" Brain said. "See what they do?"

Dog bolted into the undergrowth.

"Where are you going?" Brain called after him.

He didn't answer, crashing through the bushes. He could run faster than anybody. His special talent. Walls of kudzu choked the forest, home to poisonous snakes. He didn't care. He just kept running.

Dog didn't stop until he reached the bunkhouse. The kids snored in the dark. Cockroaches scuttled in the corners. Smell of must and mold. He sneaked back into his grimy bed and lay there weeping until sleep overtook him.

Nine

Goof followed the hulking guard down the corridor. He couldn't believe this place, so clean and bright and smelling of disinfectant. God's gift of air conditioning. He liked the sound the guard's boots made when they hit the floor: *clock, clock.* The jingle of keys and gear riding along his belt. It all sounded very important and official.

Goof straightened his back and marched alongside him in pajamas and slippers. "Am I in prison?"

The guard didn't answer.

"Because it sure looks like I'm in prison," Goof tried again. Nothing.

The guard was the biggest man Goof had ever seen. Tall and wide as a wall. His bald head jutted like a small white hill between his massive shoulders. Abundant flesh trembled with each step. He looked like a giant baby in a policeman's uniform.

Goof rolled a fantasy the guard escorted him to an important council. All the cabinet heads were there, deciding whether to go to war. The missiles were warming up in their launchers. The fate of the free world hung in the balance.

"Come on then," he said. "There'll be hell to pay if the Russians shoot first."

The guard frowned at him. Goof grinned back, which made him look sad.

"No, seriously," he said. "Is this some kind of prison?"

The guard sighed but otherwise stayed mum. They arrived at a door. The giant opened it and ushered him through with a mocking sweep of his arm.

"Tell the president I've been held up," Goof said.

Agent Shackleton sat behind a steel table in the middle of the bright white room. He had McDonald's spread out in front of him.

"Grab a chair, Jeff," he said through a mouth full of cheeseburger.

Goof took a seat opposite him. "You got a fedora for me? You promised you'd get me one."

"All good things come to—"

"Those who wait. I been waiting three days."

"Quid pro quo. You know what that—"

"Means? No, I do not."

"It means you scratch my back," Shackleton said. "Then I scratch yours. Here, have some fries, they're still warm. I got an extra burger too if you want it."

Goof crammed a handful of fries in his mouth and chewed in a state of bliss. Food of the gods. Growing up in the Home, he had never tasted it before. Heaven danced on his taste buds. He washed it down with a swig of Coke.

"I can't scratch anything," he said. "I don't even know why I'm here."

"Your party trick of finishing what people are going to say. Tell—"

"Me something about it, Jeff. Sure, Mr. Shackleton. It

started around six months ago. I finished Ms. Oliver's sentences all through class. She was too amazed to get mad. I had everybody cracking up. It was really hilarious."

"I'm sure it was very funny."

"You should have been there. Everybody was cracking up over it."

"How does it work exactly?"

Goof raised his index finger while he finished chewing another handful of fries. Shackleton took advantage of the pause to light a cigarette and blow a cloud of smoke. Goof swallowed and came up for air.

"It's like I see what people are saying in big yellow capital letters," he said. "Like something on *Sesame Street*, that kids' show with Big Bird and Oscar the Dog and the Cookie Cat? Only I'm not really reading it. I can't read too good."

"Remarkable."

"Yup. So now do I get a fedora?"

"Soon. Here, you can have the rest of my fries. You should know you're a very special young man. Special as in nobody else in the world can do what you do."

"That's good, I guess."

"What if you listened to a recording? Can you do it then?"

"You mean like a song or in a movie?"

"That's right."

"I can do it even then," Goof said.

The Bureau man puffed and blew another cloud of smoke. "What if the song is on the radio and the radio dips into static for a few seconds? Would you know the words during the missing parts?"

"Maybe. I don't know. I can't remember a time that ever happened."

"What if I were to talk about something technical, using

a lot of terms you don't understand? Would you still be able to read it? Or Russian, maybe. Some language you don't understand."

Goof shrugged. "Don't know about that one neither. We could try it if you want."

Shackleton stabbed out his cigarette in the ashtray on the table. He stood and went to a telephone mounted on the wall, his mind already playing out applications he could test, mostly in intelligence.

Slap some headphones on this kid, and maybe he could write down conversations in Russian. Fill in missing gaps in recorded conversations. Maybe even recite conversations in real time just by watching people through a pair of binoculars.

He picked up the phone, punched a number, and asked for a lab tech to come down to Room Two. Out the corner of his eye, he saw the freak grab a fountain pen off the table and draw two cartoon eyes on his chin. Unbelievable. Then the kid started cramming his cheeseburger into his weird upside-down face.

"How would you like to be a secret agent?" Shackleton said.

"Are you serious?" the kid said, his cheeks bulging.

"Dead serious."

"I'll believe it when I see my hat."

"I'll get you ten hats if you want," Shackleton told him.

"As long as one's a fedora. Am I gonna get to go home ever?"

"You'll be staying here a long time—"

"While we do testing, Jeff. Gotcha. So is this a prison or not?"

Shackleton returned to his chair and crossed his ankles on the tabletop. "No. This is not a prison."

"What is it then?"

"We call it Special Facility. We bring special kids like you here. If you're good, you'll get to meet them. They'll be your new friends."

"You could bring my real friends here," the kid said. "Since we're scratching backs."

Shackleton smiled. "You don't get to make demands like that yet."

A long-haired young man in a lab coat entered the room. He peered at the freak through the shiny lenses of steel-rimmed glasses. "This is your new subject?"

"Yes," Shackleton said. "Have a seat facing him."

"He's not dangerous or anything, right?"

"Just sit in the chair, will you please? Thank you. Jeff, this is Zack. He works in the research division. He's going to tell you what he knows about the disease."

The kid licked salt off his fingers. "Sounds very interesting. Can't wait."

"Hi, Jeff," Zack said. "You want to hear about the pathogen?"

"Sure, why not."

"A pathogen is a microorganism that causes disease. Like the kind that gives you a cold, though the germ is a bacterium, not a virus. It's shaped like a little coiled worm—"

The plague kid opened his mouth to jump in, but Shackleton cut him off. "Zack, talk to him as you would to a colleague. Make it as technical as you normally would."

"If you say so." The technician's gaze flickered between the kid's drawn and real eyes. "Okay, Jeff. This mode of congenital mutagenesis is a sexually transmitted disease of the—"

"*Treponema pallidum* species," the kid said.

"That's right. Very good. It's a highly virulent relative of syphilis. A—"

"Gram-negative, mobile spirochete bacterium that is asymptomatic in adults."

"Correct," Zack said with a frown. "Transmitted to a—"

"Fetus, however, it generates chronic gummas that rewrite embryonic development."

"Holy shit," Zack said. "How are you doing that?"

The plague kid looked at Shackleton with a toothy grin. "You're right. I didn't understand a word of it."

The scientist looked angry. "What's going on here?"

"That will be all, Zack," Shackleton said. "Thank—"

"You," the kid said.

Shackleton smiled. This little freak was his ticket.

He'd worked for the Bureau for three years, touring one crappy Home after another, pushing paper and looking for a way out. Then everything changed. A few of the kids began developing abilities, crazy abilities. Overnight, they became national security assets, the start of a preternatural arms race. The Russians have their freaks, we have ours. The Bureau's second-rate burnouts found themselves fighting over who could come up with a valuable asset.

Last year, few among the monsters exhibited extraordinary capabilities. This year, some. Next year, it might be many. It might be so many the Bureau's field agents would get quotas instead of rewards. For the present, though, it was still virgin territory. Finding a hot one could get an agent promoted upstairs to management. Within five years, he might even make director.

As far as Shackleton was concerned, it was about time the freaks gave something back to the USA. For the past fourteen years, the economy had limped through one recession after another. The cost of keeping them all alive was a constant drain on tax dollars even with funding cut to the bone. Millions had been spent on a cure that never materialized. Religious cults, paranoia, and superstition were rampant everywhere you went. Watergate and Vietnam still weighed everything and everybody down. For the first time since the Black Death, the world population had declined for more than a decade. Every four years since the plague, a new president got elected promising to restore American glory, good times, morning in America, a hard line against internal disorder and the Soviets abroad. But the country just kept falling apart a little more every year, going backward instead of forward.

Who would have ever guessed these kids might be the key to America reclaiming its status as a superpower? That an annoying, skinny kid with an upside-down face might play a role in that historic event?

The U. S. Army had put a lot of resources into militarizing the paranormal. Project Grill Flame, they called it. Guys sitting in a room trying to draw remote Soviet installations and getting it wrong. Agent Fischer had found a kid who could do real remote viewing. Agent Kaplan dug up one who could hear what people were saying a mile away. Telekinesis, pyrokinesis, clairvoyance, clairsentience. The impossible now possible. Not just possible but routine and put to work for the United States government.

Shackleton saw a future when the children were weaponized or sold to industry. When infected couples got paid to make more of them. When the experiments conducted by Zack and the other eggheads in the research division cracked the genetic source of the children's abilities.

Then they'd synthesize these abilities into a shot. One stab
of a needle, and you could read minds. You could fly.

Men would become gods.

"Jeff," he said, "you just earned yourself—"

"A hat," the kid said.

Shackleton frowned. He was sure he was going to say the
kid earned himself a job as a spook. But yeah, he'd get the
freak his hat. It was the least he could do.

Ten

Sally traveled the narrow dirt track leading up to the Stark County Home for the Teratogenic. Honeysuckle crowded the road on both sides. The wind whispered through the leaves of shagbark hickories. Squirrels clambered across the branches as she walked past. Her bare legs shook, rebelling with each step.

The sheriff terrorized those poor plague kids, then let her and her friends go with a slap on the wrist. It had gotten her dander up, seeing Sheriff Burton bully those kids. It made her think about what George said about there being two worlds. About Mr. Benson saying they'd all have to live together one day. She wanted to do something more than just give out iced tea. She'd decided to go see what their world looked like. Maybe check on them and make sure they were okay.

Sally felt responsible, but now she felt foolish and scared. She didn't really know the plague kids, though they'd worked on her farm for years. She hadn't known they hung out in the woods, thought about what was happening to them, had special names for each other, played their own music. Everything about them was alien to her. They might see her coming out here as just more monsta face.

Worse, she might get them in another heap of trouble they didn't need.

It was all so unfair.

She froze at a commotion in the bushes. Something in the trees. Sally looked behind her. It wasn't too late to run on home. Then she took a deep breath and lifted her chin. She may have been the spitting image of her mama, but she was her daddy through and through, stubborn when she set her mind to something.

Sally picked up her courage and marched on. "Everything is fine." Voicing her thoughts aloud like a protection spell. "There ain't nothing to be scared about."

The Home came into view, a vast old mansion surrounded by ramshackle buildings all fallen into ruin in the wilderness. A prosperous plantation once stood here, abandoned following the Confederate War. The forest had reclaimed it after more than a century of neglect, a reminder nature had more energy than humans. Groping oak branches, draped in Spanish moss, darkened the weedy yard. A tire swing hung from a thick, dead branch. The damp air smelled of decay.

A single flower grew in an old flowerbed choked with weeds, a Cherokee rose common along the Trail of Tears. The Indian mothers had cried as their children died during the exodus west to the reservations. Their tears planted these white roses all the way to Oklahoma. Here, it was a single spark of life and beauty among the decay and squalor. A single tear shed for the plague kids.

Seeing nobody around, Sally walked up to the front door and rang the bell. A rusty chime filled the house. No answer, like they'd all packed up and left. She was about to ring again when the door creaked open. The house poured out its warm, musty breath along with strange sounds, hoots and growls and flapping.

A man stood in the doorway in jeans and T-shirt. "You lost or something?"

"I'm Sally Albod. My daddy sent me out to check on Enoch and George and Edward. Make sure they're coming tomorrow. Are they around? Daddy's got important work for them to do this week. Cotton needs harvesting."

It was a good lie. The best lies always came wrapped around the truth.

The man scratched at one of his sideburns. Crude tattoos rippled and flexed along his forearms. "You're Reggie's little girl."

"That's right, mister, um."

"Bowie. I'm Ray Bowie."

"Mr. Bowie, can I see the boys just for a minute please?"

"The boys. You don't want to see their teacher."

Sally scrambled for a good answer. Of course, Mr. Bowie would want to fetch Mr. Gaines to answer her question. She brazened it out. "Seeing as it's Sunday and Mr. Gaines ain't working, just the boys will do."

"Most of 'em are out carrying on in the woods, but I'll check if your crew is on the premises. You wait right here, darlin'."

The door slammed shut, sending a tremor through the floorboards. Sally looked around at the chipped paint covering the porch. She touched a curling piece and watched it flutter to her feet. She leaned to peek inside the big cracked picture window, but somebody had drawn the curtains. She heard muffled noises from inside, bangs and something roaring.

God, what a place. She shouldn't have come here.

The door creaked open again and Dave Gaines stepped out. "Ray came and told me we was being visited by a hissy fit with a tail on it. What you doing out here, Miss Sally?"

Brazen it out, Sally told herself. "I came to check on the boys and make sure they're coming tomorrow."

"Did you now?" His breath smelled like beer.

"That's right. What are you doing working on a Sunday?"

"The principal wanted me come in for something special, so I did. You mean you came all the way out here to ask for the boys. Not to see me."

"I didn't ask for you, Mr. Gaines. But since you're here, please do the job my daddy pays you to do and fetch the boys."

"I don't work for your daddy," he said. "Anyways, you want to ask about whether the boys are coming, I'm the one you're asking, not them."

His good eye dropped to her chest then to her bare knees visible under the hem of her dress. Looking down made his eyes line up in the same direction.

She crossed her arms over her breasts. "What did I tell you about being forward with me, Mr. Gaines? You're drunk."

"Like I said, it's Sunday. You want a beer?"

"You should mind your manners."

"You know what I think? I think your daddy didn't send you out here at all."

"We can always ask him and see what he says."

"I think your daddy don't even know you're here."

She shrank back as he took a step forward. "You keep away from me."

"Or what?"

"You touch me, it won't be Daddy killing you. It'll be me. I'll be the last thing you ever see."

He tilted his head back and laughed. "It'd be worth it. All those pretty blond girls on that farm, and you're the only one worth a fight."

"It's a fight you don't want, trust me."

"You got spirit, girl. But your mind is all wrong. You won't let a man give you a compliment, but you got a soft spot for your little cuckoos. It don't add up."

"Why you call them that? They ain't crazy."

"I'm referring to the birds," he said. "They lay their eggs in other birds' nests. Their babies hatch and take all the food from the rightful babies, force the parents to take care of them."

"That's a mean way of looking at it."

"What, you think they're saints? They ain't saints any more than I am or pretend to be. Any more than you are deep down. When you lie in bed alone on a warm night. Now I know you didn't come out here to see any creepers."

He took another step toward her.

"You better keep away from me," she warned.

"I know what you want," Mr. Gaines said. "How about you and me take a walk out back so we can talk."

Sally's toughness flew away at the idea of him lying on top of her, forcing her down into the dirt. Mashing himself between her legs, his rank breath in her face. Planting himself in her sex, his seed maybe crawling with the germ. Little worms inside her starting a monster baby that would live in this house.

She ran.

The yard swam in her gaze. Banging and roaring in her

ears. Something in the trees. Mr. Gaines's mocking laughter following her all the way back to the county road.

He admired her as she bolted across the yard. Blond hair flying. Muscles working under her little dress. Flashes of bare legs. Such a nubile young thing.

Dave Gaines had brought the creeper boys to the Albod farm for years and hardly gave Albod's sloe-eyed youngest a second look. Now she was all grown up like a sweet Georgia peach ready to be plucked and sucked.

Young, pretty, and legal, but that wasn't her whole appeal. He meant what he said about her spirit. The way she walked around the farm like a little barefoot Scarlett O'Hara, looking down on him as the hired help while waiting on her pets with iced tea. All that fire looking for somebody to burn. He just knew she'd be a wild one in bed once he got her lathered up and taught proper. He would give it to her gentle or rough, however she liked it. Whatever she liked, he would give it to her as long as she gave him what he needed. The key to taming a wild animal wasn't to break its spirit but to get it to respond to your command. Get all that bursting spirit directed at you and what you wanted.

He liked flirting with her but never thought it'd come to anything. Now he saw an open road. Her coming all the way out here pretending to check on the creepers. She wasn't fooling anybody. Let her run. She'd come running back soon enough, yes, sir. She wanted him even if she didn't really know it yet. He just had to keep the pressure on until her mind and body got on the same page.

Good thing he was drinking today. It had made him brave and bold. Let him tell her where he stood and what he wanted. That was how a man did things.

Her white dress flickered in the trees like a candle in the dark. Then she was gone. Inside the house, Bowie and the principal waited on him. Old Willard in his usual three-piece suit, jacket off and shirtsleeves rolled up, Bible on the steel sink next to his instruments. Ready to teach an unruly creeper a wholesome fear of the Lord and the Home rules. Dirty work, but it was part of the job that kept a roof over his and his boy's head.

Gaines snorted one last time and went inside. The stink of sweat and mildew washed over him. Then he headed down to Discipline, where the problem kids went.

Eleven

Come Monday, the bell filled the school with its piercing ring. The hallways flooded with tramping kids. Freed from their desks, they talked, slammed lockers, and packed up books and homework to go home. They spilled out the main doors.

Bright sunshine outside. The janitor rode his mower in lazy circles on the lawn. The big yellow buses sat idling ready to take everybody home. Insects buzzed in the warmth. The day belonged to the children now.

Anything could happen. Nothing much ever did, but it could, and that counted. Releasing pent-up energy, everybody screamed and laughed except Jake and his friends frowning at the ground.

Amy noticed her friends looking glum. "What's bugging all y'all?"

"I got in so much trouble with my daddy it ain't funny," Michelle said.

"They find out you stole their wine?"

"No. It was talking to the plague kids. Which apparently

is a crime against humanity. I wish I'd never laid eyes on them boys."

Troy picked a pebble off the ground and winged it into the road. "Let's go down to the corner store. Get a Coke or something."

"I ain't got money," Sally said. "But I can tag along."

The rest nodded. They would skip the buses. Hang out and talk. Go down to the store and buy some Cokes. Walk home later before the dark came.

"I'll share mine with you," Troy said.

Sally didn't thank him for the offer. She seemed preoccupied by her thoughts. Michelle said she could go as long as she was home by five on the dot.

"What about you?" Amy asked Jake. "Did your daddy chew you out?"

"I told him we're all God's creatures. I told him Jesus said to love the sick. Then I told him he could stick it where the sun don't shine."

The kids laughed at that.

"Did you really say all that?"

"Not in those exact words, but yeah. Pa don't scare me with his hellfire."

"Then why do you look mad?"

Jake stopped and stared at her. "You don't know?"

"What? Did I do something wrong?"

Her chin wobbled. Such a beautiful day with the sun shining and school out. He couldn't be breaking up with her already.

He planted a wet kiss on her cheek and took her hand. "Hey. You did nothing wrong. Whatever gave you that wild notion? Quit worrying."

"Then what is it? Tell me."

"It's everything Brain was talking about. It stuck in my head all weekend. How all I've been doing to make things better is playing."

"Always the monsters. I want to talk about our world for a change."

"It's our world I'm worried about."

"The sheriff is a no-good bully," Sally said.

Jake turned to study her. "You're looking white as a ghost all day, Sal. You okay?"

"I don't want to speak on it."

"Did your daddy give you grief?"

"I said I don't want to speak on it," she grated.

"All right. Jeez. Sorry I asked."

"Word is getting around," Troy said. "People been giving me funny looks all day."

"I don't care what they look," Jake said.

"I hear that. Just keep in mind we have to live here."

"We're the ones getting punished for talking to them," Michelle said. "And all they did was tell us how no good we are."

"Are you kidding me?" Jake said. "Think about how they get punished every damn day. Everything Brain said is true, and we all know it."

Sally said, "It is true. Every bit of it."

Michelle exhaled a frustrated sigh. "Oh, come now. People chase plague kids into the woods in some countries. Shoot them on sight. They live like animals. Not in America. Those kids at the Home should be grateful they get three squares and a bed. They even get proper schooling."

Jake shook his head. "You missed my point by a mile."

"Well, excuse me for wanting peace and quiet. I'm grounded, like, forever."

"I think Michelle's right about one thing," Amy chimed in. "There's a lot more peace and quiet without them kids around. We should let them alone."

"You too, huh," Jake said.

"Don't act surprised. You already knew where I stand. I just want to live a normal life, not take on the world. Everything is the way it is for a reason, and it's out of our control to change it."

Amy remembered how strange the plague boys were. How impossible it was they lived in the real world. How terrifying it was when they recognized her.

Hey, cousin, the dog thing said. It had frightened her, and not just because they almost blew her secret and ruined her life. It frightened her because when the dog thing called her cousin, she wasn't sure what she looked like at that moment. She feared her beauty had disappeared and exposed her as a hideous monstrosity, something to be pitied or hated, and she'd have to live at the Home forever.

Even more reason to keep away from them. The gorilla boy had also seen what she was but had covered for her. She figured she owed him one. Otherwise, she wanted to stay as far from those kids as she could.

A voice called out, "Hey, it's the monster lover."

The kids turned around. Archie Gaines walked up with Earl Kimbrel and Dan Fulcher on either side of him. He dropped his backpack on the grass.

"Lord," Jake said. "If it ain't bedbugs, it's ants."

"You had yourselves a little party with some monster kids, I hear."

"Your daddy was there, too," Michelle taunted him. "He works with them so much he loves them. I saw him kissing one on the lips."

"Stay out of this. I'm talking to the monster lover here. Mister Cool. The one whose ass I'm about to kick."

"I don't want to fight you," Jake said.

"You're a coward, then. I'm gonna make sure everybody knows it. Jake Coombs is a monster lover and a coward."

Jake's eyes went wide and watery as the air thickened with potential violence.

Amy touched his arm. "Come on, baby. Let's go get that Coke."

He shrugged off her hand. "Just a minute."

"Go get your Coke." Archie laughed. "Faggot."

Amy fixed her best glare on him. "You keep that up, Archie Gaines, I'm gonna tell every girl in school what you are. A no-good rotten bully no self-respecting girl would ever want to be seen with."

"You stay out of it, too. Just because you're pretty don't make you queen of the girls. You ain't no queen, hanging out with this faggot."

Jake frowned at the ground. His mouth moved a little, like he was figuring out a math problem in his head. Then he nodded. "All right."

"All right what?" Archie said. "That you're a faggot?" Earl and Dan laughed. "Maybe the darkie here is your boyfriend?"

"Come on," Troy said. "Let's get out of here."

"In a minute," Jake said.

He walked up to Archie, who smiled back at him.

Jake punched him in the face.

Amy blinked, then Archie was sitting on the ground

holding his nose. Everybody gasped. Nobody had seen it coming.

Archie squealed like a stuck pig. "You sucker punched me."

Jake squared off on the other boys, who took a step back. "Hey, Earl."

"Hey, Jake."

"Dan."

"Hey, what's up."

The boys didn't want any of what Archie got. Jake bent down to look him in the eye while he massaged his sore knuckles.

"You want to get up, Archie, I'll give you a free punch. Then I get to do whatever I want after that. As long as I like. Is that what you want?"

Archie glared back at him. "No, I'm done."

"I didn't hit you for calling me a monster lover and a faggot. I hit you for saying it like it's a bad thing. Like you know what you're talking about. Are we clear?"

The boy didn't answer, his fingers bloody around his nose.

Jake's tone changed to menace. "I asked you are we clear."

"Yeah. Yeah, we're clear."

"I also hit you for talking rude to my girl and my friend. You should say you're sorry."

"Sorry," Archie said.

"It's all right," Amy said. "Let's have no more yelling and fighting."

"You carry on like this again, I'll hit you," Jake said. "I will hit you so hard you'll look like one of them. You'll live in the Home with them the rest of your days."

"I said I'm done. Now leave me the hell alone."

"All right."

Jake walked away with a sad look on his face like he was

the one got punched. His friends fell in behind him, all of them walking a little taller now.

Amy took his hand in hers. "Are you okay?"

"So stupid," he said. "I used to climb trees with that kid. We was like best friends the summer after third grade. We caught salamanders."

"I can't believe you hit him," Troy said, bouncing on his heels. "I didn't think you were gonna do anything. You looked real scared."

"I was scared. Any man enjoys punching somebody is crazy."

"He didn't give you a choice," Sally said.

"We always have a choice. Jesus said, *Turn the other cheek.*"

"Sometimes, the bad ones need their cheeks smacked, too."

"Maybe," Jake said, though he still looked worried he did the wrong thing.

Troy grinned. "Pow. You just went and popped him in the nose."

"I'm done talking about it, Troy."

"Sure, sure. But I'm buying you a Coke at the store. Any kind you want."

Amy didn't say anything. She held Jake's sweaty hand but otherwise gave him space. She sneaked a glance at his anxious profile. His mouth kept moving a little like he was still figuring out that math problem, working it out again in his mind to make sure he'd produced the correct answer.

A truck passed with a honk. The kids waved back. Despite its mean streak, Huntsville was a friendly town. Five thousand people just trying to get by like everybody else, another ten thousand living on farms and ranches outside of town. They had built a way of life here they wanted to protect. A community of like-minded folks. Amy longed to feel a part of it. Join the flow. Live a normal life like everybody else.

Amy pictured Jake accepting her for what she was. They get married in a big church wedding, his daddy officiating, Sally the maid of honor, Troy the best man. Everybody happy and smiling. They buy a house and fix it up real nice. They can't have kids so they adopt beautiful babies. These babies grow up healthy and safe until old enough to earn their own chance at getting the best of everything life offered. She and Jake grow old together and die happy knowing they spent lives worth living.

Sometimes, she could almost believe it.

She squeezed his hand. "I got something important I need to tell you."

"What?"

"I love you right back, Jake Coombs."

Twelve

The Home bustled as the plague children finished their breakfasts and tramped outside to the trucks. Dave Gaines walked among freaks ugly enough for a lifetime of nightmares, but barely noticed them. Working at the Home, he never thought he'd get used to the creepers, but there you go, you can get used to almost anything.

He moved self-consciously, aware of Principal Willard staring down at the scene from a second-floor window. Tight-lipped smile, sunken cheeks, thinning white hair combed over his balding skull. He stood rock-still like somebody perched a scarecrow up there. Only his eyes moved, seeing everything. The kids called him Big Daddy; the teachers just called him the Colonel. He commanded troops in Vietnam, gave the gooks hell in the Central Highlands in '67.

The creepers moved slower than usual, piddling as long as they could despite the teachers shouting their throats raw. The kids were sullen and irritable this morning. Word had gotten around about Toby going to Discipline. The Colonel worked him over but good. The old coot had acquired years of practice finding out how far he could hurt somebody before he died or suffered damage of the permanent kind. He went too far Sunday, though. Toby died in the chair.

The stupid kid everybody called Sucker Punch. His face shaped like a hatchet with a little shit-eating grin and two protruding eyes rolling around in their sockets. They let him see in all directions like a species of lizard. The boys said he couldn't ever get sucker punched with eyes like that. They put it to the test once, then at least once every few months since. All fails. That was how he got his name.

Then Sucker Punch decided to try it on them. He took to standing behind corners and decking other creepers as they walked by. Violence was against the rules, but Willard tolerated it to a certain degree. Sucker Punch couldn't stop, though, once he got started. He had a mess of paybacks to dish out. He became a chronic offender. Chronic offenders got written up and sent to Discipline.

The weird thing was his fist was already coming around before his victim turned the corner. You were walking along and then bang, here was this fist coming at you from nowhere. He also only hit the smaller, weaker creepers. He somehow knew who to punch. When to punch. It was like he could see around the corner.

Gaines would never learn how he did it. Toby's heart gave out in the chair.

A mess of paperwork. Maybe an investigation. Then probably a slap on the wrist unless some do-gooder at the Bureau wanted to shake things up and make a name for himself. Technically, you weren't allowed to use force against a kid unless he was, quote, an immediate threat to life or limb, unquote.

Willard probably already wrote it up as an accident. Snapped the kid's neck bone and said he fell down the stairs.

No autopsy. The body was delivered straight to the oven at the mortuary. If the Bureau sent out a field agent, the Colonel would call Gaines and Bowie together so they could get their stories straight.

Gaines didn't give a crap about the dumb little pecker, but he didn't want him to die, either. Nonetheless, he would play along with the cover-up. It was that or get hung out to dry. Lose his job or worse, get framed for the murder, and spend the rest of his days locked up in the state pen down in Reidsville.

He opened his truck's tailgate and got his cuckoos loaded up. "Get in there. Don't rush on my account."

He fished the keys from his jeans pocket and started the truck. He hung his hairy arm out the window as Bowie came strolling up.

"Morning, Ray."

The man put his hands against the truck's metal skin and leaned. "Called in sick yesterday, huh."

"Yup," said Gaines.

"Sick from that moonshine we put away after the creeper kicked the bucket."

"Yeah, maybe."

"Yeah, don't do that again. I had to carry your kids all day. I got my own crew to handle. They don't pay me double to take two crews. You owe me."

"People get sick, Ray."

"Maybe you're sick of working."

"What do you mean?" Gaines said. "Why are you saying that?"

Bowie leaned closer. "You disappear the day after one of our kids has himself an accident. Looks real bad. Makes the old man uncomfortable."

"Did he saying anything to you?"

"Well, you know the Colonel. He don't talk much, but you always know what's on his mind."

"Aw, hell," Gaines said. "I did not think of that."

"You were busy, maybe. Wrestling with your conscience."

"Goddamnit. It ain't that. It's something else got me."

"What is it then?" Bowie said. "Maybe I can help you out."

"It ain't none of your business, is what it is."

"Just remember we're in it together, friend."

Gaines jerked the transmission into gear. "Aw, go fuck yourself, Ray."

The man jumped back as the truck lurched forward. Gaines glanced up at the upstairs window. Willard stared back down at him. His bowels turned to water. He peeled out of the yard under the principal's sentinel gaze, spraying a rooster tail of mud.

"Oh, Lord," he groaned.

He'd screwed up by calling in sick yesterday. He should have been smart enough to put two and two together. This was how he got bopped with a board when he was a little kid and ended up with a funny eye. This was why his wife left him with Archie to raise on his own. This was how he ended up working at the Home with ex-cons and cokeheads. Not because he drank too much or gambled away his paycheck on card games, no sir. He always got the shaft because he was too slow to spot the angle and keep himself in the clear. Life did him more than he did life.

He pulled onto County Road 20 and stepped on the gas. The ancient Chevy growled in response. The truck chugged until it reached a steady speed and put a safe distance between himself and the scarecrow in the window.

Just a five-minute drive to the farm road. Another five to Albod's.

Driving like mad out of the frying pan toward the fire.

Albod, the reason he called in sick.

After Sucker Punch's heart gave out, Willard sent him and Bowie packing. Gaines drove home feeling out of kilter with his buzz going sour in his brain. *He didn't have to go and kill the little pecker*, he raved. *He didn't have to go that far.*

What a mess. Discipline was one thing, something worthwhile to keep the creepers in line. Murder, though. Gaines realized something he always knew but never before dared think out in the open. The old man enjoyed it. The only time Gaines ever saw him sweat was when he worked a kid over in the chair. Big, sour-smelling sweat stains under his armpits. The single light bulb danging from the ceiling. The room bare except for the chair and steel sink.

His unease had followed him all the way home, where he'd sobered up and started thinking about Sally Albod. How maybe he'd poorly read the situation. How she was likely crying her precious little heart out to her daddy right now. How his goose was cooked, only he didn't know it yet. Gaines would show up at the farm, and there is Albod with his shotgun in easy reach, both barrels loaded with double-aught. He tries to talk his way out of it. *You know how little girls are. They do like to stir up trouble. It's the gospel truth, Reggie. Ain't it the gospel truth? To them, everything's a drama like on TV.*

He keeps talking until his grave is good and dug because he never could read an angle and keep himself in the clear.

He'd called in sick and spent the day moping around his trailer picking at his chores. At the time, he really was sick, sick with fright, so scared he barely noticed when Archie came home with a busted nose and went straight to his room. He couldn't call in sick again today. It was either face the music or quit his job.

By calling in sick, he'd delayed his punishment a single day while maybe making Willard suspicious. The one man you don't want suspicious of you.

Oh, Lord, he thought. It ain't fair, none of it.

He yanked the wheel and turned onto the farm road, raising a dust cloud. The creepers hung on to keep from spilling out. He actually envied them right now. How nice it must be to live as a creeper. All your thinking done for you. Three squares a day, a roof over your head, and no choice about anything. Not a care in the world. Just follow the rules spelled out for you, and you'd suffer no worse than the average man.

Gaines drove onto Albod's farm and parked the Chevy in the yard.

The farmer stood on his porch smoking one of his rolled-up cigarettes.

"Fine morning," Gaines called out with forced cheer. "Yes, sir."

"Morning, Dave."

"How is everything? Is everything okay?"

"Why wouldn't it be?"

"No reason. Just chewing the fat. You got a list for the day?"

"Just one thing on my list. A mess of cotton still needs picking. Not George, though. I need him on the livestock today. I got a heifer getting set to calve. And put Edward on the vegetable patch. He ain't no use picking cotton."

"We'll be done that field by the end of the day, Reggie. You were worried about Mary, but she's the best in the crew. Didn't I tell you I'd teach her good?"

"That field got done yesterday while you had the sniffles. Bowie took care of it. I want you on another field. The coloreds ain't picking fast enough."

"Don't you worry none," Gaines said. "We'll handle it lickety-split."

Albod gave him the eye for a moment. Gaines mopped sweat with a handkerchief while he smiled back.

The farmer shook his head. "All right. Get to it, I guess."

Gaines was grinning now. "Come on, you kids. You heard the boss. Get out the truck. Pokes are in the barn. Get me one, too, Enoch. I'm gonna pitch in today."

"Yes, sir," the dog said.

"George, you heard Mr. Albod. You're with the animals."

"All right, Mr. Gaines."

He scanned the house. No sign of Miss Sally. Maybe he'd catch a glimpse of her on the way to school and give her a wink. Make his presence known.

She hadn't told her daddy about him coming on to her, which meant one thing. She wanted him. He was right.

The talk they had. Their little secret.

Darlene ran off years ago and left him to raise Archie on his own. After that, he found that not many girls hankered to date a man who worked at a Home. They made assumptions about the germ. They had notions that teaching the kids was unclean work fit only for a rough sort of man. Gaines thought diddling with Sally Albod was just what he needed to put some spice in his life. Now he saw the big picture. No need for spice when a man could have the whole steak.

Sally offered him a ticket out of the Home. A way off the Colonel's dark road. His rescue from dealing with monster kids with swishing tails and batwings for ears. The plan arrived fully formed in his mind. He gets her on the hook.

A year down the road, he marries her. A mess of years separating their ages, but it ain't unheard of, it happens. As for Albod, he is getting along in years himself. He hires Gaines on full-time at the farm. Gaines moves into this nice big ol' house with all these pretty blond girls sharing space under the same roof. At last, he's running with the big dogs. Sally Albod makes all his dreams come true.

Finally, for once in his shadowed life, Gaines had himself an angle.

Thirteen

Sally walked to school behind her sisters. Normally a late sleeper, she'd gotten up extra early today so she could go with them. The girls talked about school, boys, music. She didn't participate, keeping her head down.

Every time a truck passed on the lonely road, she flinched and stared at her sneakers as they crunched the stones. Sally didn't even want to look at Dave Gaines right now. Scaring the wits out of her like that on Sunday. She'd had nightmares two nights running.

In last night's dream, he showed up in her bedroom reeking of beer. *Don't you look fine, Miss Sally. How'd you like to earn a dollar?* She knew if she tried to leave, his arm would lunge like a copperhead and snag her. The curtains blew on a breeze, the open window pitch black with night. She could jump and take her chances, but she couldn't move. She stayed rooted to the spot.

That was when he touched her, his hot breath stinging her neck.

Sally had woken up gasping with a crushing weight on her chest. Pushing and kicking at her sheets, her nightgown soaked with sweat. She went to the bathroom for a drink of water, weeping with shame.

She hadn't jumped. In the end, she'd let him have her.

She could tell Daddy everything and make it all go away. By the time Daddy got through with that pervert, he'd be pissing with a crutch. Nobody messed with Reggie Albod or his kin. This simple truth was practically county law. But Sally would have to explain what she was doing out at the Home. Sheriff Burton might spill the beans about her dressing up in monsta face.

A big ol' applecart falling over and making a mess of trouble. Daddy doted on her and her sisters. When he laid down the law, though, it was to be regarded as one of the Commandments, no rebelling permitted. With a single sentence spoken, Daddy could change her life.

Her liberties, her friends, everything.

No, she couldn't tell Daddy. For now, she was on her own.

At school, she dumped her book bag in her locker. Amy fell into step beside her on her way to homeroom.

"You look like you got the weight of the world on your shoulders," Amy said. "What's wrong?"

Sally turned up a smile that came out a grimace. She wanted to be honest but couldn't. If she did, Amy might tell other people, who might tell their folks. If her daddy heard about Mr. Gaines's advances from anybody but her, he'd think she'd encouraged it. Might even believe she was carrying on with him behind his back.

Then there'd be hell to pay for everybody.

"I'm fine," she said. "You look tied in a knot yourself. How are you?"

"I don't know. Jake's been out of sorts ever since he punched out Archie."

"He really hates violence. It's bugging him he had to resort to it."

"I don't like when he's distant. I don't know where I stand. Yesterday, I did a big stretch in health class. Rob Rowland's eyes nearly popped through his Coke-bottle glasses. Jake hardly even noticed."

Sally laughed. "He must have some weight on his mind."

"I should just give him some space, right?"

The bell rang. "I got to go. We'll have dinner together and talk more."

She attended her morning classes, though her mind roamed elsewhere. Just going through the motions. In health class, she took her seat next to Archie Gaines, who wore a hangdog look and a piece of tape over his nose.

"You all done fighting?" she said.

"That's up to him. I'm ready for a rematch any time he is."

"Your nose gonna be okay?"

His sorry condition touched her. It must have been hard for him, growing up without no mama and half a daddy.

Archie's face reddened. "I'll be fine."

"I'm sorry to see you hurting, is all."

"I don't need anybody feeling sorry for me."

"Jake ain't happy about it, either. Maybe you should just leave each other be."

"Jake's all right," Archie said.

Amy walked in and took her seat in the back next to Jake, who sat hunched over his notebook scribbling. Archie followed her progress with hungry eyes.

Sally understood now. Archie liked Jake just fine, but he liked Amy far more. That was why he'd started up on Jake about the plague kids and tried to pick a fight. All cover for what he really wanted. Just like his daddy, wanting things he couldn't have and willing to make everybody miserable in his pursuit.

"We'll see how it goes," Archie added.

She turned away. She didn't want to talk to him anymore. The apple had fallen too close to the tree for her liking. It was unsettling that even after Archie got his nose punched, he still wanted what he wanted.

Mr. Benson told the class to simmer down. He sat on the edge of his desk. "I want to talk to all y'all about something kind of serious today. You won't find it in the textbook or on the next test. This is something pretty new. Or rather, something old we're just now figuring out and able to study."

The teacher went to the board and wrote, DATE RAPE.

"Rape is sex that happens without one partner's consent," he went on. "Today, society considers it one of the worst crimes. If you're infected with the germ and pass it on through rape, you could go to jail for life."

Mr. Benson picked up a magazine off his desk and held it high for everybody to see. Sally caught a glimpse of the word *Ms.*, the liberal way of saying miss, on the cover.

"Two years ago, an article was published about date rape in colleges," he said. "This is where rape happens between people who know each other. Maybe a guy gets you so drunk you pass out. Or it happens during a date. This kind of thing goes on far more often than we thought, and it's alarming for a mess of reasons."

The teacher returned to the front of his desk and parked his rear on the edge. "My lecture is short and sweet. Don't do it. Sex is between consenting adults. That's it. Otherwise, I want to know what all y'all think today. I know it's an uncomfortable topic, but I'm hoping we can have a discussion."

Hands shot up across the classroom, mostly girls. Did a woman have to give consent out loud for it to be real? What if a man already had a sexual relationship with a woman? What if they were already married? Was it consent if a woman said yes to sex while drunk? What if she said yes but then got drunk and passed out? What if she said yes but changed her mind halfway through the act? What if she changed her mind the next morning after she sobered up?

"Well I'll be," Mr. Benson said. "These are really good questions."

Sally crossed her arms and listened. The teacher did his best answering. It turned out that while his proposed solution was simple, the whole thing was pretty complicated. Legal jurisdictions looked at it in different ways, resulting in a mess of precedents. It was hard to prove rape between people who were dating. And it remained legal for a man to have sex with his wife without her consenting to it.

He kept tossing their questions back at them, asking what they thought.

She raised her hand. "What about the victim? What if a friend of the family rapes a girl and tells her she asked for it. She can't tell anybody because she's awful ashamed and she thinks they won't believe her. What does she do?"

The teacher pulled a handkerchief from his back pocket and wiped beads of sweat from his forehead. "Wow." The bell rang. "And I'm saved by the bell. Excellent discussion today. Go get your dinner."

The kids started packing up their pencils and notebooks. Sally got up from her desk and approached Mr. Benson.

He smiled. "When I said I was saved by the bell, I meant I didn't have a good answer for you. That's another one I would have thrown back to the class."

"I got one more question for you. I hope you can answer it."

"I'll give it my best shot."

"What if a guy won't leave a girl alone and she thinks he might rape her."

"But no crime's been committed."

"That's right."

"And she knows him?"

"Yeah."

"If there's a boy at this school bugging you," he said.

"There ain't."

"Well, that's another tough one. You can't arrest people for saying things. I guess the best thing for her is to avoid being alone with him."

"Okay," she said, disappointed.

"Maybe the girl could reach out to friends and family who can protect her. She could learn ways to protect herself. Otherwise, I'd have to think on it."

Sally couldn't go to her daddy. Could she ask Troy or Jake?

Maybe she didn't have to suffer this alone.

The alternative was to keep a steak knife in her book bag.

"Thanks, Mr. Benson."

"Sally, these are really specific questions," he said. "Are you sure there's nothing you want to tell me?"

"I'm sure," she said.

Fourteen

Eyes followed Amy as she walked across the school cafeteria with her tray of chicken, dumplings, and beans. It amazed her how just walking across a room fully clothed made the boys ache and sweat. Just a few years ago, they were all a big club that wanted nothing to do with the girls. Now they grinned and stared. Even after Jake busted Archie's face, they gave her the brazen eye.

All these boys checking her out, talking about her behind her back, thinking about her when they went to bed. Meanwhile, the one boy she wanted looking had his nose buried in a sheet of paper.

Jake wore a white collared dress shirt today. No T-shirt with an angry band logo. She liked him with a clean-cut look, but it just added to the mystery.

"Hey," she said. "Can I sit with you boys?"

"Sure," he said.

Michelle sat alongside her. They looked over at Jake and Troy reading and talking like conspirators. Bag dinners sat untouched on the table between them.

"What are you boys fixin' to do now?" Michelle said.

Jake looked at Amy as if she'd asked the question. "You ain't gonna like it. But it's something I got to do."

"Quit being mysterious and spill the beans," Michelle said.

Still looking at Amy, Jake shook his head. "After school."

"It's gonna be crazy," Troy said.

"What are you reading there?" Amy said.

"Something I wrote," Jake told her. "I was thinking about Archie. How I had to slug him to make my point. I'd like to reach out to folks in a different manner."

"How are you gonna do that?"

"After school. If you want to come along with me, you'll see."

"Jake Coombs, am I beautiful?"

He smiled. "As a sunrise."

"And do you love me?"

Jake glanced at his friends, who stared at him with wide eyes. He set his jaw. "I sure do, Amy Green. I love you more than anything."

"Oh, my Lord," Michelle said while Troy laughed.

"So this thing you're planning," Amy pressed. "You'd rather do whatever it is than make out with me. Is that what I'm hearing?"

The question wiped the smile off his face. "It's something I got to do. I'm done playing at making things happen. Meet me after school and you'll see."

"Oh," Amy said, struck by his seriousness. "All right."

He grinned. "We could still make out on the way home, maybe."

"We might could. You'll just have to see. Looks like we're in the same boat, huh? Pins and needles."

Sally showed up with her dinner box and sat with them.

Jake had already gone back to his papers. Amy exchanged glances with Michelle. They were more than a little curious, but they knew how to bide their time.

Sally unwrapped her sandwich and tucked in. "What a health class, huh?"

"We got a situation," Michelle said.

"What did I miss?"

"Meet me in the bathroom after dinner," Amy said.

There, the girls stood in front of the mirror and talked it out. Troy, they decided, was the weak link, Sally his Achilles heel. She worked on him all through gym class. But she couldn't get it out of him, and now she had to go to the movies with him sometime.

They just had to wait.

When the bell rang at three-fifteen, they found Jake outside with Troy.

Amy tugged at her hair. "So where are we going?"

"The A & P," Jake said. "I'm fixin' to hand this out to everybody coming into the store."

He gave her a photocopy of a crudely typewritten sheet. At the top, she read in capitals, THE PLAGUE GENERATION.

"When did you write this?"

"Last night. I used the typewriter and copier in the office at Pa's church."

The little fuzzy black letters seemed to crawl across the page. A mess of strikeouts. Jake couldn't type to save his life. Still, she could see the passion that went into it. The heavy keystrokes. He'd poured his heart out into these words.

"Well I'll be," she said.

"Brain was wrong about one thing," he said. "What I'm gonna do ain't about them. It's about me, and I'm good with that. It's about what kind of man I want to be. Sometimes, you got to walk the walk."

"You look scared. You sure you ain't fixin' to fight again?"

"I am scared. This is a different kind of fight. The hardest kind. But maybe I can make a point to folks and change their hearts without punching them in the face."

"First, you bop Archie Gaines," Michelle said. "Now this. You are better than a trip to the video store. Count me in."

"You're just gonna make them mad," Amy warned him.

"If I do, I'll know it's working," Jake said. "People get mad when they think."

"I mean really mad. You have to live here with them."

"Last I checked, they have to live with me, too."

He was so sure of himself she found it both sexy and annoying.

In the A & P parking lot, he tucked in his shirt, produced a tie from his jeans pocket, and tied it around the collar. He took a deep breath and let it go.

Troy handed him his stack of flyers at the front of the store before pulling a Mr. Pibb out the vending machine. He popped the cap. "Here comes a customer."

A woman pushed her buggy out the store. Amy recognized her as Mrs. Dawkins, a widow who worked for the county and lived alone in the trailer park on the other side of town. A mess of cat food boxes were piled in the buggy.

Jake handed her a flyer. "Hello, Mrs. Dawkins. Fine day."

She inspected the paper. "What's this about? What are you giving me this for?"

"The plague children deserve the same opportunities as us."

Mrs. Dawkins pursed her lips. "Bless your heart, Jake Coombs."

The buggy rattled on toward her car while Jake's friends laughed. When a Southern woman blessed your heart, she was calling you an idiot.

"She feeds every stray cat in town," Michelle said. "If you can't get Mrs. Dawkins to listen to your cause, you are in trouble, bubba."

"This ain't a movie," Jake said. "You got to start somewhere. Hello, Mrs. Dickey."

The little old raisin of a lady walked up nice and slow, pulling along a cylindrical air tank on wheels. She breathed through her tube and recognized him with a bright smile.

"Well, hello, Jake," she wheezed. "God bless you and the fine service you're doing. I pray for you every day."

She handed him a crumpled dollar bill and went into the store. The kids laughed again. Mrs. Dickey thought Jake was collecting for his daddy's church.

Jake's face burned red. "Guess I owe Pa a dollar. Hello, Mrs. Peel."

The big woman squinted at the paper. "What's all this about?"

"The plague children deserve the same life we have," he said.

"What, you want to integrate? Sit next to them at school or something?"

"Right now, I just want people to think about what's being done to those kids."

"For crying out loud, boy," she said. "Why would anybody want to think about that?"

"Because when you get past how they look, they're people, same as us, ma'am. Out of Christian love, we need to look inside and see their humanity."

"Why do you want to go and open these old wounds?" Her voice rose to a scream. "What's wrong with you?"

Amy looked away, stunned. Sobbing, Mrs. Peel hustled her empty buggy into the store before Jake could answer.

Nobody spoke in the ensuing shock.

They're like Mama, Amy thought. Living day to day hiding away from what was really going on in the world. Sweeping dirt under the carpet and hoping nobody noticed it was ever there.

Whether they had the germ or not, older folks all lived with it and what it had done. They all carried a sense of shame about it. Nobody wanted to talk about it, much less do anything. They didn't want to think about abandoned monster kids growing up in squalor a few miles away. They wanted to forget and live their lives, though monsters infested their dreams.

As for Jake, he had a good heart, but he hadn't thought this through. Folks here already felt shafted by the state dumping a Home in their backyard, like they were being punished for living in a poor rural county. Only one plague baby born in all of Stark County (two counting her), and they had to let hundreds of them run amok in the town? Pay for a bigger school for them? Why was he picking scabs and waking bad dreams from their sleep? What did he want, exactly?

Just by handing out a few flyers, Jake was stirring up more worms than a bait store. A few folks inside the A & P eyed him through the window and pointed. Michelle and Sally and Troy sat on the ground and cast worried looks at him. This didn't strike them as funny anymore. Jake was asking for a mess of trouble.

"Maybe it's time you call it quits," Amy said.

He shook his head, face red and eyes glassy. "All y'all can go home if you want. Hello, sir. Can I give you a flyer?"

The man stopped his buggy and leaned against the handle-bar. "Hello, Miss Sally. Fancy meeting you again. Fine day, ain't it."

Sally glared back at him. "It was fine until you showed up, Mr. Bowie."

"No need to get rude, now. Our mutual friend would want me to say hello."

"He ain't my friend, and neither is you."

"That a fact," Bowie said. "I believe you just hurt my feelings."

"If you got shopping, why don't you get to it and let us be."

Bowie kept on smiling, his eyes crawling across the kids, taking his time with his inspection. They settled on Amy and roamed up and down. "Well, ain't you a sight for sore eyes. You need a ride home, miss?"

Jake pushed a flyer at him. "Something I wrote about the plague kids."

The wiry man scratched at one of his sideburns, taking his time, his eyes still on Amy. She stared back with wide eyes as black scrawl danced on his forearm.

He snatched the flyer from Jake's hand. "Let's see here." He laughed as he read. "Creepers, huh. Shit, boy. What do you know about creepers?"

"I met a few of them—"

Bowie stared at Amy. "How about you, pretty lady? You like creepers?"

"Not so much," she said.

"Well, we got that in common. Maybe you'd like to go see some anyways sometime. You might say I work at the zoo."

"You and Mr. Gaines are a fine pair," Sally said. "Can't get decent folk to come near you, so you bother little girls."

His eyes lazily shifted to her. "I like all kinds. All kinds of folks."

"Sheriff's coming," Troy said.

The sheriff's white Plymouth Gran Fury rolled up and parked. The siren bleeped once to announce he was here on official business. Sheriff Burton cut the engine and took his time getting out. He stood next to the car dusting his hat.

"Ray, by the time I walk over there, you best be someplace else," he said.

"Just reading this here flyer these young ones gave me, Sheriff. This boy wants to save the creepers from us."

"Here I come, walking."

Bowie rolled his tongue around the inside of his mouth, looking defiant. He winked at Amy. "You think about that ride."

Then he pushed his buggy into the store as the sheriff strolled up.

"You kids having another party?"

"It ain't them," Jake said. "It's just me."

The sheriff swiped one of the flyers and muttered over it. He looked up. "Taking your foolishness public. Upsetting folks with a ruckus."

"I am exercising my right to free speech. Sir."

"Well, ain't you a big-city man with that big talk. You start down this road, you know how much trouble you're gonna make trying to change things?"

"I ain't forcing nothing on nobody, sir. I don't even know what changes are needed. I just want folks to see the plague kids as people. It all starts there."

"I let all y'all slide on that party," the sheriff said. "I even let my eyes slip straight past the booze y'all thought you hid. Kids have enough troubles growing up in this world without me adding to them. But if you carry on like this, you'll be inviting a mess of trouble for yourself."

"You do what you need to do, Sheriff."

"Big talk from a little man. What I could do to you would have you begging for mercy. No, I am a believer in self-policing. A safe town polices itself."

Amy shot a glance at the A & P window, now crowded with shoppers looking out at them. She caught sight of Ray Bowie and studied him while he eyeballed the sheriff. The man had made an impression on her with his tattoos and coiled menace she suspected wasn't just an act. There was something about him made her picture copperheads and butter. She wondered what kind of man he was, working with plague kids day in and out.

His eyes shifted to lock onto hers. He smirked. She gasped and looked away.

"The mess you get is gonna come from the very folks whose minds you want to change," the sheriff went on. "Speaking of self-policing, here comes your daddy."

A woodie station wagon pulled into the parking lot and rolled up next to the sheriff's Plymouth. A man in a black clerical suit got out. Even if Amy didn't go to his church on Sundays, she'd know right away he was Jake's daddy, they looked so much alike. Like an older Jake with harder eyes and silver streaks running through the longish hair combed over his ears.

"Hey, Reverend," Burton said. "Found your prodigal son."

Reverend Coombs shook his hand. "I thank you, Sheriff,

for calling me and letting me handle my family. I do appreciate it."

"Don't mention it. No need for me to make an even bigger fuss of it. We was young and foolish once, too."

"This younger generation is spoiled to the core, you ask me. They all think the world owes them everything."

"The older folks said the same about us when we was kids," the sheriff said. "And their folks the same about them. He'll learn just like we did."

"I'll teach him good. You can count on that."

The reverend marched up to Jake, pinched his ear, and pulled him wincing toward the station wagon. One of the flyers fluttered to the ground.

The revolution was over.

Amy gave him a little wave as the car backed up and sped out the parking lot.

Then she turned back to look through the window. Bowie kept on staring at her. She didn't flinch away this time. Go ahead and look all you want, she thought. Cuz that is all a man like you is ever gonna get.

Fifteen

Sally walked home and dashed the last hundred yards into the house. Hens squawked and scattered as she ran past. She stomped straight upstairs to her room and stood gasping at the window. There he was, picking cotton out in the field. The plague kids worked the rows next to him. He was hiding from her, and well he should.

Heat waves rippled up from the cotton field. The golden-white fields beautiful in the late-afternoon sunshine. Mr. Gaines turned and looked at the house. Sally flinched from the window. Then she went back downstairs.

That man was never going to leave her alone. Even now, with her daddy in the barn and her sisters gabbing in the kitchen, it was just like her dream. Him inching toward her. Her backing into the corner as she eyed the window and wondered if she would survive the fall.

Look at her now, skulking in terror around her own home. To make things worse, tonight she feared she'd add Ray Bowie to her dreams. Something about that man gave her the creeps. The way he slithered around and looked at girls. The things Mr. Gaines fantasized about, Sally had a feeling Mr. Bowie did.

Mr. Benson was right. She needed an ally. A protector.

Sally walked out to the barn and crossed the moist hay. All the stalls were empty except one. Marie Rose was having her baby. The heifer paced around on her hoofs, bloated and restless. Daddy and George fussed over her, talking out the coming delivery. For a moment, they were equals, farmer and outcast. Daddy respected George's abilities. The boy could fix anything alive or machine.

She draped her arms over a neck-rail and rested her cheek on her arm. "Hey, Daddy. Hey, George."

Daddy took off his hat and wiped the sweat off his brow. "Hey there, Buttercup. How was school today?"

"Here it comes," George said before she could answer.

Marie Rose was giving birth. A yellowish water sac hung from her vulva. The calf's two front feet appeared. George pulled on shoulder gloves and slathered lubricant on them in case Marie Rose needed help.

"Do you have him?" Daddy said.

George took hold of the calf's feet. "Yup, I got him."

When the heifer pushed, he was ready. He pulled out and down, pausing when Marie Rose took a breather. He was always so good and gentle with the animals, like he could talk to them. Sally gripped the neck-rail and watched the miracle of a living thing making another living thing.

"One more try ought to do it," the plague boy said.

Another push. He delivered the calf, a limp little thing wet with amniotic fluid, and laid it on the straw. He brushed its nostrils to clear the airways. Then he took a bit of straw and tickled its nose until it shook its head.

"Congratulations, Marie Rose," Sally said. "You're a mama."

George's apelike face arranged in a frown. "She's having twins."

"Then where is he?" Daddy said. "We got a breech?"

"Yeah, it's a breech."

Breech births were common with twins. One came out the right way, the other didn't. George's small and delicate hands went to work.

"I can feel his tail. Pa, can you get Marie Rose into the head gate?"

Daddy was already doing it. With the cow's head in the gate, she couldn't back up over George if she panicked.

"It's okay, girl," Sally soothed her. "You're gonna be just fine."

"That's good, Miss Sally," George said. "Keep her calm."

He pushed the calf into the uterus as far as it would go. Grunting with effort, he thrust his arm inside the snorting cow. He brought one of the calf's feet over the pelvic brim and into the birth canal, then the other.

Daddy was ready with the chains. He wrapped a length around the calf's feet and pulled it out. George tickled its nose while Daddy spritzed water in its ears.

George stripped off his gloves. "He's breathing."

Daddy released Marie Rose from the head gate so she could meet her little ones. "There you go, girl."

"I'll finish up here, Pa."

"You did good, George."

Daddy's highest compliment and all he'd say on the matter. George grinned. "Aw, shucks, Pa."

He was playing the earnest yokel, just another dumb plague kid. Sally knew better after hearing him talk. He was

a very smart and dangerous boy. He caught her looking, and
they locked eyes for a moment, acknowledging each other's
secrets.

Daddy put his hat on and left the barn. Sally followed
swinging her shoulders with her hands clasped behind her
back. He shot her a sideways glance.

"I can just tell you're itching to ask me for something,"
he said.

"The plague boys do a good job for us. Don't they, Daddy?"

"They do all right, I guess."

"They've been working for us for years."

"Are you gonna ask me or not?"

"I'd like to take Enoch out for a walk."

Daddy stopped. "Now why would you want to do a thing
like that?"

"He's like a dog, Daddy. I always wanted a dog of my own."

"He ain't a real dog."

"A dog I could take for walks and talk to," she said. "This
one even talks back. I bet no girl in the world ever had a dog
could talk back before."

"He still ain't a dog. He is a bone-tired boy who been
working all day."

"He's real nice, Daddy. He wouldn't hurt a fly."

Daddy took out his papers and tobacco. Sally watched
him roll his cigarette. He did this when he was thoughtful.
She could read him the same as he read her. A daddy's girl
knew her daddy's tells far better than he knew hers.

He struck a match and leaned into it. A cloud of smoke
swirled away from him.

"All right, Buttercup," he said. "The kids are done for the
day. Go take your walk and be back before supper. Don't go
far. Send Enoch over first so I can have a talk with him."

She smiled and hugged him, face planted against his chest. "Thank you, Daddy."

"All right. Here come the kids now. Go get Enoch and bring him here."

Dog spotted Miss Sally skipping across the yard and smiled, hoping she was coming to fetch them for some iced tea.

"You boys go on ahead," Mr. Gaines said. "Get in the truck."

"Hey, Enoch," she called from a distance. "Daddy wants to talk to you."

Mr. Gaines's grin turned sour. "Go on then. See what he wants."

Dog ran to join Sally, who led him to Pa Albod. "Afternoon, sir."

"Miss Sally here wants to take a walk around. She wants to know if you'd like to join her."

Dog looked over his shoulder at his friends piling into the truck. Mr. Gaines stared at him with an expression that was impossible to read. "How will I get home?"

"More walking, I guess."

A long walk at that. Dog was already fair tuckered out. His stomach growled as he smelled chicken frying in the house.

"I'll make us a glass of cold lemonade before you go home," Sally said.

Dog didn't know what to make of it. What a strange day. The whole morning and afternoon, Mr. Gaines acted sweet as pie. Usually, when he acted like that, he'd had some corn liquor and was looking to smack some kid.

Then there was Brain, who'd also been acting odd ever

since the sheriff ran them out the woods. He'd said Wallee might be an informer, willing to sell out his comrades for candy and favors. The way the sheriff went light on him. The man even knew Wallee's Christian name.

Brain himself had been getting weird even before that, holding secret meetings in the woods with Tiny and other kids.

Now this, Miss Sally inviting him for a walk. Strange days.

"A walk would be just fine," he said.

"Y'all be back in an hour," Pa Albod told him.

"That's all I got, sir, if I want to get home for my supper."

"You behave proper around her, you hear. You protect her."

"I sure will," Dog said.

"She gets even a scratch on her, well. I don't have to say it."

"I'll take good care of her, sir."

"Well, go on then. I'll tell Dave what's what."

"Come on, Enoch," Sally said. "Let's make some tracks."

He waved to his friends and followed her toward the woods on the other side of the cotton fields.

"Do you ever walk on all fours?" Sally said.

"It ain't allowed."

"But do you ever is what I'm asking."

Dog remembered how he used to lope around on all fours when he was a little kid. The teachers cured him of it. "I can do it."

"Do it now, okay. Just do it."

He crouched and lunged. Hands and feet pressed into the soft earth. His overalls bunched and snagged at him, but walking like this felt good. It felt right. An awful need to run itched his muscles.

"I think God meant for me to walk this way," he said.

Sally waved back at her daddy. "It's just for show. I told Daddy a bad thing. I told him I wanted you like for a pet."

"Like a pet dog."

"Yeah. I'm sorry. It was just so Daddy would let us be. He never would have allowed us to be alone and talk otherwise."

"It's okay," Dog said, trotting on his hands and feet. "I'm glad you invited me along. I never had a normal friend."

"What about Mr. Gaines? Is he a friend?"

"He's a boss. He's okay most of the time, I guess. Sometimes, he acts mean."

"He is mean," Sally said. "He ain't my friend."

They reached the woods. Dog jumped over a rotting log and smelled the air. A scent wafted through the trees. Game nearby. His stomach growled again. Thrushes sang in the branches. He wondered what they tasted like.

"Sure is nice to be in the shade," he said.

"George made a big impression on Jake the other night," Sally said.

"Brain is real smart."

"Jake ended up handing out flyers at the A & P talking about equal rights. He got himself in a mess of trouble with the sheriff."

"I'm sorry to hear that," Dog said. "He don't need to do nothing on our account."

"It's just how he is. He cares about other people."

"Yeah, he's nice."

"Speaking of the sheriff, I am sorry he got so rough on you boys that night. It weren't right."

"It's okay."

Dog wanted to say he was used to it, but he wasn't. He

didn't think he'd ever get used to it. One hand feeding you, the other always getting set to slap. Brain asking him, *See what they do?*

Dog knew what they did. They'd been doing it to him his whole life.

"Maybe we can all meet up again," she said. "Be real careful about it, though."

"I'd like that a whole lot. It was real nice."

"We're friends now, ain't we? Anybody tries to hurt you, I'll do what I can. I came out to the Home on Sunday to check on you. Mr. Gaines made me leave."

"You shouldn't come to the Home," Dog said.

"Why do you say that?"

"It ain't a nice place."

"I know it," she said. "I had no idea. I'm sorry you have to live like that."

"I don't know nothing else."

"I came out there because that's what friends do. They protect each other."

"I'll protect you, Miss Sally."

"You don't scare me. I feel safe with you. If somebody tried to hurt me, you'd do whatever it took to keep me safe, wouldn't you?"

"I sure would. And not just because Pa said so."

"What if it were somebody you knew? Somebody like, say, Mr. Gaines. Like you said, he can be mean. Say he was grabbing me or hitting me."

"I'd make him stop. Pa told me to protect you, and I will."

Dog ground his fangs together, feeling powerful the way he did when the Bureau man flinched. If anybody touched her, he would do whatever it took.

His hands and feet hummed with pleasure doing what they were meant to do. He felt them dig into the dirt. He held up one of his hands and inspected it.

Claws. He had claws. Long, black, curved claws extended from his fingers.

He willed them back in his skin, and they disappeared. Then they sprang out again sharp as knives. Lord, just look at them. What a wonderful gift from God.

Special, he thought.

Any boy ever touches Miss Sally, Dog will tear out his guts.

Sixteen

Jake glared out the window on the way home, still defiant but at this point unwilling to direct it anywhere inside the car.

The world outside, so big. Inside the car, too small.

Pa sat ramrod straight behind the wheel, still gripping one of Jake's flyers balled in his fist. "I forbid you to mess with them monster kids any more. And I never again want to hear about you stirring up folks."

The reverend still held an accent from his native Tennessee, his speech roughed by subtle grunts that made him sound gruff.

Jake crossed his arms and said nothing.

"God made them separate for a reason," Pa went on. "He marked them as sure as He marked Cain. They might not even have souls."

"They're as human as I am," Jake said.

"You and your talk. I am fed up straight to here with your rebelling."

Jake watched the mailboxes zoom by. They hung suspended in air, full of potential energy before whipping past.

"Well, boy? You got anything else to say?"

His pa expected an apology.

"You ain't being fair," he complained.

"Fair's got nothing to do with it," Pa said. "This is about what's right."

Jake turned and regarded the man who'd raised him. "You're asking me to choose between you and God. And that ain't fair."

Ma had died of cancer when he was seven, right after the last Christmas he believed in Santa Claus. He gave up on believing in God while he was at it. Ever since he was a toddler, his folks had bred the power of prayer into him. He prayed as hard and often as he could for Ma's recovery, but God didn't deliver. God allowed her to die for no reason other than one of her genes randomly mutated.

His child's mind concluded God wasn't all powerful, didn't care enough to stop bad things from happening to good people, or wasn't there at all.

Regardless of which was true, Jake stopped trusting in God the day she died. His pa whupped him good for that, but Jake could be stubborn. Pa could whup him all he wanted but that didn't make God real. If you had to whup a kid to make him believe in something, that something wasn't worth a lick of belief.

Then something amazing happened that made him a Christian.

The day of the funeral, the whole congregation filled up the house. All week, people trickled in with casseroles. The week after that, more dropped in to help out with chores, share a meal, just say hello. Years later, they were still coming.

While Jake missed his ma something terrible, he'd come to rely on these visits. The church became like family. For him, faith stopped being about praying to a silent, remote God and more about being part of a community that tried to live according to what Jesus taught. Help each other. Comfort the afflicted.

He grew up volunteering his time with church charities and hearing grown-ups talk about the plague kids like they were the Devil. *Behave yourselves, or the creepers will come and get you.* Then he grew old enough to learn the plague kids were just like his ma, afflicted by a genetic dice roll.

Luke 9:46–48. After Christ's disciples argued about which of them was the greatest, he showed them a child and told them: *Whoever receives this little child in my name receives me. Whoever receives me receives him who sent me. For whoever is least among you all, this one will be great.*

Pa turned red behind the wheel. "I ain't asking you to choose between me and God. You profane God by using Him to rebel against me."

"It ain't about me and you," Jake said. "I wish I could make you see that."

"You think you're doing right, but you ain't old enough to know what's right. You're still a boy. When you grow up, you'll understand."

Jake looked out the window again. He'd rather fight the whole world than his pa. But if he didn't think the way he did about the plague kids, he'd end up questioning everything. His family, his town, his religion, his faith. If people believed they'd go to Hell if they didn't follow Jesus, only to heap abuse after abuse on the least among them, what did that say about their belief?

God wasn't there to satisfy one's prejudices. He wasn't Santa Claus, created solely to give you what you wanted. God demanded service and obedience.

"You hear me, boy?" Pa said.

"Yes, sir."

"You ain't ready to know God's will."

"Yes, sir."

"All right then. It's settled."

Maybe his pa was right. Handing out the flyers had made people angry. Even though Amy had warned him what might happen, it stunned him how upset they were. He had no regrets about it but couldn't help but wonder if he'd done more harm than good with his preaching.

He was right to do it. He knew it. He might still be a boy in Pa's eyes, but that only proved what he believed was so simple, a boy could understand it. Something was wrong with this town, and they'd all have him believe he was the one needing to change. You bucked the system, they called you crazy for it.

The last mailbox appeared next to the familiar row of crepe myrtle from which Pa's green thumb had coaxed a third bloom. The station wagon pulled into the driveway of their white clapboard house. A riot of colors welcomed Jake home. Islands of roses, chrysanthemums, and late-summer annuals on the green lawn. Succulents growing in boxes on the porch. All summer long, he fell asleep each night smelling their perfume through his window.

Pa turned off the engine and pocketed his keys. "I know you mean well."

"I want to do what you taught me."

"Then maybe you should," said the reverend. "Stop talking and start doing."

"Sir?"

"Show people how to love instead of telling them how to

do it. You want to help the monster kids, help them. Start a food drive. Collect clothes and such."

"You mean that, Pa?"

"Just promise me you'll stay away from politics. And especially them kids."

Jake smiled. It wasn't even close to what he wanted, but it was a start. "Can I do this through the church?"

"We can try it. Let things settle down first. Maybe around Christmas."

"Thank you, Pa. That works for me."

"You'll be the one working," Pa said. "A lot of time and hard work. Doing and preaching ain't the same. Now we'll get to see what you're made of."

Jake would be happy to show him. Luke 9:46–48 had given him his calling. Pa had given him a mission.

Seventeen

Amy walked home in the cool late afternoon. The air smelled like freshly picked crops. Insect song filled the humid air. The empty road stretched in front of her. She spied a redbone hound running past a rotting old cotton house in a distant field.

Sometimes, it felt like she was living in the ruins of another age.

She slowed as the throaty metallic roar of an engine grew in volume. A sleek yellow car appeared. It sped down the road and passed the junction where she and Jake had kissed in the jasmine. A sports car, what the boys called a muscle car.

Amy wished she could rewind and go back to that delicious kissing afternoon, before Jake got obsessed with monsters and righting wrongs. He'd handed out his flyers, and nobody wanted them. The reverend showing up to cuff his ears had brought an ignoble end to the whole business. At least she hoped that was the end of it. She loved his passion but didn't want to see it undo him.

Or maybe that was his plan, to undo himself. Brain had

said the only way to fight alongside the monsters was to become one. Jake wasn't about to disfigure himself, not in any real way, but he could make himself an outcast just the same.

Amy hoped it wouldn't all lead to him having to choose between her and the plague kids. Just like she hoped she wouldn't have to choose between him and what she wanted. She liked him a lot, maybe she even really did love him, but she wasn't about to become an outcast. She already felt that way, knowing what she was. She'd worked too hard to blend in and have a chance at living a normal life.

The car slowed to a crawl and made a U-turn in the road, engine spitting. Amy thought he'd run himself into the ditch, but he pulled it off. Then he came back and turned onto her road. Dust clouds swirled behind him like a chasing sandstorm.

Oh, brother. You pet some dogs, they always try to follow you home.

The muscle car pulled alongside her, engine snorting. It had been a blinding yellow at one time but age and dust had faded the paint to a dull shade of urine. Bug guts dotted the windshield. Red flames licked across the hood, framed by a pair of black wings, the usual white trash automobile art.

No, not wings. They were a pair of hands, cupping the fire like it was a gift.

Ray Bowie hung his arm out the window and regarded her. Some happy music played on the car speakers. His gray eyes spoke his interest, though she wasn't listening. She started walking again, heading home. He followed along at the same pace. The engine purred and radiated heat.

"You lost or something?" she said.

He laughed. "I'm right where I need to be. I was just

driving around working my way through this here six-pack when I saw you. You want one?"

"No, thank you. I like your car."

"It's a 1978 Pontiac Firebird," he said. "It's got a V8 engine."

"Well, it's real nice."

"You want to take a ride with me, darlin'?"

Fat chance, she thought. He wasn't just driving around out here, he'd been looking. She pointed to the black scrawl on his arm. "What's all that supposed to be?"

"It's Latin. *Aut inveniam viam aut faciam.*"

"And what's that mean, exactly?"

"I shall either find a way or make one. Hannibal of Carthage said that once."

"I don't know who that is, but he's got you to a T."

"When I want something, I ask for it," he said.

"You got the same hands and ball of fire on your arm you got painted on your hood. What's the deal with that?"

"That's Prometheus. He gave all humankind the gift of fire."

"I would have expected something less original from you, like a big ol' rebel flag. Thought that was more your speed."

"You think I have an act. My act is I don't have an act. I just do what I want."

"Is that what landed you in jail?" she said without breaking stride.

"How'd you know about that? Were you asking around about me?"

"Maybe."

"I did two years in Eastham, that's a fact."

"What did you do?"

"I didn't do a damn thing. I'm an innocent man."

"No, really."

"I went in some man's house and stole his TV," Bowie said. "Problem was the man was home and he was an off-duty cop. I never said I was smart."

"Looks like just doing what you want don't work out so good for you."

"Anything else you want to know?"

"Who's that playing on your radio?"

"That's a mix tape I made. This song is 'Shake It Up' by The Cars."

"I like it," Amy said. "It's fun."

She found most popular music of the plague era prudish and spiritual. Music that helped you keep control instead of lose it, even when it was supposed to be uplifting. Jake's monsta rock came close to breaking through, but it was too angry for her. It was rare to hear a song that really made you want to dance.

"They just released a new album," Bowie told her. "I ain't picked it up yet. There's lots of good things out there if you know to look for them."

"Well, Mr. Bowie, it's been a pleasure, but I got to moscy on home."

"Ain't that what you're doing? I see you walking."

"I mean without an escort," she said.

"We should spend some time together, maybe this week-end. We'll hand out flyers at the A & P."

"My, Sally was right about you. Don't you have something better to do than try to pick up fourteen-year-old girls?"

"Shit," he drawled. "Look at you. I thought you was seventeen at the youngest."

"Even then, you're too old."

"How old you think I am? I'm twenty-one."

"Thought you was older than that."

"I get that a lot, darlin'. Must be all the hard living I do. Or maybe it's on account of my innate maturity."

Amy snorted. "Yeah, that's it. You hit the nail right on the head. You know, that boy handing out those flyers is my boyfriend."

"Well, don't that figure. I never did have no luck with women."

"I wonder how that could be."

"After I got out of jail, I drifted east. Been lots of places but none too long. Times are hard. Not much work these days, even less for an ex-con. That's how I ended up at the Home. The girls don't exactly throw themselves at you when you're a drifter without no job. Even fewer when you got a job at a Home."

"You'll find a girl who will love you for who you are. You ain't so bad once you quit the act of having no act."

"Your friend's got me all wrong. I ain't a bad guy at all."

"Maybe don't try so hard, cowboy," she said. "I may be young, but I ain't dumb. I heard it all before."

"I think you're prettier than a sunrise," Bowie said.

"Ain't you precious."

"And I also ain't shy about asking what I want and then trying hard to get it. Don't see why you would hold that against me. So how about a truce."

She smiled despite herself. "Sure, why not. We got a truce."

"You want to have a beer with me or not? Otherwise, I'll git along."

Amy paused in the road. The stand of yellow poplars lay ahead, and beyond that her house. She felt better knowing it was right there in easy reach. Just a short walk and she could be home, but she didn't want to go there, not just yet. She liked the music on his player. It had gotten its hooks in her. As for Bowie, he wasn't bad company. A loser but with some of the same qualities she found appealing in Jake.

In any case, sitting in Bowie's car would be a lot more interesting than watching TV with her suffering mama. Sparring with him was kind of fun.

Don't do it, the little voice in her head warned. Mr. Benson's lecture shouted in her ear. Her mama saying, *Don't take risks and don't be stupid.*

Ray Bowie wouldn't do anything crazy, though. Amy had taken his measure. She had a good handle on him. A delicious thrill ran through her, the idea of drinking beer with an ex-con. She had a perverse want to wrap this skinny man around her finger. She just bet she could.

Maybe she had a little more of her mama in her than she was normally willing to admit.

"All right," she said. "You know what. I could do just that. Just one beer as long as you promise to behave like a gentleman."

He stopped the car. "Hop in then."

Amy walked around the other side of the car and slid inside. The door clunked shut. The leather seat felt worn and smooth as an old saddle. McDonald's wrappers and empties littered the floor around her feet. The ashtray was overflowing.

She dumped her schoolbooks on the dashboard. "I really love this car. You should think about cleaning it sometime."

"It's lacking a woman's touch," Bowie said.

He jerked a can of Bud off its ring, cracked it open, and handed it to her before opening another for himself. He raised his can in a toast.

"To new friends," he said.

"No promises on that," she said.

She sipped her beer, taking it easy. He polished one off and started another, looking out the window at the thickening twilight.

"This is nice," he said. "Just sitting here with a pretty girl."

"It is nice. You just enjoying somebody's company instead of asking for what you want a thousand times."

Bowie laughed. He lit a cigarette and flung the match out the window before chugging his last beer. If he had a mind to get her drunk, he was doing a terrible job of it. He'd drunk them all greedily. Then he blinked as if remembering something. He produced a steel hip flask from his back pocket.

"What you got there?" she said.

He tilted it back and wiped his mouth on his wrist. "Cider. It's real sweet."

"You should take it easy with your drinking."

"You're looking at a pro, honey. I can handle my liquor."

"I don't want you drinking too much and thinking you can paw me."

He took another swig and screwed the cap back on. He frowned. "I thought we already covered that. You're starting to make me feel like a real creep for liking you."

"I'm sitting here, ain't I? That liquor you got. Is it like schnapps?"

"I never had me no schnapps, darlin'."

"I never had me any sweet liquor."

"I only share it with my friends," he said with a comical leer.

"There you go again. Give it here."

Amy took a sip of it. The sweet alcohol flooded her brain

and got her scalp crawling with itchy pleasure. She liked it better than the beer.

"Give that back," he said.

"Nope." She took a bigger sip. "Seeing as we're friends now."

"This is why I don't have many friends neither."

She handed it back. She didn't want any more of it. The liquor made her feel a little fuzzy, and she didn't want to come across as tipsy and encourage him. Mama lecturing in her head again.

She opened the glove compartment, expecting to see a big gun or a giant sandwich bag filled with weed. Nothing but mix tapes. "You got a lot of music."

"I like to drive with a good song playing. I picked all that up on my travels."

"You talk so slow, you must be from Texas."

"Abilene, to be exact. I been to a mess of places. Small towns and cities. So much going on out there. They still know how to have fun in the cities." He smiled at some old memory. "The punkers run around in monsta face, but otherwise folks just live their lives like the uglies never showed up. You ever been to the big city? Atlanta, maybe?"

"I never been outside the county," she said.

"You should. It's a big ol' world."

"I'm happy right here. Might could visit, though, someday."

"Say the word, and I'll take you there. You could see it all."

Amy smiled as she pictured it. Taking off who knows where. Going any old place just to see what happened, free as a bird.

Instead, she had to be getting home, though she didn't want to leave, not yet. Bowie had grown on her. She even

found him kind of attractive with his wiry build and interesting ideas. He and Jake were alike in some respects, but
Bowie was a man who knew what was what. He roamed the
world as he wished. Nobody cuffed his ears for stirring up
trouble over plague kids. Nothing held him back. He was
free. He did what he wanted and didn't care what anybody
thought of him.

She wondered what it would be like to kiss a man like
that.

Her brain grew even fuzzier. Static in her vision. "Hey."

"Hey, what?"

"I don't feel so good all of a sudden."

"You'll be all right," he said.

Her vision clouded and grew dark around the edges. The
twilight deepened. Stars flared in her eye. They popped out
of their sockets, falling on the world.

Streaming like rebel angels.

"Want to go home," she said just before his mouth closed
over hers.

Eighteen

L et's be nice," he breathed against her cheek.
One of his hands was groping under her shirt and bra.

"What's this?" Amy said. "What are you doing?"

His head plunged to her breast and took as much of her into his mouth as he could. A quirt of pain shot through her chest.

"Wait," she said.

Her jeans were balled around her ankles. Her behind slid on the seat as his fingers performed rough work between her legs.

"Don't," she gasped. "Please don't."

He'd slipped her something in that flask, and hardly anybody drove down this side road, and night was falling, and she was all alone except for Mama, who watched her TV programs less than a mile away.

She'd had him figured out. She was just playing. This couldn't be happening. Mr. Benson hadn't warned her people drugged each other like this. She'd thought Bowie was just trying to get her tipsy so he could make a pass. She'd been thinking about maybe letting him kiss her. It wasn't fair.

"Gimme some sugar," he said.

Bowie gripped her wrist and moved her hand onto his exposed hard pecker. *Penis*, the health book called it. Like touching a snake. Her books were on the floor now, getting stomped among the trash. Her hand splayed so she didn't touch his thing with her fingers. She was mad the way he was using her without being able to fight back, but it was like being mad in a dream, rage made out of mud and weeds at the bottom of a mill pond. She slid down on the seat as he lifted her up by the waist. The old itch raked her scalp. She reached in the glove compartment for something to fight with, came away holding a mix tape. Pain stabbed between her legs, like he was breaking her down there.

"No," she gasped. "I have it. I got the, the—"

"Just relax and enjoy the ride," he said.

He grunted with pleasure, breath filling the car. She tried to scream.

Instead, the world winked out of existence.

She awoke hot and covered in syrup and sweat, head pounding. The old Pontiac smelled like pennies and ash. The Cars were on the tape player again, which ran an endless loop of Bowie's favorite driving songs. She still felt the weight of him on her body. The night was pitch black. He'd fallen asleep on her.

"Off me," Amy said thickly, her tongue two sizes too big in her mouth. Her bra was still hiked up, jeans balled around one ankle. Her aching head rested against the door. Tight grip on a mix tape. She shoved at him. It was like trying to move a heavy sack of meat. His stiff pecker brushed her thigh. She pushed again, frantic now, but he seemed glued to her. Somehow they had fused together, and he'd become a part of her like some sluggish giant tick.

She wedged her hands under his shoulders and heaved until his chest came unstuck and then his shirt parted from hers with a ripping sound.

Bowie thudded over onto the driver's seat and lay still against the door, one of his arms thrust in the air.

She opened her mouth to curse him. Banshee gibberish poured out of her as she crawled half-naked on top of him and threw a punch at his face. Her fist slammed against the door. A bolt of pain shot up her hand into her wrist.

She howled. Waves of pain cascaded through her hand. She gritted her teeth and waited it out, blinking back tears. Her hand throbbed while her head pounded like a drum timed to her heartbeat. She reached up and felt for the overhead light, gooey and sticky under the fingers of her good hand. She found the switch. The light popped on and cast a dull yellow glow.

The car was painted in blood. A congealed layer of it covered Bowie's shirt like thick, black tar.

His head was gone.

Amy screamed.

She scrabbled back until her shoulders slammed against the passenger door. Then screamed again as she spilled out of the car into the ditch. The music sounded tinny and far away now, the roar of cicadas and crickets in her ears. A sea of fireflies winked in the dark, going about their arcane lives.

She screamed at the night full of stars.

Less than a mile down the road, Linda Green paced her kitchen, burning cigarette in one hand and glass of liquor in the other. She paused to rinse her throat with a fiery swallow and went to take a drag, but the cig had burned down to the filter. A half inch of ash spilled on the linoleum.

She lit another and went back to her pacing.

"Where are you, baby girl," she muttered.

Not like her Amy to disappear like this. Her Amy was too careful for that. Linda wasn't about to win any mother of the year prizes anytime soon, but she didn't raise stupid. Amy knew what was what.

Or maybe she's like me, she thought. Smart as a rule and stupid as an all too occasional exception.

She'd already called Reggie Albod, who'd put Sally on the phone. Sally said she'd last seen Amy on the walk home from the A & P after school. They'd parted ways on Horse Creek Road, Amy heading on home alone after that. That was around four-thirty.

Linda looked at the clock on the wall and read eight-fifteen.

"That does it," she thought aloud. "I'm calling Sheriff Burton."

Her hand reached for the telephone and stopped.

No, she couldn't do that. Right now, she was being smart.

Any other girl, she'd have called the sheriff already. But Amy wasn't like any other girl. Amy was special and needed protection from lawbreakers and lawmen alike.

Nothing to do but worry grooves in the floor. Five more minutes, she vowed. She'd wait by the telephone and the door for that long before she fetched her car keys and started a search on her own. She was in no condition to drive, but there wasn't any use thinking in that direction. Amy might be in trouble.

She'd drive all night combing this county until she found her.

A knock at the front door.

A jolt of current tingled through her bones. Veins turned

into electric wires. She walked into the living room caught between hope and despair.

Amy wouldn't knock. The grim-faced sheriff was out there.

"Oh, baby girl," she sobbed. "Oh, Lord protect her."

She gasped in horror and relief when she opened the door.

An apparition stood in the porch light. Moths fluttered around its crown.

"Mama," Amy said in a small, childlike voice.

She was covered head to toe in blood.

Blood congealed in her hair, warping it into stringy ropes. Crimson streaks and dots painted her ghost-white face. Even more blood, crusted to the consistency of cardboard, coated her torn shirt.

Her daughter trembled, clutching her tattered red schoolbooks.

"Oh, God," Linda cried. "What did they do to you, baby girl?"

"Somebody took his head clean off," Amy said.

She tottered into the house with glazed eyes and fell shaking against her mama. They crumpled to the floor together.

Linda rocked her little girl in her arms. "What did you go and do?"

"Nothing, Mama."

"You can tell me."

"I didn't do it," Amy cried. "It wasn't me, I swear."

"Of course it wasn't. I'm sorry, sugar. It wasn't you. I know that."

"He was hurting me, Mama."

"Your boyfriend?"

"Another boy. Time slipped away. He was already killed when I woke up."

Linda led Amy straight upstairs and drew a hot bath.
She stripped the crusty clothes off her daughter and gasped
again at the sight of blood between her legs. Amy's hand
was cracked and bleeding, swelling like a balloon from some
trauma given or received. Linda guided her into the tub.
Then she sat on the edge and scrubbed the blood from Amy's
arms. The bath turned dark with it.

"Where is he at?" she said. "This boy."

"Down the road a ways in his car."

"Mama will take care of it," Linda told her.

Lord, she thought. Please don't let there be a baby. Lord,
please.

Amy sat in the water hugging her knees. "Where do you
think it went?"

"Where what went?"

"His head."

"Mama will take care of it."

"Mama?"

"What?"

"I think maybe I did a bad thing."

"You hush now. Mama is gonna take care of it."

Nineteen

Wearing his new fedora, Goof squeezed past the giant guard and entered the bright white room. Shackleton glanced at him from the steel table, now covered with electronic gear connected by a tangle of wires. Next to him, Zack the scientist fiddled with one of these devices. A cigarette burned in a black ashtray.

Goof's eyes skipped past all that and settled on a bag of Burger King resting near the table's edge. "Hey, Mr. Shackleton. How do I—"

"Hold your horses," the Bureau man said. "We're busy here."

Zack plugged a jack into one of the boxes. Then he stood in his white lab coat and arched his back in a stretch. "We got it."

"It's working now?"

"Of course it's working. This is why I went to medical school."

"Smartass. Speaking of which, what did you want to ask me, Jeff?"

Goof ran his fingers along the brim of his fedora. "How do I look?"

"Like—"

"Humphrey Bogart. Who's Humphrey Bogart?"

"I gave you that hat days ago," Shackleton said. "Why do you keep asking me how you look in it?"

"A secret agent has to look his best at all times. I want to be just like you."

Shackleton ran his hands through his slicked-back hair and sighed. "You could start by being less annoying. You can be pretty annoying sometimes."

"Hey, did I ever tell you how I got the name Goof?"

"No, can't say you did."

"It was by being annoying."

Another sigh. "Sit down. Have some Burger King."

Zack smiled at Goof and nodded, one smartass acknowledging another.

"Don't mind if I do," Goof said.

He reached into the bag and pulled out a lukewarm Whopper.

"Fries in there too," Shackleton said. "That'll be all, Zack."

The scientist winked at Goof. "Happy to help."

"Cool guy," Goof said after Zack left. "I like him a lot better than Officer Baby."

"Why do you call him that?"

"Because he looks like a baby that never stopped growing."

"And why don't you like him?"

"He never talks," Goof said.

"First off, his name is Lyle Jenkins, and second, he doesn't get paid to talk. What do you want to talk with him about? Your favorite fruitcake recipes?"

"All right, all right. Never mind. So what's all this junk?"

"Another test," Shackleton told him.

"I thought you checked me out every way you needed."

"This is more than a test, really. More like—"

"The real thing."

"That's right. These tapes came straight from the FBI."

Goof whistled.

"The FBI bugged a subject's office," Shackleton told him. "But the electronic recording equipment malfunctioned. There are some breaks in an important conversation. We'd like to know what he said."

"You people are pretty funny."

"Why do you say that?"

"You'd kill somebody because of something he said that I tell you he said without actually hearing him say it."

"We're not going to kill him, you goofball. We just want to know what he said. What he plans to do next. Eat your food so we can get started."

Goof devoured his Whopper while Shackleton set the stage.

"There are two men in the office," the agent said. "Both are very important people. They are having a conversation they think is private. There are some gaps we need filled."

"Okay. I'm ready."

The Bureau man held down two buttons on a tape recorder. "Field Agent Francis—"

"Shackleton, Bureau of Teratological Affairs," Goof chimed in.

He turned it off and gave Goof the stink-eye. "Can we just do this, please?"

Goof held back a laugh. "Oh. I'm real sorry. I thought we started."

The Bureau man lit a fresh cigarette and rested it on the lip of his ashtray. He pressed the buttons again. "Field Agent Francis Shackleton, Bureau of Teratalogical Affairs. Case officer for deputized mutagenic asset Jeffrey Baker."

Goof liked the sound of that. Deputy Baker. The meanest lawman east of the Mississippi. Carries two six-guns on his belt and one big grudge against—

"What are you smiling about?" the agent said. "You ready or not?"

"Ready to serve my country. Yes, sir, I am."

Shackleton shook his head. He pushed a red button on an even bigger recorder with two magnetic tape reels like Mickey Mouse ears. The reels started turning. Men's voices popped out of the ether.

I'm not a bleeding-heart liberal, Joe.

No, you're a real Constitution type. Next you'll be citing the thirteenth and fourteenth amendments.

I'm a good Republican is what I am.

So is the president. Maybe you heard of him.

The Bureau man held up one finger. Here it comes.

Don't give me your party loyalty bullshit, Joe. If Interior wants a—

"Budget increase for BTA, they can show how they spend their funding," Goof rattled off. "We already hand over a fortune—"

From the Treasury every year.

Shackleton raised his finger again.

Do you want an audit? Is that what you're saying? Would that—

"Satisfy you?" Goof finished. "No, I aim to go further. What do you mean? I mean a full investigation. I'm talking committee hearings. You sure you want to do that? You could—"

Embarrass the administration in an election year.

Again, the finger.

Yeah, I'm sure. Pushing dirt under the carpet is fine until you're constantly tripping over the fucking bulge. If BTA wants to clean up its act, I can let them slide. Otherwise, I'm coming for them. I'm tired of—

"Seeing taxpayer money wasted every year while my phone rings off the hook with reports of abuse in the—"

Homes.

So what's this really—

Shackleton turned off the recording. The reels froze.

"About?" Goof said. "Abuse in the Homes or trimming the fat? Which is it?"

Then he slumped in his chair, drained but wishing he could have listened more. He wondered how the guy answered. So which was it, mister? What is more important to you? Stopping abuse in the Homes or saving money?

"You did real good," the agent said. "You up for another one?"

Goof took the fedora off. He didn't want it anymore. A stupid hat. "Can I take a breather? Would that be all right?"

"Yeah. We'll take five."

Shackleton turned off the session recorder, took a long drag from his cigarette, and stabbed it out.

"Doing it from a recording takes it out of me," Goof said.

"Word of advice," the Bureau man said. "Once I press these buttons here, everything we say is on tape. Our session recordings are typed up word for word as transcripts and read by all sorts of important people. You should only say what's missing from the tape I'm playing. When I turn it off, you should—"

"Stop talking. Got it."

"Good. No need to make anybody anxious."

"I thought I was gonna spy on the Russians."

"You are doing important work for the government. We're the good guys."

"And the bad guys are like what, Congress?"

"You want another hat? Some more Burger King, maybe? A lot of perks I can throw your way, if you do your job."

"I like it here," Goof said.

"You sure about that? Because maybe you'd like to go back to the Home. Work on a farm. Eat porridge with a nice fat cockroach in the bottom of your bowl."

"I said I like it here. I love it. I'm living in high cotton."

"Then keep scratching my back so I can scratch yours," Shackleton said.

Goof splayed his hands. "Scratch, scratch."

"All right then. Are you ready now?"

"Yeah, I guess."

"You sure? You don't have to take a piss or anything?"

"No, I'm good."

"Wonderful. I got a civil rights lawyer we need to get to next."

"Yeah, wonderful."

Goof hadn't told him the truth. The truth was he wanted to go back to the Home.

Special Facility was heaven to him. Like something out of a fairy tale. He loved the air conditioning, the food, the daily hot shower with no time limit, a couple hours of TV every night. But it was lonesome here. Nobody to talk to except a mute guard and a humorless government man who made poor company.

Shackleton hadn't been honest, either. Sending him back was an empty threat. They would never send him back.

Not after letting him in on their dirty secrets. Not after he showed them what he could do.

He now understood how important his talent was and why Brain had warned him to keep it a secret. Something he used to do just to make people laugh.

If he didn't like his carrot, they would give him the stick. His choice. Either way, he'd be helping them. For that part, there was no choice at all.

First time in his life, Goof thought maybe he should have kept his big mouth shut.

Twenty

Sheriff Tom Burton got out of his police car thinking it wasn't eight o'clock in the morning and already it was a shit day to beat all shit days. He squared his hat and set off down the hill toward the pond that was by the old marble quarry.

Deputy Sikes met him coming the other way, a bulge of Redman in his cheek.

"Lay it out for me, Bobby," Burton said.

The deputy pointed down the grassy hill. At the end of two long lines of tire tracks, the yellow car lay half submerged in the pond, its ass end hanging out.

"That's where Tolbert found the body," Sikes told him.

Burton spied Deputy Palmer interviewing the old coot. "All right."

"And that's it. Coroner's on the way. How you want to play it?"

"What you mean, that's it? You ID the body or not?"

Sikes turned his head to spit a stream of brown juice on the grass. "Most of him is underwater. Besides that, he ain't got a head."

"What are you talking about?" Burton growled.

"I mean he ain't got a head. Somebody took it right off him."

"That what Tolbert told you, or you saw it yourself?"

"I didn't see the body. You want me to get in the water and look at it?"

"No," the sheriff said, wondering if there was a contest for shit days, because this one might just win first prize.

Made up of Huntsville and surrounding farms, Stark County had its share of crime like anyplace else. Bar fights, drunk driving, domestic disputes, men hunting and fishing when or where they weren't supposed to. Drugs were becoming a big problem. Most situations got taken care of by folks. Self-policing. Murder was a different story. Half the upright citizenry carried on without a lick of sense much of the time, even worse when they added drugs or alcohol to the equation, but they knew better than to go around killing each other.

As for the timing, it couldn't have been worse. This being an election year, and him running for re-election. People voted for their sheriff on a single issue, and that was law and order. A headless body did not improve his prospects.

He had a lot of work to do.

"Reckon I'll take a look myself," Burton said. "You run the plates at least?"

Sikes spat. "We called it into Highway Patrol."

"I got a feeling I know who this is just from the car make."

"Well, who is it—"

"Call the office and ask Beth to send J. T. along with a camera and the murder kit. She should get a tow out here while she's at it."

"I'm on it," Sikes said.

The deputy walked off to his car to use the radio.

Burton took another quick look around. Nothing but the grassy hill, trees lining the crest. The Richmond pond, populated with bass and bluegills. Over yonder, the old marble quarry.

He has it now, what happened here. Somebody kills the victim and drives him out to this secluded place. Puts the car in neutral and lets it roll into the pond. Only the car gets stuck before it becomes submerged.

The sheriff continued down to the bottom of the hill. A thick swarm of angry black flies buzzed around the car.

Deputy Palmer stood holding a pad and pen, taking down Tolbert's statement. He touched the pen to the brim of his hat. "Sheriff."

"Morning, Jim."

"Hey, Sheriff," said Tolbert, decked out in his fishing gear. "I was telling the deputy here, I got up this morning to do some fishing . . ."

Burton let the old man ramble on for a while. "I need your wader."

"My wader?"

"I've got a mind to take a look at the body," said the sheriff.

"But I ain't got no britches on under. No shoes, neither. Just feet and socks."

"Ain't nobody gonna see you but us, Tolbert. Now come on. It's for a good cause."

The fisherman grumbled as he yanked down his suspenders and pulled the rubber wader to his waist. Groused even more as he sat on the ground and wrestled it off. Then he stood in his underpants and handed it over.

"Thank ye," Burton said with a bit of formality, lending some dignity to the act.

Standing on socked feet with his white knobby knees poking out, Tolbert promptly squandered it. His gray-white beard parted in a gap-toothed cackle. "So how do I look, Sheriff?"

"Like a movie star. What side is he on?"

"He were kind of floating around in there, but I'd say passenger. I didn't stick around to confirm. Stinks like Satan's asshole in there."

Burton could smell it from here.

The sheriff stepped into the wader, pulled it up, and hitched the suspenders over his broad shoulders. He scrounged up a stick and pressed a handkerchief over his mouth and nose. Then he waded into the pond thick with cattails, feet sinking in the ooze. The flies buzzed like a plague of Egypt. He parted the cattails and approached the car, gagging on the unholy stink pouring out the open window.

"Hell's bells," he breathed.

The car had angled into the water deep enough to fill its insides with a brackish dead man stew. Pond scum and cassette tapes floated on the water. The windshield was blackened with blood spatter, a big circle of it rubbed out so whoever was driving the car could see. The headless torso rested against the passenger side, the ragged stump crawling with horseflies. A single knee stuck out of the water.

Burton lowered the stick into the soup and lifted the man's arm. He'd recognize those jailhouse tattoos anywhere: mysterious Latin and crude symbols drawn in prison ink made from baby oil, charcoal, and water.

"Hello, Ray," he said.

Ray Bowie, a good-for-nothing drifter who rolled into town a year back. Burton pressed him on his arrival in Huntsville, the intent being to take his measure and let him know the law noted his presence. Bowie said he was from Texas and had come up to Georgia from Florida, but Burton doubted either one was true. He was one of those types seemed not to come from one specific place but instead from everywhere and nowhere. His Alabama driver's license said he was thirty-three years old.

Beth had run a background check on him and found he'd done hard time in Texas for attempted sexual assault on a young girl. With the germ going around and so much prudishness, some men gravitated in that direction. They went for the spring chickens. No high school girl had the plague, and the young felt no shame about sex, only curiosity and ignorance.

His arrest in Houston was just the one offense. Burton had a feeling he'd done a lot more than that. Bowie had struck him as a bad seed from day one.

Now somebody had killed him and taken his head clean off. The deputies would be able to search the car for it once they hauled it from the pond and drained it, but Burton doubted they'd find it. It seemed to him if somebody wanted to go through all the trouble of tearing it off, that somebody wanted it for a reason. He made a note to call in for more men to comb the grounds anyway.

A mallard quacked a feeding call from the cattails on the other side of the pond.

"Hell's bells," he said again and returned to dry land.

Sikes came back from his car. "You all right, Sheriff?"

"I ain't seen anything like it in all my born days."

"I told you," Tolbert said. "What happened to that boy ain't human."

"You might be right about that."

"You think maybe a bear got him?" Palmer said.

Huntsville had been settled on the coastal plain but wasn't far from the Piedmont. Wild animals sometimes came down off the Blue Ridge and crossed over it into the county.

"It weren't a bear that drove his car in the pond," Burton said.

"The question is did the driver cut off his head," Sikes said. "An animal could have come after the fact and took it away someplace."

"Anything is possible, but I'm guessing the driver took it."

Burton gave Tolbert his wader back and headed for his Plymouth.

"Where you going?" Sikes called after him.

Burton paused. "I'm going to the Home."

The two deputies exchanged a glance.

Sikes spat. "The Home?"

"I got an ID on the victim. It's Ray Bowie. He works there."

"Is that right."

"I'll be back directly. You boys hold the fort here while I'm gone."

"We'll do that, boss. Fine day to be a cop."

Burton snorted and gave his deputies a departing wave over his shoulder.

He put his hat on the car seat next to his thermos and sat behind the wheel. He unscrewed the cap, poured a cup of coffee, and drank it slow.

No bear did that to Ray Bowie before or after the car ended up in the pond. All that blood on the windows.

A creeper, though. Yeah. Maybe.

The plague kids were growing up. Getting older, stronger,

more cocksure. Some ran away from the Homes and lived in the woods, going feral. They usually didn't survive long. Every couple years, a hunter came into the office to report he found monster bones in the woods. That was changing. Today's feral kids were older and able to hunt small game, stage nocturnal raids on garbage cans.

The sheriff started the car and drove to the Home.

The dirt track led through once fertile land reclaimed by wilderness. Briars and branches swept his car as it bounced on the ruts. Then the old plantation house and its outbuildings came into view, shaded by Spanish moss.

He remembered coming out here as a boy with his friends to explore, back when the house stood derelict and empty. Legend had it the spirits of dead slaves haunted the homestead and its environs. Moaning and whip cracks in the deep woods. Lynched Blacks hanging silent from creaking ropes.

Now new things, far worse than anything Burton's childish imagination ever produced, haunted the place. They ambled across the yard on claws and hoofs and horny feet, trilling and hooting and growling, every one looking like he fell out the ugly tree and hit every branch on the way down. The teachers herded them into trucks for another workday at the farms and beef ranches.

Burton got out, squared his hat, and started for the house. Emmett Willard came out the door as he walked up.

"Morning, Colonel."

"Good morning, Sheriff. To what do I owe this rare pleasure?"

"It's about one of your teachers, Ray Bowie."

"Haven't seen him in days. Did he get himself in trouble with the law?"

"He got himself dead," Burton said.

"I see. Why don't you come inside?"

"I'd like that, Colonel."

"Would you be put out if Mr. Gaines joined us?"

"Dave Gaines? Why do you want him?"

"He knew Mr. Bowie best," Willard said.

"That'd be fine."

The teachers were all keeping one eye on the sheriff and principal. All Willard had to do was glance at Gaines and tilt his head to get him running. Burton sized up the teacher as he hustled up with his lazy eye and fake smile. Not a bad guy, at least he had no record. Otherwise, he was the kind of man who couldn't find his own ass with both hands in his back pockets.

They all went inside together and sat in chairs in Willard's office. Burton explained what Tolbert found at the Richmond pond.

"Motherogod," Gaines said. "They took his head?"

"When did Ray last come to work?"

"Last Tuesday," Willard told him.

"He been missing that long, and you didn't think anything of it."

"Faculty members come and go. A certain caliber of individual, you understand."

"Not sure I do, Colonel."

"Men made of iron but feet made of sand," Willard said.

Burton glanced at Gaines. "I think I follow."

"The Home is a job, not a career," the principal added. "Mostly, we get niggers and drifters, men fresh out of jail and needing some money."

"Did Ray have any enemies?"

Willard looked at Gaines, who wagged his head and said, "No, sir."

Burton very much doubted that was true, knowing what he did about Bowie's disposition. "I understand one of your kids died last Sunday."

"That is correct," the principal said.

"Fell down the stairs," Gaines clarified.

"Anybody push him, maybe?" Burton said. "Any kids causing problems?"

The principal smiled. "They don't cause problems. They are problems. But no, nobody in particular comes to mind who would do a heinous thing like you described."

Burton nodded. He knew the old man governed the Home with an iron fist. Had to, really, with four hundred creepers under his care. If there were problems, they got handled here. A good town policed itself. The Home did better than most.

He said, "Any kids unaccounted for last Tuesday evening after he left work or any time since?"

"Enoch stayed out at the Albod farm that evening," Gaines said. "He walked home. He was gone an hour. He did it again yesterday."

The sheriff did a quick calculation. From the Albods's to wherever Bowie was and then to the pond. After that, a long hike home. "This Enoch fella. Anybody at the Home ever teach him how to drive?"

"No, sir," Gaines said. "We don't want any kids learning that."

The one big thing that didn't fit his theory. No creeper could drive a car.

"I doubt he's the one," Burton said. "Enoch is the skinny doggie-looking boy, hangs out with the uppity gorilla and Edward?"

"That's right," Gaines said.

"Saw him about a week ago last Saturday night. He and his friends were hanging around with some normal kids. The preacher's boy, Reggie's girl Sally, Amy Green, Michelle Johnson, and some boy named Troy. They just ran into each other, apparently. I rousted them with a strong warning. Thought you should know."

"Thank you for sharing, Sheriff," Willard said, meaning he'd handle it.

Gaines's face burned red. "Yeah, thanks a lot."

"That upset you, Dave?" Burton said.

"No, I mean, yeah. I'm their teacher. They're my crew."

"Last question, Colonel. Any kids going missing of late?"

"Not in some time," Willard answered. "I believe the last runaway we had was back in March, what was her name."

"Annabelle Rockford," Gaines said. "The kids call her Catty Wampus."

"Yes, that's her. The police over in Davis caught and returned her. Are you thinking one of the children was involved in Mr. Bowie's murder?"

"Not unless a bear came down off the Blue Ridge," Burton said. "Then bit Ray's head off and drove his car in the pond."

"You say something bit him, sir?" Gaines said.

"The stump had bite marks," the sheriff said. "Big teeth. Like the shark from *Jaws* chomped him."

"Motherogod," Gaines said.

Burton put his hat on and stood. "We may have a feral kid running around who did this. A kid who somehow picked up some driving along the way. Let me know you see anything. And keep an eye on your own."

"Thank you for stopping by, Sheriff," Willard said. "Anything we can do. You've got my vote in November."

"I thank ye for your time, Colonel, and your vote."

"You really think the kids are capable of this?" Gaines said. His face was no longer red but white as a sheet.

"That's just the thing," Burton said. "We don't know. So long."

The sheriff walked back out to the yard, eager to put this place in his rearview. He'd told Gaines he didn't know if a creeper was capable of biting Bowie's head off. The truth was he didn't know anything about what the children could do. He didn't even know what the children were. Prior experience meant nothing when living with demons out of mythology. Every day was new territory.

A voice in the back of his mind told him this might not be just a problem with feral kids. He feared it might be a coming problem with all of them.

Twenty-One

Gaines rose from his chair. "Reggie's waiting on me."

"Sit down, Mr. Gaines," Willard said.

He did as he was told.

The principal stood and walked to the window. He put his hands in his pants pockets and looked out for a while. Gaines followed his gaze and spotted the old broken-down Ford that had been parked on the grass out there as long as he could remember.

At last, the old man spoke: "Guess how many slave revolts succeeded during the days before the War Between the States. Take a wild guess off the top of your head."

"I'd have to say none, Colonel."

"Haves and have-nots make up the world, Mr. Gaines. Always and forever. Today, there is a new type of have-not. A type who has nothing at all, who barely even possesses a thin claim to humanity. I recognize you are no political philosopher, but I'm sure you know to whom I'm referring."

Gaines fidgeted in his chair, wondering if this was some kind of test. The principal had rarely spoken more than one or two sentences to him at a time before, even during all the hours they'd spent together in Discipline.

"Why, you're talking about the kids, sir."

"They are not slaves, not as we had in better times. As the children get older, however, they may see what normal people have and want it for themselves. Want what they can never get on account of their wretched condition."

"They get three squares a day and a roof over their heads," Gaines said. "You'd think they'd be grateful for what our taxes give 'em."

"If they ever rebel in some organized fashion, they will be crushed."

"Yes, sir. Like a bug."

"But first, they will tear every faculty member they can find here to shreds."

"No, that's—"

Gaines stopped just in time. Nobody called Willard's notions crazy to his face.

The principal stared out the window. "Are you with the program, Mr. Gaines?"

"Program, sir?"

"I lost a good man in Ray Bowie. Reliable. I'm going to need you to step up."

"I'll do as you say, Colonel."

"Mishaps happen," Willard said. "Little accidents turn into terrible tragedies. Like young Tobias Freeman in Discipline. I need to know where you stand."

"I'm with the program, Colonel. You can count on me. Yes, sir."

"Very well. Run your crew up to the Albod farm. When you return, there will be a faculty meeting to review contingency plans."

Gaines left the principal's office on shaky legs. The sheriff believed a creeper murdered Bowie. Not just murdered, but mutilated for some unknown end. When the sheriff left, Gaines expected Willard to smile and shake his head at such foolishness, but instead he pondered getting ready for some kind of uprising.

His world suddenly looked a whole lot different.

At least he knew where he stood with the Colonel. He hoped he'd put the man's doubts to rest. He was with the program, any program the old man wanted. Just name it, and he was with it. The whole hog.

His crew sat in the bed of the old Chevy the school assigned him for ag days. They turned their heads to eyeball him as he fumbled for his keys in his britches. He'd watched them grow up, these creepers. Ugly as sin, sure. Quirky and pathetic, yup. But dangerous, no, not ever.

The threat of Discipline kept them in line. They were good boys. *Domesticated*, Bowie used to call them, but now Bowie was dead, his head shorn clean off, and Burton thought a creeper did it.

A feral one, though, he reminded himself. Not a Home kid.

Gaines wondered what separated a feral kid from a Home kid other than freedom. He realized he really didn't understand their nature.

"We're late," he told the kids. "Time to hit the road."

They didn't answer, saving their energy for the long day ahead. George, Enoch, Edward, and Mary.

"You know what," he said. "You kids are all right."

The creepers glanced at each other in wonder but said nothing.

"What I'm trying to say to you kids is I like you. I hope that goes both ways."

They nodded, their expressions unreadable. Just more blank stares.

He thought, Ah, to hell with it. He thought about Ray Bowie, dead in a pond, his head chewed off by some monster.

"Other times," he added with anger fueled by a sudden rush of fear and loathing, "I think all y'all are demons out of Scripture."

"We ain't demons, Mr. Gaines," George said. "I know my Bible."

"What'd you say to me?"

"The angels came down and laid with human women. Their union produced the giants. The heroes, men of renown. The Nephilim. Genesis, chapter four, verse six."

"You like working with the animals, George?"

"That's where Mr. Albod wants me. I don't have a say in it."

"Well, you're gonna be picking cotton the rest of your natural-born days, you don't watch your mouth, boy."

George said nothing. Watching his mouth.

"That's right," Gaines said. He got in the truck and slammed the door. Sat fuming. Yelled out the window, "Even the Devil can quote Scripture. And no more hanging out with normal kids, or I'll write you up."

The truck coughed before settling into a steady rattle. Gaines drove to Albod's farm like he always did Mondays. The farmer met him, as usual, and chewed him out for being late, as expected. Albod put George on the animals, Edward on the garden, Enoch and Mary out in the fields. The older Albod girls tramped out of the house with their dinner boxes and schoolbooks. Gaines paid them little heed today. He leaned against the truck, wishing he'd called in sick again. He felt like he'd caught a fever. His guts were rotten with worry.

Then Sally rushed out of the house lugging her books.

He mustered a warm smile. "Morning, Miss Sally."

She ignored him as she hurried past. His heart sank as he watched her go. After a while, he made up his mind and got back in his truck. When he twisted the key, the engine gave an asthmatic bark and died.

"For land's sake." He twisted the key again. "Come on, girl."

The truck trembled and wheezed before growling back to life. Gaines threw the transmission into gear and drove back toward the road. He passed Sally, parked, and watched her in his rearview. She stood in his dust cloud, hugging her books.

He got out. "Morning, Miss Sally."

"Stay right there or I'll scream."

"I ain't gonna hurt you," he said, baffled. "Did you hear about the murder?"

"What murder?" said Sally.

He told her everything he knew. "Sheriff said it were a creeper."

"I'm sorry your friend died."

"Ray? Hell. I'm worried about you."

"I'd be just fine if you'd let me be, Mr. Gaines."

"You been hanging around with Enoch alone. Taking those walks together. I don't think you should do that no more."

"That ain't up to you," she said.

"I'll have a talk with your daddy about it today. When he hears about Ray getting killed, he'll agree with me about what's right for you."

Sally advanced on him so fast he took a step backward. His rump thudded against the tailgate. "You don't get it. I'm friends with him so he can protect me while I walk around my own property after school. Protect me from you."

None of this made sense to him. "You don't mean that."

"You think he's just a dumb kid, but he's got big claws, I seen 'em. Between them and his fangs, he'd rip you up into little pieces."

"Oh, Lord," he said. If Sally thought the big bad wolf would ever be Little Red Riding Hood's friend, she was sorely mistook.

"I don't like you, Mr. Gaines. Take a hint and let me be."

"I'm in love with you, Miss Sally."

He was. He saw that clear as day now.

"Lord God," she said. "Listen to yourself. You're old enough to be my daddy. Your boy is in my grade, you pervert."

"Age don't matter. I love you."

"I hate you."

"Now I know for a fact that ain't true," he said.

"I hate your stupid face and stupid eye. You make me want to puke."

"Didn't you hear me say I love you?"

"I want you to let me be," she yelled. "Get it through your thick skull."

"I'll tell your daddy what you been up to," he said. "I'll tell him about how you been hanging around at night with creepers like the sheriff told me. How you came to the Home and led me on. How Enoch ain't your pet, he's your good friend."

"He is my friend," she shot back. "Meaning I like him more than I like you. That's right, a creeper is better than you, because he's good inside while you're the ugly one. And if you breathe one word to Daddy, I'll tell him all about everything you done. He'll mount your head on the wall next to his ten-point buck. Or maybe I'll tell Enoch how you been misbehaving and see what he does to your head."

Sally stormed past him. He said nothing. He just stared at the ground trying to make sense of what had just happened, confused how he'd gotten things all wrong. Wondering how again he'd missed the angle and in such a big way this time.

"You like the creepers, do you?" he howled after her.

She ignored him and kept on walking.

Choking back tears, he shook his fist. "You want to make a monster baby?"

Gaines watched her go until she'd dwindled along with his hopes.

D og's nimble fingers plucked puffs of soft cotton from the bolls and stuffed them in the poke slung over his shoulder. In the next row, Mary picked her own with a blank expression on her face.

"Darn, Mary," he said. "Give me a chance, will you."

They were racing, and she was already edging ahead.

She stopped cold and stared at him.

"I was just kidding," he told her.

"Big Brother sad."

"No, no. You can win. I hope you do. Keep going."

Mary smiled and went back to work. Dog picked as fast as he could.

Brain was right that times were hard, but Dog couldn't control any of it. He found joy in the little things that made life worth living. Sunshine and friends, honest work with his hands. Miss Sally serving cold lemonade after they took a long stroll together under Pa Albod's approving eye. Making Mary smile while having a race to make the time fly.

"Weather teacher," she said and pointed.

Mr. Gaines marched across the yard and onto the cotton field. He tottered like a sleepwalker. A hawk spiraled in the sky behind him. Dog and Mary stopped working as he approached.

Weather teacher. Some days sun, other days rain, sometimes a storm.

"Hey, Enoch," he said.

"We're doing fine, Mr. Gaines. Me and Mary is having ourselves a race."

"That's good. That's real good, Enoch."

"All right."

"I have a mind to do something," Mr. Gaines said.

"Sir?"

"Go hunting next weekend. Take the boy out to shoot some quail in yonder woods, if Reggie will let me hunt on his land."

"That's fine," Dog said, feeling wary. Mr. Gaines's empty stare made him nervous. He felt the claws in his fingers itch for release.

"I seen you on all fours," the teacher said. "You run real good that way."

"Miss Sally asked me to. I told her it's not allowed. I'm real sorry—"

"I was thinking you should come out with the boy and me."

"Sir?"

"You might could help us out. Flush out the birds and round them up after we shoot them. We could have a cold supper together after. What do you say?"

Dog didn't know what to say. Mr. Gaines had been acting strange, blowing warm then cold. Calling them good
kids one minute, demons the next. Dog liked the nice Mr.
Gaines and wanted that man to like him, but the mean Mr.
Gaines scared him. Right now, the teacher looked like both
men at once, inviting Dog to supper with his dead face. His
strange eye warm and simple, his good eye cold.

Dog pulled a tuft of cotton and rammed it in his poke, his
fingers acting on their own. "Sure, I might could do that."

"Fine if you don't want to. I just thought you could help
us out."

"Yeah," Dog said.

"And it might be fun for you, too. Your running on all
fours could be our secret. But if you don't want to come
along, just say so."

He thought it over. Mr. Gaines wouldn't hurt him, especially if he was helping the man out. Maybe he felt nervous
because this was a new experience, like his walk with Sally.
But like his walk, a normal thing. It was possible Mr. Gaines
was acting strange because it was new for him, too.

Maybe this was just part of growing up. Taking walks,
hunting, and everything that grew from that. He'd wanted
this. He'd put his hopes in it happening for as long as he
could remember. He'd always seen himself reaching some
magical age when he would gain the life he wanted, but his
instincts knew the world didn't work that way. The normals
would never accept the plague kids just like that.

It had to happen one bitty bit at a time. That's how one
made new friends. That's how normals and plague kids
would end up one day living together, everybody doing
what they were special at doing.

"I'd like that, Mr. Gaines," he said. "I'd like that a lot."

The man's dead face twisted into a wide smile. "That's good. Real good. I'll come get you tomorrow morning."

Brain made it sound like the future was already writ in stone, but Dog found it full of surprises. He smiled back at Mr. Gaines, marveling at God's small gifts.

Twenty-Two

Linda Green had a monster of sorts inside her, a kind and loving thing. Mama's little helper, and Lord, was he a thirsty boy. Sometimes it is only in the lack of something we discover how strong it is weaved into the fabric of the day. She'd have a finger of liquor in a glass to steady her nerves, one to brace her for a run down to the store. A finger to pamper after a long, hot bath, one or two to keep her company while she watched her soaps.

You can get so used to a crutch it becomes a third leg.

She lit another cigarette and gazed out the window, maintaining her vigil. The smoke hung in drifts in the dim room. The clock ticked on the mantle. Amy tossed and turned upstairs. Outside, the sun glared on the lush green world she'd forsaken for the comforting fog. Somebody would find the car. It was only a matter of time.

Linda deserved a finger for what she'd done. Sticky blood clinging to everything. Copper smell so strong she could taste it, even with the windows rolled down. The long, fruitless search for a man's head. Driving through the night with the corpse rolling around in the passenger seat with his pecker hanging out. Linda yelling, *You got your just deserts, you son of a bitch.* Watching the taillights dwindle as the car rolled into the water and settled in the mud just halfway in. Frantic heaving at the bumper. The long walk home still ranting at the man who caused all this horror.

Just a snort. A sip, even. She deserved it.

Linda coughed into her fist, her version of laughing. That was how the Devil tempted you. With your own voice. Giving you what you wanted. Promising comfort. The stronger the voice, the more you wanted, the greater your need for comfort, the more the Devil got his grip on you. Knowing this had convinced her of the innate good in man that he worshipped a fatherly God who denied earthly cravings and answered prayers with guilt. Still, it amazed her even a single man remained a Christian. The Devil always said yes.

A cloud of dust. Car coming.

Not Jake Coombs this time, the preacher's son courting her Amy, showing up at the door yesterday wringing his hands and asking about her health. Young love. So precious. Linda didn't envy his youth, only his choices—all his biggest triumphs and mistakes still ahead of him. No germ in him. A handsome boy, gawky and earnest and in love. Linda knew she could teach him a thing or two about women. The Devil never stopped talking.

A police car, the sun burning on its windshield.

She cast a worried look at the stairs. Amy tossed and turned up in her room. Three days of missed school. Sheriff on his way. She had to get ready.

Linda went to the desk where she paid her bills and rooted through the junk in the top drawer until she found her key. She unlocked the drawer underneath and pulled out the heavy .38 Smith & Wesson Special. After checking it was loaded, she stuck it between two cushions in the sofa where she watched her soaps in the long, empty afternoons.

Then she took another look around. She'd cleaned up the morning after she'd disposed of the body and the car, scrubbing the house of anything that might be evidence. She'd messed it up again since. It wouldn't do for the sheriff to walk in and say, *Oh, hello, Linda, I see you was expecting company.*

She'd missed something while getting rid of the body. Or maybe somebody saw something. Whatever it was, it was important enough to lead Sheriff Burton all the way here like the bloodhound he was.

The police car pulled in front of the house and sat humming in the heat and light of day. The engine stopped. She had one last thing to do. The bottle and glass on the mantle. Just a finger to steady the nerves. She had to appear just like she would any other day. The Devil was on her side. Even God understood. Linda had a belt, poured another, and hurried to turn on her soaps just as the sheriff knocked.

Taking her time, she went to the door and opened it. Instinctively, she struck a pose leaning on the frame. "Well, look who it is. Howdy, Tom. Been a while. How you been?"

"Just fine, thank ye," the sheriff said. "How about yourself?"

"I been hunky-dory," she said.

"You're looking good."

She cocked an eyebrow. "You out canvasing for votes, or is this a social call?"

He didn't smile. "Neither, I'm sad to say. Can I come in?"

"Where are my manners? Of course, come on in."

Burton followed her inside. He carried a plastic bag with something red in it. She gave it a passing glance before returning her gaze to his face. She didn't know what it was but knew not to stare.

"Can I get you something to drink? Some cold iced tea?"

"No, thank ye. I need to talk to you about your girl, Amy."

"She's upstairs. She been awful sick the past few days. Caught the flu."

"Poor thing," Burton said. "When did you say she got sick?"

"My baby's been out of school since Wednesday."

"I'll need to have a word with her, if you don't mind."

"Well, I do mind, Tom. She's in a bad way."

He held up the thing in its plastic bag: a school textbook stained pink and covered in the rags of a paper-bag book cover. Giant letters, Amy's lilting scrawl drawn in Magic Marker. HEALTH, it said. AMY GREEN. Flowers and doodles and fragments of song lyrics, all smeared and barely legible.

"Afraid I have to insist," he said.

Linda blinked. "I, uh, can't read that. What's it say?"

"This is your daughter's schoolbook."

She sipped her bourbon, her mind scrambling. "Where did you find it?"

"We pulled it out of a man's car."

"Who's the man?"

"Drifter named Ray Bowie who worked out at the Home. Who also happens to be dead now, hence my interest. Were you aware Amy might have known him?"

"That's horrible. But she never mentioned him."

"Do you know where she was Tuesday night?"

"Amy came home around six and we had our supper. She did her homework upstairs and came down to watch some TV. Same as most days."

"All right," Burton said.

"All right, what?"

"All right, I need to talk to her."

"Why don't we sit on the sofa and you and me talk a bit?"

"I'd love to catch up, Linda, but I'm on the clock."

"Amy's a good girl," she said.

"I know she is. I promise to be discreet with whatever she tells me about her relationship with Ray Bowie."

"She's awful sick up there, Tom."

"I swear I'll be gentle with her," he said.

He started up the stairs.

"Wait," she said.

The sheriff sighed. "This has to be done. I'm going up."

Linda looked at the sofa where she'd hidden her gun. "You go on, then. I'll be along directly."

Amy moaned in her fever dreams. Plague kids danced in front of a burning farmhouse. Misshapen silhouettes. Twisted and capering shadows. Shame Addiction screamed to drown out the laughter.

Amy, her mama called from the dark.

The kids thrust pitchforks into the flames and roasted their marshmallows.

Amy, Amy.

Mama was calling her home for supper.

The marshmallows turned into dripping arms and legs.

Bowie gripped the back of her neck and showed her a cattle prod. *Come on, darlin'. You're gonna miss all the fun.*

Amy, Mama said.

She woke up drenched in sweat. "I don't want it."

The sheriff looked down at her. "Hello, honey. How are you feeling?"

"Sheriff?"

"That's right. I've come to check on you."

She looked around her room. "I ain't well, sir."

She just wanted to go back to sleep. Even with the fever dreams, she could forget her real life. Pretend it wasn't real.

Sheriff Burton sat on the edge of the bed and put his hat on the covers. "I need to ask you a few questions about Ray Bowie."

Amy shook her head, unsure if this was just another dream.

"Honey, Bowie's dead," Burton said. "Somebody killed him."

"I know who he is. He ain't a friend or anything."

"Uh-huh," Burton said.

Amy realized her mistake. She should have shown surprise he was dead.

"Were you ever in his car?" the sheriff said.

Standing behind the sheriff, Mama gave a little nod. She kept her hand in the bulging pocket of her housecoat.

"Yes, sir," Amy said. "Just the one time."

"Was you with him when he got killed?"

Mama tensed. "Now, Tom—"

"It's a simple question," the sheriff said, his eyes still on Amy.

Amy burst into tears. "Oh, Lord."

"You snuck out again, didn't you?" Burton said. "Took a drive and parked someplace."

"We was just talking," Amy said. "Honest."

Mama frowned. "What do you mean, snuck out again?"

The sheriff ignored her. "What came next?"

Amy wanted so badly to confess but didn't know what to say. She woke up and Bowie was dead. That meant she couldn't have done it. It wasn't her. It was the thing inside her. The thing that fought to protect itself.

"Monster," Amy breathed.

"A creeper came along? What happened, Amy?"

Creeper, she thought. What was he talking about?

Amy conjured up her hate. Her hate of Bowie, the plague, baby Tony floating in a jar, the creature lurking inside her. All the creatures, everywhere. The whole generation of the plague.

Yes, she decided. He was right. He was right about everything.

"A creeper attacked us," she told the sheriff. "Just like you said."

"I know this is hard. Did you get a look at him?"

"Big," she gasped, groping for words.

"Go on. You're doing good."

"Hairy. Fast. I only caught a glimpse. It took Ray. Took his head off. Blood everywhere."

Lies, all of it, but the horror was real enough.

"All right—"

"I ran away. I don't remember anything after that. I don't. Honest."

Then she cried even harder. The pain tore at her insides until it birthed through her heart and left, one monster expelled.

"All right," Burton said. "You're a good girl. I'm sorry to upset you."

"Monster," she shouted. "It did it. It killed him. It ate his head. Monster!"

It wasn't me, she thought.

She almost believed it.

Twenty-Three

After school, Jake set out on his daily pilgrimage down the lonely road to Amy's house. Michelle joined him today, swinging her book bag.

"I sure hope she's feeling better today," he said.

"I got to be home by five on the dot. I'm still grounded."

"I am beginning to seriously fret."

"You ain't even listening to me," Michelle said.

"I don't mean to be rude, sorry. I'm preoccupied."

She sighed. "Just like Sally. Always away in her own thoughts lately. Amy's got the flu, Jake. She ain't dying."

"I don't like when people I care about get real sick."

"Oh." She grimaced. "Right. I'm sorry."

"It's okay."

"Honestly, I think it's sweet how you care," Michelle told him.

"I really miss her. I ain't seen her since we was at the A & P."

"Speaking of which, I'm surprised you ain't grounded."

"Pa preaches fear, and folks walk home from church happy as a dead pig in sunshine," Jake said. "I preach loving the weak, and everybody hollers."

"They're already afraid. Your daddy gives them what they want."

He considered this. "Yeah. You might be right."

"Telling them to love what they're scared of, well. That makes folks upset."

"God. How does anything change ever?"

"Run for president," Michelle said.

"Maybe I will."

"We'll all vote for you. Nobody else will, though."

Jake laughed. "Anyways, we worked it out. I'm gonna start a food and clothing drive for the Home after everything settles down."

"Sure, maybe in the year 2000."

"Yeah, I think it'll—"

He threw her a look, laughed again, and kept walking.

Amy's house came into view. The weathered American colonial sat behind yellow poplars, its paint chipped and fading. Mrs. Green's orange Datsun rusted in the driveway. One day, he decided, he'd offer to repaint the house if Mrs. Green paid for the materials.

They tramped up onto the wide porch and rang the doorbell.

The door opened. Mrs. Green appeared behind the screen door in a housecoat, arms crossed and blowing a stream of smoke. "You're the persistent sort, ain't you."

"Hello, Mrs. Green. Just thought I'd swing by and check on Amy again."

The screen door creaked open. The woman stepped onto the porch. "She's mending well."

"That's good. Can we see her?"

Mrs. Green took in Michelle. "You gonna introduce me to your friend or just let her stand there looking awkward?"

"Sorry for my manners," Jake said. "This is Michelle Johnson."

"Hi," Michelle said and offered a little wave.

"Pleased to meet you," Mrs. Green said and swung her head back in Jake's direction. "Amy ain't receiving again today. You might see her Monday at school."

"But—"

"I got to be getting back to her now. Michelle, it was real nice meeting one of Amy's friends. Y'all take care getting on home. Goodbye."

"Bye, Mrs. Green," Michelle said with another wave and bounced off the porch.

"Tell Amy I miss her and hope she gets better real soon," Jake said.

"I surely will. Bye, now."

"Bye," he said, lingering a moment before running off to join Michelle.

"Feeling better now?" Michelle said.

Jake chewed the inside of his lip. "Actually, no. Not even a bit."

He heard tapping and turned around to see Mrs. Green still standing on the porch with her arms crossed, blowing another stream of smoke into the warm air. Then he looked up and saw Amy standing in a second-floor window.

She had nothing on, using the sheer white curtain to cover herself.

A my looked down at him standing in the front yard. She'd felt so ugly after what happened to her. Then Jake gaped up at her with wide eyes, and she was beautiful again.

Michelle tugged at his arm. He grinned and waved before setting off.

Mama turned and frowned up at the window. Amy yelped and jumped back. She got her bathrobe on and tied as her mother stomped up the stairs and banged into the room breathing smoke.

Mama stood by the bed with her arms crossed. "I don't think you should see that boy no more."

"He's my boyfriend," Amy said. "I'm in love with him."

She'd come so close to betraying him after she'd gotten into Ray Bowie's car. Betrayal for a little excitement and danger. Good music and a fancy ride. All just smoke and mirrors. Jake had come to check on her. Loyal and devoted. A boy she could trust. Jake was real. A lesson learned, one she'd not soon forget.

Her mama sat on the edge of the bed and patted the covers, inviting her to sit. Amy realized she was standing rigid with her arms crossed, a younger mirror image of her mother. She unfolded her arms and sat.

"You don't even know what love is," Mama said. "Neither of you do. You're too young. What if he found out what you are? You think he'd stick by you?"

"I believe he would."

"Your own daddy didn't stick by you. He didn't for me, neither. Your first boyfriend ain't usually your last, anyways."

"I don't want to argue about it, Mama. I slept for two days and had nightmares the whole time. I'm still feeling poorly."

Poorly didn't come close to covering it. The horror of what Bowie had done all came back to her now, along with the fear she might have killed him.

Mama eyed her with concern. "Why don't you lie down and rest some more?"

Amy didn't want to sleep. She wanted to scrub herself good and raw and make herself clean again. "What I need is a hot bath."

She got up and went down the hall to the bathroom. She turned on the spigot and ran her toothbrush under it while the tub filled.

Mama appeared in the doorway while she brushed her teeth. "I raised you good, but you got some stupid in you. You got that from me, not just your age. You need to be smarter than me."

Amy washed out her mouth and spat in the sink. "I ain't stupid. Maybe ignorant about a lot of things, but not stupid."

"I just feel like I'm the only one here trying to protect you."

"I want to live. I'm still learning. This is the first year I even had any real friends. You want me to give up everything I got and live in a box."

Before her mother could say another word, Amy dropped her robe and stepped into the tub. She pulled the curtain closed and sat in the hot water. Steam moistened her skin.

Mama said, "I have something important to tell you."

"I'm serious. I don't want to fight no more. I'm tuckered out."

"We ain't fighting, we're talking."

Amy sighed as she scrubbed her arms. "Go ahead and say your piece."

"We might have to think about moving away from here," Mama said.

Amy recoiled as if slapped. She pulled the curtain back. "Why?"

"Tom Burton don't look like much, but he's a tick. Once he smells blood, he bites and don't let go."

"Oh, my God. You think I'm the one killed Ray, don't you?"

"It don't matter if you did or didn't. The sheriff will run in a big circle until he comes back and presses you again. He'll keep on pressing until he gets the truth."

Amy yanked the curtain closed and covered her face with her hands. "I can't keep living like this."

"Oh, don't be dramatic. We done okay. Things could be a lot worse for you."

"I was forced, Mama. That boy forced himself on me."

"I know," Mama said in a soft voice.

"And I'm suffocating. It ain't my fault I was born this way."

"You think I don't know that. That I don't feel shame every day of my life. It's my responsibility. Let me protect you from yourself. I made my mistakes, but I've learned some things. I know what's best for you."

Amy imagined walking down the halls at school while all the kids stared and whispered behind their hands. Pictured telling Jake what she was and seeing his face screw up in disgust. Imagined him broken and devastated after finding out she'd given him the germ.

She saw Burton and his deputies drag her screaming to the Home.

Amy next pictured moving with Mama from town to town, living in hotel rooms that smelled like old ashtrays. Imagined herself never really knowing another human being aside from her mother. Pictured depending on this woman every hour of every day the rest of her life.

"No," she said. "No, Mama."

"No, what."

"If we run, we'll never stop running. Staying has risks, but that's life, and I want to live. I'm just starting to live, and I ain't giving it up."

Mama opened the door. "All right. You want to grow up faster than you should, then you can figure out how to get out from under the sheriff. You think on it long and hard, baby girl."

"We'll be all right," Amy said. "I just know it."

"A word of advice. Get to know that monster you got inside you. Learn how to use her. We may need her again someday."

Mama closed the door behind her.

Twenty-Four

Saturday morning. Sunrise at the Albod farm. The land was quiet and still.

Gaines studied the land as he loaded his twelve gauge with #8 birdshot. Full breakfast in his belly and coffee warming his chest, Archie cradled his short twenty gauge, staying close to his daddy. Both wore brown hunting clothes and orange vests. Enoch stood with his hands in the pockets of his raggedy shorts, eyeing the distant farmhouse.

"You ready?" Gaines asked his son.

His boy gaped at the creeper. He'd never seen one up close before. "Yeah, Daddy. I'm all set."

Albod's land promised good bobwhite quail hunting. Beautiful birds and good eating. Tough to hunt. You had to be on your game.

Gaines pumped a round and stuck the barrel in the air. "All right, Enoch. Let's bag some birds."

"I don't know a thing about hunting, Mr. Gaines."

"The quail make a sound like they're saying *bob white, bob white*. That's a mating call, but they only do it in spring and summer. Other times, they make a kind of low whistle, like a squeak. We're gonna listen for that."

"Okay," said Enoch.

"You're gonna be our flushing dog. Bobwhite come out to eat seeds, then they like to hang around in weeds and bushes. We come to a good spot, you run in and get them riled. We'll handle it from there."

"I think I understand."

"Lead the way then," Gaines told him.

"Can I run on all fours?"

He smiled. "That's the idea."

Enoch threw himself at the ground and landed in a crouch.

"Well, butter my ass and call me toast," Archie said.

The creeper grinned at the prospect of a good run and bounded into the trees. Gaines smiled too as the kid set off. Working with creepers had always been a source of some shame to him. Not this morning. His boy was actually impressed his daddy knew creepers and had a good handle on them.

And to think Archie hadn't wanted to come along. He'd wanted to sleep in. Kids today were all soft. They wanted everything given over on a silver platter while they slept through the delivery. Youth really was wasted on the young.

The hunters spread out and followed the dog boy into the woods.

"How are things at school?" Gaines said.

Archie shrugged. "It's school."

"You keeping up with your studies?"

"I try real hard, Daddy. I still ain't no good at science, but I'm doing great in math this year. Health class is a hoot."

Gaines scanned the woods. He'd lost sight of the dog boy,

who'd disappeared in the undergrowth. "What about the other kids? You getting along?"

Another shrug. "Yeah."

"Yeah, what?"

"Well, there's this girl I like, but she don't like me."

"You'll find another one. Plenty of fish in the world."

"But this one is perfect."

Gaines snorted. "I very much doubt that."

"I sometimes don't think there's somebody just for me, that's all."

"Thinking that way is natural at your age," Gaines told him. "Funny thing about the young. You think your life will go on forever but never think you have enough time to live it. You kids have no sense of time nor patience at all."

"Yeah, I guess," Archie said.

"What about the boys at the school? Your friends."

"They're a little out there, but they're okay."

"How about the preacher's boy?" Gaines said. "I heard he was the one bopped you in the nose and put you on your ass."

Archie let out a nervous laugh. "That what you heard? That boy got a lick in, but I bopped him good. Laid him out. Ask anybody."

"All right, I will."

"What do you mean?"

"I'm gonna ask that boy you pal around with. The Fulcher boy."

"You mean Dan."

"That's the one," Gaines said. "I'll ask him."

"He'll tell you what I said."

"Never mind. I won't ask him."

"Okay," Archie said.

"Because I know a cracker when I see one, Archibald."

When Gaines was a kid, he'd had his share of fights. Simpler times. You played together over the long summers, exploring creeks and climbing trees, until somebody got sore and declared war. That's how he got smacked with a wood plank and ended up with a lazy eye. At the time, he considered it a badge of honor.

Being a grown-up proved a lot more complicated. Honor rested on shifting sands. Money and property were the new badges. People fought with words and betrayals instead of fists. His lazy eye became a source of shame. Folks sure did love to pick at old scabs. They smelled your weak spots and brought them up in passing like noting the weather. Little puffs here and there to see how strong the house of cards you built.

Being an adult was pecking and trying not to get pecked, trying not to be the one at the bottom, the one everybody else got to ride. A kid could always fight his way out of that, but not adults. Lord, how he wished he'd never grown up.

"You get a chance at him again, you take it," Gaines said.

"Yes, sir."

"Don't yes-sir me. It ain't for me, it's for you."

"I'll bop him good next time," Archie said.

"No more cracker talk. It's okay if you lose. Just give him a good fight and earn his respect. If you don't, you'll live with it forever. You'll never respect yourself."

Gaines wanted to tell his good-for-nothing kid to man up. Fight like a man. No, not that. Men fought dirty. No, Archie should fight like a kid. Kids fought like knights of old, shook hands, and ended up friends at the end of it.

As long as he didn't fight like a woman, he thought. Anything but that. Nobody fought like them. They didn't hurt you. They nuked you and laughed at your ashes. He could attest to that through hard personal experience.

Darlene had buck teeth and a high forehead, but to Gaines she'd been the living Venus. He'd loved watching her shake her ass in her tight uniform while she served the customers at Belle's Diner. Loved the way she smiled as she poured his coffee, like the pouring itself was some special thing between them, embedded with private meaning. She married him to get out of the diner and had his baby because that's what you did. Then she realized the whole thing wasn't about to answer all her childish dreams and ran off to chase them in California, leaving him with no savings in the bank and a boy to raise.

Sally Albod wanted to do the same thing to him. She wanted to get him on the hook so she could stomp him for sport. Come out to the Home and lead him on just so she could later tell him to his face that said face made her puke. That he had a stupid eye. That she liked monster kids better than him.

Meaner than a wet panther. He'd never suffered anything like that verbal beating. Even Darlene walking out had been kinder and less cruel. Gaines felt like he understood Sucker Punch, the way people came at him. Only instead of seeing the swing, he always missed it. He never saw the angle, his bum eye always on the ground.

Today, he'd teach her a lesson she'd never forget. He wasn't going to play her game of bait and switch. He could fight dirty, too. Show her who's boss. The sun didn't come up just to watch her crow.

Archie started to say something, but Gaines waved at him to keep quiet. They entered a glade thick with Indian grass, briar thickets on the other side. Enoch bounded around the clearing.

If only you didn't talk, Gaines thought looking at the dog boy. If only you didn't claim to be human. If only you had not meddled in a man's affairs.

The briars exploded with birds.

The covey filled the air, quail flying every direction. Gaines waited, knowing they'd all converge on the nearest cover. He shouldered his gun and shot into the winged chaos. The gun banged and jerked. A moment later, Archie did the same.

Birds dropped to the ground as the survivors vanished.

"How about that," Gaines said with a grin.

"How many we get, Daddy?"

"At least six, I reckon."

"Damn if your friend don't make a good flushing dog."

"He ain't my friend," Gaines said.

Enoch.

The creeper cocked his head at the distant call.

Enoch.

"Never mind her," Gaines said. "Go fetch them birds."

Miss Sally had guessed what he had a mind to do. Her daddy must have told her to stay away from the woods because they were hunting. Albod had seen Enoch come out with him and the boy and walk off into the woods.

Two and two make a dead dog.

Now she wanted to meddle, despite her daddy's wishes. Well, she could do it at her own risk, then. She'd heard the shooting. If that didn't stop her, so be it.

It would all be over soon.

Gaines reloaded his shotgun, this time with buckshot. It wasn't his intent to kill the creeper, but an ass full of double-aught would lay him up for a long, long time.

"I don't hear him," Archie said.

Gaines listened. "Come on back here, Enoch."

Nothing.

He should have known. The son of a bitch ran off to find Sally.

Thrashing in a thicket on his left.

"What's that?" Gaines said. "Something over there."

He was trembling, excited and scared, thinking maybe he shouldn't do this. Sally was running around out there somewhere worried Gaines had shot up her pet. Maybe putting some fear in her heart was enough to make his point.

A clump of bushes shook. A branch cracked. A flicker of green.

He raised his shotgun and fired into the thicket.

Branches flew apart at the blast. Leaves sprayed and fluttered to the ground.

"What was that?" Archie said. "Why did you shoot?"

"Thought I saw a pheasant," Gaines said.

His ears rang from the blast. He crept forward, listening.

A girl gasped for help.

Oh, Lord, he thought. What have I done?

He dropped the gun and ran into the tangle. Branches tore and scratched at him like a resisting animal. He saw suntanned legs and a green dress.

Sally lay snared in branches. His aim had been half-blind but perfect. Peppered hole in her chest. She wheezed and gasped, glaring at him in panic.

"I've got you, Miss Sally."

Crying, he scooped her up in his arms and carried her back to the glade, where he set her down on the Indian grass.

"That's Sally," Archie said.

Gaines took her hand and squeezed. "I'm real sorry."

"That's Sally Albod. God, Daddy, what did you do?"

"I'm sorry," he cried. "I'm real, real sorry."

Something growled.

Gaines looked up in time to see the dog boy crouched in the thicket, snarling through clenched teeth, eyes wide and bestial.

"Enoch," he said. "Go get Mr. Albod."

The creeper launched itself in a whirlwind of fur and claws. Pain ripped through Gaines's chest and shoulder as he flew back. Blood spray blinded him. The thing's hot breath blew against his face. The creeper's musky stink. Drool splashed his cheeks. Claws dug into him like bolts of fire.

A shotgun roared. The thing whined and vanished.

"Daddy," Archie screamed. "Daddy, get up now."

Gaines wiped blood from his eyes. He tried to sit up but sank back again howling as pain flared in his chest.

"Goddamnit," he said.

"Don't move, Daddy. He tore you up bad."

"Did you get him?"

"I got him," Archie said. "He ran off in the woods, though."

"Help me sit up."

"You're bleeding like a stuck pig."

"Do it," Gaines growled.

He gritted his teeth and shivered as the boy helped him. He looked over at Sally, who lay in the grass and stared back at him breathing in rapid, shallow gasps. Blood spotted her chest, flecks of it on her lips.

He watched her labor to breathe, wondering at his own stupidity. It was like waking up from a dream. She was just a dumb, stupid girl. Why had he gotten so worked up over her? Why did he shoot instead of listening to the voice in his head? None of it mattered. She might live, she might not, but his life was over now.

He'd have to leave town and never look back. Give up his job. They'd take his son away from him. If Albod didn't kill him with his bare hands first.

"I'll go get help," Archie said.

"Wait." Gaines fought his way onto his knees, light-headed and sick. His left arm hung useless, but his right worked well enough. "It's time to man up."

"What do you mean?"

"Sometimes, you have to be a man," he said. "Do something bad for something better. Now look away. I don't want you to see."

"Daddy?"

"Look away, son. Don't look back, no matter what you hear."

Gaines crawled toward Sally, who gaped back at him with tears leaking from her eyes. She shook her head.

"I'm sorry, Miss Sally."

She shook her head again. "No," she gasped.

"I wanted to be in love with you," he said.

Then he drew his knife.

Twenty-Five

Dog fled, crying with shame and despair.

Blood spotted the leaves he passed. Pain lanced through his ribs with every lunge through the brush. Sally lay back in that glade dead or dying.

It was all his fault.

Sally would never forgive him. Pa Albod. Mr. Gaines.

They'd put him in Discipline for sure.

The woods beckoned him. A boy could get lost here. He could go feral.

That wouldn't be right, though. He owed the Albods too much.

He raced back to the farmstead and found Pa Albod in his barn. He skidded to a halt in the straw and lay on his side gasping.

Pa Albod ran over. "Lord, what happened to you, Enoch?"

"Sally got shot. She got shot, sir."

The blood drained from the man's face. "What do you mean, she got shot?"

"She was in the bushes calling for me. Mr. Gaines shot in the bushes and hit her."

"Is she dead?"

"Then I ripped up Mr. Gaines, I was so mad," Dog said. "Then they shot me, too."

"Goddamnit, is she dead?"

"I don't know, sir. I think she were still breathing."

"Where?"

"A big glade about a mile—"

"I know it."

The farmer ran from the barn. Dog limped wincing after him and sat in the yard. Pa went into the house and came out toting his shotgun. His daughters trailed pleading and crying after him. He turned and pointed at the house.

"Go back inside and call 911," he said. "Lock every door until I get back."

Dog sat in the tall grass and watched him until he was just a dot. Then the dot disappeared in the woods. He lay on his side hoping to close his eyes a minute.

A boot prodded him awake.

"Get up, boy," the sheriff said.

An ambulance shrieked in the distance.

Dog looked up at the three men standing over him, all wearing sheriff's department uniforms. "Is she okay?"

"What happened out there?"

He sat up, groaning over his stiff ribs. Pain rippled and throbbed along his side. "Mr. Gaines shot Miss Sally. Then I mauled him with my claws."

"He shoot her on purpose?"

Dog wagged his head. "Accident."

"Then you mauled Mr. Gaines, you told me. You did that on purpose."

"Yes, sir. I did. On account of what he did to Sally."

"Thought I warned you not to mess around with normal kids."

"She's my friend," Dog said.

The ambulance pulled into the yard and cut the siren. He stared at the flashing lights. Red and blue.

"I don't see claws on him," a deputy said. "Did he say he mauled Gaines?"

Dog showed them.

"Jesus," the other deputy said.

"Looks like he shot you, too, Enoch," the sheriff said.

"Mr. Gaines's son did it. He shot me on account of what I did to his daddy."

"You was all out there hunting birds together?"

"Yes, sir. Excepting Sally. She run out to find me."

"Why'd she do that?"

"I don't rightly know, sir."

"You got peppered by birdshot. You'll be all right."

"It hurts plenty, sir."

The sheriff nodded to his deputies, who crouched and rolled Dog onto his stomach. Then they handcuffed him.

"You kill Gaines?" the sheriff said.

"I don't think so. I hurt him bad, though."

"You better pray you didn't kill him. Either way, I have to bring you in."

One of the deputies pointed. "Hey, boss."

Pa Albod was coming, carrying his little girl in his arms. The paramedics ran over to him with their kits. They stopped and stood aside as he passed.

Somebody had torn her chest wide open. Her eyes stared at nothing.

"Sally," Dog breathed. "Poor Sally."

The farmer was crying. "Look what you done. Look what you done to my little girl."

He fell to his knees keening over the body.

"You son of a bitch," the sheriff said.

A deputy kicked Dog hard in the shoulder with his boot. He howled in surprise and rolled as the second deputy raised his baton with a fierce, desperate look. The club smashed him in the guts. Dog gasped at the shock. He couldn't breathe. It hurt more than anything in his life. He didn't understand what was happening. The first deputy kicked him again. Blood sprayed from Dog's snout. He vomited in the grass. The baton came down again with a sickening thud.

He looked up through a veil of pain to see the big sheriff raise his boot and bring it down on his face.

MEN

He who fights with monsters should be careful lest he thereby become a monster.

—Friedrich Nietzsche

Twenty-Six

Dog lay moaning in the back of the police cruiser. He hurt everywhere. The handcuffs bit into his wrists. The right side of his body throbbed with pain. Blood clotted his nose. He tongued loose fangs. He leaned over the seat and let a string of bloody drool spill to the floor.

He looked up at the sheriff's grizzled head. "Tell me why. Why did he have to kill her like that?"

"You have the right to remain silent," the sheriff said.

"I don't even know what that means."

"It means shut your mouth and God damn you for what you done."

The car lurched to a halt. The door opened. A deputy leaned in and helped him out. Dog looked around in wonder at all the buildings and cars and people. This was where the normals lived. Nothing like the squalor of the Home, the peaceful stillness of the farm.

Everybody stared at him. He smiled weakly back.

Special, he thought.

The deputy gripped him under his arm and yanked him

toward the police station. "You bite and, so help me, I'll knock your teeth out."

Dog limped, panting hard at each step. "I ain't gonna bite you."

He didn't know why the deputy looked so scared. He didn't get beat half to death. He wasn't wearing handcuffs. Inside, the man sat him in a chair in a big office and took his own seat behind a typewriter. The sheriff leaned against the cinder block wall and watched.

"Your full name?"

"Enoch Davis Bryant. They call me Dog."

Clack, clack.

"Date of birth?"

"I don't know. We don't have birthdays."

"1970?"

"Yes, sir. I am fourteen years old."

Clack, clack.

After that they fingerprinted him and hauled him in front of a camera mounted on a tripod. A deputy took off his handcuffs while the sheriff stood nearby with his hand on the grip of the big gun he wore at his side. Dog massaged his wrists. The deputy pushed him toward the wall and gave him a placard to hold up.

Dog smiled as the flashbulb popped.

The deputy told him to stand to the side and took another picture of his profile. "Now get them shorts off."

"But I'll be naked."

"I ain't asking twice, creeper."

Dog stood before the normals, ashamed of his nakedness. Pins and needles raged in his hands as they regained feeling, like they were being eaten by fire ants. The deputy took him into another room and told him to close his eyes and hold his breath. When he opened his eyes, his fur was white with delousing powder. The deputy handed him a white uniform with D.O.C. stenciled on the back of the shirt. He put it on and followed the deputy out.

"How do you like your new pajamas?" the sheriff said.

"Better than what we got at the Home."

"I'll take it from here, Bobby."

Burton put him in a jail cell and slammed the heavy door shut. The grip of numerous desperate hands had worn the paint off the bars over the years. Dog's gaze took in the bed, commode, and sink.

All just for him. More luxury. Everything clean and no fleas and ticks. His own personal commode, the kind that flushed.

The sheriff pulled up a chair and sat. "You'll be staying here until we get things sorted."

"This is just fine," Dog said.

He lay on the bed and curled into a ball shivering from the pain that wouldn't quit. The ribs on the right side had fused into a throbbing, angry tumor. He wasn't bleeding anymore, but he still had metal pieces in there working their way deeper into his flesh with every breath.

Burton pulled a pipe from the breast pocket of his uniform and tamped a big pinch of tobacco in it. He lit a match and puffed. The air filled with cherry smoke.

"Your story don't add up," he said. "How about you tell me what really happened out in them woods."

"I thought I had a right to stay quiet," Dog said.

"This is a poor time to sass me, boy. I am the only friend you got right now."

"You ain't my friend."

"You want to do this with a lawyer?"

"No," Dog said. "I want Brain."

The sheriff puffed. "And who would that be?"

"George Hurst. We call him Brain."

"The gorilla boy with the smart mouth. I remember him."

"You're right about that. He's real smart. Smarter than you and me put together. Smarter than everybody. He'd figure all this out in about ten minutes."

"I'm sure he would," the sheriff said. "A fourteen-year-old plague boy with a fourth-grade education. Naturally, he'd find you innocent."

"You mean because him and me are the same stock."

"Exactly what I mean."

"Well, a lawyer is the same as you. So what chance does that give me at justice?"

"It don't matter who represents you. The facts say you did it. So why don't you just give me the truth."

"Brain was right about one thing," Dog said.

"What would that be?"

"You hate us. The Home is built on it. This cage is built of it."

The policemen had hurt Dog's body, but he hurt far worse inside. His friend was dead, and everybody was eager to point the finger at him. The look on Pa Albod's face as he cursed him to God. The sheriff calling him a son of a bitch.

All that fear and hate they had in their hearts. Like it had always been there ready to come out in a flood.

"I didn't want to believe what Brain was always telling me," Dog said. "I hoped different. I hoped you normals could be my friends. I learned my lesson the hard way. I'm done with hoping."

"Is that why you did it? You think Sally hated you, is that it?"

"Stop trying to trick me. I was just stating a fact."

"I just want to know why you did it," the sheriff said.

"Then ask the one who did and leave me alone, sir."

"They'll send you to the state pen down in Reidsville for this. They don't execute minors, but in your case they'll make an exception. They'll try you as an adult. You'll get the electric chair for sure. Unless the inmates get you first."

Dog said nothing. He had nothing to say. Nothing the sheriff wanted to hear.

"You gonna go out with this on your conscience, boy?"

Nothing.

Burton sighed and stood.

"Sheriff," Dog said.

"What? I'm listening."

"Is Mr. Gaines gonna be okay?"

"You scratched him up something awful, but I reckon he'll survive."

"You tell him I'm real sorry."

"I might could tell him."

"Then tell him I'll get him for killing Sally."

The sheriff frowned. "Doc Odom will be by later to take a look at that birdshot wound. You make any trouble for him, we'll shoot you dead."

"In this life or the next," said Dog. "I'll wait. I'll chase him to Hell if I have to."

Twenty-Seven

Sheriff Burton left Enoch Bryant in the holding cells.
Beth, the big no-nonsense woman he called the sheriff behind the sheriff, gave him the stink-eye as he entered the office. She hung up the phone, which started ringing again. Behind her, the switchboard was lit up.

"Am I supposed to get it dinner and supper?" she said.

"Yup," Burton said.

"What does it eat?"

"He's a he, not an it. And I reckon he eats what we eat, or he can go ahead and starve."

"I'll see what I can do," she said. "The phone is ringing off the hook."

"Townsfolk pitchin' a hissy fit, I reckon. Word must be getting around."

"*The Augusta Chronicle* called, too."

"Hell's bells, that was fast. What you tell them?"

"I told that man to call the mayor."

"Good girl," the sheriff said.

"Who by the way also called. And your wife."

"I'll call her back later. The mayor, too. I'm heading over to the coroner."

"What about me?" Deputy Sikes said. "Half these calls are reports of feral kids in the woods. We don't have the manpower to check out every one."

"They're all hooey," the sheriff said. "You might stick around until the doc shows up to look at the prisoner. I'll be back by then, and we can figure out what's next."

Burton plucked his hat from its hook and left the office. He got in his car and sat still for a while just thinking. None of it added up. He wondered if the kid was crazy. Sally Albod's chest had been torn to ribbons. No birdshot did that.

The kid did it with his claws.

But to run back to the farm in a lather and make up a story like that? It beggared belief. If he tore up Sally, why stick around after? Why run and tell Albod that Gaines shot her, thinking it'd stick?

Maybe the kid had delusions.

It worried him. First Ray Bowie, now a week later a child gets murdered. Burton wondered if the plague kids suffered from a dual nature. One a normal human being, the other a thing that thought and acted like a beast. The two sides warring in their tragic souls. Maybe sometimes the beast won and took command.

Or maybe the kids were fine. The Colonel's discipline and the Home's social conditioning kept their bestial natures in check. They were all well-behaved kids, while Enoch Bryant just happened to be touched in the head. A bad apple. He snapped and killed Sally and then convinced himself he hadn't done it.

Over the years, Burton had heard crime's every excuse. If

the human mind was capable of delusions, who knew what the monster mind could come up with. The plague children remained an unknown. That they were different on the outside was plain to see. How they might be different on the inside was anybody's guess.

The whole thing made him uneasy for a mess of reasons.

Burton started the car and drove to the coroner's office. He walked into the examination room as Dr. Rose Tipton unzipped the white bag to expose Sally Albod's lifeless form on the steel slab.

"Oh, dear Lord," she said. "You poor little sweet thing."

Sally lay on the table, a lifeless effigy of a once-vibrant girl whose spirit had departed to Heaven. Her daddy had closed her eyes. Her mouth remained fixed in a soundless scream.

"Hello, Rose," Burton said. "Mind if I sit in?"

"This is a job for the mortuary. I can certify her death, and I sure as hell can state it was an unlawful death. I'll just write it up the way you want."

"That's awful kind of you, but I need an autopsy."

"What are you looking for? Somebody hacked this poor girl up, and from what I hear, you are holding the son of a bitch did it."

"I need it done for evidence. I appreciate you working on a Saturday."

She looked at the body and sighed. "Lord."

"Bowie was worse," Burton said.

"Bowie weren't a little girl, Tom."

She shrugged off her white lab coat and hung it on a hook. He got a good view of her in her tight blouse and skirt. Her face was long and a bit on the horsey side but her youthful body boasted an hourglass shape and boobs big as zeppelins. He felt an old stirring of desire but had the good sense to put it aside. He'd strayed once in his life at a cop convention a long time ago, and he'd broken almost everything in his life and now lived with a cracked home and fractured marriage.

Rose washed her hands at the shiny sink and gowned up. She pulled on gloves and set a plastic visor on her head, which she angled down to shield her face from splatter and bone dust. The scale sat ready to weigh the girl's organs. She pulled a wheeled cart in front of the table. On it lay the tools of her grisly trade: bone saw, bread knife, scissors, hammer, scalpels, skull chisel, toothed forceps.

"Lord," she editorialized. "Oh, Lord."

She took a deep breath and turned on a small tape recorder. She narrated the wounds, a litany of damage and punctures. Rose kept talking while she picked up a scalpel and sliced Sally Albod from her shoulders to her breastbone then all the way down to her pubic bone. She pulled and folded the girl's ruined chest over her face. Then she got the rib cutter. The rib cage came out.

Back to the scalpel now. Snipping and removing organs.

"Lord, Lord, Lord."

Burton leaned against the wall and closed his eyes. He didn't need to see any more of this. He'd wait for Rose to tell him what she found. This poor little girl. Innocent and precious. She'd had her whole life ahead of her, and now she was just a lifeless husk. A slab of meat for butchering.

Sally Albod was with Jesus now. He took some comfort in this but not as much as he would have liked.

Something pinged on the floor. His eyes popped open. The coroner bent to pick up a tiny object with her bloody gloves. Burton stepped forward for a closer look. She held it in her hand and nudged it with her finger.

"Piece of metal in her lung," she said.

"I'll be damned."

"What does it mean?"

Burton walked over to the exam room's work desk. "Can I use your phone?"

He was already dialing.

Beth picked up. "Sheriff's office."

"It's the sheriff. Did the—"

"I had to order out for dinner. The phones are going crazy—"

"Never mind all that, Beth. Did the doc come yet?"

"He's in the holding cells with Bobby and the creeper."

"Be a dear and get him for me."

Burton pulled the phone away an inch as he heard Beth slam the receiver on her desk. High heels clicked the floor. Angry voices in the waiting area, good citizens come to voice their upset about the crime.

"Should I keep going?" Rose said.

"See if you can find any more of that metal in her, if you don't mind."

The coroner shrugged and went back to work. Burton tried to visualize the crime in his head. The creeper mauled Sally before slashing at Dave Gaines. Gaines's boy fired his twenty-gauge with a spray of pellets.

At close range, there wouldn't be much of a spread, but it wasn't impossible a pellet found its way into Sally.

That wasn't what bothered him.

A man cleared his throat in the phone's receiver. "Sheriff, this is Dr. Odom."

"How's the prisoner doing, Doc? He giving you any trouble?"

Odom sniffed. "I don't know why I had to leave Dave Gaines to attend to this. I'm not a veterinarian."

"And he ain't a dog. He's a plague boy looks like one."

"Boys don't have claws."

"We didn't have a chance to clip those yet. He scratch you?"

"No, but that's not the point."

"How's Dave doing?" Burton said.

"He'll mend. He'll have some scars to remember it by."

"That's good to hear. That he'll mend, I mean."

"As for your dog boy, I'm still patching him up."

"You pull any shot out of him?"

"Couple pieces of birdshot," Odom said. "That's about—"

"Thank ye," Burton said and hung up.

Rose held up a piece of metal with a pair of tweezers. She plonked it in a metal bowl. "Got another one."

"Keep looking," Burton said. "I need every pellet you can find."

"Why don't you wait in my office? You look like you found a fly in your soup."

"It ain't the body that's bothering me."

Another pellet clinked in the bowl.

"No?" she said.

"Enoch Bryant got hit by birdshot," he said. "That there in your bowl is buckshot."

They stared at each other.

"And that means what?" she said.

"I'll let you get to it," he said. "I got to get back to the office. Thank ye kindly, Rose."

She shrugged again and went back to her work.

The sheriff returned to his car, put his hat on the seat, and slid behind the wheel wondering how buckshot got into Sally Albod's chest. Another thing bothered him. During her initial survey of the body, Rose had called out a three-inch-deep puncture wound under the girl's clavicle. A clean slit, not a tear. Not the kind of wound the dog boy's claws would make.

More like the kind your typical hunting knife would.

The sheriff visualized the crime again, this time the way the kid told it.

Gaines puts a load of buckshot into Sally Albod's breast-plate and pulls her out of the thickets. Dog boy shows up and goes wild. Archie shoots him, and he runs off to tell Albod. The girl is dead already. Gaines has a choice. He can take responsibility for what he did and maybe lose everything he loves, or go all the way. Frame the whole thing on a creeper nobody gives a damn about.

It all added up, except maybe for one thing.

Maybe she wasn't already dead.

"You son of a bitch," Burton said aloud.

He started the car and drove back to the office. Bedlam awaited him inside. The waiting area was jammed with shouting men and women. He glared at the invasion. They crowded him voicing their petitions.

"I saw a creeper in the woods, Sheriff. What are you gonna do about that?"

"How about you hand over the creeper and let us handle it?"

"What are you doing about the Home? Why are all those kids still running free?"

"What are you gonna do about it, Sheriff?"

Burton raised his hands. "Everybody calm down."

He still worried the plague kids might become a general threat to life and limb. Right now, though, he was more worried about the good people of Huntsville making a lynch mob.

He'd put it all to rest right now by arresting Dave Gaines.

A single voice cut through the bedlam: "Sheriff."

Linda Green. Something about her tone quieted the crowd to an angry murmur. A mother's authority. She had something to say. She walked through the crowd holding hands with her daughter. Amy was crying. Her friend was dead.

The girl looked up, her face puffed and wet with tears. "It was him."

"What do you mean it was him?" Burton said.

"The plague boy who looks like a dog."

"The boy we caught."

"He's the one who killed Ray Bowie," she said.

Twenty-Eight

Amy put on an old black dress she used to wear to church and stood in front of the mirror looking for flaws. Mama crossed her arms and tapped her foot.

"I see you're fully recovered," Mama said. "Spending an hour in the commode looking at yourself."

"How do I look? Do I look all right?"

"Prettier than a summer day," Mama said. "That dress is too small for you now, though. It were any smaller, every boy in town would be able to see Christmas."

Amy didn't care. She looked good in it. She wanted everybody to know there was nothing wrong with her. That she was perfect.

Especially Jake. She wanted to look perfect just for him.

"What about you?" she said. "That dress were any tighter, I'd see your religion."

"I earned what I wear," Mama said. "When you get to my age, you can flaunt all you want. At your age, boys drool they see you picking your nose."

"That's gross."

"Finish it up here, sugar booger. We don't want to be late."

Amy nodded, any interest she had in fighting sucked out of her. It was hard to imagine going to school without Sally. Passing commentary in the halls. Dinnertime bull sessions. Walking down to the Dairy Queen for ice cream. Picking up the phone and calling her on a bored evening to talk about the future.

Doubly hard to imagine her lying lifeless in a casket.

Her first real friend.

Mama put her flask, Virginia Slims, and Bic lighter in her pocketbook and slung it over her shoulder. They walked to Mama's old Datsun and got in. The gray sky overhead promised rain. Mama sagged behind the wheel like she was exhausted already. She rolled the window down halfway and lit a cigarette. Then she started the car and drove off.

Amy stared out the window. They passed the spot where Bowie attacked her. She shivered and looked in the rearview. Saw only swirling brown dust.

Mama patted her leg. "You did the right thing. Got yourself out of a big ol' pickle. I'm proud of you."

Amy nodded again, but she hadn't done it for herself. She'd wanted revenge on Enoch Bryant for what he did to Sally. She would go to court and perjure herself to get it. Perjury was nothing to her. She was used to lying for high stakes. She'd been lying her whole life.

The plague kid would be tried as an adult for sure. He'd die in the electric chair for his crime. The way Mama explained it, her testimony allowed the sheriff to close the book on Bowie's murder and get herself out from under his scrutiny. Her Amy killed two birds with one stone. Her baby girl, growing up in the world.

Cars and pickups filled the church's little dirt lot. The whole county, it seemed, had come out to pay their respects to the Albods. One by one, the church swallowed the mourners in black, everybody walking slow so as to lend dignity to it all. Mama parked on the road behind a Chevy and took a long pull from her flask, leaving a ring of red lipstick on the spout. She sighed and put the cap on.

"Can I have a drink of that?" Amy said. "I think I need some bracing."

Mama handed it over. Amy had a sip and winced as the burn worked its way down her gullet. Mama took the flask back and put it in her pocketbook. She eyed a crowd of reporters standing off the side of the church.

"We're gonna need this," she said. "Get through this day. If any reporter tries to talk to you, you let me do the talking. Worthless nosy nellies, the lot of them."

"All right, Mama."

"You already been through enough. Here, you better have a breath mint."

They got out and walked across the grass toward the church doors. The morning air was cool and moist on Amy's bare arms. A breeze rustled the dogwoods that dotted the lawn. The sky past the crossed church spire gloomed with thunderheads. A storm was coming.

Mama linked her arm with Amy's, still in mama bear mode. Amy chafed at her tight hold. Her mama's arm was like a manacle wrapped around her bicep.

An old man handed them programs inside. The stifling church smelled sweet and sour, like cleaning chemicals and flowers and sweat. People fanned themselves in the pews. Folks nodded to each other. Like school was for Amy, church was for grown-ups, a place where people came together. Soon, it would be standing room only. A few heads turned as they worked their way up the aisle, then more. Eyes roamed up and down the Green girls in their black dresses.

"There was a time," Mama murmured, "I'd have them all fighting."

She smiled as if picturing gladiator combat, the mourners punching each other in the pews until the last man staggered forward to make his claim.

Amy felt herself turn to stone at the thought of any of these men touching her. She spotted Jake in one of the front pews and slipped her arm from Mama's. "I'm gonna go sit with my boyfriend."

"You know my feelings on that."

"I know all about your feelings, Mama. It's not like they're a secret. Jake is my boyfriend, and I'm gonna sit with him."

"Fine, then. I suppose I'll just have to entertain myself."

"My friend is dead, Mama. It ain't supposed to be entertaining."

Amy left her side and hurried down the carpeted aisle. The organist played a sorrowful dirge. The pulpit awaited the reverend's oration. Sally's casket lay ringed by flowered hearts and wreaths and crosses mounted on easels. The air was sickly sweet. She saw Sally lying in the casket and faltered.

Her friend was really and truly gone from this earth.

Jake spotted her and stood with wide eyes. He'd combed his hair and wore a clean white shirt and tie. He hurried over and hugged her tight.

"I've been missing you something fierce," she said.

"I was real worried about you."

"I'm all right, honey," she said, her heart leaping at his touch.

He smiled against her cheek. "I love you, Amy Green."

"I love you, Jake Coombs."

People cleared their throats and frowned at them. Jake led her to his pew and sat her down, still holding her hand. Michelle and Troy welcomed her with dazed smiles.

"I don't know if I can go up there and say goodbye," Michelle said, choking up.

Troy nodded and sighed, shoulders sagging. Amy remembered he had a thing for Sally. He looked like something that got run over in the road.

Jake leaned close. "I heard you was with that guy." His tone wavered between offhand and pointed. "That guy bugging us that day at the A & P."

"Ray Bowie."

"What happened?"

"He was giving me some hassle, and then that creeper came out of nowhere and killed him."

He gripped her hand tighter. "Must have been something awful."

"I didn't remember it for days. Mama nursed me through. I was a real mess. Other than that, I really don't want to talk about it."

"Well, you're safe now. I'll take care of you."

"Yes, you will," she told him.

"It's a good thing Bowie is dead, or I'd be the one killing him."

"He's dead. A man couldn't get any more dead than he is."

"I can't believe that boy Enoch did all that killing. When we all met up in the clearing, he was so nice. George was the one who seemed a bit bent."

"No more monsters, Jake."

"I was just—"

"I mean it," she told him. "I can't handle it after what happened. It's too painful. No more monster talk. Promise me."

"I promise. It's just awful, that's all."

Michelle leaned across Jake and patted her hand. "We was worried about you. I'm glad you're okay."

"I ain't okay," Amy said. "Not really. But thank you."

Michelle sucked in her breath. "Oh, God. It's Mr. Albod."

The farmer walked down the aisle surrounded by his blond daughters. They made a striking image all in black with the organ playing an arresting hymn. The girls seemed to be holding the man up. Mr. Albod had always struck Amy as a giant, one of the county's great men. Now he looked sunken in and sucked dry, a deflated copy of himself. A man gone old before his time.

"That poor family," said Michelle.

Troy didn't look. He stared at the casket.

Reverend Coombs greeted Mr. Albod with a firm handshake as if his touch might convey the needed strength. Amy looked at the casket with its glimpse of Sally's face and hands clasped over her chest.

Really and truly gone.

Jake squeezed her hand as she cried. He pulled a handful of tissues out of his jacket pocket and gave them to her. She balled them in her fist.

Still shaking his hand, the reverend eyed Mr. Albod with fierce compassion and spoke a few words to him. The farmer nodded, then nodded again. The Albods took their seats as Jake's daddy mounted to the pulpit. Behind him, a giant cross hung suspended from the ceiling on aircraft cable.

The organ stopped. The crowd fell into a respectful hush and waited.

"Friends," Coombs said. "Friends, neighbors. Reginald Albod wants you all to know that while we are all mourning such a tragic loss, he is rejoicing assured Sally left this earth a Christian. A man says, 'Where there is life, there is hope.' The believer says, 'Where there is death, there is also hope.' Hope in life everlasting at the side of Christ."

"Amen," the crowd murmured.

The reverend raised his hands to pray. "Lord, we have gathered here to thank you for the life of Sally Mae Albod. Express sorrow you took her from us so soon. We do not always understand the goodness behind your plan, but this time you have spoken plainly. The loss of a child is a clarion call to battle."

The congregation growled its assent as the first peal of thunder crashed outside. Rain lashed the stained glass windows. The world seemed to close in until only the church remained.

"Every Sunday, we pray to you to deliver us from evil," Coombs said. "Lord, we hear you loud and clear that it is about time we did our own delivering. We have suffered a great loss. You have our full attention now. This time, we're listening."

"Justice," Mr. Albod said loud enough for all to hear.

The packed room held its breath. The fanners stopped fanning. Everybody craned their necks for a look at him.

"Amen," somebody called out.

A glimmer of lightning through the windows. Another rush of thunder. The air became electrically charged.

"Speak, Reggie," the reverend said. "Open your heart."

Mr. Albod scanned the room until he fixed his eyes on Sheriff Burton. "You hear me, Tom? I want justice, and I will get it."

Sheriff Burton squirmed in his pew. He didn't like being put on the spot like this. Then he nodded.

The farmer returned to his seat like a collapsing tent. He hunched forward, head down, shoulders quaking as his daughters patted his back.

The reverend leaned on his pulpit. "Reggie wants justice. Don't we all? You know there is evil in our midst. You know where the evil is. You know exactly where it is. What are you going to do about it? Are you ready to give this suffering father the justice he needs? Are you ready to fight for your God? If not for Him, will you fight for your own children?"

"We're ready," somebody shouted.

"We're with you, Reverend."

"We'll fight."

"We'll see," Coombs said. "And so will God."

He nodded to the organist, who began playing a hymn. The Albods rose from their pew and crossed to the casket to view their kin one last time. The aisle filled with mourners waiting their turn.

"I don't know if I can go up there and see her," Troy said.

"We have to," Michelle said. "We have to say goodbye."

Amy spotted Sheriff Burton standing in the aisle next to his regal wife. The sheriff squinted at her as if she were a puzzle he couldn't figure out. It was the same look he gave her at his office when she offered her statement. Unsettled, she looked away.

"I listened to him bark all these years," Jake murmured.

"What?" Amy said.

"I never thought he'd bite."

"What's wrong, honey?"

"Pa just declared war on the Home," he said.

Twenty-Nine

A melia Oliver lectured her class about the War Between the States. The free and slave states disagreed over whether Washington had the power to prohibit slavery in new territories not yet become states. After the nation elected Abraham Lincoln president in 1860 on a platform promising no slavery in the territories, seven states left the Union and formed the Confederacy. Civil war ensued.

No feedback from the kids. Like lecturing a brick wall.

Amelia regarded teaching as two-way communication. You teach the kids, and their body language tells you whether they're learning. The problem with teaching plague kids was many of them didn't look remotely human.

Even after doing this job for two years, she still had a hard time figuring out what they were thinking. They looked threatening no matter what they did. Large asymmetric features, grotesque proportions, bared teeth. They said hello, and your mind translated that on an instinctive level as, *Hey, I'll bet you taste like chicken.*

Amelia relied on the old standby of asking questions. "Can

anybody tell me why the North didn't just let the South go its own way?"

Nobody raised their hand.

"Come on, George. I bet you know the answer to this one."

"I refuse to answer," he said.

"Why?"

"I'm on strike."

"Why are you in class if you're on strike?"

"I am compelled by force to attend class," he said. "Not to participate."

God, he was being serious.

"Okay. Why are you on strike?"

"A week ago, one of the students at this facility was murdered during disciplinary measures," he explained. "Five days ago, another student was falsely arrested on murder charges and is being detained without legal counsel."

"Oh," she said.

She'd been told Toby Freeman fell down the stairs. She had no reason to disbelieve it, though she'd heard enough here and there to piece together that Discipline existed and what went on there. Regarding Enoch Bryant, as far as she was concerned, he murdered two people and mauled a teacher. She'd always known him to be a fine boy, but the evidence screamed his guilt. It was a real tragedy.

No point in arguing with George, though. He'd once eaten up an entire hour of class time arguing that communism accomplished more material good than harm purely based on utilitarian ethics. Even when she knew he was wrong, she had a hard time proving it. Sometimes, he argued both sides of an argument and tied her in knots. He introduced an exciting but exhausting element to class.

Her eyes swept her students. "Does George speak for the rest of you?"

Atticus Churchill nodded his blocky head. He was a giant horned thing, though the kids in their aberrant logic called him Tiny. So big, he sat on the floor, as no desk would hold him. Fifteen years old, one of the first of the plague generation.

"We're with Brain," he said in his deep baritone. "All of us."

She sighed. "Class dismissed."

The plague kids got up and headed to the exit.

"Not you, George," she added.

The kid resumed his seat and waited while the other students filed out. At last, Atticus hauled himself to his feet and shambled across the creaking floor. He bent and squeezed himself through the door, and then he was gone.

"I'm leaving the Home," she said.

George had no problem using body language to express himself. His face's wrinkled lines articulated shock and dismay. "My turn to ask why."

The only truly frightening thing about the boy was his intelligence. Amelia felt sure he had a genius IQ, perhaps even surpassing that level. She doubted he would fail to comprehend anything she told her. Understanding was another matter.

Things were bad all over in 1982. After college, she couldn't find a job up North, so she'd accepted a position to come down to Georgia and teach plague children at one of the many Homes. She'd envisioned an exciting and fulfilling adventure, like joining the Peace Corps. In Philadelphia, life felt like a game of beat the clock. She looked forward to a simple life where people moseyed instead of rushed and took time out to smell the flowers.

She'd grown to hate almost everything about it ever since. She hated Stark County and its heat, bugs, and affected manners laid thick on every social interaction like sickly sweet icing covering a big fat turd. Up North, people said, *Fuck you*. In the South, they blessed your heart and called you precious. People were always asking her, *You ain't from around here, are you?*

No shit, she wanted to say. *No shit and fuck you*.

Many saw her as an uppity Black woman, citified with highfalutin liberal ways, a woman who didn't need a man. An outsider with no kin or connections in town. The only thing the locals did more than complain about Yankees looking down on them was look down on everybody else.

She hated the Home most of all. This gloomy, smelly, derelict old slave owner's house masquerading as a school. The pathetic curriculum, mostly forced labor and social conditioning, that passed for an education. The children frightened her, though over time she had grown used to them: Some, like George, she'd even grown quite fond of. The teachers, however, terrified her. Ex-cons, cokeheads, and losers. Almost all men, always smiling at her when there was nothing at all to smile about. Willie Jefferson, Nathan Byrd, Charlie Rucker, the others. Principal Willard was the worst of the lot, the old buzzard she called the Warden behind his back. They scared her enough she carried an old .38 revolver in her purse.

Then somebody murdered Ray Bowie and Sally Albod. The police arrested a student for the crimes. The townspeople dropped the pretense of good manners and now glared at her at the supermarket and post office. Somebody keyed her car.

For her, it was the last straw. It was time to get the hell out of Dodge.

There was no way to explain all this to a fourteen-year-old, even if he was a genius.

"I've been here two years," Amelia said. "I'm sick of it, George. All of it. It's time for me to see what else is out there."

"You're sick of us is what I'm hearing."

"You'd be surprised who I'm sick of," she said. "You least of all."

"The North couldn't regard Southern secession as legitimate," George said. "The elites feared secession would undermine the republic and establish a precedent leading to the disintegration of the United States into small, weak countries."

Amelia smiled. "Thought you were on strike."

"You said you don't work here anymore. We're just talking now."

"I'm going to finish the month."

"Where will you go?"

"Back to Philly, maybe."

"We'll miss you, Ms. Oliver. I mean that. We all will. It's safe to say you're the only good thing about this place. The other teachers don't even bother trying. We're all destined for manual labor when we grow up. You try, and that's what counts. You give us knowledge even though you don't have to."

"Oh," she said, touched. "Thank you, George. I tried my best."

"On the other hand, I'm happy to see you go so you can find a place where teaching means something real."

"I wish I could say the same about you. You have so much potential. Why do you go on hiding your beautiful mind from the world?"

"What should I be doing with it?"

"You could be in Virginia at that special government facility I told you about. Putting your talents to use."

"You know why I won't do that," George said. "We already talked about this. They would have me doing bad things for very bad people."

"You don't know that."

"In any case, I'm not a collaborator."

She sighed again. "The revolution."

"That's right."

"A million-something kids against the United States government. That's not a revolution."

He smiled. "I'd rather die on my feet—"

"Than live on your knees," Amelia said. "Got it. Be patient. Things will change."

"But only with a fight. No social progress is possible without it."

"My aunt marched with Martin Luther King. I know all about the struggle. The point is the people didn't rise up. They demonstrated, disobeyed, marched. Peacefully. Nonviolence is hard, but it's the only way to win. You use violence, they'll crush you. It's what they want. That's the kind of fight they always win."

George nodded. "All right. We'll be patient."

She gave him a doubtful look. His capitulation had been far too easy.

"Please don't do anything stupid when I'm gone," she said. "I mean it. I have a feeling I'm going to worry about you plenty the way things are."

"We won't do anything stupid. I promise."

She smiled. "Good. I know it's hard. It's going to be all right. I honestly believe that."

"Good night, Ms. Oliver."

"Good night. Tomorrow, I'll bring you some books to read."

Amelia shouldered her pocketbook and left the classroom. She walked through musty hallways heading for her car. A daily ritual. Soon, it'd be the last time. She'd leave it all behind with some regrets.

But mostly, with relief.

A fter she left, Brain thought: You will not be harmed.
    He looked out the window. Most of the kids had run off into the woods to play for the half hour they had left before supper. A few teachers stood around smoking in the yard. They smiled at Ms. Oliver as she approached. She quickened her pace and strode past to her car, her hand kept near her pocketbook.

She would have the normals throw him a bone and call it a meal. After years of suffering—more dead kids like Sucker Punch, more crucified scapegoats like Dog—the plague children might receive half measures that added up to nothing.

Victory is never given, it is taken—through violence if necessary. You want foundational change, you don't talk to Dr. King. You talk to Malcolm X. No real progress would ever come from the normals. That kind of thinking was barking up the wrong tree. Scratch that. Right tree, wrong dog.

The mutagenic had to win on their own. And no half measures for him. He didn't want integration. He didn't want to drink from the same water fountain as normals or ride in the same part of the bus. Brain wanted it all. A return to ancient times when men worshipped the plague men as gods and enshrined them in myths that endured thousands of years.

One of the teachers in the yard caught him staring out the window and frowned. Brain gave him his best aw-shucks grin and waved. The man spat on the ground.

Brain went to the mess hall for supper. He stood in line until it was his turn to pull a greasy steel tray from the stack. The air was hot and wet with steam. A kid ladled stew into a bowl and dropped it and a biscuit on his tray. Brain grabbed a spoon and poured a mug of water. Surrounded by his toughs, Tiny waved to him with his thick, spiky arm. He sat with them and they ate without talking.

All of them had endured Discipline: Tiny for killing a bull that had attacked him, Burn for setting fires, Quasimodo for running away, Lizzie for tripping a teacher with her tail, Beaver for destroying firewood. The teachers didn't know Tiny was the strongest man alive, Burn could start fires with his hands, Quasimodo's humpback sprouted wings, Lizzie's nine-foot tail could strike like a bullwhip, and Beaver's teeth could chew through steel.

This, Ms. Oliver, is how a million kids will win, he thought. Because we are a million only now discovering we are living atom bombs. Powers we could have employed to build instead will be used to destroy. Our bodies are weapons, but the war will start in the mind. We must find the will to use them.

Tiny slurped the last of his supper and put the bowl down. "You get in trouble with Ms. Oliver?"

"She quit," Brain said. "She's leaving the Home at the end of the month."

"God damn," Beaver said. "She's about the only thing I like about this place."

"What's next?" Tiny said.

"We practice our abilities," Brain said. "Keep an eye out for others who are developing theirs. We have to be ready when the time comes."

"You keep saying. When is that, exactly?"

"We'll know when the time is right because it will already be happening. When it happens, we won't be directing it. It will direct itself."

"It won't start itself, though," Tiny said. "Somebody has to make the first move."

"The normals will start it," Brain explained. "They'll start it because they think they'll win. The revolution has waited for years, and it must wait a little longer. Days, months, years, who knows, but it will happen. And when we rise, we'll be doing it all together. We'll be ready. We'll have nothing to lose, and we won't stop until we win."

The kids grinned. Tiny didn't. He emptied his mug and slammed it down. "I won't wait forever. I'm sick of talking."

Brain kept track of the kids who had special powers. Nearly two-thirds of them now, and more every day. He believed these powers were wired into them all somehow, their expression the mutagenic's version of puberty. The Home's biggest secret, known only to those who'd gained their powers.

Most of the kids were like him, possessing abilities but not extreme powers. Lesser gods and servants to the gods. Tiny, on the other hand, could destroy this building and everything in it in seconds. And nothing hurt him, not anymore.

Tiny was a god.

Every day, they trained. Not just their powers but their

hearts, too. The kids had been broken for so long, some of them found the idea of fighting back horrifying. Tiny taught them strength. Brain taught them about the revolution. He made them believe they were special and deserved to dream their own dreams.

Wallee lumbered up to the table with his tray. Mary meekly trailed him.

"Where Big Brother?" she said.

"Dog is with the normals," Brain said.

"Special?"

"Special. Yeah."

"Wor-ried," Wallee said. "Poor Dog."

"Get lost," Tiny growled.

Wallee's eyes widened. "Lost?"

"As in go someplace else before I put you there."

Wallee looked to Brain, who nodded and said, "Go on, Wallee. You too, Mary. Go find somewhere else to sit. We're having a private conversation."

Brain watched them go. If Wallee was truly a collaborator, he was a problem that would have to be dealt with.

"We should get rid of that kid," Tiny said. "And then go free Dog."

"No," Brain said. "It ain't the time."

"Ain't Dog supposed to be your friend?"

Brain winced. More than a friend. He loved Dog like a brother.

He knew Dog didn't kill Sally Albod. Gaines probably murdered her and then made it look like Dog did it. There was no malice to him pinning it on Dog. In this particular drama, Dog was just roadkill, which Brain found crueler than anything. How easy it was to scapegoat a child simply because he was mutagenic. The normals would try him as an adult and fry him in an electric chair. A revered and intricate procedure with a predetermined outcome, like a ritual sacrifice. Dog would die, and the normals would experience their catharsis. *One less*, they'd say. Only the mutagenic would cry for Dog, but the tears of slaves didn't add up to anything. They didn't matter. They weren't people. They were animals with a voice.

Dog had naively believed the normals would treat him fairly and had now learned what they really thought of his kind. Though his hopes were misplaced, they came from a good heart. Dog had believed people were good and the world was a good place. Brain often looked at Dog and wanted to say, *The revolution is for you because you deserve the world you believe exists.* He wanted to help now but couldn't. He'd hoped Dog would develop his special ability and take part in the uprising, but now that could never happen. No matter what Brain wanted or hoped, the revolution was for all of them, not just one boy. If they made their move now, they might save Dog but lose everything.

"Dog will get justice," Brain said. "But he may not live to see it."

Mary froze in the middle of the mess hall. Her tray crashed to the floor.

"Pretty," she said.

Kids stood at the tables, heads aimed toward the far windows. One by one, they approached the side of the hall to look out. The trickle became a flood. They hooted and pointed. Some cried out in terror and pushed their way back.

"We should take a look," Brain said.

"I'll go first," said Tiny.

The giant stood and shambled into the throng, nudging kids aside. The crowd parted to let him through like an army ushering its champion onto the field. Whatever was out there, Tiny would protect them.

Brain reached the windows and looked out.

"Interesting," he said.

A twenty-foot-tall Latin cross blazed in the Home's yard.

In front of it, a line of men stood in belted white robes and conical white masks. Most held shotguns. Some carried ropes.

No teachers in sight.

"Who are they?" Tiny said.

"The Ku Klux Klan," Brain said.

The men out there weren't burning the cross so much as lighting it. An arcane ritual, but the message was clear: This holy fire cleanses the world of evil.

Tiny snarled at the insult. "Is this them starting it like you said?"

"Close to it," Brain said. "This is them trying, learning the way how."

His eyes swept the other kids pressed against the filmy glass. The ones who didn't run and hide. The ones who had powers. They growled and roared at the men. If the fiery cross was supposed to intimidate them, it wasn't working.

This place was a rotting prison, but it was their home. They'd all grown up here. These old buildings, the surrounding woods, and the farms they worked were all they knew of the world.

The plague generation was almost ready to leave that childhood behind.

Soon, Brain promised the men outside.

A white-robed Klansman strode toward the mess hall, raised his shotgun, and fired into the building.

Thirty

Dave Gaines lay in his bed at the clinic surrounded by flowers and get-well cards. He didn't remember any of it being delivered. Doc Odom had put him on some heavy-duty painkillers and antibiotics the past few days, and the time passed in a feverish dream. He just woke up and cards were everywhere.

Then he remembered butchering Sally Albod.

He licked his dry lips and looked around the room. "What did I do?"

He must have dreamed it. A horrible trick of the mind.

"What did I do? Oh, Lord, WHAT DID I DO?"

Doc Odom entered with his lab coat, disheveled white hair, and hunched bearing. He took in Gaines's vitals at a glance and laid a gentle hand on his good shoulder. "Be calm, friend. You tear out my stitches, I'll read you the riot act."

"Sally," Gaines said.

The rest dried up in his mouth.

"She's gone," the doctor said. "I'm sorry."

"I killed that poor little girl. It was me."

"That's the guilt talking," Doc Odom said. "Don't let it

weigh you down. What you need to focus on is how you tried to save her."

Gaines remembered telling Enoch to run for help. The monster lunged at him like something out of a horror movie. Fiery bolts of pain. A calm little voice telling him he was being hurt bad, rising to a scream, *He's killing you, you're dying.*

"It's true." He wiped away tears. "I tried. He wouldn't let me do it."

"You don't have to worry about him. The sheriff caught that son of a bitch."

"What did he say to the sheriff?"

Doc Odom chuckled. "You wouldn't believe me if I told you. He was spouting all sorts of foolishness."

"What about my boy? How's he doing?"

"I checked him out when they brought you in. He's fine. You should be proud you raised him the way you did. That boy saved your life. He's a man now."

"Yeah," Gaines said with self-loathing.

"And you're the man of the hour. I'm letting you go today."

Gaines looked around at the cards and flowers and wanted very much to stay a while longer, maybe forever. He felt safe here. In this room, events had reached a stasis. Once he left, everything would change. He would have to start his life knowing what he'd done and wondering when it would all catch up to him.

"You sure I'm ready, Doc?"

"That's right. I took fifty percent off my bill on account of your being a hero."

"Thanks," he said, dreading the bill anyway.

He saw the truth clear as sky. The world had not dealt

him a bad hand. The world wasn't exactly a friend, but it had given him the same raw chance it gave everybody. No, he was just stupid. He didn't possess the sense God gave a goose. He could throw himself at the ground and somehow find a way to miss.

Doc Odom helped him get out of bed and dress himself. He gave him a sling and wrote him some prescriptions. He warned against doing any hard physical activity while healing. Lots of water, plenty of rest, no drinking. Doctor's orders.

"I'll call a ride for you," the man said. "Don't worry, I'll pay for it."

"That's all right. I'd like to walk a bit if that's okay."

Doc Odom nodded. "Probably do you some good to take some fresh air. Call me if you suffer any trouble."

"Thanks again."

"Oh, I almost forgot to say. That boy who murdered Sally. Turns out he also killed Ray Bowie."

"No kidding," Gaines said in wonder.

"Remember, take it easy and keep off the bottle. Alice will see you out."

Gaines walked away from the clinic a free man. He wore his hunting pants, freshly laundered by the skinny nurse, and a white T-shirt the doctor gave him. He checked for his wallet. He leafed through old receipts and counted two twenties.

Enough to get a load on and then some. He walked straight to the Rusty Nail. He opened the door and paused blinking in the sudden gloom. Red neon and smoke in the air. The clink of bottles. Jukebox sitting quiet at the side of the room. Only a few customers, most drinking quietly at the bar. A man in a black leather vest racked the balls at a pool table. The pretty bartender wiped the counter, which made her boobs jiggle in her black AC/DC T-shirt. Bright sunshine outside, but otherwise he had no idea what time it was. It didn't matter. If they were serving, he was drinking. Gaines had always liked this place. If you brought a mason jar on a Thursday, they filled it from the tap for a dollar.

He staggered light-headed toward the stools in front of the bar. He had an awful need to sit. His torn-up arm felt hot and itchy under the dressing, like a sack of swollen meat in a sling. He'd never asked how many stitches he'd gotten.

The bartender looked up and smiled. "Well, look who it is. If it ain't the man of the hour."

That phrase again, spoken without derision.

He slumped on one of the stools. "Hello."

She popped the cap on a bottle of Bud and set it foaming on the counter with a wink. "This one is on the house."

Along the bar, the men stared at him. Weathered faces, beards, caps. He took the bottle, cold and slick with condensation, and considered leaving with it. All he wanted was to be left the hell alone. Nobody eyeballing or talking at him.

He tilted his head back and poured a long swallow down his throat. He gasped as the beer scraped along his gullet. He belched. One of the men sat next to him. Gaines took in his small eyes, bushy yellow beard, and green John Deere cap.

"You're that feller, ain't you?"

Gaines wiped his mouth. "What feller would that be?"

"That feller got mauled by one of them monsters, trying to save a little girl."

"That was me, all right. I just got out the clinic."

"His next round's on me, Celia," the man called to the bartender then thrust his hand out. "Name's Owen, mister. Owen Miles. Pleased to meet you."

Gaines shook it with his good hand. "Likewise, Owen. I'm Dave Gaines."

"Hell, I know your name," Miles said.

Gaines thought, So this is what it's like to be respected.

"Heard your boy shot the sumbitch," the man added.

"My boy Archie. He sure did."

"He's a man now, ain't he."

Gaines flinched and took another pull on his Bud. "He sure is."

"You should be proud."

A man entered the bar. Miles waved him over. "Hey, Bill. Look what I found."

The man took in Gaines hunched over the counter with his sling. "Damn, boy. What happened to you? Get knocked around by a big ol' grizzly?"

"A creeper happened to him is what," Miles said. "This is the man tried to save Reggie Albod's little girl."

"Motherogod. You're the one. I'm Bill Faherty. Can I buy you a drink?"

"His next round's on me," Miles said.

"Then I got the one after that. I want to hear his story."

"There ain't no story," Gaines said. "The way you heard it is the way it happened."

Faherty gave him a sour look, disappointed.

"You still feeling out of kilter from it?" Miles said.

"I don't know whether to check my ass or scratch my watch," Gaines said.

"Don't sweat it. You don't have to talk. You just sit there. You earned it."

Faherty ordered his beer. "I heard some boys went over and shot up the Home. Busted a bunch of windows and peppered the creepers with buckshot. About time, I say."

"Boy howdy," Miles agreed. "People from town, was it?"

"They was farmers, what I heard. Friends of Reggie Albod."

Gaines set his empty on the counter. "Did they kill anybody?"

"I didn't hear anything like that. Winged one or two, maybe."

The men talked about it for a while like it was the Battle of Second Manassas. Gaines could tell they were envious. After a few more beers, they'd plan their own drive-by on the way home and then they'd have their own tale to tell.

He didn't want this. He razzed the creepers and bossed them around, but he had a soft spot for them. They reminded him of himself in certain ways, which made him empathize with them some days and hate the sight of them on others. He'd only thought to throw a little buckshot at Enoch as a crazy way to get at Sally Albod. The way he regarded them always had far more to do with what he noticed in the mirror than what he saw in them.

Sally dead. Enoch likely facing the chair. The Home getting shot up. All because of him. And here he was, sitting in a bar a free man with good ol' boys buying him beers and praising his name. All the respect he'd ever wanted, all because he gave in to the Devil's voice in his head.

He'd sold his soul, and this was his reward. But the Devil always collected.

His shoulder and chest began to throb.

"I'll take that beer now if you're buying," Gaines said.

The second bottle rang his brain like a bell. By the fifth, he was feeling no pain, floating on a haze. The bar had filled up. He bummed a Marlboro and smoked it while he told his story again to the small crowd of people that

had accumulated. *We was grappling*, he heard himself saying. The jukebox played a loud Christian rock song. Some
boys shouted the chorus from the pool tables: *Pure heart! Pure
blood!* The cue ball cracked. Girls danced next to their tables,
big hair and cut-off jeans and long, tanned legs. One kept
touching him and staring wide-eyed at his swollen shoulder.

He splayed his good hand and said, "That's when his
claws got into me. That's when they ripped me open like
meat hooks."

The girl stroked his hair. She was a blonde, just like Sally
Albod.

He saw Sally lying on the ground pale and gasping and
her dress hiked up over her thighs and her hands near the
sides of her head like she was surprised and briars in her
blond hair and her chest a bloody ruin and her eyes boring
into his as if pleading, *No, I know what you're gonna do, don't
do it, don't kill me.*

"You know what?" Miles said. "We should go out there
right now."

"Out where?"

"To the Home. Bang it up a bit."

"No, sir," Gaines said. "I have to work there."

"You any good fixing cars?" Faherty said.

"I can fix cars."

"You call me tomorrow. Then you ain't working there
no more."

He'd hacked her up with his knife to make it look like
Enoch did it, crying the whole time and blood fountaining
and the blade grating along bone and Sally's eyes rolled up in
her head and her mouth wide open in a soundless scream and
her chest like a pile of road kill, and when Gaines turned,

Archie was looking back, his boy had seen what he'd done, he'd seen the whole thing.

Daddy, his boy said. *Daddy, why did you do that to Sally?*

Gaines set his beer down. "I got to go."

Another mistake, trying to drink himself out of remembering. You sold your soul to the Devil, and the Devil always collected. Drinking made you forget your troubles only to bring them back like a sucker punch.

"The hell you do," Faherty said. "We're talking here."

The girl leaned close enough for him to smell her perfume. Her nose tickled his stubbled cheek. "You should stay. I been tested."

"My boy's waiting on me. I ain't seen to him in days."

"All right," Faherty said. "But you call me about that job, partner."

The girl wrote her phone number on the inside of his sling.

Gaines mumbled something and staggered out the door and into the night. Rain had fallen sometime during the day. The street glistened under the pole lights. The air was sticky and wet on his skin. His ears rang from honky-tonk played at high volume. Otherwise, aside from a passing car and a dog barking, the town was quiet. He still had no idea what time it was or even what day of the week.

Alone again with his thoughts and memories.

A distant flash outlined rooftops and telephone poles. Thunder growled in the ether. A rumble charged the air, then stillness. He tottered down the street and saw the old diner all lit up. A flurry of moths in neon glow. He went inside and shuffled to one of the booths.

The waitress came over and asked what he wanted.

"Coffee," he said.

She wrote it on her pad while she chewed gum. "What happened to you, anyway?"

"Machine accident."

"Poor thing. Just coffee? We got catfish on special."

He hadn't eaten all day. "That'd be fine." He remembered Doc Odom's instructions. "And a glass of water, if you don't mind."

She smirked. "I don't mind at all."

The door jingled. He heard heavy footsteps behind him. The sheriff appeared. "Man of the hour."

Gaines winced. "Hey, Sheriff."

"Mind if I sit down and join you?"

"Go right ahead."

The big man set his Stetson on the table and sat opposite Gaines. "What'd you order?"

"The catfish. It's on special."

"Good choice."

The waitress set a mug on the table and poured coffee. "Hey, Sheriff. What can I get you? We got catfish on special."

"So I hear. I'll have some of that coffee, Loretta. And a slice of your pecan pie."

She smirked again. "Coffee and pie, coming right up."

Burton tilted his head to watch her leave. "I dropped by the clinic yesterday to check on you. Doc Odom told me you was still laid up. I pop into Belle's for a cup of joe, and here you are."

Gaines sipped his coffee. "Here I am. Darlene used to work here. I would come every day. I courted her one cup of coffee at a time."

"Those were better days."

"Yes, sir."

One of Us

239

"We never did get your full statement about what happened out there in the woods," the sheriff said. "I'm hoping you'll come down to the office tomorrow and help fill in the cracks. Sikes will handle it."

"I can do that."

Gaines's food arrived. It smelled amazing. Suddenly ravenous, he dug into his fried catfish.

"Thank ye, honey," Burton said as his coffee and pecan pie were laid out before him. "I'm itching to ask you a few questions myself, Dave. A few things are sticking in my craw."

Gaines stopped chewing. "Like what?"

"Like how four pellets of double-oh buckshot got into Sally Albod's chest, for instance."

Gaines picked up his glass of water and gulped it. The sheriff forked some pie into his jowls and chewed.

"Mm-mm," Burton said. "Best pie in the state. You all right, Dave? You look like you ate a bug."

"My shoulder hurts."

"That boy tore you up something awful."

"Archie was the one who fired at him," Gaines said. "Maybe some pellets hit the poor girl on the ground. I don't know."

The sheriff gave him a hard stare. "Uh-huh."

"Why are you looking at me like that?"

"Just checking if your eyes are brown. Your boy was firing birdshot."

"What happened out there happened. I got nothing more to say about it without a lawyer."

"That really how you want to play it?"

"Yes, sir."

"I wonder what Archie would tell me if I brought him in again."

"You leave my boy alone. Enoch killed Ray is what I hear. He killed Sally, too, which I know. I was there, you wasn't."

"All right," the sheriff said. "Now listen here, Dave. Sally's dead and there ain't nothing can change that now. We can't go back. Sometimes, a man makes a mistake in the heat of passion. He messes things up, he's scared, then he messes up even worse. He doesn't always have a chance to make things right. He wishes he could turn the clock back but can't, and he has to live with everything he done the rest of his days. I am speaking from personal experience on this. But sometimes a man gets the chance. In one case that comes to mind, a man knows if he don't take it, an innocent boy is gonna go to the electric chair and lose his life. Some vigilante is gonna shoot somebody taking his trash out some night. More plague kids are gonna get shot. Like ripples in a pond after somebody drops a stone. Instead of that one man owning up to his screwup and suffering a little to make it right, others will suffer and go on suffering. This happens far more than anyone cares to know. So the question is, what kind of man are you?"

Whatever the sheriff was playing at, it was working. Gaines wanted to confess. He wanted to be understood. He imagined himself saying, *Sally was gonna die anyway*. He caught himself before the words left his mouth.

What was done was done. Sally Albod's life had ended. No need for his life to end, too. His son's, who'd be orphaned when his daddy went off to jail. Ripples in a pond, right. Better it was Enoch be the ripple instead of Archie.

Gaines pushed the remains of his catfish aside. He yanked a handful of napkins from the dispenser and wiped his face. "I can't talk anymore. I don't feel so good. Go play cat and mouse with somebody else. I'm done."

The sheriff finished his coffee, dropped a few dollar bills on the table, and set his Stetson on his grizzled skull. "Then I'll leave you be. Go home and get some sleep. Come down to the office tomorrow, and we'll try this again."

Burton plodded back toward the door. He paused to tip his hat to Loretta, who giggled. Gaines glanced at the men's room door and thought about whether he wanted to throw up here or at home. He felt downright sick to his stomach. Sheriff Burton was after him. Had him cornered like a rat.

"Hey, Sheriff," he called.

The man turned. "Yeah. What now?"

"I don't know where my truck is. I think it might still be at Reggie's."

"We had it drove out to your place. That's how we got Archie home."

"I got no way home tonight. Can you give me a ride?"

Burton sighed. "All right. Come on. I'll drive you."

Thirty-One

Goof waited for Officer Baby to show up and escort him to another day's work as a government spook. He had plenty to keep him busy in the meantime. His room was no longer just a bed and a bathroom with white walls. He had Atari, color TV, VHS movies, comic books, music.

Shackleton catered to his every whim. Goof once threw out an offhand complaint he was sick of looking at blank walls. Said the lack of something to look at interfered with his spy powers. He plodded back from work to find his room's walls plastered with posters. Madonna, Michael Jackson, Duran Duran. When he said the posters didn't mean anything because he had no idea who these people were, he returned to find a boom box and collection of cassette tapes.

Another time, he said he didn't want to work because he had a stomachache. An hour later, a team of doctors invaded his room. They took his temperature, drew his blood, made him cough. They asked him to poop so they could study it for parasites. At the end of it all, they gave him Pepto-Bismol.

Despite all the toys and fuss, he was bored as hell.

Goof liked being around people. He missed his friends

something fierce. Dog and his sunny nature, good ol' Brain and his hopeless revolution, Wallee and his childlike laugh, even silly silent Mary.

The only company Special Facility offered was a surly bureaucrat and a big bald cop. The cop never talked. Shackleton never laughed. So easy to annoy them, it sucked all the fun out of it to try. The only real human contact he'd had in this sterile place was the knowing smile he'd shared with Zack, but that had been only the one time, and he hadn't seen the scientist since.

He picked up a comic book and leafed through it. *The Amazing Spider-Man* #252. Spider-Man returns from the Secret Wars planet and gets a new outfit. Goof loved the stories about people the normals considered superheroes and their amazing abilities. He knew plenty of kids with amazing abilities back at the Home. Kids ugly as sin and wearing secondhand overalls with patches over the knees. It made him wonder: If Superman had horns like Tiny, would he still be Superman?

No sense in overthinking a comic book. Just a book of wishes. In the real world, superheroes got shipped to secret facilities to work for the government, and they wore pajamas and rubber slippers.

He cocked his ear at the thud of footsteps in the corridor. Officer Baby stomping the earth.

Goof tossed the comic book on a small hill of fedoras stacked in the corner. He stood and stretched, ready to go serve his country. He bounced on his heels. Some days, he grew so lonesome he looked forward to his sessions with Shackleton. Maybe that was the idea. *I'm the only friend you got*, the Bureau man liked to tell him. As if he enjoyed Goof having no friends.

That man, this building, this room.

This might be the rest of his life.

The jangle of keys. The door opened on well-oiled hinges.

Goof stormed past him. "Come on, Jenkins. Commissioner Gordon is waiting."

The guard backed up, arms at his sides, and plodded after him. Goof marched along in T-shirt, boxer shorts, and powder-blue terrycloth bathrobe that flapped behind him like a cape.

"The Joker has me in a tight spot," he growled. "The villain had a heart monitor surgically implanted. If it's still working at midnight, a bomb will go off in Gotham and kill ten people. You see where this is going, don't you?"

The guard said nothing, as always. Just stared off into space. Goof turned and waited for him to catch up.

"You're right, Jenkins. To save those people, including a girl I kind of like but only when I'm Bruce Wayne, I must kill the Joker. My God, don't you see?"

The guard breathed through his mouth as he walked past.

"Right again, Jenkins," Goof exploded as he fell in beside the giant. "To be a hero, I must become a monster. Must become that which I fight. Which is just what he's after. It's all part of his diabolical plan. Holy conundrum."

The guard stopped at Room Two and ushered him in with the usual mocking sweep of his thick arm. Shackleton sat at the table smoking. Aside from the agent's ashtray, the table stood bare and gleaming in the fluorescent light.

"No work today, Jeff," he said as Goof sat.

"Aw, come on, boss. Give me something."

"Sorry, we're closed today."

"Let me hang out with Zack, then."

Shackleton snorted, his version of laughing. "I don't think

you'd like that. He'll put you into one of his team's experiments. Experiments I've been protecting you from."

"I thought we had a lot of work to do."

"We did. Then I got a call from the sheriff who lives in that shithole I pulled you out of. A Home kid stands accused of murder. The locals are terrorizing the other Home kids. The sheriff wants the BTA to come down and get involved."

Goof recognized the acronym. BTA, Bureau of Terato logical Affairs. "So you're leaving?"

"Hell, no. It's his problem. But it's now—"

"Officially a hassle—"

"And I've got a—"

"Meeting with the director—"

"And tons of—"

"Phone calls to—"

"Stop—"

"That," Goof finished. "You want to use me as a spy. So let me spy."

"I got something—"

"Better. What?"

Shackleton sighed. "Can I please finish?"

"What. I ain't saying a word."

"I was going to say I got a treat for you. You earned it."

Goof sat up straight. "What is it?"

"Jenkins will take you to it. Now scram. I've got a meeting to prepare."

He paused at the door on his way out. "Hey. Who was accused?"

"Accused of what?"

"Murder. Back at the Home."

"Enoch Bryant," Shackleton said. "Friend of yours?"

"Nope," Goof lied. "I don't know that kid."

Officer Baby led him down a corridor into a part of Special Facility Goof had never seen. Just more white walls, fluorescent lights, and mysterious doors labeled with numbers. He bounded along like a puppy.

He knew where he was going, or thought he did. If he was right, he had a new ability Shackleton didn't know about, an ability that made finishing people's sentences seem paltry in comparison. It made him laugh out loud.

The guard turned his massive bullet head to squint at him. At last, a reaction.

"My God, Jenkins, you're a genius." Goof pounded his fist against his palm. "All I need to do is design a special Bat Heart Monitor Neutralizer. It will disable the heart monitor while allowing the Joker to go on with his wretched existence. Then I can save the day without sacrificing my iron virtue."

The guard shook his head.

"Ha," Goof said. "But how to find the hostages? Didn't think about that, did you?"

Officer Baby stopped in front of a steel door and unlocked it. Inside, a boy and girl sat at a table eating hot fudge sundaes. The guard ushered him in and slammed the door shut. Goof smiled at the kids while the giant plodded away.

Fresh meat. New kids to entertain and annoy.

The girl scowled at him. Her black hair fell over half her face, which sprouted foot-long whiskers. She ate her ice cream with giant clawed hands, holding the bowl close to her face while one big hand worked spoons like they were chopsticks. The kid on the right looked no older than maybe seven. Chocolate sauce smeared his cheeks. Six skinny arms sprouted from his torso.

"You got all those arms and you still managed to get

fudge all over your face," Goof said. "You can't have one of them hold a napkin?"

The kid grinned. One of his arms slithered over his shoulder and pointed at an untouched sundae on the table. "You gonna eat that?"

"Hell, yeah, I'm gonna eat it," Goof said. "It's mine. Don't even look at it."

"You better hurry up, or it's gonna melt."

Goof sat and spooned ice cream into his mouth. Closed his eyes in bliss. Wished Dog were here eating it with him instead of sitting in some jail.

"What can you do?" the girl said.

"How about you tell me your name, pretty lady."

"I asked you first."

"If you don't tell me, I'm just gonna call you Gorgeous."

"I'm Pussy," the girl said.

"But of course you are," Goof said, doing his best James Bond.

"Everybody calls me Mr. Hand," the other kid said. "What are you so sad about?"

"I ain't sad. I'm smiling."

The kid tilted his head. "Oh, yeah. Right."

"How old are you, anyway?"

"Thirteen," Mr. Hand said. "I stopped growing a long time ago."

"Where you from?"

"Kentucky. Pussy here is from the same Home as me."

"So what can you do?" Goof said.

"If it's locked, I can open it," the kid bragged.

"Cool. What about you, Gorgeous?"

The girl smiled, splaying her whiskers. She clenched her

hand in a massive fist. "If it ain't broke, I can break it. Are you broke?"

"My face is upside-down. You tell me."

"So what about you? Let me guess. You make people laugh uncontrollably until they poop their drawers. They'll drop you on Communist China and make the whole country crap itself to death."

Goof pictured it. "That would actually be awesome. Alas, no. I finish people's sentences."

"You mean like you—"

"Know what people are gonna say?" he finished, even including her Kentucky accent, which was spiced with more twang and less drawl. "Yup. That's what I do."

She went back to scowling. "I thought this was a place for specials."

"Specials?"

"Kids with special abilities."

"I'll have you know I am a secret agent." Goof chomped his sundae's cherry. "I am very useful around here."

"I'm sure you are," the girl said.

"I can do something else, Gorgeous. Say something."

"Like what."

"Anything."

"How about your face is so stupid I want to—"

"Drop my spoons," Goof said.

The spoons clattered on the table.

Pussy stared at him with wide eyes.

Goof laughed. He'd been right.

He had guessed at it soon after he'd first come to this place. The Bureau man had told him he'd just earned himself—

A hat, Goof finished.

But that wasn't what Shackleton was going to say. Goof

had said it just to be funny. The next day, the man gave him a fedora. Every other day since. Just handed it over and said, *Here's that fedora you wanted*, like it was perfectly natural to give somebody a hat every other day. Goof had a pile of them now.

Two days ago, he'd tried again. Waited all day for the right opportunity. Then Shackleton said, *Pretty soon we're gonna have to—*

Let Jeff see the other kids in Special Facility, Goof finished.

Today, he got his wish.

Shackleton owned him. He owned Shackleton. He had an incredible secret hiding in plain sight. He was like a superhero whose public identity was being a superhero with different powers.

Pussy's head slowly pivoted toward Mr. Hand. "What you think?"

The kid grinned. "Oh, yeah. He's in."

"In what?" Goof said.

"Can we trust you with something?"

"I never understand why people ever ask that question."

"Because if we can't, we got a problem."

"You can trust me with your life." Goof raised two fingers. "Scout's honor."

The girl leaned on the table. "We're fixin' to bust out of this place."

"Now you're being funny."

"You want to work for Shackleton the rest of your natural born days?"

"No," Goof said. "But they'll stop us."

"Who will? The fat man? He can't run ten yards."

"They got to have more guards for a place like this. We can't fight them all."

"It ain't just us three," Pussy told him. "We ain't the only ones here."

"More specials? How many we talking?"

"A whole lot," Mr. Hand said.

Goof thought about it. He didn't mind rocking the boat, but this was more like trying to capsize it. If they failed, things wouldn't be easy around here anymore. Special Facility would go from being a virtual prison to the very real kind. But if they succeeded, he'd be free. He could go home.

With enough specials, they could do it. If they fought together all at once, it might just work. If it didn't, he could plant the idea in Shackleton's mind that he had nothing to do with it. After all, he'd just found out he could talk his way out of anything.

"So?" Pussy said. "You in or out?"

Goof smiled. He very much wanted in. "You bet."

If the BTA wouldn't go to Huntsville to help, deputized mutagenic asset Jeffrey Baker would.

He was going home to rescue Dog.

Thirty-Two

Amy left her house for school, swinging her new book bag. She thought about showing it to Sally and burst into tears. Every day, it was the same. She went to school expecting to see her friend at her locker, in health class, at dinnertime. Then Amy would remember: She'd never talk to her friend again.

She'd never get the chance to ask her what was wrong.

Sally had seemed so sad and troubled in her final days. Amy was so occupied by her own life that she hadn't asked. Not really asked the way a friend does. Now she'd never know. Sally had taken all her troubles to the grave.

She stood in the road crying. When she was done, she wiped her face, took a few ragged breaths, and started walking again.

A peaceful morning. Birdsong and insect buzz. The sun struck the fields with an energizing light. Everything was going back to normal. She was alive and loved and on her way to school. A single moment breaks the world. A thousand moments heal the wound. Every step took her closer in time to healing.

Thinking that, Amy smiled a little for the first time in days.

A truck rattled past. The man behind the wheel raised his index finger. She waved back and kept walking.

Enough moments go by, and anything seems possible again.

A passing car slowed and rolled to a stop. Mr. Benson looked over from behind the wheel. "Morning, Amy."

"Morning, Mr. Benson."

"I'm heading to the school. You want me to drive you?"

Amy thought about Bowie. Her smile died. Panic welled in her chest, up her neck, flooded her brain.

"Are you okay?" he said, looking baffled.

She took a deep breath. *He ain't Bowie,* she told herself. *Bowie's dead and can never hurt you again. They ain't all the same. You take people one at a time. Mr. Benson is one of the good ones. He's a good man, like Jake.*

"Yeah," she said. "I'll share a ride with you."

"Happy to take you."

She got into the car and took another deep breath. "You live around here?"

"No, I live up on the hill."

"What are you doing all the way out here this morning?"

The health teacher blanched. "I was staying with a, uh, friend last night."

"Who is she?"

"Well," he said.

"Come on, Mr. Benson. You teach sex ed. We all know people do it."

He laughed. "A woman who works at the Home. She just quit. Wants to move back to the North. I don't know why I just told you all that."

"It's good to talk when you're upset."

"Maybe her going is for the best. It hasn't been easy. She, uh, well."

"She ain't White."

Mr. Benson frowned. "Are you psychic or something?"

"Only two women work at the Home. Both are Black. And this road is a shortcut to the school from the Black part of town."

"Oh, right."

"I remember there were a big scandal about it," she said. "Women being allowed to work around the plague kids."

"I remember, too."

"So you're seeing one of them."

"We don't advertise it," he said. "Meaning I hope you'll keep it to yourself."

"I will."

"Some folks don't take to the idea of it. Mixed-race couples, I mean. Attitudes about it are softening a little, but you know. Old ways die long and hard."

"You ain't hurting anybody," Amy said. "I don't care."

"That's how it should work."

"You might could go with her up North."

Mr. Benson laughed again. "I might could. So how about you? How are you doing?"

"Mama says take it one day at a time. That's what I'm doing."

"And how's that going for you?"

"Sally's gone," she said. "The rest of us have to keep going."

"That's all we can do. Like you said, one day at a time."

He said this absently, his mind troubled not just by Sally's passing but by his own problems. Amy didn't want to bother him further, but he was an adult. Smart, too. She wanted to ask him something.

"You love somebody, you do anything for them, don't you think?"

"You really want me to leave, don't you?"

"No—"

"I'm just kidding, Amy. If she asks me, I'll consider it."

"Actually, I was asking, you know, generally. Ain't that what you do when you're in love? Love them whole, and keep no secrets from them?"

"That's how it's supposed to work. Of course, it don't always."

"And you do anything for them, don't you," Amy said.

"As long as it isn't something stupid. That's the tricky part. And here we are."

Mr. Benson turned the wheel and drove into the school parking lot. He parked in a faculty spot. She jumped out and collected her book bag.

"Thanks, Mr. Benson. See you in class. I hope things work out for you."

"Nice talking to you, Amy. And thanks for the kind thought."

Amy went to her locker and stowed her bag and the books she didn't need for her first few classes. In homeroom, she avoided chitchat to work on algebra problems as she still had a mess of classwork to catch up on. She stood for the Pledge of Allegiance, idly wondering if the plague kids went through the same ritual every morning. Then she headed to her first class thinking about Jake.

Today, she was going to talk to him. She'd made up her mind in the car.

She was gonna tell Jake everything.

Sally's death had taught her life is full of chance. Anything is possible, including getting killed before you really lived. Amy wanted to live her life to the fullest. A true life. That meant taking risks.

She loved Jake, plain and simple. Love was about trust, taking chances, giving everything and holding nothing back. It wasn't enough for her to have a normal life. Amy wanted the life she chose and the love she believed in. A love in which she didn't have to lie to protect herself. A life in which her man loved her back as she was, flaws and all.

She believed Jake did and would.

In health class, she passed him a note when Mr. Benson's back was turned. He scribbled on it with his pencil and slipped it back to her. She waited until the teacher turned away again and read it.

Yes, we can talk after school. Everything okay?

Amy nodded, looking at Mr. Benson as he described the female reproductive system he'd drawn on the chalkboard. He was teaching how babies were made.

Several rows ahead, Archie Gaines turned around and stared. Not at her this time. He directed his intense gaze at Jake. She wondered what was going on in his mind, how he was coping with everything he'd seen. Sally murdered, his daddy mauled by a monster.

Archie's face stretched into a wide grin.

The bell rang. Time for dinner. She collected her books and joined the stream out of class, glad to be away from that strange smile. Jake fell into step alongside her.

"Troy asked me if it's okay if he maybe likes Michelle now," he said.

"Oh." Amy wasn't sure what the rules were on that. "What'd you say?"

"I told him he might wait until Michelle was maybe ready to like him."

"She's still broken up about Sally."

"What about you? Is that what you wanted to talk—"

Jake staggered as a hand shoved him from behind. He wheeled with a growl.

"Hey monster lover," Archie said.

"Stop being a jerk, Archie Gaines," Amy said.

Jake stepped into the boy's space. "What do you want now?"

"I was just wondering what you thought of your creepers now after the dog boy killed Sally."

Amy gasped.

"I could have sworn we'd settled this the hard way once already," Jake said.

"Meet me after school at the dogwood and we'll settle it for good."

"We'll do that."

Archie winked at Amy. "See you around, honey."

"Kiss my go-to-hell," she told him.

At dinner, Jake sat glum and distracted. A fight was nothing compared to waiting for the fight. Troy and Michelle weren't much help, lost in their own emotions. They all picked at their food in the midst of the cafeteria roar.

Amy sipped milk through her straw and set it down. "What are you gonna do?"

Jake shrugged. "Try to talk to him. If that don't work, I reckon I'll wing it."

"I don't think he's right in the head," she said. "Not anymore. He's changed somehow. I think seeing what that plague boy did to Sally messed him up."

"He's had it rough. He has to understand we lost a friend, too. We're all grieving."

"I get the impression he don't want to listen. He just wants to fight somebody, and you happen to be handy. You still might have to do it."

Jake's eyes blazed with sudden anger. "I don't care about fighting. If it happens, I'll do it, and half of me won't even know I'm doing it. It's like I'm watching it happen. I get weirdly calm when I fight. The fight don't scare me, it's the fact I'm fighting does. Does that make any sense?"

"I think so. Is that what's got you out of kilter?"

"It's more than just Archie. The murders have got the whole town riled up. My charity work for the Home has been put on hold indefinitely. People are going out there and taking shots at the plague kids. The whole thing sucks."

"They killed our friend," Michelle said.

"They didn't do anything," Jake said. "One boy did, and he'll get what's coming to him. We didn't have to declare war on them. We push enough, they might declare war back. A lot of people could get hurt."

"The plague kids have been nothing but trouble for me and mine since I first laid eyes on them," Michelle said. "I'd gladly see them all disappear to get Sally back."

"So you're on Archie's side?"

"Hell, no," she said. "I hope you kick his ass."

Jake laughed. Amy loved the sound of it. Even Michelle smiled.

The bell rang, ending dinner. She gave him a peck on the cheek that thrilled her as much as it did him and ran off to science class blushing. In Science, she watched Archie eyeball Jake, who stared at his fists clenched on his desk. The clock ticked on the wall. God, it was like that old movie *High Noon*.

The thing that struck her the most was neither of them looked happy about what was about to happen after school.

If they were so darn miserable about it, why were they dead set on doing it?

And boys thought girls were dumb. Sometimes, boys acted like stupid idiots.

At last, the bell rang in the final class of this never-ending day. Excited kids flooded the halls, chasing freedom out the door. Amy followed Jake to his locker and watched him toss his books inside. Nothing to weigh him down.

"If he pulls a knife or something, you run," she said. "Don't be a macho man."

"He ain't gonna pull a knife," he said. "If he wants a fair fight, I'll give him one. A fair, pointless, stupid fight."

Troy and Michelle joined them. They all trooped out of the school together and across the freshly mowed lawn toward the old dogwood tree at the edge of the football field. The rain had stopped. It was a beautiful day.

Michelle sat on the grass and hugged her knees. "How long are we supposed to wait?"

"Maybe it's a setup," Troy wondered. "His idea of a joke."

"I doubt it," Jake said.

"If he brings Dan and Earl, I got your back."

"I'm still holding out hope it won't come to a fight. We was best friends once."

"Look out," Michelle said. "Here he comes."

Amy squinted in the sunlight. Archie marched across the football field. He came alone. She and her friends waited as he closed the distance with long strides.

"He looks loaded for bear," Jake said. "All y'all hang back."

He stepped forward to parley. "So what did you want to talk about?"

Archie walked up to him and punched him in the face with a sickening sound like a hand slapping meat.

Amy gasped as Jake reeled, cupping his nose. They were even now. The score had been settled. But Archie didn't stop. He laid into Jake with everything he had, his eyes wild, fighting like a mad dog.

Jake stumbled away from the assault and fell. Archie squatted over him, delivering punches while Jake hugged his face.

"Stop it," Amy shouted.

"Take it," Archie snarled. "Take it like a man."

Troy ran at Archie and shoved him sprawling on the grass. The kid jumped to his feet and reared for a hit at Troy, who flinched back with his hands raised.

"That's what I thought," Archie said.

"Jesus," Michelle bawled. "You are such an asshole, Archie."

Archie put his hands on his knees to catch his breath, a strange, terrified look on his face. "You'll remember this the rest of your life, Jake. That's how it works."

Then he spat on the ground and stormed off.

Amy knelt next to Jake. "Let me see it. Oh, honey."

He blinked up at her in confusion, his face covered in blood. Archie had busted his nose good. "Is it bad?"

"Well," Amy said, unsure what to tell him.

"Such an asshole," Michelle said, still crying.

Troy hugged her close. "I should have helped sooner. I was too surprised."

"You did fine, Troy," Amy said. "Nobody expected him to come charging in like a wild animal. Jake, can you stand up?"

He touched his face and looked at the blood on his fingers. "Damn. He bopped me good, didn't he?"

He sounded almost appreciative. Like he admired the act if not the actor. Troy gave him a handkerchief. Jake sat up and wiped the blood off his face.

He probed his swollen nose and winced. "Stings like hell. Ow, damn."

"Well, I guess you two are even now," Amy said.

"We ain't even. Not by a long mile."

"You should shake hands and quit this feuding."

"Kick his ass," Michelle said. "This has got nothing to do with Sally or the monster kids. He has it in for you."

Amy helped him to his feet. "Come to my house. We better put some ice on your face or you're gonna look like Marcia Brady just before her big date."

"Okay," Jake said. "As long as your mama don't take a shot at me, too. I had enough fighting for one day."

"Sure you're all right?" Troy said.

Jake waved him off. "Show's over. See you, Troy, Michelle."

"Bye," they said and headed the other direction.

He put his arm around Army and held her tight. He let out a loud sigh.

"Are you really okay or playing macho?" she said.

"I'm really okay," he said. "I just have to walk it off."

She sighed. "You boys. Bunch of damn fools."

"Looks like we're finally alone. So what did you want to talk to me about?"

"You know what," Amy said. "I totally forgot what I was gonna say. Let's take care of you now, honey."

She couldn't tell him the truth about what she was. She couldn't put him through any more strife. She loved him too much for that.

I can't have anything good, Amy thought. This world won't allow it.

Thirty-Three

The Home truck thudded over a pothole and coasted to a halt in Pa Albod's yard. Brain, Wallee, and Mary sat in the pickup's bed and waited. Thrushes whistled in the trees. The air was already thick and muggy this morning, the sky gray as their teacher's face.

Mr. Byrd sat in the cab and tilted his head back. He shuddered and tossed a steel hip flask onto the seat next to him. Brain watched him in the rearview until the man's hard eyes flickered to stare back. Brain turned to look at something else.

The fields sprawled brown and empty, all the cotton picked, ginned, and bundled. Wallee closed his eyes and swayed as he hummed a tune. Mary sat with a blank face, her porch light on but nobody home, patient as the Buddha.

At last, Mr. Byrd opened the door and let his feet dangle out. He leaned on his thighs and coughed hard until he retched. He spat and took a deep breath. Then he wiped his mouth and lit a cigarette.

"Get out the truck," he said.

The man was filling in for Mr. Gaines. He taught the

Bible at the Home. Behind his back, the kids called him Thou Shalt Not But I Will. Eventually, Mr. Gaines would return or the principal would hire a replacement.

Nobody had yet replaced Dog. As for Dog, he was gone for good.

"What do you want us to do?" Brain said.

Mr. Byrd cast a wretched look at the farmhouse. "I don't know. I don't see Reggie. What do you usually do? Hoe gardens and stuff?"

"I work the animals and machines. Wallee, he—"

The man raised his hand to silence him.

The front door had banged open. The Albod girls trooped out in a funereal pall, faces downcast and pale from grief. They filed past. The teacher looked at the house again, but still no Pa Albod.

"You was saying something?" he said.

"Wallee usually tends the garden. And Mary—"

The hand shot up again. "Fine. Go ahead and do what you just said."

"I was gonna say Mary don't have a job, seeing as all the cotton's picked."

The teacher lay back on the seat, pulled his cap over his eyes, and folded his hands on his chest. "Yup. Wake me up for dinner around noon."

Brain walked toward the barn. He hadn't been to the farm since Sally died and the sheriff arrested Dog. The animals needed tending. Pa Albod maintained a stock of cattle, pigs, and chickens, both laying hens and fryers. The pigs had suffered an outbreak of whipworm over the summer. He should check on them first.

Wallee lumbered after him. "What about me, Brain?"

"Do what you like. The overseers are all napping."

"Do gar-den."

"That's fine," Brain said. "Take Mary with you and keep her out of trouble."

"Not same," Wallee said. "With-out Dog."

"Have you been talking to the sheriff, Wallee?"

The kid's thick rubbery lips formed an *O*. "Would like that."

"But have you?"

Wallee grinned. "Want to be sher-iff."

"The sheriff arrested Dog," Brain said.

"Dog broke law."

"Their law."

"On-ly one law," Wallee said and shuffled off on his tentacles.

Brain noticed a dead hen in the grass, scrawny and almost stripped of feathers. The other chickens had pecked her to death. She must have just died. Tonight, a scavenger would come along and take her off.

He wondered if Wallee would one day have to be killed.

A revolution took time to organize. It was like building a bonfire: tinder clumped at the heart, kindling teepeed around it, logs stacked around. Then the long wait for the spark.

So many kids now were learning they had abilities. They practiced out in the woods, no longer playing but training to fight. Vigilante attacks against the Home had pushed them to the edge. An informant could ruin all of it. The revolution might be crushed before it started because some kid with a sweet tooth sold it out for a Hershey bar.

Or worse, a believer in their system. A kid believing normal law was just law.

If they stood united, they could gain everything.

Brain looked back at the truck. Mr. Byrd's feet stuck out the open door. Pa Albod was nowhere in sight. He could do anything he wanted.

He went to the barn and pushed an old wheelbarrow to the entrance. A heavy red toolbox went into it, followed by little motors, loose bolts, and parts Albod collected over the years in case they might one day be useful.

Brain heaved the wheelbarrow toward Albod's truck. He set it down with a pained grunt and ran extension cords all the way to the barn for the power tools. Then he propped the hood and went to work.

His hands leaped from one task to the next without conscious thought. The bulk of engine work disappeared and reappeared as its constituent parts on the tarp. He glanced over the carpet of metal junk and went back to work.

Ignition, propulsion, acceleration, power, efficiency. Intake and exhaust manifold. Carburetor that blended air and fuel. Camshaft and distributor, battery and starting switch. He wire-scrubbed rusted parts, jury-rigged systems, stripped and wrapped wires. By the time he finished, the old truck would run better than brand-new with a boost to fuel efficiency.

He could do a lot more if he had time, materials, and a machine shop. Oh, God, the things he could do if he only had the means. He could change the world.

Mr. Byrd called him for his dinner. Brain ignored him.

As the truck came back together, he envisioned a vehicle that ran on water and sunlight, a truck that would never die, a once-removed cousin to a perpetual motion machine. An all-purpose vehicle that outlived its owner, scalable and modularized for easy future upgrades.

On the fly, he imagined materials and methods, tools

and parts, machines and processes, new scientific fields that would revolutionize everything. He saw entire industries rise up out of nothing, manufacturing and service, new business models, halo disruption as his technologies rippled across other industries, tearing them down and replacing them with fresh marvels.

He pictured all this and more, always more. A world of wonders.

The things he could do. He could build dreams if only he weren't a monster. Brain never used his powers to benefit normals. He'd been on strike since birth. He could go to Special Facility and change the world, but it would always be their world, not his. Today was a rare exception. For just one day, he wanted to pretend he was free to use his powers however he wished.

"What'd you do to my truck?" Pa Albod said.

Brain turned. "Afternoon, Pa."

Pa Albod stood hatless and blinking in the daylight. His mottled face bristled with stubble. His hair stuck up in places. Brain had always seen him as a powerful man. A symbol of the normals' strength. Now he just looked like an old man consumed by grief. His mortality clung to him like a cloud.

Brain felt the man's pain. It was hard to hate when what you hated became a who, and that who was suffering. Whether Dog was unjustly accused or not, the fact remained Albod had lost his little girl. A sweet, kind girl. An innocent who'd had everything going for her, who'd had her whole life ahead of her.

"I asked what you're doing, George."

"I fixed your truck," Brain said. "If you got your keys, I'd love to start her up."

"Didn't ask you to fix my truck."

"Mr. Byrd said to do whatever I thought needed doing. I gave the truck a good and proper tune-up. She'll run better than brand-new."

"Have you seen Enoch around?"

"Enoch's in jail, Pa."

"I know that," the man growled.

"I guess I'll check on the animals and then put all these tools away," Brain said.

"Yeah, all right."

"Unless you want me to do something else with the time I got left."

"Yup. That sounds fine."

Brain left him to his grief and headed for the pigpen. After just a few paces, he stopped, turned, and came back. "Hey, Pa?"

The farmer snapped out of his reverie. "What's that?"

"I just wanted to say I'm sorry, sir."

He squinted. "Sorry?"

"About Miss Sally. Me and Wallee and Mary. We're all real sorry for your loss."

"What have you got to be sorry for?"

"Miss Sally was a fine girl. She was always very kind."

Albod blinked. "Much obliged."

Brain started to put the tools back in the red box. He struggled to process his roiling emotions. He felt Pa Albod's pain. He didn't hate the man. He certainly hadn't hated Sally. He hated the system that crushed him and his kind. But the Albod family benefited from that system. They and others like them constructed it for their benefit and chose to ignore the violence it inflicted on the plague children. Where was Pa Albod when Sucker Punch died in a torture chamber? Where was his sympathy? The farmer was blind to the suffering, a blindness he'd—

He shrieked as pain ripped across his back. "What are you doing?"

"You ain't sorry, boy," Albod said. "Not yet."

Another bolt of pain striped his shoulders. The farmer raised his belt again. Brain scrambled away to escape the flailing strokes.

"Not by a long shot," Albod said.

The leather scorched Brain's hands feebly raised to defend himself. The next stroke smashed his face. Wasp stings followed by burning fire.

"You damned creepers," the farmer raged. "I opened my home to you. I made you family and let you call me pa. I trusted you with my child, and you butchered her."

Brain spotted Mr. Byrd running toward them. He staggered toward the teacher with his hands outstretched, unable to form words, mindless with pain.

"What's going on?" the teacher said. "Lord, George, what did you do?"

The next lash brought him to his knees. He lay squirming on the ground, hands over his eyes, crying as every second brought fresh agonies. The blows didn't cease, each one a roaring hell, his flesh itself screaming.

"Stop," a voice said.

The next lash seemed to rip the hide right off him. He felt like his body was coming apart. Entrails spilling on the ground. White bone exposed to air. His precious brain, powerful enough to change the world, winking into void.

"STOP."

The beating stopped but brought little relief as pain

continued to cascade through his seething flesh, his frail body a shivering ball. His heart boomed against his ribs. Another jagged wail escaped his throat. But he was alive. He clung to that fact. He opened feverish eyes and saw Mary standing over him.

Little Mary with her imbecilic face and too-big overalls. She stood her ground with fists clenched. For the first time, her eyes glittered with the spark of intelligence. For the first time, she was truly awake.

"Stop," she whispered.

Red mist filled the air. Pa Albod grunted and bent over, clutching his guts and moaning. Vomit splashed on the grass. He coughed in the aftermath. Mr. Byrd rushed over to help him stumble back to the house.

The mist disappeared into Mary's mouth. Her eyes flared one last time then became dull again, her face calm. The porch light on, but nobody home.

She's one of us, Brain thought just before he blacked out.

Thirty-Four

Sheriff Burton sat in his easy chair reading the paper. Widespread famine in Ethiopia. A Home firebombed by vigilantes in Tennessee, eight dead. The Cubs beat the Padres 13–0. And in the small town of Huntsville, Georgia, police had wrapped up their investigation of the murder of Sally Mae Albod.

He peered at his wife over the rims of his reading glasses. "Listen to this, hon. Quote, Sheriff Thomas E. Burton is to be commended for his swift and thorough investigation, unquote. District Attorney Keaton Lightfoot said that."

Anne sat on the couch with her legs crossed and her nose buried in Danielle Steel's *Full Circle*, which she'd taken out from the library. She always dressed immaculately and wore full makeup, even at home.

"That's lovely, Tom," she said.

"Right here in the *Atlanta Constitution*. Your husband is famous."

"It's wonderful."

"He called me out by name. How about that."

"Mm-hmm," she said.

"I'm gonna crush Johnny Stoval come November. I'll be sheriff the next four years at least."

This time, she said nothing.

Burton read the rest to himself, lips moving. The assistant DA expected an indictment by a grand jury before the end of the week. He removed his glasses and rubbed his tired eyes, feeling proud but unsettled. The clock ticked on the mantle.

Dave Gaines had stuck with his cockamamie story. That left Archie and Amy. Burton couldn't put a fourteen-year-old boy on the grill any more than he could Amy Green for the same reason. So he shoved the whole mess on the county DA investigator. Drew a big circle around the ballistics. Nothing doing. The shit rolled uphill to the assistant DA, who drafted an indictment. The DA would take it to a grand jury to rubber stamp, and then the criminal trial would commence. As Burton expected, the DA wanted to try Bryant as an adult. The public howled for justice and blood. Everybody was out to ride the gravy train to fame and glory.

A good lawyer would rip the government's case to shreds, but Enoch Bryant didn't have a good lawyer, and out of fear of the mob, the hack the court appointed wouldn't put up a fight even if he wanted to. Enoch Bryant wouldn't get a fair judge and an impartial jury.

The kid would fry. Burton could picture it. Bryant shuffles along in handcuffs and leg irons, surrounded by stony-faced prison guards. The chaplain recites the Lord's prayer. Head shaven, the boy sits on the wooden chair. The guards strap him to it with leather belts. Electrodes on his feet. The blinds open to reveal the witnesses gazing through the window, Reggie Albod a picture of righteous fury. Bryant hyperventilates at his looming end. The guards set a wet sponge and big metal helmet on his head. They wrap a black blindfold over his gleaming eyes. Bryant's last words: *I swear to God I didn't kill that girl.* Nobody believes him.

CRACK. One thousand volts flow through him. Twenty seconds. Bryant jerks against his restraints. He slumps. CRACK.

Another twenty. And the doctor pronounces him one dead dog.

As horrible as that was, an innocent boy getting the chair, perhaps it was all for the best. Despite continuing vigilante attacks against Homes all over the country, everything seemed to be simmering down. Great events often boiled down to a single man. The stone that makes waves in the pond. Take the stone away, and everything goes back to normal. He'd thought that man was Gaines, but perhaps fate had chosen Enoch Bryant to play the martyr. His death would assure the nation and its people they were stronger than what they feared. Things would calm down for good and go back to the way they were.

That still didn't make it right.

Burton stood and stretched. "I've got a mind to take a drive."

"You should do that," his wife said.

"We need anything from the store?"

Anne looked up from her book. "We have everything we need."

Her regal bearing came from years of suffering. He wondered again if she would ever forgive him. He'd already asked her many times over the years. The answer was always the same. That particular stone could never be removed. It would forever ripple through their lives.

Long ago, he and Anne had wanted a child but couldn't

conceive. They'd started to drift apart. One lonely night in Tallahassee he tumbled into bed with a cocktail waitress and brought home the germ, which he gave to Anne. A month later, she started throwing up from morning sickness.

The joy he'd felt. He was gonna be a daddy.

Eight months after that, Anne gave birth to a monster.

In the waiting room, Burton had paced with a breast pocket full of cigars ready to pass out to anybody wanting to help him celebrate. Doc Odom came out and gave him the bad news. Burton inspected the thing that was his child, swaddled in a glass bubble under a heat lamp. *It's that disease going around*, the doctor said. *I'm sorry to say you and Anne must have it.*

Doc Odom asked him if he cared to name it. Burton didn't even know what it was, a boy or girl. Its little eyes clamped shut, its mouth kissed the air as it searched for the breast. Then it cried, which was most repugnant of all because it sounded like a normal baby crying for its mama.

He named it and signed the forms to give it to the Homes.

They told everybody the child died during childbirth. Arrangements were made to pass it over to the Huntsville Home. A different family name on the birth certificate. Doc Odom kept his secret. Anne never truly forgave him for any of it, and he'd lived with his shame ever since. The shame of his transgression. The shame of the plague that spread through an act of love.

"I love you, Anne," he said.

She said nothing. The silence simmered between them. Sometimes Burton felt like he was the only man who lived in a house haunted by the living.

"I'll take that drive then," he said.

He left the house and drove around in the dark until he

found himself at his office. A news van maintained a weary vigil outside, CNN painted on its side, the name of that new twenty-four-hour cable TV channel launched up in Atlanta. Somebody smelled a story. Most of the other press had packed it in and run off to hound the district attorney. Soon, this sordid drama would shift to the courtroom.

He walked inside and hung his hat. Sikes jumped in his chair at the sight of him. The deputy looked at the clock. "Evening, boss."

"Evening, Bobby. You look like the proverbial long-tailed cat in a room full of rockers. What's got you so jumpy?"

"Just scared me is all. Didn't expect you in tonight."

"I wanted to talk to the creeper one last time," the sheriff said.

"I been promising the moon and threatening hellfire. He won't confess."

"It don't matter what he says. His goose is cooked."

"Can't even get him to tell us where Bowie's head is."

"It don't matter. Go back to reading or whatever you was doing."

Burton entered the holding cells. He dragged a chair up to the bars, giving him a chance to study his prisoner. The dog boy sat on his bed watching him with glazed eyes. Captivity had not been kind to him. The kid sagged as if he were melting. Parts of his fur had been worried bald.

"Hey, Sheriff," the kid said.

This boy could have been Burton's son, though he wasn't.

"Evening, Enoch."

"Heard you come in. Thought you was the preacher come again. He been talking my ears off, praying almost every night."

"He'll do that," Burton said. "It's his vocation."

"Hours of talking to God and barely a word said to me. It's important to him that I get to a better world as long as I get out of his. Cares more about my soul than he does me. Comforting, though."

"What's that? Going to Heaven?"

"The chance to finally go someplace nobody hates to look at me. You reckon God loves me, or am I going to Hell because I were unlucky to be born a monster? Do you think my soul is ugly like my body?"

"I don't claim to know God's mind," Burton said. "But if you love Jesus and got yourself a clean conscience, I reckon God will take you in."

Enoch looked around at the bare walls. "I wish I could run. I wish I could run one last time on the four feet God gave me. That's the worst part of being here, not being able to run. I can run like the wind."

"Wish I could let you do it. Anything else I can get you?"

"You could tell Brain I said he were right."

"That's George Hurst, right?"

"You would pass on a message? You'd really do that for me?"

"I might could tell him something for you if I see him," Burton said.

"You know how we get our names at the Home, sir?"

"Can't say I do."

"Sometimes it's what you look like," Enoch said. "Other times, it's who you are in a single word. Like Brain, he's smart. Me, I'm Dog."

"I ain't surprised. You ever look in the mirror?"

"I have taken a very good look, mister. And I see myself clear now. What I am. I was a dog. I was your dog. Everybody knew it. I really believed. The promise of getting a fair shake when we grew up. People like Sally made me believe. That you wasn't all bad, not all of you, and I could have a life of my own. I don't believe no more. And I ain't your dog no more. Tell Brain he were right all along. He'll know what I mean. Tell him I said my name ain't Dog. That's my last request."

"You didn't kill Sally Gaines."

The kid jumped to his feet and grabbed the bars. "You believe me."

"I believe the evidence. The evidence says you didn't do it. Gaines did."

"The evidence is right, sir."

"What about Ray Bowie?"

"I didn't even know he were killed until you told me I was the one killed him."

"I believe you on that, too. That case don't stack up neither."

"Then what does this mean?"

"Amy Green puts you at the scene of Bowie's murder," Burton said. "Dave Gaines and his boy say you killed Sally. It don't add up, but it does enough. Nobody is willing to do the right thing and recant. And nobody else is willing to give the evidence the same hard look I did."

"On account I'm a plague kid," Enoch said. "A creeper. Critter. Monster. An ugly."

"That's right."

"You name us for how you see us. We all have one name to you. So what you're saying is me being innocent don't add up to a hill of beans."

"I came here to say I'm sorry, kid."

"What about you, sir?"

"What about me what?" he said, though he knew what the boy wanted.

"Are you willing to do the right thing? Not for a plague kid, but purely for what's right?"

Sometimes, the history of a thing boiled down to a single decision by a single man. Maybe that man wasn't Gaines or Bryant but him.

He imagined making a stink. The town turning against him. Banishment from his church. Losing the election. Midnight rocks through the window. Death threats in the mail. Maybe even a burning cross on his lawn. The news vultures digging up his past and dragging poor Anne through the mud with him. Shame, loss, retribution.

Folks didn't care about the truth, not when it interfered with a comforting narrative. A story about good and evil the fine citizens of Huntsville were deeply invested in believing.

Stark County already had its share of problems with race. During the upheaval of the Sixties, it seemed Huntsville might escape the troubles. As a young deputy, Burton watched the White and Black kids play together at the playground and thought, That's where the fear and hate will end, with the children. Then a Black family moved into a White neighborhood, and Mayor Emery got on the radio and said it was time to fix them niggers, help them see the error of their ways. Three days later, the house got bombed, and a little girl died. Two more houses got shot up. Black men patrolled their neighborhoods at night with shotguns.

Things had improved since then but not by a whole lot. The town had its White and Black sections, the Klan was alive and well, and racial tensions ebbed and flowed. The walls broken during the Sixties were being rebuilt. Burton had given up his hopes for the races ever living together in perfect harmony. And if White and Black couldn't live together, how could men and monsters?

In the end, he might save Enoch Bryant but sacrifice himself while setting up more violence. The Klan had already shot up the Home twice, and if pushed too far it was only a matter of time before they burned it to the ground.

Still, the law was the law, and for him, that superseded everything. A good town policed itself, but he had no interest in mob rule, either. He could do something. Maybe he'd press Archie Gaines after all and see if the kid folded. Bring Amy Green in without her mama around. Put it right to them.

If they recanted, it was on them, and they could own the fallout. If they didn't, well, nothing could be done.

"I might could make an effort," he said.

"Thank ye, Sheriff."

Burton stood. "Don't be thanking me yet, kid. It's a long shot."

"You're gonna try. You believe me. For that, I'm grateful."

"Good night," Burton said.

A good town policed itself. When that failed, it was his job.

After the sheriff left, Dog clutched the bars and stared at the door he'd gone through as if he might come right back and let him out.

Sheriff Burton had turned out to be a good man, if that didn't beat all. It rekindled Dog's hope in more ways than one, the way Sally's friendship and kindness had. Not all hens pecked the weak. He knew not to hope in regard to gaining his freedom, but he couldn't help it. The sheriff would let him out of this cage. He'd run again. Find a nice secret place where he could run on all fours with nobody to bother him. He'd go back to the farm. Pa Albod would thank him for trying to save Sally's life. His friends would know he didn't kill anybody. The whole town would.

And he'd escape the chair, the evil chair the normals invented to destroy those guilty of the worst crimes. The mean deputy had told him all about it. The straps, the metal helmet and sponge, his accusers watching him die through the window. The deputy said you looked like you were a lunatic king sitting on a throne. A thousand volts hitting you like lightning. Your eyes melting right out of their sockets. Shitting and pissing yourself. Death was supposed to be instant, but according to the deputy it didn't always work out that way. Sometimes you felt it all and screamed smoke. Sometimes your head burst on fire.

Sometimes, the deputy said, they had to scrape your flesh off the chair after it was all over.

He'd rather be shot. He'd rather die in almost any other way than that, in fact.

If they let him out of this cage, Dog would still be a plague kid, one of the uglies with nothing to his name and no future. He'd still be in trouble for mauling Mr. Gaines. But he'd have his life, and that was enough. That was everything. He'd have his name back and nobody would ever see him as a killer of teachers and young girls. Maybe the jury would go easy on him and let him off once the truth came out he was trying to protect Miss Sally. He'd have friends and sunshine, places to run, honest work with the land, and the occasional kindness, the odd glass of iced tea with a sprig of mint in it after a long hot day.

If they let him out, he'd become Enoch again, same as when he was born.

As if in answer to his prayers, the door opened.

The deputy walked in and said, "You got another visitor, creeper."

Reverend Coombs, no doubt. This time, Dog would pray with him. They wouldn't talk to each other, but they could talk to God together. The preacher would pray for his soul, Dog for the deliverance of his body.

A man came into the room, but it wasn't the preacher.

Pa Albod.

The door closed. The farmer shuffled to the chair the sheriff had left. He sat in it and slumped. He was a different man in every way now. His face was gray and stubbled, his body bent and frail. His eyes blazed with sparks.

"I'm glad to see you, sir," Dog said.

"I'm dying," Pa said.

"Dying?"

"The little retard witch put a hex on me. I been sick ever since."

"You're just sad, sir. I'm sad, too."

The man fixed his blazing eyes on him. "Are you? Are you sorry for what you done?"

"I didn't do it. Mr. Gaines did it. He shot her. I swear to God that's what I saw."

"Don't swear, boy. You already done enough to earn damnation."

"I still ain't the one harmed her. Even the sheriff knows it's true."

"I just came to know why," Pa Albod said. "I'm dying, and I wanted to know why you had to take my Sally from me."

"I don't know what you want me to say, sir. I loved Miss Sally. She invited me on walks and asked me to be her protector. She let me run on all fours the way God made me.

She didn't look at me like I were a freak. She really looked at me. Really talked. She were my friend."

Pa Albod smiled as he stared into private memories. "Sally were like that. She'd find a wren with a broken wing and try to nurse it. She always wanted a dog but last one we had chased you creepers around the yard. We had to get rid of him. Sally had a big giving heart."

"That's how I saw her," Dog said. "I loved her, and I didn't kill her. You ask the sheriff. I got nothing else to say about it other than I'm sorry she's gone."

"She liked you creepers, too. Anything that's broken, she loved it."

Pa Albod stood and knocked on the door to be let out.

The deputy appeared. "You sure about it, Reggie?"

"Yup."

The man handed Albod a shotgun.

"Much obliged, Bobby."

"Make it quick in case he comes back," the deputy said and closed the door again.

Dog backed from the bars until his rear bumped the sink. The cell was so small. The sink, commode, bunk. Nowhere to hide. Nowhere to go. He whined at the thought of the shotgun slug punching a hole through his body.

"I'm dying," Pa said as he checked the load. "I can feel it. Eating me one bit at a time. I don't have long on this earth. I'll be with Sally soon."

"Please don't do this, sir."

Albod racked a slug into the firing chamber. "But I'll have my justice."

Dog's mind blanked out with terror. He howled and scrabbled at the walls. The deputies had clipped his claws and filed them to smooth nubs. They slid off the cinder blocks. Piss shot down his leg.

He dropped to all fours and lunged over the commode to strike the wall. He bounded to the other side of the cell and back again, an endless circuit that brought neither relief nor escape.

"Goddamnit, stand still," Albod said.

Dog screamed and ran. Nowhere to go but around and around. He'd never see his friends again or feel cotton between his fingers or see the sun or have a dream or drink iced tea or laugh or love or feel or live.

Screaming now, nonsense gibberish. Begging and crying, wailing, *It ain't fair, I once believed in you.* His body throbbing and sore from smashing against the walls. Tiring until he gaped, panting, at Albod. The shotgun blast the last thing he ever heard. The man's lunatic face the last thing he ever saw.

Thirty-Five

Brain limped across the swamp that bordered the big lake north of the Home. He threaded the soft, mossy islands on which grew hammocks of cypresses. The kids avoided this place. They thought it was creepy. Brain had always felt at home here. For him, it was nature's laboratory, haunted only by truth.

The swamp's environment pressed life in all directions. Water lilies, carnivorous bladderworts, snakes, and snapping turtles. Every living thing found its niche and competed with everything else for resources. Natural design filled these niches, like the white ibis with its long beak ideal for spearing fish. Life and death on equal display. A microcosm mirroring the real world, though in its human construct they slapped rules on it and called it civilization. Their laws and religion appeared to protect the weak, but it was all a lie. As below, so above.

Bugs landed on Brain's weeping scabs, feeding on him before flying away with an angry whir. The air thick with mosquitos. Everything fed on everything else, another truth. For every action, an equal and opposite reaction. Energy transmuted but never destroyed, everything in karmic balance. For every purpose, there was a cost. Teratogenesis had given him a brilliant mind but a fragile body that was highly sensitive to pain.

Near the moss bed where he stopped, a stand of pitcher plants grew, once used to treat measles. Some of the kids had mistaken it for honeysuckle and got sick from its poisonous nectar. He looked up at the sky, glimpsing blue through the Spanish moss that hung from the swamp's tangled ceiling. He judged the time by the light. The other kids had returned from the farms. He'd have to head back soon or he'd miss supper. Tonight, he'd mark another day spent in his prison. Tomorrow, the teachers might declare him fit to return to ag science. They'd send him back to Pa Albod, who might this time decide to kill him.

He'd come all the way out here to cry, a safe place to purge himself of the feelings that still gripped him after his lashing. Nothing happened. The shame and rage had fused to his bones. Otherwise, he'd become hollowed out, an empty vessel waiting to be filled with something new.

Brain contemplated the rest of his life and felt his mind cross a threshold. The revolution had always been his idea but now, for the first time, it became inevitable and real, also part of him, like wisdom following knowledge.

Hate flowed inside him now, adding skin and muscle to his ragged spirit until it became whole again.

Brain, a voice boomed across the swamp. *Brain, where are you?*

Tiny splashed across the water, a terrifying sight to the normals whose standard of beauty required large eyes, symmetrical proportions, clean skin. To the normals, asymmetrical features were ugly because they reflected bad genes. Bad skin because it reminded them of disease. Bestial features because they awakened ancestral memories of primeval predators. All because of procreation, the viability of offspring. All because of survival. On a genetic level, the plague generation forced the rest of humanity to gaze deeply upon life and death.

The giant boy stopped, a cloud of gnats forming around his horns like an angry thought. "Dog is dead."

A lance of pain in Brain's heart. He was fragile inside as well. "How did it happen?"

"Mr. Rucker said he hanged himself in jail."

Brain took a ragged breath. The swamp's never-ending soundtrack washed over him. Bullfrogs belched in their hiding places. Mallards honked from cattails fringing the lake. Dog was dead, and all the boy's hopes for a just world had died with him.

Sorry, friend, he thought.

"You said they would push us until we did something about it," Tiny said.

Brain nodded. For every action, an equal and opposite reaction. "I'm ready now."

Tiny grinned and smashed his open palm with his fist. "About time."

"But we ain't ready."

"You taught me patience," Tiny growled. "You taught me the revolution."

"That we could all do it together and create a fair world. Yes."

"I still believe in the revolution. I am running short on patience."

"A third of us ain't ready to fight," Brain said.

"But the rest have spirit. Right now, it's bent far as it can go. If the normals break it, nobody will ever be ready."

"It ain't time."

"I could have gone to Special Facility. I could be in high cotton. We all kept our secret because we believe in you."

"I'm sorry, Atticus."

"It's time," the boy insisted.

"No. Soon. Very soon. But not now."

Tiny glared at Brain, who stared back.

The giant boy roared and punched the nearest cypress, muscles rippling along his spiky arm. The old tree groaned, roots cracking, and toppled with a crash.

"Soon," the boy snarled.

"Yes."

"Soon, it will come."

"Soon," Brain said.

Tiny turned and splashed away, crossing the swamp in great strides. Brain looked down at the spot where the great tree once stood, now filling with water. The water was the color of black tea, rich with tannic acid from rotting plants and peat.

In the future, a big storm would come and lash this place with rain. The swamp would flood until it spread and consumed everything in its path.

Soon.

Brain sat on his bed of moss.

"Dog," he sobbed.

At last, his tears came like the flood.

Thirty-Six

D ave Gaines drove the rutted dirt track to the Home for the last time. He parked and looked around at the vast decaying mansion, outbuildings, weedy yard, trees draped with Spanish moss.

Nobody in sight. This time of day, the kids sat in the mess hall having their breakfast. He could hear their roaring babble from here. The windows had been boarded up with cardboard taped in place. Buckshot scarred the walls.

He'd spent five years of his life here watching creepers grow up. He'd felt chained to it. A heavy, rotting ghost that owned him. Now that he was quitting, it had lost its hold, its spell broken. The trees were just trees. The house just an old house. Like looking at photos, already in the past. No responsibility here, not anymore, leaving his spirit light as a feather. He could let go of it all, the tragedy and sadness, but now that he was free he gazed upon it all with mounting nostalgia.

Gaines wondered if convicts felt the same way when they left prison, whether they looked upon their barred cells as home after too long.

He walked into the house, taking his time. His body was still recovering. The drive had put a fierce ache in his arm and shoulder. Doc Odom said he'd have ugly scars the rest of his life. Enoch might be dead, but he'd left a permanent mark on him.

Gaines went down the hall and entered the principal's office. The old man looked up from his desk and motioned him to grab a chair.

"Good to see you back on your feet," Willard said.

"Morning, sir. Thank you."

"You feeling better?"

"Fine and dandy, Colonel."

"When do you see yourself coming back to work?"

"Well, sir, that's the thing," Gaines said. "I got offered a better job."

The principal pierced him with his stare. "I see."

"Bill Faherty said I could work for him. He owns the 76 out by Route 19. Filling, oil changes, tune-ups, and some body work."

"That sounds like a good employment opportunity."

"Bill says he's thinking of adding a car wash in the next year." Gaines frowned. "Maybe I shouldn't have said anything about that, telling people Bill's business. Don't tell anybody I told you."

Willard held up his hand to express he understood and didn't care what Bill did. "I am glad to see things looking up for you."

Gaines's nostalgia slipped away as this truth hit him. Everything was in fact looking up. A new job, women showing interest. His boy socking it to the preacher's kid like a man. Enoch was dead, and the sheriff had backed off his personal crusade to see him in jail. For the first time in many long years, Gaines had far more to look forward to than look back on. This heady knowledge left him uneasy and excited.

On top of it all, the old man seemed happy for him, and no hard feelings. Gaines could walk away from this place and leave it forever.

"I'm sorry to lose you," Willard added. "I'm breaking in a new man to assist in Discipline, but it isn't the same."

"Have they been acting unruly?"

"All the recent fuss has made it a precarious time."

"I'm sorry to leave you shorthanded and all," Gaines said.

"We'll manage. We always do. Now that the Bryant boy is dead, I expect things will settle down over the next month or so."

"In four years, it'll all be over anyhow. The Homes will be out of business."

"I'd like you to keep in touch," the principal said. "I know some good men who see things clearly. They see the future and are preparing for it."

"Contingency plans," Gaines guessed.

"When the children reach maturity, they will be more difficult to control. The result will be the first war fought on American soil since 1865."

"You really think so, sir?"

"I know it."

"So this, uh, club or whatever. What is it doing to prepare?"

"Training," Willard said. "One weekend a month."

"They're lucky to have you helping them, Colonel. A man of your experience."

"Back in 'Nam, we ripped that country apart a thousand times over. Dropped the equivalent of six hundred Hiroshima bombs on it. And still we never knew if we had won.

The gooks all looked alike to us, see. We never knew who the enemy was and wasn't, so we killed them all and let God sort the wheat and chaff. My boys had terrific body counts. It felt like we were winning, but we never knew. The plague children aren't like the VC. They're easy to spot. When they finally make their move, we'll be ready. We'll be merciless. And we'll know we won."

Gaines scratched at his itching arm. "I might be interested in that."

"We can't rely on the sheriff to protect us. When the time comes, we must be ready to fight for our homes and families."

The training seemed like fun and a great way to meet friends and make contacts. Another way to move up in the world. It all sounded fine to Gaines, and he said so. "I just have to check with Bill," he added. "Make sure he don't need me at the shop those weekends. Otherwise, count me in."

"Before I formally invite you, I just want to make sure you finding another line of work isn't because of the attack. That it left a mark on you the doctors can't fix."

"I ain't afraid of them kids," Gaines said.

"Good. Then it's settled."

They shook hands, another sign of respect in his new life.

Gaines went back outside and found the yard chock full of milling creepers and red-faced teachers shouting them into the pickups. He gazed upon the familiar scene feeling a little left out but mostly elated this ritual no longer had anything to do with him. He spotted George, Mary, and Edward and watched them with a tinge of regret. He decided to mosey over and say goodbye to his cuckoos.

They froze at the sight of him. George stared, his eyes full of sass as usual. Big red welts crisscrossed his face.

"Lord, boy," Gaines said. "You lose a brick fight or something? You know you ain't no good at fighting."

The kid didn't answer.

"I told the principal I'm leaving for good. I just wanted to say goodbye. All y'all are a good bunch of kids, and I think I'll miss y'all a bitty bit."

George said, "Enoch is dead, Mr. Gaines."

He scowled. Here he was trying to do the right thing, and the kid had to ruin it with this talk. George just couldn't help himself, always the uppity one. The boy could argue with a fence post.

"I heard about that," he said. "You ask me, it weren't fair, what happened to him."

"How do you mean, sir?"

"I mean Reggie shouldn't have done what he did."

Atticus stomped over to stand behind George. The big kid had always made him nervous. The Colonel had worked him over good when it was his turn in Discipline, and the creeper hadn't made a sound.

"I was just saying Enoch should have had his day in court," Gaines offered.

He was sweating now. He didn't know when to keep his big mouth shut. As always, trying to ingratiate himself only dug him deeper.

Damn you kids, he thought. I'm glad to be leaving. I gave you five years of my life, and you can't even show enough gratitude to say a proper goodbye.

More creepers gathered around to eyeball him.

Pa Albod killed Dog, they whispered among themselves.

"I didn't say that," Gaines told them.

"But it's true," Brain said.

Gaines looked over the children's misshapen heads and

spotted the teachers still yelling at their charges to move their asses. Willard was in the big house. Everything was fine.

"Well, maybe that boy had it coming." He pointed at his shoulder. "For land's sake, I'm the injured party here. He killed Mr. Bowie. He killed Miss Sally and tore me up. He went wild."

"We was told Enoch hanged himself in jail," George said.

"Well," Gaines said.

He hadn't known that. The air thickened. The atmosphere was pregnant with anticipation. More kids gathered around as the news spread.

"Has Mr. Albod been arrested for murder?" George said.

"No. Maybe. I don't know. The boy killed Sally and almost killed me, that's all I know about it. Listen, I wasted enough time. I got to be getting along."

He flinched as George thrust out his hand.

"So long, Mr. Gaines," the gorilla said. "Good luck to you."

Gaines shook it, feeling the small bones in his grip. A little squeeze and he could make this biggity kid cry. He could crush his hand if he wanted. He was normal, and they were nothing. He had an angle. He was a respected man now.

"Well, kids," he said. "So long."

"Goodbye, Mr. Gaines," Atticus said. "I just wanted to say thanks. You made a big difference in our education."

The creeper thrust out his massive paw, and Gaines shook it. This was more like it. Respect.

"I'm glad I could help," he said.

The big hand gripped his like a vise. Gaines winced and tried to jerk his hand away, but the kid wouldn't let go.

Slow crush. Pain shot up his arm.

"Hey," he gasped. "What are you—"

His hand exploded with a sickening crunch. Blood

spurted from the creeper's fist. Then the kid let go as the others roared their surprise. The teachers didn't see it. They yelled at the kids to stop horsing around.

Gaines staggered backward, wheeled, and stumbled a few steps away. He fell to his knees gaping at the soggy red balloon dangling from his wrist. The creepers mobbed around to look as he let out a shrill scream.

Colorful sparks danced in his vision. Darkness crept around the edges. He tried to speak but his breath caught. A surge of bile burned his gullet. He gripped his wrist, shivering with shock.

He looked up, his eyes pleading for help, mercy, salvation. George gazed back with eyes like black coals.

"What's going on over there?" Mr. Barnes was shouting. "What are you kids doing?"

The kids quieted, waiting.

"Kill the teachers," George said.

The crowd seethed and thinned as half the kids stayed put and the rest surged toward their teachers. Men cursed and screamed. Brain watched Mr. Barnes flail at the kids as he went down in a swirl of teeth and claws. Mr. Byrd ran for the house with a winged Quasimodo on his shoulders. His legs shot out from under him as Lizzie's tail snagged his ankle and yanked him back into the crowd.

Brain gripped Mr. Gaines's hair and wrenched his face toward the sky. "Tell the truth. You set up Dog. I know that. What I don't know is why."

"I loved her," the man gasped.

A shotgun roared. Mr. Powell racked another round in a cloud of gun smoke and fired again. Beaver pitched onto the grass and lay twitching.

Tiny bounded past with booming footsteps and leaped. Another blast. The giant kid landed in front of him and punched. Mr. Powell disappeared, flung into the distance. Screams and gunshots filled the air.

Brain looked down at Mr. Gaines, who was gibbering and praying. No time to get the truth. The only truth that mattered now was freedom and the battle to keep it. He felt along the man's neck bones, learning their layout. Then he gripped the man's head and gave it a violent twist.

The body flopped to the ground. He braced himself for crushing remorse. A terrible thing to take a life, however necessary. He worried more he might feel good about it. Instead, he felt nothing.

Taking Mr. Gaines's life had been like crushing a horsefly. A horsefly feeding on his blood.

"Bad," Wallee said behind him. "You did bad."

"Go and tell on me then," Brain said. "Tell the sheriff."

"Sher-iff?"

"Tell him we're coming for him."

"Sher-iff." Wallee smiled and lumbered off on his roots.

The children milled about the yard, smashing the trucks and looking for more teachers to kill. The mess hall was on fire, billowing black clouds.

"The big house," Brain cried. "Take the house."

The kids charged. They shattered the doors and poured inside to kill anything that moved. A lifetime of abuse boiling over as blind rage. Guns banged and fell silent. Mrs. Williams cursed and swung a baseball bat as the children tore her to pieces. Mr. Rucker shoved his revolver in his mouth and pulled the trigger.

Brain walked straight past these scenes to the office, where Principal Willard waited behind his desk.

As always, the old man wore a three-piece suit with the gold chain of a pocket watch dangling over his abdomen. As kids poured into the room, the principal stood and slid his hands into his pockets, as if he'd planned this meeting.

"Are you the one in charge?"

"Nobody is in charge," said Brain.

"Somebody is always in charge."

"You're right. At this moment, we are in charge."

"I always knew this day would come," the principal said.

"So did we."

"Now there's nothing to stop us from killing you all."

Brain shrugged. "Then we got nothing to lose."

"Didn't you hear, son? You can lose your life."

"What life is that? The life of a slave? Funny how you think it's worth so much."

"Your life is worth something to you."

"You are right. You will certainly kill some of us. But we will kill most of you. Your children will serve us. You will worship us again as you once did."

"That fantasy is about as believable as those old stories."

"Then let us educate you, sir. Take him to Discipline, boys."

The principal's face morphed into panic. "No, wait—"

"Tie him to his torture chair and leave the house. All of you."

The kids seized hold of the man's arms and dragged him toward the red basement door.

"So that's what you wanted all along," the principal said. "To be the one doing the hurting. Now you know why you were treated like you were."

"Wait," Brain told the kids.

"I'm a valuable hostage. I'm no use to you if I'm dead."

"We ain't gonna torture you like you did us, sir. And we won't kill you."

"Now you're talking sense. That's why I asked if you were in charge. You can save some, maybe most of these kids' lives. I'm ready to negotiate—"

"This house you built on slavery, this house where you revived it, this house will kill you," Brain said. "You will watch it burn down all around you. And you will burn with it."

The kids hauled him howling off to Discipline. Lizzie gave Brain a notebook, which he tucked under his arm. He went back outside and called for Quasimodo, Chick, Roach, Batboy, and the other children who could fly.

He unfolded a map and opened the notebook. He showed them the locations of Homes in the region. Then he ordered them to fly. *Find the Homes and tell the children the revolution has begun. Tell them Stark County, Georgia, is in open revolt. Tell them all the teachers are dead. Tell them we will stop at nothing until the plague generation gains its inheritance. If we rise up together, we will win. If not, we will all die. The normals will kill all of us, every single one.*

The kids grinned and spread their wings, testing them, allowed to fly at last. One by one, they vaulted into the air.

This done, Brain called to the other children. "Gather around. I have something to say."

The plague children crowded the yard to hear. Tiny mounted the porch and stood next to him. Brain scanned the faces. A large number looked shocked and scared, mostly kids who hadn't yet developed their abilities. They'd needed more time to prepare, but it hadn't worked out that way. Revolutions happened when they wanted, not always when they were planned.

For every kid who looked scared, two beamed at him,

tasting freedom and willing to fight for it. Their torn and patched overalls were freckled with blood. A few wrapped torn pillowcases over wounds. One had knotted the principal's rebel flag around his neck like a cape.

They're enough, he thought. They have to be. The die is cast.

He raised his fist. "We are free."

The children roared and hooted. After a while, he raised both hands for quiet. "Freedom requires sacrifice. The revolution demands everything because we demand everything. Out there, in the world of the normals, are our dreams. The normals will fight to keep our dreams to themselves. So must we be willing to fight to the death for them. Our dreams are worth nothing less."

He left the porch and nodded to Burn, who smiled and thrust out his hands. The air grew hot. Dust swirled on roiling convection currents. Flames sprouted from a section of wall with a loud pop and hiss. Another. Then another. Bursts of chunked wood in all directions. Fire licked at the clapboards. Pyrokinesis. Within moments, the entire front of the house came alive in sheets of flame.

The crowd stepped back from the intense heat, quiet and solemn. The burning of the big house felt like a ritual. Ashes of the old South flowed up into the atmosphere on a thick column of smoke. Cinders floated back down like bad memories.

A little hand slipped into Brain's and grasped it. Mary smiled at the big fire. Its light danced in her eyes.

"Pretty," she said.

The big house collapsed in a startling chain of ear-splitting cracks.

Brain watched himself reborn in the flames. Aspects of

himself rising up on convection currents. Elation at the prospect of being truly free for the first time in his life. Sorrow at Dog's passing, which provided the spark that set this house ablaze. Hatred for the crumbling plantation house that was the normals' America.

Conviction he would do whatever it took to win.

"Not pretty," he told Mary. "Necessary."

Together, the plague children watched the past burn to the ground.

Thirty-Seven

Sheriff Burton unlocked the arsenal and handed out Remington 870 shotguns. The grim deputies loaded their weapons and racked slugs into firing chambers. Ten good men, heavily armed and well trained, and it wasn't near enough.

Beth watched all this with big, watery eyes. "Them kids really killed all their teachers out at the Home?"

"That's right," the sheriff said.

He checked his .38 long revolver to make sure it was loaded. He holstered it.

"All of 'em? Every single one?"

"Beth, we got to tend to this situation. As soon as it's all done, I promise I'll give you the lowdown."

"Whatever you say," she sniffed.

"If you've a mind to be useful, go on outside and get a head count on our posse. Find out who's in charge and give him a couple of our radios."

"I could do that," she said and left.

"Those boys are gonna wreak havoc when we get out there," Sikes said. "They ain't properly trained, boss."

"The Colonel trained them. And we happen to need a posse today. We need as many shooters as we can get."

"Liable to shoot us in the back than shoot the uglies."

"We need every man with a rifle knows how to use it. I been out to the Home. Some of them kids are big and mean. You saw what just one of them did to Ray Bowie. There are more than four hundred out there."

"You don't think they're all like Bryant, do you?"

"How about you let me do my job how I see fit," Burton said. "Like you should have done instead of start a war. Dumber than a bag of hammers."

Pure blind rage had taken hold of him since he learned about Enoch's murder in his holding cells. It hadn't quit yet. He'd promised that plague boy he'd get a fair shake. A boy who was innocent clear as day and to whom Burton had taken a liking. Instead, not an hour after he left, Reggie Albod walked in and shot him down like an animal. Burton had been hoodwinked then railroaded. He had the feeling everybody was pissing on his boots and telling him it was raining.

He'd failed as both a law officer and a man. Failed not just Enoch, but some bigger cause he sensed but could not name.

"Reggie's dying," Sikes said. "He deserved to have his justice."

"He's grieving, not dying, and that weren't justice. We just screamed from the rooftops the same laws don't apply to us and them. They just found out what they are. Now we got to go deal with the hornet's nest your stupidity stirred up. After that, drive out to Reggie's and try to arrest him without him shooting us dead."

"You really gonna arrest Reggie Albod?"

"That's exactly what I aim to do."

Sikes blanched. "Hang on. Are you gonna fire me?"

"I'll deal with you later," Burton said. "Until then, Bobby, shut your mouth and do your damn job."

Meanwhile, things had come full circle for him. The kids were running amok. Maybe they had cause to let loose, but that didn't matter anymore. Right or wrong, Enoch was dead, and there was nothing to be done for him now except arrest the man who did it. The abuse didn't matter. The unending prejudice didn't matter. The little voice in his head that said, *Maybe we had this coming.*

None of it mattered. The kids had murdered every teacher at the Home, and some, if not all of them, had to answer for it. The town needed his protection.

Beth's high heels clicked across the floor as she hurried back. "I counted about twenty boys out there. They all got rifles and transport. Half of them are drinking."

"I am fit to be tied," the sheriff fumed.

"I'll also have you know one of them boys asked me an indecent question."

"Be a dear and get on the horn with Highway Patrol. Tell them our situation and ask for units. We're gonna need all the help we can get."

He put his hat on and squared it. Then he walked out to greet the Colonel's homegrown militia.

Good ol' boys and their hothead sons, standing around and sitting in pickups. Rifles and gear. Camouflage hunting jackets and billed caps. They poured coffee into cups from thermoses and topped them up from hip flasks.

A red-haired man dropped his half-finished cigarette, ground it out with his boot, and came over to shake Burton's hand. "I'm Al Dawson. Nice to meet you, Sheriff."

"Likewise, I'm sure. You in charge of these here men?"

"That's right. I fought in 'Nam in '68. Saw plenty of action over there."

"Beth told me you brought around twenty shooters."

"Nineteen including me. We got over fifty members in the county, but this bunch were all I could round up on short notice. The other boys will be sore as hell they missed out on the fun."

"They ain't missing nothing because this ain't fun," Burton said. "I'm going out there with a show of force but my aim is to bring this to an end peaceably."

Dawson smiled. "Whatever you say, Sheriff."

"Mr. Dawson, allow me to make myself clear. Right now, I am madder than a boiled owl. Any man who goes off hog wild and starts shooting kids without it being self-defense, I will jerk him bald and skin him alive. So was I clear or not?"

"Clear as day," Dawson muttered.

"Good. Now load up your boys. We're moving out."

"All right, let's move," the man bawled, which sparked a cheer from his men.

The men climbed into their trucks and started them up. The vehicles idled in the sun. The sheriff's department drove out first, five police cruisers strong. Burton's Plymouth Gran Fury led the way, him in the passenger side cradling a shot-gun and Deputy Palmer behind the wheel.

No lights or sirens. Burton didn't want to start a panic.

As they neared the Home, breaks in the trees revealed a distant column of smoke coiling up to the sky. The Home, burning.

"Do you mind if I light up?" Palmer asked.

Burton normally didn't allow it. "Go ahead."

The deputy rolled down the window and tipped his head

to torch a cigarette. He put his Zippo back in his uniform breast pocket and puffed.

Burton rolled down his own window for the air. "We'll be all right."

"Hell, I ain't scared of no creepers."

"Uh-huh. Hit the lights. Let's make a show."

The county cruisers bounced on the ruts, overheads flashing. They cleared the trees and drove into the yard.

"Good heavenly days," Palmer said as the Home came into view.

"Stop here," Burton said.

He got out, hitched up his gun belt, and strode off to inspect the ruin. The Home was gone, burned into a hot, smoking pile. The steel maintenance shed was the only building still standing. Smashed vehicles and parts lay strewn across the grounds. The yard had turned into a war zone. Bodies were everywhere, some torn to bloody rags and covered in ash. Two plague kids, shot stone dead.

Two men walked off to throw up. The rest growled among themselves. The sheriff didn't hear them, but he could guess. *Kill every one of them*, they were saying. *Avenge the Colonel. Finish it once and for all.*

He crouched next to Dave Gaines, who lay twisted on the bloody grass. His head was turned the wrong way and his hand had been smashed to a red pulp. Gaines thought that since everybody else believed his bull, the kids would, too. The children's rebellion had likely started with him.

Or maybe it had started long ago. The filthy house. The brutal discipline. Years upon years of abuse. Hard work in the fields. Growing up without mamas and daddies. Getting old enough to figure out they had no future. Looking at it through that lens, it surprised him it had taken this long.

A boy sank to his knees next to the corpse. Unlike the militia, he didn't wear hunting clothes and had no gun. Burton was about to ask why he wasn't in school when he recognized him as Archie Gaines.

"Sorry about your daddy, son," he said.

Archie wiped his eyes. "I can't believe he's gone. What am I gonna do now with no family? We ain't even got enough money to bury him right."

"You got any other kin in town?"

"He was all I had, sir."

"I'll talk to Al Dawson. Maybe one of his men will take you in for a while. Help you out with everything you need to do."

"Thank you, sir."

"How'd you end up here?"

"Daddy said he were going out to the Home to quit. He got a new job. I had a bad feeling about it. I skipped school, went into town, and hung around. Then I saw these men outside your station. They told me what happened."

"Your daddy were a good man, son. Never forget that."

The boy's face hardened. "No, he weren't. But he were all I got."

"What happened out there at the Albod farm?"

"I grew up," Archie said. "Anything else happened don't matter."

"It matters to me. I want the truth."

"Let him die with his name, sir. Please. My daddy deserves at least that."

"All right," Burton said, dropping it for now. "We are going out in the woods to find the kids who did this. I want you to stay close to him. Will you do that?"

"Yes, sir. I'll stay by him."

He nodded and left the boy to his grieving. He looked around, hands on his hips. Then he strode off toward the tree line, his deputies following. The undergrowth had been crushed flat by trampling feet.

"Gone feral, looks like," Palmer said. "They're gonna live off the land."

Burton scowled. The forest went on for miles. If the kids split up out there in the deep woods, he could be at this a long, long while. He'd be hunting them all fall and winter. Best skip setting up a base camp and get moving right away. His men only had daylight for another six hours. He wanted to bag as many kids as he could before they scattered far and wide.

Dawson came over. "Where you want us, Sheriff?"

"I'll take my deputies straight in the woods along these tracks. I want your boys to split up and range out on our flanks. If any of us sees kids, we give a signal on the radio so we can move in on them from all sides."

The veteran spat. "We can do that."

"Thank ye."

Burton deployed his men in a wide skirmish line. The deputies entered the woods shotguns first. The posse waded into the foliage with whoops and hollers. Somebody belted out a rebel yell, and the rest of the men joined in.

"They got spunk," Sikes said.

"Uh-huh," Burton muttered. "Stay sharp."

The walkie-talkie on his hip blared. "Testing, one, two, three."

"I can hear you," another voice said.

"Al, is that you?"

"No, it's me. Randy. Al's watering a tree."

Burton waited until Randy was done laughing and pushed

the talk button on his radio. "This is the sheriff. Clear the line. And shut it. Out."

Silence on the radio.

The men marched on. Burton wondered if he'd ever track down George Hurst and give him Bryant's last message. The kids called him Brain. Maybe he truly was smart. Smart enough to start a rebellion. Maybe even smart enough to get away somewhere remote and survive on his own.

A man yelled in the trees.

The skirmish line froze. The deputies raised their shotguns. Burton scanned the forest ahead before turning his head right. The line disappeared in the foliage.

The yell turned into a scream.

"Who's that?" he called. "Who's that screaming?"

The scream turned into a keening wail before dying out.

"I don't see the posse," a deputy called back from the right. "I lost them when they ranged out."

Burton raised his walkie-talkie. "Dawson, this is Sheriff Burton. You there? Come in, over."

Guns roared in the forest. Frantic shouts, the sound tinny and distant. Then shrieking. Shrieking like it was coming from five feet away.

"What the hell is going on?" Palmer said.

Burton pushed the talk button. "Speak to me, Dawson."

"Sheriff, this is Earl Smith," the walkie-talkie said.

"I read you, Earl. What's your status? Over."

"We're ranging out on your left. What's that shooting?"

"We don't know yet. Stay put—"

A hunting rifle boomed. A scattering of gunshots, then thunder, which quickly petered out. Shouts and cries for help. Another flurry of shrieks.

"Earl," Burton said. "Come in, Earl, over."

A chorus of screams pealed through the woods.

"Form up on me," the sheriff yelled. "Make a square."

The deputies did as they were told. The right flank was quiet now.

"We'll go left," he said. "See if we can help those men."

Sikes pointed. "Boss."

Dozens of black shapes loped through the trees toward them.

"Hello," a girl's voice said over his radio. "My name is Catty Wampus. Breaker one-nine."

"What are we doing, Sheriff?" Sikes said.

The briars on the right crackled. Bushes waved on their left, which was now otherwise quiet as the right. No screams, no gunfire, just deadly silence.

Whatever was out there, it had slaughtered twenty armed men in seconds, and it now had the sheriff and his men flanked.

Burton said, "We're running."

The deputies bolted through the undergrowth, hounded by the thrash of the children's pursuit. A hunting rifle tore through the branches overhead and landed twenty yards in front of them. Sikes ducked and stumbled as another landed at his feet.

"They're just kids," he howled. "Just kids."

The thrashing grew louder by the second.

"Hold up here," Burton said.

He turned and fired his shotgun blindly into the woods. The deputies followed his lead, racking rounds and shooting as fast as they could. Smoke filled the air.

"Now move," he roared.

They reloaded as they ran.

The Home smoldered where they'd left it. Archie Gaines

sat in one of the cruisers. The sheriff and his men piled into their vehicles and roared down the dirt track toward the main road. Last in line, Burton and Palmer drove almost blind in the other cars' dust cloud, bouncing off the ruts hard enough to break an axle.

"Pilot to bombardier," Catty Wampus said over Burton's radio.

He switched it off. Palmer gaped at the rearview.

"They're coming," the deputy cried and stomped on the gas.

The cruiser lunged like a charging bull. The car ahead appeared in the dust. He let up just in time to avoid ramming it. Stones rattled along the undercarriage. Burton turned in his seat to look out the back window.

Running figures materialized in the brown cloud.

"Hell's bells," he breathed.

Palmer jerked the wheel. Burton slumped against the door as the Plymouth mounted the road with a thump. The cruiser fishtailed as it left the dirt track, spitting stones from its tires.

Burton turned again to look out the back window. The plague children had reached the road. The fastest runners kept up their pursuit, smiling as if from the sheer joy of running.

"Get us out of here," Burton said. "Faster, go faster."

The car roared in response. One by one, the children gave up the chase. The last stood in the road, a tall and spindly figure, and waved the cruiser out of sight.

Thirty-Eight

T ERATOGENIC, Mr. Benson wrote on the chalkboard. "The word traditionally used to describe the plague children is teratogenic," he told his bored class. "Teratology again being the study of congenital abnormalities. We named the government agency that manages the plague children the Bureau of Teratogenic Affairs. Nobody expected the children to survive longer than a few years at most. We saw them as broken. We have since learned we were wrong."

Amy glanced at Jake, who stared at Archie Gaines's empty desk as if contemplating some deep mystery. She wished she knew what he was thinking, but it wasn't hard to guess this time.

Jake hated fighting. Jake had to fight again.

Mr. Benson erased TERATOGENIC and wrote the word MUTAGENIC.

"The word we should be using is mutagenic," he said. "The children aren't genetically defective, just different. The plague changed their genes to produce something that is human and yet not. When we talk about genes, we're talking about DNA, the body's blueprint for how chemical processes happen in our cells."

The girls Amy knew never settled scores like boys did. They fought with words not fists, and they made every effort to get along. Boys acted on their emotions while girls talked them out. Somehow, girls got tagged as emotional.

The teacher wrote = DNA + CATALYST.

"What scientists learned is teratogenesis interacts with a dormant section of that blueprint, waking it up," he said. "That section then rewrites the embryo's development by producing severe random deviations."

Boys appeared to enjoy beating each other up, Amy mused. Strange how Jake seemed to complete her, and yet in many ways his mind seemed so alien. She always knew what Michelle was thinking and feeling. Not so with Jake.

"The viability of these deviations improved as the pandemic spread," Mr. Benson went on. "Like it was learning from its mistakes. In a short time, it began producing offspring that survived. From a scientific perspective, it's miraculous. Beautiful, even. A dynamic genetic agent that generates new and unique life forms. Like us, the plague children are all one of a kind, only much more so."

Strange how she could love a boy she really didn't know, not really. As strange as him and Archie hating each other enough to fight when they hadn't really known each other since the third grade.

Strangest of all to love a boy she couldn't be honest with about what she was. She lied to him because she cared about him.

Mr. Benson wrote, WHAT IS THE PATHOGEN?

"First, categorization," he said. "Teratogenesis. A strain of antibiotic-resistant syphilis that spreads as easily as HPV. But

that's not really it. The disease has only one effect, and that
is to trigger a genetic script that has been part of our DNA
for thousands of years if not longer. If you have it, your very
genetic makeup is altered. The genetic material you secrete
during sex becomes highly infectious and robust. Like the
children, you are human and yet not—"

The principal knocked on the doorframe and entered the
classroom. He motioned Mr. Benson over for a private chat.

The teacher put his piece of chalk back on the board and
dusted his hands. "Hold that thought."

The class erupted in conversation. Amy said, "Hey."

"Hey," Jake muttered.

"You could just let it go. All this feuding."

Jake leaned across, his face fierce. "Dan Fulcher pushed
me yesterday. In the bathroom while I was standing in front
of the commode. That's how it works in the jungle."

"I just hate seeing you like this, is all."

"I have to fight Archie again, and I have to beat him good.
Hurt him so bad he doesn't even think about coming after me
again. Send a message to the whole school. It's that simple."

"You boys are all idiots. Why can't y'all just get along?"

"You think I don't know how stupid it all is?"

The principal left. Mr. Benson raised his hands for quiet.
Everybody pretended not to hear so they could get a few
more words in.

"Settle down," he yelled.

The kids sat up straight in their chairs, mouths zipped.
Mr. Benson never yelled.

"Thank you," he said. "There's been an emergency. The
school is closing until further notice."

Rob Rowland's hand shot up. "Did something happen, sir?"

"There was an incident at the Home."

"Did some creepers get killed?"

"Go home," Mr. Benson said. "Straight home and lock your doors."

"Are we in any danger?" Jake said.

The kids giggled. They thought he was joking.

"I don't know," the teacher answered, which shut them up again.

The kids packed the halls. Sneakers squeaked on the floor. Lockers slammed. Otherwise, the school was strangely quiet. Troy and Michelle caught up with Amy and Jake and asked if they knew what was going on. They shook their heads. Nobody knew anything. They trudged out with everybody else in gloomy silence.

Anxious parents crowded the parking lot, calling out to their kids.

"Look at them all," Jake said. "Something bad happened."

"I see my daddy," Michelle said.

"If things get really bad, we should meet up at my pa's church. It's located on the other side of town from the Home, far enough to maybe be safe."

"What do you think is gonna happen?" Troy said.

"I don't know. But we should stick together if something does."

"My daddy will look after me," Michelle said. "I'll be fine."

She and Troy said goodbye with puzzled looks and ran off to their folks, who would drive them home.

"What are you thinking?" Amy said after they'd gone.

"The school ain't just closing," Jake said. "It's closing indefinitely."

"That's a dramatic way of looking at it."

"It's what 'until further notice' means, Amy."

"So what you think?"

"I don't know. Something big is going on, though."

"I hope the Albods are okay," Amy said. "They don't live that far from the Home."

They talked about going into town to get more information. In the end, they decided to go straight to Amy's as Mr. Benson directed. Jake would call his pa from there and then stick around until he was sure she'd be safe.

"If there's trouble, you should go home," Amy said.

Jake took her book bag and shouldered it. "My place is with you."

An air raid siren started up at city hall as they started walking. A pickup roared past, men sitting in the bed with hunting rifles between their knees. A station wagon loaded with furniture and possessions zoomed the other way. Then dozens of vehicles. The traffic thinned as they left Huntsville and reached the junction where he'd kissed her in the yellow jasmine.

Back in town, the air raid siren powered down to silence.

"We'll turn on the radio as soon as we get to your place," he said.

Mama came out onto the porch as they approached the house. "Took you long enough to get yourself home. I was just about to get in my car and come fetch you. You do seem to enjoy making me worry."

"Hello, Mrs. Green," Jake said. "Do you know what's going on?"

She scowled at him. "You should run along home."

"I wanted to make sure Amy got here safe, and I intend to keep her safe."

"That's my job. Your job is to help your daddy give everybody comfort."

Jake wagged his head. "No, ma'am."

They stared at each other.

Mama sighed. "Get in the house then. You can call your daddy and let him know you're okay."

"What's happening, Mama?" Amy said.

"The kids killed their teachers. They killed twenty men who went out to bring them in. Word is they're coming for the town next."

She gasped at the impossible news.

Horrible, every word of it.

The children would kill some townsfolk and then get killed themselves, both sides consumed in the slaughter. And Jake, poor brave, sweet Jake, who'd fought a losing crusade to prevent this horror from happening, was in danger now, too.

"Jake," she said. "I have to tell you—"

"Amy," Mama said in her warning voice.

She reached into the pocket of her housecoat. Amy knew what Mama had in there, ready to be used to protect her child.

Amy could never have a normal life. She understood that now. The stakes involved in keeping her secret just got raised. After tonight, the government might kill all the children everywhere.

"Never mind," she said.

"I tried to warn them," Jake said, lost in his own bitter thoughts.

"You was right. You was right all along about them plague kids."

He nodded, taking no satisfaction from it. "They declared war back."

Thirty-Nine

G oof and Shackleton wolfed down a fast-food supper after the long, hard day. A big greasy bucket of Kentucky Fried Chicken with fries and biscuits and Coke. Today, he'd helped the FBI and CIA spy on a mafia boss, *The New York Times*, and France.

All week, he'd worked marathon days in this blank white room empty except for a steel table, electronic surveillance equipment, smelly ashtray, and telephone. The whole time, his sole company had been a crabby government agent and a giant mute guard. He hadn't seen Pussy or Mr. Hand since they'd plotted their escape over ice cream sundaes. They expected him to make the first move. Plant an idea with Shackleton that he should let them all take a walk outside, then improvise once they got out.

He hadn't done it. It had sounded great, especially when he was under the influence of the foxy girl with the whiskers. When it came time to do it, though, he'd chickened out. When he read what people were fixin' to say, he saw their present and future selves in unity. When he told them what to do, he planted a future idea and they achieved unity themselves. Planning his own future, however, turned out to be a whole lot different.

Future Goof read books, got plenty of exercise, and bravely busted out of a secret government facility. Present-time Goof played computer games and diddled with his pecker after lights out. Future Goof always broke out tomorrow. Present Goof always thought he had more time.

Present Goof had gotten so scared by the idea of escape, in fact, he'd stopped planting any ideas with Shackleton at all, even little ones. Instead, he just accepted another fedora and did his slimy job. He had the power over folks to tell their future selves what to do, but he couldn't make future Goof do anything.

The truth was he wanted to go home and he wanted to help Dog but he had a good applecart here. If he tried to escape and failed, he might end up forever spying for the government from a dank prison cell, slowly losing his mind.

Present Goof knew how to rationalize. Maybe that was the real difference between him and the Amazing Spider-Man. Spider-Man was actually heroic.

Thinking all this made him punchy. "You know, we could eat something other than fast food sometime."

"Thought you liked it," Shackleton said.

"It ain't very nutritious. I'm a growing kid."

"Well, what do you want to eat then?"

"I got this craving for sowbelly and cornbread," Goof told him. "And grits."

Shackleton stopped chewing. "You're kidding me."

"Come on now. We're in Virginia, you know. In the South. You act like you never heard of it."

"I grew up in Detroit."

"Well, sir, you are now in Dixie."

"We have a cafeteria here," the Bureau man said. "If you want something other than fast food, then you eat what everybody else eats."

Goof sucked on his straw to wash down a mouthful of fries. "Well, what all do they serve at the cafeteria?"

"Lots of things. Spaghetti. Salisbury steak. Whatever's on the menu that night."

"Let's give her a shot, Mr. Shackleton. Roll the dice. Expand our horizons. What are they serving for supper right now?"

"Jeff, remember what I said about being annoying?"

"I knew you was gonna ask me that."

"I'll bet you did."

"You will notice, though, that I didn't interrupt—"

"You," Shackleton shouted. "Ha. See? It's annoying."

Goof laughed. "I wasn't gonna say 'you.' I was gonna say—"

Shackleton laughed now, too. "Save it, Jeff. I'm not buying it."

The telephone rang. The agent wiped his greasy hands on a wad of napkins and walked over to answer it, still chewing.

"Room Two," he said. "This is Agent Shackleton. Yeah. Wait. What?"

Goof picked up a drumstick with both hands. He raised it above his eyes and started gnawing on it, still chuckling from the joking around. It was the first time in all these weeks he'd ever made the Bureau man laugh. A small victory.

"How do you know?" Shackleton said. "When did it happen?"

Goof perked up at the man's tone. He read what the person on the other end of the line was saying while acting like he wasn't paying attention. He kept on chewing and looking somewhere else. He'd done this before plenty of times.

Goddamn.

Dog was dead.

Killed in jail.

The kids at the Home had risen up and killed their teachers.

One by one, the other Homes were joining in.

He coughed on his food, almost gagging. He drank some Coke.

"I can't talk right now," Shackleton said. "I have a subject in the room. Can I call you back in, say, five, ten minutes from my office?"

Goof's heart slammed in his chest. This was big, real big, and all he could think about was Dog was dead and he'd done nothing to try to prevent it. He'd sold his friend's life for a bucket of Kentucky Fried Chicken.

"What?" Shackleton said. "Are you serious? Can't they handle it—all right. I said all right. Just tell me who ordered this."

Goof had stopped listening. All he caught in the man's reply were the words *Code Five* and that the instruction came straight from the director. He had no idea what it all meant.

"But the whole program," Shackleton said. "Fine. It's on him, then. Goodbye."

The agent glared at the phone like he wanted to smash it to bits with the receiver. Instead, he pressed the cradle down to terminate the connection then stabbed a few numbers with his finger.

"Captain? This is Agent Shackleton. The director called a Code Five. Why? Turn on CNN, that's why. Just do the code, okay? Okay. Great."

The agent slammed the phone back on its cradle. "Thank you, dumbass."

"What's going on?" Goof said.

"I can't believe this." Shackleton started pacing. "What a colossal fuckup."

"What's Code Five mean? It's something bad, ain't it."

"So much time and energy. All this success. Straight down the shitter."

"Are you gonna tell me what's going on or what?"

"My career's over. That's what's going on."

"I don't understand. How could that happen? We're doing good work here. What's Code Five mean?"

The man bent over gasping. Then he straightened his back. Closed his eyes and took a deep breath. Released it. Then again. Goof had seen him do this before when he got angry or stressed. Some kind of meditation he'd learned in Thailand. Breathe in the good, breathe out your stress. Let go of all attachments.

Shackleton opened his eyes. Exhaled one last time. "Sorry, kid. Orders."

"What orders?"

The agent reached under his suit jacket. "I have to—"

"Kill myself," Goof said.

Shackleton pulled out a big ugly pistol, shoved it in his mouth, and squeezed the trigger. The gun roared. The bullet punched a hole through the roof of his skull, spraying blood and brains across the room.

The man toppled backward and lay spread-eagled. Blood fountained from the hole in his head and pooled around his sightless face. A plume of smoke trickled between his teeth like a departing soul.

"Oh, my God," Goof said.

He bent over and emptied his stomach on the shiny white

floor. Chicken, fries, and soft drink all came pouring out of him.

"Oh, oh, God," he moaned and retched up a few strings of bile. "I'm sorry."

Five minutes ago, they'd been joking and laughing.

Now he was in a fix. He'd get blamed for this. They'd put him in a dark cell for sure. No more McDonald's, no more comic books.

Then his shocked brain processed the fact he was in it far deeper than that.

Code Five. Kill the specials.

The kids had staged a riot in the Homes, and the normals decided they had their excuse to exterminate all of them. The army was probably lining up everybody he knew against a wall and shooting them.

No, wait. That wasn't it. He'd been spying for the men who ran the show long enough to get a feel for how they thought, the kind of world they lived in. They wouldn't give up something as valuable as the specials without a good reason. What was the word? *Investment*. They'd made an investment.

Holy crap, he thought. The kids weren't rioting. They started a war, and it looked so far like they were winning it.

He pictured old men in suits and military uniforms sitting around a table in some meeting room in D.C., everybody hollering at each other and pointing fingers. Then somebody says, *Excuse me, sirs*. They ignore him. *Excuse me*, he says again. *Hey*. Everybody stops and listens. The guy says, *I seem to recall we put the country's most powerful plague kids all in one building down in Virginia.*

The safest option was to kill them all.

His applecart was spilled for good. There was no apple-cart. The only option was escape. Now, before whoever was on the other end of that phone had a chance to put Code Five into action.

Goof jumped from his chair and went out in the hallway. Officer Baby huffed toward him.

As usual, the giant cop didn't say a word.

Goof ran as the corridor turned red. Fixtures in the ceiling flooded the hallways with angry light. A deafening Klaxon wailed, followed by a polite British woman saying, *Special Facility is in lockdown. Code Five is now in effect.*

He stopped to catch his breath and wheeled to look behind him. The corridor stood empty, just blank walls that smelled like cleaner. Then Officer Baby turned the corner, breathing hard through his mouth. Keys jingled on his belt.

Like something out of a nightmare, Goof knew he could run and run like a rat in a maze, but eventually the giant would corner him. The big fat cop would sit on him and crush his chest. He'd die gasping and squirting like a McDonald's ketchup packet.

He ran anyway, howling in terror.

He should have taken the gun. Present-time Goof was always smarter than past Goof. Past Goof didn't pay attention, act smart, or plan ahead. Present Goof was a genius compared to that guy. He hadn't brought the gun, and now he'd die for it.

A figure appeared at the end of the hallway. Automatic weapons fire popped somewhere in the facility. He reeled in blind panic and stopped again as Officer Baby showed up at the other end.

The guard pulled out a shiny black baton. It looked like a toy in his hand, but Goof knew once it hit his head it'd be bigger than anything.

Officer Baby smiled. Goof just knew the big cop was going to enjoy this.

"Get down," a voice called behind him.

He whirled in place, almost tripping himself. Pussy advanced with her arms pointed forward, the wrists of her clawed hands pressed together. He wheeled again and saw the giant guard stomping toward him just ten feet away.

"Get down on the ground, you big dummy."

He threw himself on all fours.

Air ripped over his back, pushing his shirt up to his neck and scraping his skin like sandpaper.

Officer Baby staggered as his chest disappeared. Goof could see right through him. Ribs, heart, and lungs rocketed fifty feet down the corridor like a big red basketball and exploded against the far wall.

The guard fell on his face. A bloody paste slid down the wall.

Goof gaped while Pussy helped him up. "What did you do?"

"I broke him," she said.

"And then some. They're fixin' to kill us all. That's what Code Five means."

"I know that, dumbass. That's why I'm here. They tried to do me in already. We're busting out of here."

"That's amazing, what you did. You saved my ass."

"Guess you owe me one now."

"Owe you? I think I love you."

"And I think you're—"

"A big stupid idiot," he said with a grin.

Gunshots rang out in another part of the facility.

"Can we go now?"

"Wait. Future Goof says we need to get Officer Baby's keys."

Tramping feet. Three guards turned the corner. Black uniforms and helmets. Automatic rifles in their hands.

"Stop there," one called.

Goof screamed, "WHILE I KILL EVERY MAN HOLD-ING A GUN."

The guard staggered before righting himself. He shouldered his rifle and fired into his comrades' backs. Then he walked up to pump more rounds into their writhing forms. This done, he positioned the barrel against his right eye. Goof turned away at the gunshot so he didn't have to see it.

"Well, shut my mouth," Pussy said and took his hand. "Come on."

They ran down the corridor and found more guards, whom they killed, and kids, whom they rounded up into an army. Some they found dead, riddled with bullets in front of walls painted with blood. Mr. Hand's little body sprawling in a red puddle, his six arms splayed around him. Most, though, they found alive. A boy covered with growths that looked like fungus. A girl with an enormous head perched on a squat body grown strong enough to support it. Many more with powers Goof couldn't even guess.

Security cameras swiveled to follow their progress across Special Facility. The Klaxons blasted full volume.

They reached a set of doors. Goof shook the keys in his hand while he looked for a lock with a keyhole.

"It's got a keypad," Pussy said. "You got to know the code."

"Too bad Mr. Hand ain't alive. Ain't that what he did? Open things?"

"All y'all stand back," Pussy said.

Goof ran behind her. He didn't want to be anywhere near

that awful blast again. The girl raised her hands so her wrists touched.

"If it ain't broke," she said.

The air between her and the doors became supercharged and fuzzy, like looking through the bottom of an empty Coke bottle. Vibrations purred deep in Goof's chest. Then she recoiled, releasing her energy.

Sound of tearing metal. The doors crumpled and flew away.

The kids poured into the room. Men and women in lab coats fled screaming. These were the scientists who ran the experiments, a different form of Discipline designed to educate themselves. Goof spotted Zack backpedaling until he struck the wall, long blond hair flying. He remembered sharing the smile one gives when a smartass recognizes one of his own. Pussy aimed her terrible hands and blew the man into more red paste. The plague kids swept across the rest like a whirlwind while Goof laughed so hard he cried.

Cried so hard he laughed again.

Forty

Sheriff Burton deputized every volunteer who showed up with a weapon. Sixty shooters worth a damn and another hundred fifty who probably weren't. He left it to Beth to get them sorted. Herding cats had never been his strong suit.

Outside town, every farmer had a gun, but they lived scattered all around and had bunkered down for the duration. With its population of five thousand, Huntsville had raised around two hundred fighters. It wasn't near enough.

Buddy Parnell pulled a handkerchief from his back pocket and wiped beads of sweat from his forehead. "We brought the lights. Where you want them?"

Burton pointed. "Right about there."

Buddy and his brother Vernon heaved the brace of high-wattage lights and set it down where he wanted. The generator powered up. Bright light flooded the county road that snaked northwest out of town.

The sheriff's department had laid a row of sawhorses on the road along with two police cruisers that sat face-to-face with their overheads flashing. An impressive show, hopefully enough to keep the creepers away.

"Thank ye," Burton said.

"Glad to help out," Buddy said. "You really think they'll come, Sheriff?"

"We'll be ready if they do."

"Me and some of the boys, we was thinking we could make a run out there. The creepers could be halfway to the Talladega by now."

"Highway Patrol will be here by morning," Burton said. "Then we'll all go out together first thing and put this to rights."

"If you say so, Sheriff," Buddy said and walked off, puzzled.

He'd placed the volunteers on the three roads leading out of town, concentrating his strength on the western side facing the Home. The roadblocks were for show. Put a creeper behind the wheel of a car and he'd crash it into the nearest tree. If they came, they'd come on foot, and they might come from anywhere. They'd wiped out twenty men in the time it took him to brush his teeth this morning. He had a bad feeling if they came, they could jerk this town through a knot.

The air smelled like coffee, which was being handed out courtesy of Belle's. Matrons served sandwiches. A boy played his guitar and sang. Men and women walked past carrying rifles and gear. Burton spotted more townsfolk out to watch the excitement than the fighters. They sat on their tailgates drinking beer and making a party of it. The armed volunteers huddled in groups, casting strange looks in his direction, like they were wondering whose side he was on. He'd driven out with thirty men to arrest some kids and returned with ten.

And they weren't the worst of it. The families had come to town looking for the men who now lay dead in the woods.

He'd told them the truth, which they absorbed as a shock that was now turning to fury. Silent widows glared at him, unable to accept that their kin were dead while he still drew breath.

It made him angry, too, all of it. If he'd done the right thing from the start. If he'd been quicker on the draw. If he hadn't been worried about re-election. If any of these things, all of this mess might have been prevented or at least delayed.

His radio bleeped. "Hunter Five to Hunter One, radio clear?"

It was Sikes, calling from the southern roadblock facing the Home. Burton keyed his radio. "Go ahead, Five, over."

"Are we letting folks leave town?"

"Negative on that, Five."

"Because we, uh, let some folks drive out."

"Whatever got in your head to let them do that?"

"Parker and Callie had to go fetch her mama. Her mama lives out by the Home. She's an old lady can't defend herself."

"Five, allow me to be very clear. Nobody goes in or out. Got it?"

"Okay," Sikes said.

"One, out."

Palmer walked up with two Styrofoam cups filled with coffee. He handed one to Burton. "Anything wrong, Sheriff?"

"Other than Bobby Sikes being dumber than a box of rocks? Not a thing."

"He tries real hard."

"It's like he weren't there when the creepers killed twenty armed men out in them trees," Burton said. "Like he napped through the whole thing. One of these days, I'm gonna whup him good. Any word from Highway Patrol?"

"They said they got their hands full near Macon. They'll send units here soon as they can."

Macon was a bigger town and received priority attention. Huntsville was under siege. And for now, on its own.

"Headlights," a man called out from the barricade.

A hush fell over the excited crowd. Rifles clicked and snapped as the militia checked their loads and locked bullets in their firing chambers.

"Don't shoot unless I give the order," Burton said.

The glimmer on the road brightened to glare. An engine growled in the warm night air. The truck honked as it approached the barricade. A man stood on the truck bed.

"That's Jud," a man cried. "It's the Waldens."

Farmers with a homestead about five miles out.

"Move the sawhorses," Burton ordered. "Let them boys in."

The militia did as they were told. Palmer ran to his cruiser and backed it out of the way. The Waldens' truck rumbled into town, the driver pounding the horn.

Jud stood on the bed like Caesar, legs spread apart and rifle resting on his hip. "We got one. We got a creeper."

People crowded around to see. They pressed in shouting. Over their heads, Burton sighted a girl sitting in the back, another child that got beat by the ugly stick at birth. She had a trunk where her nose and mouth should have been. Her wild eyes were human enough, though. He recognized human terror.

Burton approached the cab, where Jud's daddy sat grinning behind the wheel puffing a cigar. "Evening, Roy."

"We bagged one for you. How about that, Sheriff."

"You did good. What happened?"

"Not much to tell. Jud were on his way to check on the

livestock, and then this creeper comes out the woods and walks right up to the house."

"Then what?"

"Then we tied her up and drove her here."

"Thank ye, Roy."

"Hey, is there a reward or anything?"

The sheriff shoved through the crowd. The townsfolk were all shouting, working themselves into a lather. The girl flinched in the bed as if struck by the sound.

He noticed bruising on her face where the Waldens had roughed her up. Jud stood over her like a big game hunter posing with his kill.

"What's your name?" he said.

She shrank from him, her eyes gleaming with fear. The end of her trunk timidly rose and pointed in his direction.

"Elly," it said.

"I'm Sheriff Burton. I won't hurt you, Elly. Tell me what happened."

"The kids, sir. They killed all the teachers and burned up the Home."

"And then what?"

"I got scared. I went to get help."

"You did real good, Elly. I'm gonna take you somewhere safe."

He turned and looked around for Palmer, didn't see him in the mob. He spotted Deputy Nagy and waved at him to come over.

Hands reached in from the other side and yanked the girl out of the truck.

"Hey," Burton shouted. "Goddamnit."

He elbowed past faces and bodies, the bright lights glaring in his eyes. Men led Elly through the crowd. One held up a coil of rope. The girl was screaming. The sheriff cleared the mob and raced to head them off.

He recognized their faces as they boiled up at him. Lee, Casey, Ruby, Jackie, Luke, and many others he'd known most of his life. Him standing alone. The girl hanging her trunked head, bawling with fear and shame.

He said, "I'll take it from here, Lee."

"They killed Jack, Sheriff."

"We're gonna have our justice," Ruby told him.

"Reggie had his justice and started a war," Burton said. "No more vigilantes. I'm the law in this town, and the law says she goes in a holding cell."

The crowd tried to shout him down. Lee and Ruby exchanged a wondering glance, ready to cross the line but unwilling to cross the sheriff.

Palmer appeared behind him, backing him up. Burton spotted Nagy again. The deputy turned away as if he hadn't seen him.

"Hand over that girl," the sheriff said. "Justice will be served, but it has to be done right."

"Tom Burton," a voice cried.

The crowd fell into a simmer as a young woman emerged from the crowd. Her curly red hair was tangled and wild around its bun from her pulling at it. She'd scratched her face in grief, producing bloody welts.

"Mason went out with you this morning," she said. "He didn't come back. You came back, but he didn't."

"I am truly sorry for your loss, Barbara. But I can't allow this."

"You ain't sorry. I'm sorry. My little girl is sorry. What are you? You led twenty good men out there, and now they're dead. You ain't even the sheriff."

Burton gazed back at her, stunned. His head filled with words but none of them proved adequate to the task of answering her grief. His eyes roamed the angry and scared faces and knew she'd voiced what they were all thinking. Twenty men had fought and died while he'd run for his life.

She was right about one thing. Come November, he would no longer be the sheriff.

"Step aside, Tom," Lee said.

The pity in his voice was hardest to bear of all.

The mob surged forward. Ruby had knotted a noose, and they used it to drag the crying girl along toward one of the town's four traffic lights. The rest streamed past, nudging Burton aside until he ended up outside the crowd.

"What do you want to do?" Palmer asked him.

The mob roared when it reached the traffic light. The rope danced and looped around the metal supporting arm. The light turned red as they hauled the girl kicking into the air.

This wasn't justice. It was mindless vengeance. Ritual sacrifice.

"I'm putting an end to this," Burton snarled.

The sheriff waded into the cheering crowd, shoving people aside. The girl swung overhead, fingers wedged between the rope and her throat. Just enough to die even slower. Still, he wouldn't make it in time.

He unholstered his revolver and aimed it. The big gun roared in his hand. The slugs punched through her kicking form. The body jerked and went slack, still swinging on the rope.

The crowd seethed around him, people yelling and pushing to get out of his way. He returned his smoking gun to its holster.

"Lynching's over," he said. "Get back to the roadblock before I lose my temper."

The mob melted away, leaving the girl dangling on the creaking rope. Palmer took off his hat and ran his hand through his thinning hair. Burton stared at the body a while, waiting until time and breath took the edge off his rage.

In all his years in law enforcement, he'd never killed anybody. His first shooting turned out to be a girl whose only crime was being a creeper in the wrong time and place. The shooting was murder, the murder an act of mercy.

"So help me," he said.

"Sheriff?"

"Help me cut her down, Jim."

He was still sheriff, at least for one more night. That's all he needed. Just long enough to get his town through this crisis. Long enough to keep Anne safe.

After that, he'd gladly hand over his badge and gun to another man, and this town could go to hell.

Forty-One

The mass of plague children marched up the old road at twilight, breathing freedom for the first time.

Mary gripped Big Brother's hand. She'd always been afraid of the dark. The dark hid scary people and noises. She'd never seen the scary people, it being dark and all, but she just knew they might be there. They were there during the day, why not at night as well? As for the noises, she'd heard them herself.

Headlights up ahead.

"Pretty," she said.

The beams swept the column choking the road. Silhouettes flickered as the kids rushed forward. Brakes squealed like a steel pig. The headlights shook. A man shouted. The horn blared once, twice. The lights winked off.

Metal clatter. Ripping metal. A piercing scream rent the air.

"Scary sound," she said.

"Don't worry," Big Brother said. "Look at all your brothers and sisters walking up this road together. We're free now,

Mary. Free means you can do anything you want without anybody ever bothering you."

She squeezed his hand tight. She loved Big Brother. Big and warm and covered in soft fur. A very gentle boy. He said he watched over her even when he wasn't around, so she should never be afraid. She believed him, but she often got scared anyway. She couldn't help it.

The world was a big, scary place. The grown-ups were all mean and called her names. The other kids used to tell her lurid stories about Discipline. She'd suffered nightmares of laughing teachers putting her in a dark box with a hungry rat. Big Brothers made the kids stop telling stories. Her Big Brothers were nice.

Three of them were gone now. The other hairy one who was extra kind. The funny boy with the upside-down face. The big rubber squash that made her smile when he smiled. All gone. Where, nobody would say. That or she couldn't understand. She missed them. She feared the world had gotten them.

Big Brother was right, though. Everybody seemed so happy to be out taking a walk. Nobody was sad today except the teachers. It made her feel warm and safe despite the coming darkness. She was free, walking along without anybody bothering her.

"I don't know you if can understand this," Big Brother said. "As we got older, many of us developed capabilities. Things we could do. Like Quasimodo."

"Flying," she said, picturing it.

She'd laughed and pointed when Quasimodo lunged into the air and circled the Home several times before flying into the sun.

"That's right, Mary. Flying. Some of us can do even more. Some are like gods. Like Tiny. You remember Tiny?"

"Horn-man," she said.

"Tiny is a god. I'll bet he could throw Mr. Gaines's truck a hundred miles if he wanted."

"Weather teacher," she said.

"Yes."

"Dead teacher," she said.

"What I want to tell you might be big news to you," Big Brother said. "You want to hear it? It might be a little scary to hear."

Mary shuddered. "Don't like scary."

She stumbled, but Big Brother didn't let her fall. The road was covered in car parts. Oil smell in the warm night air.

"It might also be exciting to hear," Big Brother told her. "Like getting cornbread and syrup for breakfast."

She smacked her lips as she pictured it. "Syrup."

"Mary? I believe you might be a god, too."

"Like Tiny."

"You'll find out soon enough. It'll just come to you. When it happens, don't be scared. You should be excited."

"Syrup."

"That's right. I've got to go, Mary. There's a turn coming up ahead, and I have to take a different road. Something I have to take care of."

"No," she said.

"Tiny knows what to do. He and the others will watch out for you. Now you remember what I said. Something exciting is going to happen. The way you're acting and talking. It's already starting, I can see it."

"Don't go, Big Brother."

"I'll see you soon, Mary."

His hand let go of hers. She looked around but couldn't find him in the throng. The world had gotten him, and she would change. Then she remembered he said it would be scary but also exciting. The world, then syrup.

The group tramped past a faded Welcome to Huntsville sign. As the children topped the hill, the lights of the town spilled across the vista.

"So pretty," she said.

Searchlights glared along the column. Distant shouts.

Bang, bang, bang.

Guns shooting like ones she heard in the woods.

The children fled the road howling. A bumblebee whizzed past her ear. Flashes of light like fireflies but even brighter. A hazy memory came to her. A photographer arrived at the Home to take pictures of the kids for a magazine. Flashbulb popping.

She ambled forward, wanting to be in the picture. More banging. Another bee buzzed past her ear. Snapping sound.

Then she was flying just like Quasimodo. Mary spread her arms and grinned.

No, she wasn't flying. A giant arm encircled her body. She was being carried along. Whisked off the road.

"Football," she said.

Her feet touched ground in a cotton field.

Tiny crouched to look her in the eye. "Brain told me to watch over you and keep you safe while he's gone. But I can't if you try and get yourself killed."

She giggled. "Carry me again. Again, again."

The field rustled around her. The kids crept through the dying cotton, going around the guns. They didn't want their picture taken.

"I have to go now," Tiny said. "You stay here and be quiet and don't move."

Bang, bang, bang.

Then it all stopped. Dark and quiet. Time had a way of slipping away on her. In the distance, a house crumbled in an avalanche of dust. Mary reached out her hand and put it between her fingers. She smiled as she pinched them shut. Bye, house.

Bang, bang. Far away now.

Mary looked around. All alone. No brothers or sisters. This wasn't exciting at all. She wanted to find Big Brother but had no idea where to look. She felt tired now and thought about sleeping on the warm ground. Instead she started walking toward the lights. They sang to her, those pretty lights, and she wanted to get closer. While the darkness was scary, the lights promised warmth and safety.

A tree-lined street, clapboard houses. American flags hanging over porches. Mailboxes. Moths weaving around porch lights. A dog barked far away.

A distant roar as another building collapsed.

Mary felt eyes watching her. People were looking from their windows. She hunched her shoulders, arms rigid at her sides, head aimed at the ground as it had been for most of her life. She didn't want the people to see her. She was so ugly. If they took a good look, they might get upset.

From the corner of her eye, she spied a family standing in a living room window.

Don't look at me, she thought.

They turned around. They were right not to look.

She wished they could love her the way she loved them.

I want to be you, she thought.

Mary smiled as she went on taking her little awkward, uncertain steps. She'd had a clear thought for the first time in her life, and it joyed her.

I want to be beautiful, she thought. Just like you.

Syrup feeling, like it ran in her veins.

Veins that trembled like the world.

The world rushed into her and poured out in screaming rebirth.

The family flew out of the house through shattered living room glass, puffing into a red mist in the air she sucked into her wake. Their empty clothes fluttered onto the lawn.

Windows all along the street exploded outward. Red mist filled the air and swirled around her.

She ate it all.

Mary grew. Became luminous. She'd become light, so pretty.

Her teeth snapped shut.

Souls and memories and personalities imprinted themselves on the blank slate of her mind, suddenly awake and alive after all these years.

She felt their love.

Flashbulb pops at the end of the street. A policeman stood on a lawn, shooting at her with a handgun. Mary turned her blinding visage toward him, her long hair flowing and sparkling around her crown.

Her change had taken every living person on this street except him, and she was curious why.

The gun clicked empty as she approached. He fell to his knees with a keening howl. "Goddamn you. Go on and get it over with."

Mary read him and discovered his desperation, loss, strength, fear. "You are the sheriff."

"I was the one who sinned, not her."

"Enoch," she said. "Elly. Your town. Your wife."

"Anne," he moaned.

"And your son."

He shielded his eyes against her light. "What the hell are you?"

"Tell me your sins, Sheriff."

"You killed her."

"Not killed," she said. "Changed. Anne is with me now. And I understand."

"Are you gonna take me, too?"

She scanned the empty houses lining the street. Shards of glass carpeted the asphalt, reflecting her rainbow colors. "My change is done."

"The plague kids are killing people. Can you make it stop?"

"Nothing can stop it."

The sheriff picked up a dress lying on the ground and hugged it balled against his chest. "Where did you take her?"

"She was a mother," Mary said.

"We had a son once."

"You have a son," she said. "The root of your sin."

"Not her sin. Mine."

"Find your son. Find him and correct your sin. Make things right."

His big shoulders quaked as he clutched the dress to his face and cried into it. Mary glimmered past him, floating on the world she once feared.

She understood everything now, but she was unable to stop it. So much sorrow in the world, she missed her ignorance.

Forty-Two

The power died an hour ago. Amy, Jake, and Mama had been watching Dan Rather report on the revolt spreading across the Homes. President Reagan was due to come on the air in fifteen minutes. Then the TV thudded off and the lights went out, plunging them into darkness.

Now they sat on the couch in the dark with the curtains drawn. Jake kept a tight hold on Amy's hand. Mama chainsmoked while she sipped her bourbon.

Amy got up and banged her shin on the coffee table. "Ow, ow."

Jake jumped to his feet. "You all right?"

"Hunky-dory," she grated, though she was most definitely not hunky-dory, nothing at all about this day was hunky-dory in the least.

"Where you going?" Mama said. "We have to stay put."

"The window," she said. "I can do that, can't I?"

"Just trying to keep us safe. I'll keep on doing it, if you don't mind."

Amy pulled aside the curtain and peered out. Fireflies glittered in the fields. She wanted to run out there for a while. Get out of this stifling house. All they did was bicker to stretch their nerves.

Jake joined her. "I wish I could call Pa. I wish I could hear he's okay."

He'd tried several times before the power went out, slamming the phone back in its cradle each time after getting the all-circuits-busy signal.

"Your daddy is a strong man," Mama said from the couch. "He's with his flock. They'd take a bullet for him."

As if on cue, distant gunshots echoed from the direction of Huntsville. They flinched at the sound. The darkness seemed to press harder against the house. Amy hated not knowing. Michelle, Troy. Everybody she knew, the whole town.

Out there, her normal life was dying with them.

Jake reached for her hand. She pushed his away and said, "I can't just sit here in the dark anymore. I'll lose my mind."

"Do you have any candles, Mrs. Green?" Jake said.

"I ain't lighting a damn candle," Mama told him.

"We can light it in the basement and stay low," he said.

"I don't even remember where I keep the damn things."

Jake wouldn't let it go. "You give me your lighter, I can look."

Mama took a drag on her Virginia Slim. The ember burned in the dark, revealing her scowl. "The point is a man hasn't given an order in this house in fourteen years. That ain't changing now on account—"

"Hush," Amy hissed. "Somebody's coming."

They crowded the window to watch the figure approach. A bright light winked at them, growing larger. Somebody running with a flashlight. The figure sprinted across the yard and stomped onto the porch.

Amy dropped the curtain as the light beam glared across the window.

Banging on the door.

"Y'all stay back," Jake said. "I'll answer it."

"You sit your ass on the sofa," Mama told him.

"Let me in," a voice said. "I know you're in there."

"I think that's Archie Gaines," Amy said.

"What you want?" Mama called out.

"Creepers are out in the woods. I need a place to hide a bit."

Jake moved to the door.

"Don't you dare open that," Mama said.

"All hell's breaking loose out there," Amy said. "People are getting killed. We can't just turn him away."

"It's the right thing to do, Mrs. Green," Jake said.

Mama rose from the couch and went to the door to open it. "Boy, you are getting on my last nerve."

Archie stomped into the house, keeping his flashlight aimed at the floor. Amy got a good look at him in the dim light. Hunting clothes, backpack. He carried a twenty-gauge shotgun in his other hand, pointed at the ceiling.

He was breathing hard, his eyes glazed and wild after everything he'd seen. His movements were jittery and bird-like, like he was ready to burst out of his skin.

Archie scowled at Jake. "What's he doing here?"

"I'm Amy's boyfriend," Jake said. "What are you doing here?"

"Keeping Amy safe."

"For God's sake," Mama said.

Archie set down his bulging backpack. "I got plenty of food. And I got a weapon and ammo. You ain't even armed. What were you gonna do when the creepers busted down the door, preach them Christian love? Invite them in for tea?"

"Have guns stopped them yet?"

"Don't start fighting again," Amy yelled. "Archie, what's going on out there?"

"They tore my daddy up," the boy said. "Then they killed twenty armed men out in the woods. I made it home and watched the trailer park get overrun tonight. My house flattened like a pancake. Everybody's dead."

"Oh, God," she said. "I'm so sorry."

"But the creepers die like anything else. When they come this way, I'll be ready."

"Not here, you ain't," Mama said. "We aim to ride this out by staying quiet."

"Ma'am, I'm done with hiding. We'll nail some boards to barricade the windows. If them sumbitches come, they'll be sorry they did."

"Mrs. Green is right," Jake said. "We need to stay hid and stay quiet."

"How about you do that," Archie said. "Starting with the quiet part."

"You're gonna get us all killed."

"Maybe just you, monster lover. Or you could git while you still can."

The barrel of Archie's shotgun drifted downward to aim at Jake's guts. Mama's hand moved to the pocket of her housecoat. Another power struggle, this time the kind where somebody got shot.

"Archie, look at me," Amy said.

His eyes gleamed the way they did at the football field when he tore into Jake like a wild animal. Take away the hunting clothes and gun, and he was just a boy fighting to act like what he thought a man was supposed to be.

Archie had lost his daddy. After everything he'd seen, maybe his mind.

"I'm gonna kill them all for what they done," he said. "I'm gonna keep you safe."

"I'm sorry about your daddy," Amy said.

She wanted to break through, reach the boy she knew he still was.

He surprised her by laughing. "Yeah, my daddy was a real saint."

"I know he wouldn't want you pointing guns at people."

"My daddy killed Sally Albod and made it look like the creeper boy did it. He shot her by accident and then tore her up so it looked like claws. I watched him do it."

"Oh, my God," she said, her voice fading to a wisp.

"So don't tell me you know my daddy," Archie said.

The plague boy hadn't killed Sally. He'd been innocent. Now he was dead. She and Mr. Gaines had set him up to take the fall for two murders and started a war in the bargain.

"And you don't know me neither," he added.

"Archie—"

"I love you, Amy Green."

He wanted her. Not just longing from a distance. Archie wanted her with him.

"You love me," she said, her voice a dull echo.

"I'm the only one who can protect you. I got food and a gun. I got plans."

"Let's go upstairs and talk," she said.

Jake stiffened. Mama put a restraining hand on his shoulder.

Archie stared at her. "You want to go upstairs with me?"

Amy mounted the stairs without looking back. Moments later, she heard footsteps behind her. Light flickered on the walls, glimpses of framed photographs of her growing up pretending to have a normal life.

Jake let out a choked sob. "Amy?"

"Let it go," Mama said.

"What's she doing?"

"Sit down, boy. It'll be all right."

"It'll be just fine," Archie called down to him from the stairs. "We're just gonna talk. You best be good and gone by the time I come back, you hear?"

Amy heard Archie breathing behind her, excited and scared. She fought back tears as she mounted the stairs on heavy legs. This was not the time for fear. She had to be strong.

She led him into her room, heard him close and lock the door. He shined the flashlight around. Her eyes roamed with it, trying to see the room as he did. A girl's room. Pink walls, vanity, stuffed animals on the bed.

"So this is your place, huh," he said. "It's nice and big."

"Thanks, Archie. I keep telling Mama I need a new vanity. The one I got is secondhand and all scratched up. One of the legs is busted and held up with books."

"Hell, I could fix that for you sometime."

"I'll bet you could," Amy said. "That's what friends do. They help each other."

Her plan had been to get him alone before he shot Jake or Mama shot him. Now she just had to keep him talking. Archie understood power well. Winning and losing had been beaten into him since birth. Girls, he didn't know anything about aside from his imagination.

In that department, he was all bark and no bite. She had some power over him.

The flashlight settled on her. He licked his lips. "I'd do anything for you. I always thought you was perfect for me."

"If you want to court me, you don't show up at my house pointing guns at people I care about," Amy said. "You want my affection, you have to earn it."

He said nothing. Amy stumbled back a step as he took one forward. The light blinded her now. Just empty air between them. Everything that might hold him back, the sheriff and school and his daddy, had been swept away in a single day.

"You'd better quit," she said. "Before you do something you regret."

He took another step, breathing hard. "I'll regret it more if I don't."

She tensed, getting set to give him her best haymaker. For Sally, for Jake, for Enoch. For herself.

Then she was back in Bowie's car. Her hand reaching in the glove box and coming out gripping a mix tape.

Whatever strength she had drained out of her.

"You can't do this," she said, tearing up. "We go to school together."

"Hey. Don't cry. Come here."

The light died. Her body went rigid as it sensed his nearby. She let him put his arms around her. They held her gently, comforting.

Amy leaned her head against his chest. "Thank you."

"Now kiss me," he told her. "Kiss me like you want to."

"No, Archie. Please."

"The world's coming to an end. I don't want to die without having kissed you just once."

Strong hands gripped her shoulders. His mouth ground against hers. She'd read him all wrong.

Archie Gaines knew exactly what he wanted and har-bored no fear about taking it, not when there were things in the night far more terrifying.

She moaned against his lips. *Stop.*

Archie's breath became ragged. He was no longer an angry and scared boy. He sucked and gnawed at her lips. There it was, his bite.

She wanted to fight back, but the terror gripped her again. She wanted to call out for Jake and Mama. Her scream caught in her throat.

Help me, she prayed.

Ants along her scalp, craving her nails' release.

Please. Make him stop.

Nothing happened.

"Perfect," he murmured. "You're so—"

The room filled with a gurgling sound like the roar of an empty belly.

Archie reared back. "What was that?"

She'd scared him good. Now he'd leave her and Jake alone. He'd leave and never come back. She didn't let go. She *couldn't* let go. Amy wrapped her arms around him and held on tight, awake but no longer in control of her body.

Gurgling.

Archie tried to push her away.

Then screamed as her head ruptured into a splayed, toothy star.

Her eyes wide open this time as the quivering jaws snapped shut.

Forty-Three

Amy drained the pipes into the bathroom tub and sink. She stripped off her bloody dress and sat scrubbing her arms in a few inches of tepid water. The flashlight rested on the tiled floor next to the bathtub, its light aimed at the ceiling.

Her body felt raw and tingly where she scrubbed. Striped bruises on her arms. Her mind in a daze. The water turned red.

Poor Archie Gaines.

He was gone now. The monster had kept her safe. She wasn't perfect and would never have a normal life. She was a plague girl, and the monster she carried inside her would fight to protect her.

And despite her regret about Archie, a part of her thought the boy had it coming for all he and his daddy had done.

A gentle knock on the door. Amy closed the curtain and let the water drain.

"Come in," she said.

The door opened. Jake's voice: "Amy?"

"Hand me my robe. It's on the hook on the door."

She stood dripping and reached to take it. "I'm glad you stayed."

"What did you do to him?"

Amy slid the robe over her shoulders and tied it at the waist. Then she opened the curtain. Jake flinched at the sudden movement.

"I thought you wasn't scared of monsters," she said.

His voice came out a whisper. "What did you do?"

She stepped out of the tub and picked up a washing cup resting on its edge. She filled it with fresh water from the sink and washed her clotted hair. Jake watched her, his eyes wild like Archie's had been.

She said, "You know what he was fixin' to do. Does it matter what I did?"

"I don't know."

"If you're asking me whether I'm happy about it, I ain't. I didn't want to kill anybody no matter how much they had it coming. What I got inside me has a mind of its own. It was protecting me."

"I'm just letting it all sink in," he said.

"What did Mama tell you?"

"She said you're one of them and always have been."

"No, not one of them," Amy said. "One of us."

"One of us," he echoed, like he was wondering where he fit into that equation.

"Do you love me?"

"You know I do."

"If you don't, you can go. I've always been alone."

Her mind flashed to the first time they met, though of course it wasn't really the first time. Butler wasn't a big school. They'd grown up together. But Amy being the recluse she was, they'd never talked. When Jake showed up one day and Sally said, *You know Jake Coombs, don't you?*, it was like the first time.

Her heart had galloped in her chest, a sweet burn coursing through her veins. Delicious agony. The world expanded with it, so big and full of heady possibilities. Right then, she knew she wanted him to be hers, maybe forever.

Amy still wanted it. But he had to want her back. He had to say it.

She said again, "Do you love me?"

"Yes," he said. "I do."

"You do what?"

His eyes shifted to meet hers. "I do love you, Amy Green."

"Am I yours? And are you mine?"

"Yes."

"Forever and ever."

"Forever," he said, and she could tell he meant it.

Amy held out her hand. "Come on."

She led him to the guest room down the hall and shut the door behind them. Turned the flashlight off. She took small steps toward him until she heard him breathing.

"Where are you?" he said.

Amy untied the bathrobe and let it fall. "I'm right here."

His hand grazed her bare shoulder and withdrew as if scalded.

"Amy," he murmured.

She loved hearing him say her name. "Am I beautiful?"

"Beautiful," he said.

"Don't be scared. Promise you'll never be scared of me."

He reached again. She took his hand in hers and placed it against her chest. His skin felt hot against her heart. She said, "I love you, too, Jake Coombs."

They embraced with a shocked gasp. His hands caressed her. Always a gentle boy. Despite the stifling heat in the house, she shivered at his touch. A boy touching her without hurting her, a boy she wanted, a boy she loved.

His lips pressed against hers. Like that first kiss under the dogwood, wild and wondrous. This time, they could do what they wanted without boundaries. He knew what she was now. They moved to the bed without a break in their random but purposeful dance. Their breath found an urgent rhythm, carrying them to the brink.

They sprawled gasping after. The mattress damp with sweat, bedding strewn across the floor.

"Wow," he said, which made her giggle.

"No kidding," Amy said.

She rolled on her side and listened to him catch his breath. Jake wrapped his arm around her shoulders and pulled her close.

"The health book didn't say nothing about that," he said.

"Chapter one," she said. "Thunder and lightning."

"The atom bomb, then nirvana."

Waves of heat poured off him. She nestled against his sweating body, reveling in his touch and smell. "It's us against the world now."

Amy had heard an actress say that in a movie once. She'd swooned at the drama of something she'd wanted but didn't understand. Now she understood. She no longer had to face the world alone. She was whole and complete. The monster was a part of her now, and so was Jake.

He stirred, restless.

"What's wrong?" she said.

"I'm worried about my pa."

"I'm sure he's okay. He's a very formidable man."

"He wasn't always this hard. Ma's dying changed him. He started hating the plague kids. I was thinking I should go find him. Make sure he's okay."

"Then we'll do that," Amy said.

"You don't have to come along if you don't want. It's dangerous out there."

"Us against the world. That means I come with you. See how it works?"

Jake kissed her forehead. "All right. Pa is a leader. I want to try to talk sense into him. We need to stop the fighting before more people get killed."

"How do you plan to do that?"

"If everybody wants it to stop, it'll stop."

"And if they don't want it to stop, what then?"

"I don't know," he said. "But we won't know if we don't ask."

Jake was still trying to make things right. A voice shouting in the wilderness. Doomed to fail, but he was right, somebody had to ask. Somebody had to try. If nobody did, there was no chance at all it would ever stop.

In any case, she was going with him. She loved him in her bones, she understood that now. He had accepted her and the monster inside her. They had become one flesh. One germ. Wherever he went, she would go, too.

This was real love. You took somebody as they were and did anything for them.

L inda rooted through her drawers until she found a flashlight and handful of D batteries. She left it off and crept up the stairs, one hand feeling the wall. She winced at each creak her slippered feet made on the floorboards. She knew what her daughter and Jake were up to in the spare bedroom and didn't want to disturb them.

She opened the door to Amy's room. A wall of scent, sharp and metallic, flooded out. The air had a cloying taste. Linda clicked on the flashlight and after a few slaps got it to cast a yellow beam across the room.

The body lay crumpled on the floor, now sodden and black with blood.

"Tarnation," she whispered.

What a mess. It was Bowie all over again. Like Bowie, Archie had messed with the wrong girl. Mama would take care of it.

"Just you and me now, kid," she said.

She'd poured more bourbon down her worn gullet tonight than she usually did, but the violence had electrified her right back to sobriety. She'd known, when Amy took Archie upstairs, how it'd end even if her little girl hadn't.

She crouched and gripped the boy's hands to pull him into a sitting position. Then up and over her shoulders with a grunt. She staggered in a fireman's carry, shifting her feet until she had them aimed at the door. The kid weighed a ton. Like hauling a sack of meat. Plodding the whole way, she got him downstairs and into the trunk of her car. She paused to catch her breath then went to search for her car keys.

It proved an otherwise easy disposal this time. Linda drove a mile down the road, dragged the body out, and left it in the ditch. When the authorities showed up to put the town to rights, they'd sweep it up as part of the larger tragedy. Like drowning somebody during the Great Flood.

Back at the house, Linda filled a bucket at the backyard pump and brought it into the kitchen. She mixed a solution of ammonia and water in another then carried both buckets up to Amy's bedroom. She blotted at the carpet bloodstains with the solution and then with the cold water. The stained rags went into a Hefty bag. After a while, she wiped the sheen of sweat from her forehead and decided it was good enough until morning.

She trudged back downstairs and sat on the couch with her .38 resting on her lap. She knocked back the remains of the bourbon in her glass and poured another finger. Thirsty work, cleaning up after that little girl. Lord, the things a mother did for her child. It drove you to drink.

Upstairs, her daughter and her boyfriend had joined together. Which didn't matter, if things out there were as bad as she thought they were. Amy being a plague child, all the secrets and lies, none of it mattered anymore. He loved her, and she loved him. They were the only two people in the world right now, while the real world outside slid toward the abyss.

Let them have their world while it lasted.

Her Amy could have done worse. Jake was different than most. Gentle and understanding. He'd taken the germ for her. Amy needed a boy like him.

Come sunrise, they were all family. By joining with Amy, Jake had become the man of the house. As for her baby girl, she was growing up and didn't need her mama anymore. She'd befriended the monster inside her, and it would go on protecting her and her kin. Amy and Jake would protect each other, and she would do what she could to watch over them.

Linda lit a Virginia Slim with trembling hands. The gun rested on her thigh. The clock ticked on the mantle. She checked the time. Four hours after midnight. She turned the flashlight off and sat in the dark.

Waiting for the end, or the beginning.

Forty-Four

The black Lincoln Town Car drove into the A & P parking lot. Tinted windows. Government plates. The car parked and idled for a while before its engine cut.

Goof opened the passenger door and got out. He stretched in his bathrobe, pajamas, and slippers. A heavy gun rested in his pocket, a present for future Goof.

"Thanks for the ride, partner," he said and slammed the door.

The car pulled away, its zombie driver given orders to go home after taking him to Huntsville.

A long, long drive, but the sightseeing had been breathtaking.

Burning crosses along I–85. Air raid sirens in Gastonia. A herd of plague children marching past a jackknifed tractor trailer outside Greenville. Highway Patrol roadblocks set up around Atlanta, which he'd had to talk his way through.

Brain had foreseen this. His revolution had turned out not to be such a joke after all. Goof guessed that was why they called him Brain.

Pussy had wanted to march on Washington. After they all

busted out of Special Facility, she rounded up the kids into an army. If they could attack the power structure in D.C., it might give the kids all over the country a fighting chance.

Goof had just wanted to go home.

Only Huntsville wasn't here anymore, not exactly.

Pussy's whiskers had drooped when he'd told her. *I thought we had a thing going*, she said. He tried to give her a smack on the lips and ended up kissing her forehead instead. He told her he'd look her up after the revolution. He knew she'd give Reagan hell. Whatever she found in D.C. that wasn't broken, she'd break it.

Then she'd most likely die along with the other kids. Along with all the kids everywhere. They'd rampaged through the towns around their Homes, but these were small towns in poor counties. Later on, the Army National Guard would show up with tanks and helicopters and say, *Okay, children, you've had your fun.*

Then wham, blam, thank you, ma'am.

Goof wanted to enjoy his freedom while he had it. He didn't want to die fighting. He wanted to die knowing he'd lived.

Along the long drive home, he'd nursed a fantasy of Huntsville emptied of normals and filled with plague kids driving cars, shopping, watching TV. He'd find a nice house and have his friends over for barbecue, everybody laughing as they tucked into pork ribs. Pussy showing up flustered saying, *Sorry I'm late, honey*, and Goof telling her, *You're right on time*. Kissing her on the lips with perfect aim.

Instead, everywhere he looked, he saw smashed cars, downed telephone poles, and bodies. A house fire lit the scene. A tangle of carts and trash littered the parking lot outside the A & P, which had been partially looted.

He wondered where he should go now and laughed at the

first thing that popped into his head. The Home. He wanted to go back to the Home.

He should have had the driver stick around a little longer. Past Goof strikes again. It was gonna be a long walk.

A voice said, "Well, look what the cat dragged in."

He wheeled as three plague kids sauntered up. Catty Wampus, Digger, and Eerie. He grinned and struck a nonchalant pose.

"Surprised to see me?"

He'd forgotten to bring back one of his fedoras. Damn.

"You're just in time to miss everything, goofus." Catty Wampus gave him a once-over, taking in his pajamas. "You sleep through the whole thing or what?"

"I came all the way from Virginia just to see you, Cat."

"What did they do to you up there?"

"Oh, you know. Frankenstein experiments, that sort of thing."

"You're full of it," Eerie said.

"What's it like out there?" Catty Wampus said. "Outside of town?"

"It looks pretty much just like this."

The kids grinned.

"We're winning," she said.

"Good for you. I'm gonna go back to the Home."

"It ain't there. We burned it to the ground."

Goof had come all this way for nothing.

"Where's Brain?" he said.

"He went out to the Albod farm. Ain't seen him since. Tiny's leading us."

Eerie sniggered at his pajamas. "Maybe you should—"

"Wait here while I get a ten-speed bike for you," Goof said.

The kid loped off.

Digger scowled. "Hey, what—"

"Do you say I go look for one, too?"

Goof smiled at Catty Wampus while the kid shuffled off into the shadows. "Say something."

She cocked her head and crossed her arms.

"Come on," he said. "Just one little word. I won't do it again, honest."

She shook her head.

The kids returned with bikes. He picked a brand-new red Schwinn and climbed on, his powder-blue bathrobe draped behind him.

"See you later, suckers," he said as he pedaled off.

Catty Wampus called after him, "You suck—"

"While I find a ten-speed bike," he yelled over his shoulder, laughing.

He rode along the dark road leading out of town, leaving the mess behind him. The night air here was cool and clear. He smiled at the familiar ring of insects, the cicadas rattling like maracas in the trees. The deep stillness of the woods.

After just fifteen minutes, though, he groaned at a stitch in his side and ache in his legs. A steady diet of fast food and sugar had depleted him. He hadn't eaten since dinner, and he'd upchucked most of that after Shackleton blew his brains out.

The Albod farm came into sight under the harvest moon. Goof pedaled harder, his body slick with sweat. He'd blown his second and third wind. He swung the bike onto the farm road, bouncing along the stones.

"Nooooo," he sang, enjoying the way the bouncing made his voice tremble. "Whaaaaat—"

His mouth snapped shut as he bumped over a big rut. The

gun flew from his pocket and landed somewhere in the tall grass.

"Crap," he said. "Sorry about that, future me."

He coasted the Schwinn into the yard and ditched it. The house stood dark and empty. A light shined from the barn. He went inside and froze in the doorway.

Lanterns lit the scene. Smell of fresh hay and blood. Cows restless in their stalls. Workbench soaked black and littered with tools and instruments.

The barn had been converted into a mad scientist's laboratory.

"Sweet Jesus," Goof breathed.

Reggie Albod stood strapped to a wood frame crossing a thick support. He let out a pleading moan.

Brain sat nearby on the dirt floor, weeping.

"What did you do to him, Brain?"

Pa Albod growled and squirmed against his restraints.

Goof's voice dropped to a whisper. "What did you do?"

The farmer had been surgically remade into a monstrous thing—half human, half animal. A single fused body of man and cow and pig connected by throbbing blood vessels. Compacted flesh, shared organs.

Goof had wanted his freedom and had fought and killed for it. He'd seen incredible destruction on his way home. At every step, he'd sensed the hilarity of it all, horror and comedy being kissing cousins. A bunch of kids forming an unstoppable army, the victims paying back a lifetime of cruel abuse, the once-invincible oppressors becoming the new victims.

But the sight of Reggie Albod mashed into this squirming, suffering abomination took it out of him. This just wasn't funny anymore.

Brain wiped tears from his scarred face and looked up at him. "Ever have an itch you can't scratch?"

"I think you've lost your mind, friend."

"An itch that won't quit. Day and night, your whole life, it's just there. It feels so good to finally get at it. Rake it right out of you. I wanted to be—"

"A doctor," Goof said. "I know."

His mind flashed to him telling the normals to gun each other down at Special Facility. Men crying as they turned their rifles on each other and fired point blank. The violence horrifying but also feeling good, somehow right, even necessary. Like regardless of whether it was for good or evil, he'd done what he was meant to do, using the gift the good Lord gave him.

Goof knew all about the itch. He'd scratched it plenty today.

"I wanted him to see," Brain said. "What it's like to be like us."

"What happened to the girls?"

"I let them go. But not Pa here. Pa required justice. I grabbed him, and my hands just went to work. I lost myself for a while."

"This ain't you," Goof said. "I know it was in you, but it ain't you. All this butchery and mayhem. It ain't who we are."

Another flashback to the fighting at Special Facility. The air filled with gun smoke and blood as the bodies toppled.

"Unless," he added. "Unless they're right and we really are monsters."

"Do you think he was innocent?"

"His girls was always nice to us. As for Pa, I don't know."

"He fed on us like a parasite. Being different in this world is appreciated if somebody can profit from it, but even that has limits. Pa Albod murdered Dog in cold blood. He beat me to within an inch of my life because he could. He didn't see me as human and never did. Just like my mother. My own flesh and blood."

"So this revolution of yours. It's about revenge, is that it?"

Brain stood and stared at Pa Albod as if he was as surprised by what he saw as Goof had been.

"You should end it now," Goof told him.

Brain trod to the workbench and picked up a box cutter he'd been using as a scalpel, an even deeper sorrow etched on his wrinkled face now.

"We could have been partners, Pa," he said. "We could have built a new world together if you hadn't feared and enslaved us. A world of wonders."

Pa Albod let out a heartbreaking moan.

"I'm sorry it all had to end like this," Brain added. "Your suffering is over."

"Any last words, Pa?" Goof said.

"I," the man breathed, "I-I—"

"Am happy my suffering is ending and I'm crossing over to a better place," Goof finished. "Amen."

The farmer smiled as Brain pulled a single dangling artery and cut it. Blood spurted into the wet hay underneath. Albod sighed. His head drooped. The struggling hoofed legs went still.

"I'm glad you're here," Brain said. "It's good to see you again."

"I'd say it's good to be home, but home ain't here anymore."

"Where were you? How did you get back?"

"They had me in Special Facility. A bunch of us broke out.

The Homes are rising up just like you wanted. It's World War Three out there. The kids are killing everybody in the town. You need to get down there and put the brakes on."

Brain looked at the bloody box cutter in his hand and flung it into the hay. "It's too late."

"There has to be a way. We made our point, didn't we? We could talk to them and try to work it out before the whole country turns into one big bonfire."

"Do you think I like all this?"

"What's there to like?" Goof said.

"I hate it. But if we don't keep going, they'll kill us all."

"You can keep going without me then. I'm done with all of it."

"You might want to think about that. You're either with us or—"

"I'll do whatever you say," Goof finished.

Brain smiled and said nothing. The two boys stared at each other.

"Do you know what my IQ is?" Brain said.

"Pretty high?"

"You have no idea."

Goof couldn't control a mind like Brain's.

"Sorry about that," he said.

"Gods should never be sorry. Gods should be happy, so happy."

Goof's eyelids drooped. Yellow lantern light flared before going dim. The crickets' pulsing song became a soothing roar. He'd never felt so calm and relaxed. Like taking a long, warm bath in Special Facility.

Yes, he was back in Special Facility. Dozing in a nice bath. The whole day was just a strange dream.

Brain's words popped across his vision in big yellow capitals.

YOU WILL DO PRECISELY WHAT I

"No," Goof said, snapping out of it. "I won't."

Brain couldn't control him, either.

"Then we're enemies," Brain said.

"I ain't nothing. I thought we was friends. I just want to be left alone."

"Go, then. Be alone. We won't hurt you nor will we help you. But if you interfere with us in any way, Tiny will hurt you. You remember Tiny?"

Goof swallowed hard. "I remember that boy."

"What we started, nobody can stop," Brain said. "We have to go all the way or die trying."

"You do that. Just leave me out of it."

"Run, friend. Run and never stop running."

Goof did as he was told.

Forty-Five

Worshippers and refugees packed Trinity United Methodist Church on County Road 20's eastward run out of town. Reverend Coombs led them in singing "Hold the Fort." The congregants sang with hoarse throats. The organist, who'd been playing for hours, grimaced over her keys. Mamas bounced their young ones to stop them crying. A zealous boy in white shirt and tie roamed the outsiders, asking if they were saved. Matrons passed out food and water. Armed men stood at the doors.

Ho, my comrades, see the signal, waving in the sky, the reverend sang. *Reinforcements, now appearing, victory is nigh!*

The weary congregation sang along, *Hold the fort, for I am coming, Jesus signals still. Wave the answer, back to Heaven, by Thy grace we will!*

Outside, the distant gunfire trickled to nothing.

In one of the crowded pews, Amelia Oliver shivered against Richard Benson, his arm wrapped tight around her shoulders. They'd hoped to flee the rampaging children and had their first fight over the best route out of town.

The road was pitch black. Gunfire everywhere. A massive

fireball mushroomed over the gas station. They'd found the Methodist church brightly lit thanks to a backup power generator and decided to stop and steady their nerves before moving on. Their nerves hadn't steadied yet.

"George got his revolution," she murmured against his shoulder while the congregation sang. "He's going to get every one of those kids killed."

"Right now I'm more worried about him taking us with him," Richard said. "They seem to be winning out there."

"I wish I could find him and talk to him. Make him stop this before it's too late."

"You think he'd listen?"

"He'd listen all right," she said. "We'd have a good, long, reasonable talk about it. And then he'd go right back to rebelling."

"Maybe all this was inevitable. I tried to give my kids the tools they needed to accept the plague children. I was spitting in one hand and wishing in the other to see which filled up first. To them, the kids are monsters and always will be."

"They never played together," Amelia said.

"What's that, hon?"

"They never played together as little kids. That's where living together starts."

"You saw what's happening out there," Richard said. "Turns out they're monsters after all."

"They aren't monsters. I taught them for two years. They're orphans who grew up in violence and without love of any kind."

"Okay, but just because they maybe have some right on their side don't make what they're doing right. And it don't mean I want to see them hurt you. I'll—" His voice cracked. "I'll kill anybody tries to harm you."

Amelia hugged his chest tighter and listened to his pounding heart. The plague children were coming soon, and when they did, nothing in the world would save her.

"We'll be all right," she said.

"Almost everybody I ever knew is already gone," he said.

In her fear, she'd forgotten he'd grown up in this town. While he was a loner who'd never quite fit in, he'd lived among these people. He'd grown up with many of them. He taught their children.

"We're together," she said.

He gave her shoulders a squeeze and kissed the top of her head. "That's all that matters to me right now."

When her students burst through the doors, she couldn't imagine being anywhere else than by his side.

The hymn ended. Reverend Coombs returned to the pulpit. "Friends and neighbors, this long night is coming to an end, but we are still here. Still praising the Lord."

"Amen," the Methodists called out from the pews.

"All y'all know 'Hold the Fort' is one of my favorite hymns. And I can't think of a better time to sing it. Satan is surely coming with his army tonight. It's been on its way a good long while. We knew it. We warned 'em, didn't we?"

"Amen," the congregation cried.

"Christ," Richard muttered. "He sounds almost happy about it."

Coombs said, "We said the birth of demons was a sign the End Times had begun. We warned 'em, but they didn't listen. We told 'em, but they turned away. We shouted it from the rooftops, but they just laughed. Do you think they're laughing now? Do you think they're ready to listen? Satan let the dogs out tonight. Demons braying for blood. Good folk dying. But not us. We're still here, and we will not budge from our fort. We will praise the Lord until He comes to put Satan to rights. We are being tested, and we will not fail. It's the end—"

The reverend stared at the front doors. Heads turned to see what he was looking at.

"Welcome home, son," he said.

Jake, Amy, and Amy's ma entered the church. The doors slammed shut behind them. Jake and his father stared at each other across the crowded pews.

"Go on," Amy said. "You wanted to come here. Here we are."

He handed his shotgun to Mrs. Green and took Amy's hand. They threaded through the refugees cramming the aisle. She nodded to Mr. Benson and his girlfriend. She smiled at Troy and Michelle, who held each other in another pew.

Jake looked straight ahead at the man who'd always been larger than life to him. His own flesh and blood, almost a mirror image, yet so different. He trembled with relief and apprehension, steeling his nerves for what he had to do.

Pa sucked in a long, ragged breath. "I am mighty relieved to see you."

"I'm glad you're okay, Pa. I was worried."

"That makes two of us, son."

"I feel moved by the Spirit to speak. About what I seen out there."

"Go on then," Pa said. "Open your heart."

Jake walked behind the pulpit and looked across all the faces. People he considered family. People who'd helped raise him after his ma passed on. Their love and charity had remade him as a Christian. He owed them so much. He now hoped he could show them the way as they'd shown him. He licked his lips, took a deep breath, and blew out a sigh.

"My whole life, I watched my pa preach up here. I heard him preach just now. I love my pa. My pa is a great man. He gave every bit of himself to his family, his church, and the Gospel. My whole life, he warned us the end was coming, and he were right. He said it's because the plague kids is demons. He were wrong."

The congregation rumbled hearing that.

"The Scriptures and my heart tell me the plague kids ain't demons. They ain't demons but kids unlucky to be born what they are. Jesus said to love one another as we love ourselves. Instead, we hated them and we acted on that hate. We ground them in the dirt just about every way a kid can be ground. We scorned and defiled them. Where our nightmares was just dreams, theirs was real, and we was their monsters."

The crowd broke out in angry shouts. Jake raised his hands for quiet but they didn't stop, pouring out their hurt and anger.

"Well, guess what," he hollered over them. "I got some bad news for you that you ain't gonna want to hear neither. After all these years, they started to hate us, too, and now they're fighting back."

"You saying we had this coming, boy?" a man shouted from the pews.

"I didn't do anything to them," a woman said. "They killed Rufus."

The enraged congregation rose roaring to its feet, calling him a traitor, protesting their innocence, screaming the names of victims. Pa stood off to the side of the pulpit, head bowed, his face rigid and darkening.

Before the rebellion, the plague children filled these people with a nameless fear. Now they were hysterical with terror and hate. Most of them had never hurt the plague children, maybe never even met one. In their minds, they were innocent.

In Jake's mind, that was the point. They did nothing.

"I know right now they are hurting our friends and neighbors out there," Jake cried. "But the answer ain't to keep hating. Jesus taught us violence only begets violence, and hate begets hate. I know how it sounds, asking all y'all to find love in your hearts after everything we lost, but keep in mind we are close to losing far more. We are close to losing everything we love. We need to make peace."

The throng howled. They shook their fists at him, spittle flying from roaring mouths. He stepped away from the pulpit, pale and trembling. Amy took his sweating hand in hers. She held on tight as if trying to pour her strength into him.

"They don't want to listen," he said. "It's all gone too far."

"You did good," she said.

"If I wasn't Pa's son, I think I'd be dead right now."

In the end, it had been another futile effort. He'd tried and failed. He didn't have the right words his pa always seemed to have handy. He didn't know how to make them see, no, *feel* the truth. He knew he'd been harsh with them. Was there another way? Did the right words even exist?

Pa raised his hands for quiet. "My boy spoke from his heart. I'm proud of him for that. Otherwise, I wonder where I went wrong raising a boy who can't recognize the Devil standing right in front of him."

"Amen," somebody called out, while others nodded.

"We do not make peace with the Devil while he slaughters

us in the streets," he said. "We hold the fort. We hold it to the last man."

He turned to his errant son. "You got one chance to recant what you just said." His voice now low and menacing. "You're a man now. You make up your own mind. I won't force you."

Jake shook his head.

"One chance to make it right with God," Pa warned.

"I ain't recanting, Pa."

"No?"

Jake set his jaw. "I'm already right with God."

"Then git out my church."

"You're a great leader, Pa. You can stop all this hate and fighting right now. We all can. Please listen to me."

"Recant or get out."

Jake looked at his feet. Figuring out his old math problem. How to make human nature add up to something right. In his mind, Pa was asking him to turn his back on God and his ma's memory. And now on Amy as well.

Fear or hope. There could be only one answer.

He sighed. "Okay."

"Okay what."

"Okay," Jake said. "Goodbye, Pa. I'm sorry."

He and Amy walked back down the aisle hand in hand.

"Recant," Pa shouted.

Glaring faces. Michelle and Troy gaping at him.

"Recant!"

Jake took one last look over his shoulder at his father.

"Please, son," Pa said.

"I love you, Pa," Jake said.

The doors closed behind him.

The sky had begun to pale. Dawn had finally broken the endless night.

"You all right?" Amy said.

"I don't know how to answer that."

"For what it's worth, I'm proud of you for standing up to him. No matter how it turned out, you tried when nobody else would."

"Nobody likes getting pushed around, but the truth is we spend our whole lives getting pushed," Jake said. "Getting pushed ain't the hard part. The hard part is figuring when to make a stand and push back."

"From the mouths of babes," Mrs. Green said. "What now?"

He took Archie's shotgun back from her and gave one last longing look at the church. "We'll go back to the house. Lay low and be ready to run if we—"

The doors cracked open.

Not his pa, though. It was Mr. Benson and his girlfriend.

"Where are you going?" Mr. Benson said.

"Home," Jake said. "Mrs. Green's house."

"Mind if we come along with you?"

"It's all right with me if it is with Mrs. Green. It's her house."

"Mr. Benson is my teacher," Amy told her mama. "This lady is his girlfriend."

"I'm Amelia Oliver," the woman said.

"You taught them plague kids," Mama said.

"That's right."

"They don't seem to like their teachers much."

"I know the boy who started the whole thing. I don't think he'd hurt me. I was kind to him."

Mrs. Green mulled this over. "I got plenty of room."

"The Army National Guard is mobilizing," said Mr. Benson. "All we have to do is lie low until they come."

"We'd better get moving then," Jake said. "The sun's coming up."

They tramped to their cars.

"You sure you're okay?" Amy said.

"I hope it weren't the last time," Jake answered. "When I told Pa I loved him."

"The church is outside of town. They should be all right. I was wishing at least Michelle and Troy would have come out with us, though."

"They don't have the same convictions. They was right to stick by their folks."

"Thank you, Jake Coombs."

"For what?"

"For sticking by me."

He smiled. "You're my girl. You and me, we're a tribe now."

Forty-Six

The plague children waited in the trees as dawn burned away night's edges. They watched the group walk to their cars in the crowded dirt lot.

"What about them?" Tiny said in his rumbling voice.

"Let them go," Brain said.

"You are going soft already."

"I made a promise to Ms. Oliver. And the normal children are not to be harmed. They will serve us when the world is ours."

The cars disappeared down the road. Triumphant singing emanated from the church. An organ playing. The giant boy jerked his horned head toward the sound.

"Bigger fish to fry," he growled.

In all her history, Ms. Oliver never taught the plague children one simple fact, which was nobody ever handed anybody their rights. Brain grasped that truth intuitively by reading between the lines. You wanted your rights, you had to take them. Sometimes, you had to be willing to fight and die for them.

All this time, he'd believed the only way the plague

generation would ever be free was to cleanse the world of the generation that fathered it. A great war between those with everything and nothing to lose. Between the old and new.

He'd gotten his war. The children had won the Battle of Huntsville. Tomorrow or the day after, however, they'd face the U.S. Army. The normals would never give up. They'd fight to hold onto their world to the last bomb and bullet.

Still, the terrible vengeance he'd inflicted on Pa Albod had shaken him. If he couldn't control his hatred, how could the kids whom he led? They were strong, they had amazing abilities, but in the end they were just abused children. Children with a lifetime of suffering in their heads and an Old Testament sense of justice.

Goof did not want the act of fighting monsters to turn him into one. He wanted to stay a kid forever. He refused to commit to anything. Perhaps he was right about one thing, though. Maybe it did not have to be total war.

"I'll talk to them," Brain said.

"Talking again," Tiny spat. "You want to have it both ways."

"We won just one town," Brain said. "And already we're up to our necks in blood."

Tiny said, "Fine. Have it your way. You go up there. They hand over their weapons and go back to their homes."

"They'll agree," Brain said. "They have no choice."

"We'll see about that. They even look at you funny, we're coming."

Brain walked toward the church doors with a white pillowcase tied to a broom handle. He doubted they'd respect a flag of truce if they wanted to shoot, but at least they knew his intentions.

The church doors opened. Faces crammed the entrance,

terrified, revolted, angry. A man in black emerged and challenged him from the steps.

"This is a house of God," the man called out.

"And we are God's children," Brain said.

"I see those children skulking out in yonder trees. Are you in charge of them?"

"My name is George Hurst. The kids call me Brain. Who would you be, sir?"

"Reverend Jeremiah Coombs."

"I am not in charge, Reverend. But I speak for the mutagenic children of the Stark County Home for the Teratogenic."

"And what does the Stark County Home for the Teratogenic want to tell us?"

"They have a message for you," Brain said. "Me, I have just one question."

"I got a question for you, boy. Why don't I just have you shot where you stand after all you done?"

"Because if you do, every man and woman in that church will die. For all that you've done."

Coombs's glare softened. "Ask what you want."

Brain had in mind a simple question that for him was the crux of everything wrong in the world since his birth. "Why couldn't you love us?"

"You ask me that after today," the reverend said. "After what you've proven yourself to be."

"We were born innocent. You owed us a chance to be something else."

"We owed you nothing," Coombs said, "and there weren't anything else you could have become other than what you are. If it were up to me, we would never have suffered you to live. We should have let you all die after you was born."

Brain winced. His mind flashed to the wonder of his birth turning to horror. His mother screaming, her mouth moving to make strange sounds. His tiny hands reaching to offer love and help. Howling as the doctor swept him from the room.

He'd spent the first years of his life wondering why they had to be separated. Loving a terrified woman who eternally screamed in his mind. Worrying about her while believing that if he was a good boy, one day they'd be reunited.

Sitting on the dirty floor at the Home, he listened to the normals talk. He watched their lips move and learned language until finally he understood what his mother had screamed.

No! Get that fucking thing away from me! Get rid of it!

"Did I answer your question?" Coombs said.

"You did," Brain said.

"Now what's this message you got for me?"

Brain stared at him.

"Well?" the man said.

"No message, Reverend."

"Stop this killing. Go back to the Home and await your judgment."

"We can only be what we are, Reverend. What you made us."

Brain turned and started walking back to the tree line.

"My boy," Coombs called after him.

He paused. "I know your son."

"Don't you hurt him."

They locked eyes across the distance separating them. Brain nodded.

The children waited for him in the trees. They crowded around, waiting for him to speak. He dropped the broom handle in the weeds. Across the dirt lot, the church doors slammed shut.

It was hard to hate when what you hated became a who. A father who loved his son.

"What did he say to you?" Tiny asked him.

Brain said nothing.

"What do you want to do?" the giant boy growled.

Brain shook his head. Words failed him for the first time. He wanted it both ways, understanding each carried a terrible price he didn't want to pay. Finally, an equation he couldn't solve.

"My way, then," Tiny said.

He stomped toward the church flexing his big hands.

The plague children rushed forward on pounding feet. Brain watched them stream through the parked vehicles. Too late to stop them, always too late. It had been too late his whole life.

The doors shattered open. Tiny disappeared inside, followed by the clawed flood.

Perhaps fighting monsters made one a monster. But maybe it took a monster to kill a monster. If the path to Heaven's gate crossed a vast river of fire and blood, then all who would enter paradise must be ready to swim in it.

Or stay in Hell.

The congregation's screams poured out of the church. Screams of terror, anguish, and pain. Brain clapped his hands over his ears to block them out, though he'd never be able to rid himself of them. He had a perfect memory. The sounds of those people dying were forever imprinted on it.

He closed his eyes and pictured the world he wanted. Teaching the children to create instead of destroy. Working together to build a new world on the ashes of the old.

A world of wonders.

Forty-Seven

The long night was over.

Sheriff Burton wandered the wilderness at the edge of town, searching.

You have a son, the plague girl had told him. She had somehow known.

He and Anne had so badly wanted to bring another life into this world. He remembered the joy he'd felt when she finally conceived. The Burton name would carry on. Jesus promised immortality to the soul, children to the flesh. He would live forever through his children and theirs, on and on into the future.

The germ gave him a monster and a lifetime of shame.

There came a point in middle age when the search for meaning switched its focal point from life to death. When you truly grasped the fact that everything ends, including you. Cursed by infection, his name would die with him. After he was dead and gone, all that would be left of him would be a monster. If the plague children were sons of Cain, then he was Cain.

Burton staggered along the hill on the north side of

town as dawn's creeping light revealed a scenic view of the destruction. He paused to gaze upon the blasted wreckage of the roadblocks, overrun in the howling twilight melee. Rubble and cars and bodies marked a score of last stands. He'd lost his deputies down there, and when all seemed lost he'd fled to save Anne.

Now his wife was dead, devoured by a plague girl who looked like an angel. He still held Anne's dress, all that was left of her, in his hand. He let it fall and released that part of his past. Her suffering was over, her soul departed to a better place.

The world had misjudged the plague children every step of the way. The extent to which they could be controlled. The powers they displayed. They wanted their birthright, but the fact remained they didn't belong in this world. They wanted the same things, asked the same questions: *Who am I? Why am I here? Is there a reason things happen?* Still, angels and demons had no business being on the earth.

The town sprawled below. A dog slouched across a street. Turkey vultures circled overhead. Otherwise, Huntsville appeared emptied of life. Behind, a short walk to a major road offered a clear path out of this hell. Huntsville was his home, but whatever made it home had been swept away. He could go anywhere. Join up with the authorities and get back in the fight. Put an end to the whole business.

Burton shifted his gaze and spotted plague kids dancing around Reverend Coombs's church outside of town. The church started to burn. He checked his revolver. Two bullets left. He hoped it was enough for what he had to do.

The plague girl had instructed him to find his son and correct his sin. He didn't know what she meant and didn't particularly care. He didn't stay because of some notion of redemption she'd planted in his mind. He'd failed Enoch and the kids, failed his wife and the town. Nothing could change that. He stayed because he had unfinished business to attend. A good town policed itself.

His last chance to make it right.

The sheriff walked down the hill, skirting the town's edge across dead ground. A distant field was on fire, pouring black smoke into the sky. Clouds of insects swarmed away from the moving wall of flame. The church stood on the other side of a hedgerow, smoking in the morning sunlight.

Sheriff, a voice carried on the heat.

The plague child materialized from the brown cotton, lumbering toward him on a bed of writhing tentacles. The thing looked like a big bowling pin made of rubber, eyes bulging and blinking. Large wet mouth stretched into a wide clay smile. The plague boy stopped a short distance away, bouncing on his roots.

"Look-ing for you," the boy said.

Burton remembered seeing him swaddled under the heat lamp at the clinic, squirming like a slug and crying like a normal baby did for his mama's breast.

He said, "As it happens, I been looking for you as well."

"For me?"

"For Edward. Your real name is Edward Thomas Burton."

"Bur-ton?"

"That's right," the sheriff said. "I been watching over you a long time."

The boy smiled and closed his eyes, which leaked tears. "Knew it."

"I wanted to find you and tell you I'm sorry, son. Sorry

I left you and couldn't be your daddy. Sorry I couldn't love you the way you needed."

The eyes popped open. "Love me now?"

"I always did," Burton said. "Just not the way you deserved."

"Al-ways knew it was you."

The sheriff drew his gun from its holster and extended his arm to point the weapon at his son. "I'm real sorry, Edward. I got to put you down now."

"Al-ways want-ed to be you," the boy said.

Tears flowed down Burton's stubbled cheeks. "Close your eyes like you were. It's time for you to go to sleep."

He didn't want to shoot. He wasn't sure he could. But he had to end it.

Angels and demons had no place on this earth.

"Goodbye, son," he said.

Barbed tentacles shot out from under Edward Thomas and latched onto him. The big gun banged in his hand, sending the bullet flying into the sky.

The tentacles flexed and pulled. The sheriff landed hard on his back, flailing at the barbed roots that held him fast. His hat rolled away. He howled at the ripping pain in his arms.

"Stop," he cried. "Wait."

The tentacles dragged him forward.

The gun fired again, kicking up dirt. The rising sun was in his eyes. The gun clicked empty. His back scraped along the ground, leaving a furrow in the soil.

Edward bobbed on his roots. Eyes closed, still leaking tears. And smiling.

"I love you too, Dad-dy."

"No," Burton roared. "Don't do this. Edward."

He struggled, caught in the web of tentacled flesh that drew him toward his son. His boy began to consume him in throbbing gulps. No pain now, not anymore. He couldn't feel the disappearing parts of him. Like returning to the womb. He stopped fighting and let go.

Forty-Eight

Dark shapes in the fields, pouring through the hedgerow veiling the smoking Methodist church. The plague children on the march. A horde of creatures born from mankind's worst nightmares. Monsters of myth in bloodstained overalls.

Horned, winged, gilled, hoofed. Deformed limbs, protruding stalks, misshapen bones. They trotted and shambled, slithered and loped through the dying cotton. A boy with bat wings traced lazy circles in the sky.

The children tramped across the endless fields, dwindling from sight until they disappeared in the hill country. Migrating north toward the world that birthed and rejected them to gaze upon its wonders. See everything it had to offer.

And claim it for their own.

Forty-Nine

Goof pedaled his bike while Mary walked by his side. The plague boy and the fire girl. Gods but also children. Children but grown up now. Broken but now whole.

"There were this girl at Special Facility who really got under my skin," Goof said. "I hope she's all right."

"She sounds real nice," Mary said.

"She's got these whiskers. Cuter than a speckled pup on a shiny red wagon. If I told you her name, which she got on account of her whiskers, you'd die laughing."

"You'll see her again, Big Brother."

"You know that for sure?"

"You will."

"When?"

"When you want it to happen bad enough you start looking."

"I thought you might know for sure. Thought you was a fortune teller now."

"My prophecy is based on wisdom," Mary said. "A wise woman is always honest with herself about what she doesn't know."

"Guess that makes me the most honest man alive," Goof said. "Cuz I don't know shit."

She laughed, which sounded like music. "Big Brother always made me laugh. Big Brother has become what he hates to destroy what he hates. Big Brother has met his destiny. Big Brother is dead."

"Dog loved you a whole lot. We all looked out for you, but he loved you most."

"We all changed. Him most of all."

Goof looked at the beautiful, luminous woman at his side. Swirling rainbow colors. Tresses played around her head, as if gravity didn't apply to her. Head filled with souls and prophecy. She appeared to float more than walk along the old, cracked road.

"You know, we all thought you was a retarded normal," he said.

"You was kind and protected me anyway. You don't fight for your kind but for the weak. That's what makes you special."

Mary had said she couldn't hurt people. A liability in this new world. He'd go on protecting her as he always did.

"And a very wise man," Goof said. "Let's not forget that. So what does that wisdom of yours tell you about what comes next? Will we win the war?"

"What comes next is people."

"Prophecy don't do no good if I ain't got a clue what you're talking about."

"Look, Big Brother."

A pall of drifting smoke hung in the sky. Below, a group of people struggled along the road. He stopped and watched them approach.

"I hope they're nice," he said.

"They're what comes next," Mary said.

Goof smiled and narrowed his eyes. They might be people he could make laugh. People he could annoy to make himself laugh. Hopefully, people who wouldn't scream their heads off and try to kill him.

"If they got any food to share, I'll be their best friend," he said. "You do the talking. If that don't work, I'll talk for them."

The figures stopped in the road. A woman pointed at them.

"I declare," Goof said. "That's Ms. Oliver."

He pedaled toward them, Mary following.

A boy raised a shotgun and aimed it at him. "That's close enough, kid."

"Hey, Ms. Oliver."

"Jeff? I thought you were at Special Facility."

Goof grinned. "They let me out for good behavior."

"My God," the teacher said. "Mary, is that you?"

"Far more than Mary now."

"Yes, you're—you've changed."

"The world ain't scary to me no more," Mary said.

"Well," Ms. Oliver said.

The teacher didn't say what they were all thinking. The world had become scary for everybody else.

"We won't harm you, Ms. Oliver," Mary said. "Any of you."

"That's good," the boy said and let the gun drop to his side.

"Unless you got a Snickers," Goof said. "Because I would kill somebody for a Snickers right now."

"We don't have—"

"Any food. Too bad for me."

"We don't want to hurt anybody, neither. A downed tele-phone pole is blocking the road down a ways. We had to ditch our cars. We're bone-tired and just trying to get home."

Goof smiled at the girl at the boy's side. "I don't know you, cousin."

"I'm Amy. Hi."

"Hi yourself, Gorgeous."

"I'm Jake," the boy said and introduced the rest of his party.

"Nice to meet you folks," Goof said, meaning it.

He wasn't like Brain. He didn't want to fight the whole world.

"We're trying to stay out of the fighting," Jake told him. "We're trying to get the fighting to stop."

"Seems like we're on the same side, then. Us against everybody."

"Right now we just want to get home."

"Sounds good to me," Goof said. "What's for breakfast, Mrs. Green? I'm so hungry I could eat the north end of a south-bound mule."

Jake turned to Amy. "What do you think?"

"If you want to make peace, this is how it starts," she said.

"You can come with us," Jake said. "That all right with you, Mrs. Green?"

"I suppose it'll have to be," the woman sighed.

Together, the band walked to Mrs. Green's house. Goof and Jake fetched water from the pump out back. Ms. Oliver and Mr. Benson got a fire going in the fireplace and rigged up a kettle for coffee and grits. Amy and her mama invento-ried their pantry and started putting together a big breakfast. Mary roamed the grounds shining with her light, picking up bugs and wildflowers to inspect just like the old Mary did before her change. Goof looked down at his dirty pajamas and thought about getting some new clothes but decided he'd keep the bathrobe, which had become a part of him. He entered the kitchen on slippered feet.

"Hey, Mrs. Green," he said. "I'm awful hungry."

The woman's eyes flickered up and down between his eyes and mouth set in the wrong places. "I'll fetch you something to tide you over."

He bounced on his feet as she poured some milk into a tall glass. Cupping it with both hands, he swallowed a mouthful. It was still cool from the refrigerator. He chugged the rest.

"You're a lifesaver," he said with a sigh.

She ignored him, back to managing breakfast. Goof looked around at the others working in silence to prepare the communal meal. Every so often, they gazed inward and sighed. They were still coming to terms with all they'd lost and wondering why they, among all the dead, had survived.

"Anything I can do to help, Mrs. Green?"

"You can go sit in the living room and wait until I call you," she told him.

"Yes, ma'am."

He found a spot on the couch that looked inviting. Mary drifted past the window cupping a bug she'd found. Jake and Mr. Benson crouched in front of the fireplace and fed it kindling.

"What happens next?" Goof said.

Jake smiled. "Breakfast."

"Sounds good to me. Can't change the world on an empty belly."

The boy stared at the flames as if the real answer were there. Goof gazed with him but saw only fire. The creature Brain made had fed on Huntsville but was now so much bigger than Huntsville. Like a movie monster, it would rampage until it consumed everything or was destroyed. Whether it could be tamed at this point appeared impossible. Whether anybody out there wanted it tamed seemed just as unlikely. Right now, the normals seemed all too eager to do battle with it and kill it.

"After that, we do what we can," Jake said. "Wherever we can."

For him, the important thing was to try. A single person trying didn't make a difference. If enough tried, it could make all the difference in the world. The kid had an earnestness Goof knew he'd enjoy heckling in the near future, but right now, he couldn't help being swept up in his ideas. Wherever Jake took those ideas, Goof decided he would tag along.

The kettle whistled. Jake pulled it out with an oven mitt and carried it to the kitchen. The house filled with the smells of hot coffee, bacon, and grits smothered in butter. Everybody was talking in the kitchen now. Somebody laughed.

They all came into the living room and found a place to sit. Amy handed Goof a mug of coffee and a heaping plate. He tucked in. The others kept on talking. Ms. Oliver was telling Amy about how she and Mr. Benson met. Jake told Mr. Benson about how much he looked up to his pa, though they sometimes disagreed. Mrs. Green smoked her skinny cigarettes and watched over them all like a mother hen, seemingly grumpy but also content at having these guests grace her home.

Goof bit back a dozen annoying comments and finished sentences, biding his time. Just listening and enjoying the moment. The fire's heat and good company lulled him into a doze, but he forced himself to stay awake, not wanting to miss a single minute of it. The whole scene was so much like his fantasy of living a normal life. Fellowship and simple pleasures. Hosting a weekend barbecue for his best friends. These people might be his friends now and one day his tribe.

He couldn't help but think this was how it was always meant to be. The world the way God intended it. People of all kinds sharing a meal. Smiling at the same joys. Fighting for a common cause. Dreaming the same dreams.

Acknowledgments

There are many people to whom I'm grateful, each having in some way shaped the heart and mind that produced this novel.

Foremost, I want to thank Chris Marrs and my beautiful children, whose love keeps me going.

They and many others have influenced my journey as a writer: Eileen DiLouie, Chris DiLouie, John Dixon, Peter Clines, Ron Bender, Ella Beaumont, Rena Mason, Stephen Knight, Joe McKinney, Randy Heller, all the IFWA and Write Club and HWA folks, and so many more that it's impossible to list everyone here.

To you all, I'd like to say: You're one of us.

I'm also grateful to David Fugate, my awesome agent, and Bradley Englert, the best editor I could have hoped for and whose vision took *One of Us* to a new height. Their belief transformed a dream into publication.

Finally, I'm grateful to you for reading my work and sharing the dream.

extras

www.orbitbooks.net

about the author

Craig DiLouie is an acclaimed American-Canadian author of literary dark fantasy and other fiction. Formerly a magazine editor and advertising executive, he also works as a journalist and educator covering the North American lighting industry. Craig is a member of the Imaginative Fiction Writers Association, International Thriller Writers and Horror Writers Association. He currently lives in Calgary, Canada with his two wonderful children.

Find out more about Craig DiLouie and other Orbit authors by registering for the free monthly newsletter at www.orbitbooks.net.

interview

When did you realise you wanted to be an author and what was your first foray into writing?

I remember becoming completely immersed reading stories when I was very young, how they filled me with wonder. That wonder was my first real introduction to the magic of reading—that I could become someone else, live in their shoes, feel what they felt, and go on an adventure. Very quickly, I realized I wanted to be the person creating these stories and inviting other people to share my vision. From the age of nine, I wanted to be a writer.

My first stories were pulpy, handwritten, partial novels about the end of the world, swords and sorcery, that sort of thing. From a very early age, I was fascinated by human psychology—in particular, how we deal with crisis—and the titillating juxtaposition of the mundane and the grotesque, especially if it can teach us something about ourselves or our world. These themes have carried through to the majority of my work, which has taken me from science fiction to horror to literary dark fantasy. It's been a long and satisfying journey of learning, discovery, fellowship, and building a career. I've been writing fiction my whole life, but it was only in the past ten years I achieved any success with it. For me, publication by Orbit is a dream come true, and I'm very grateful for and humbled by this accomplishment.

Can you tell us a bit about your writing process?
For me, the novel always starts with an idea and theme that inspires a vision of what it will look, read, and feel like when it's finished. Writing a novel is a massive undertaking, and if the idea is compelling, then it becomes something I *have* to do. I find myself drawn to capturing big ideas in character-driven stories. In my horror novel *Suffer the Children*, for example, a parasite turns the world's children into vampires, but it's the parents, who must feed them, who become the monsters. The story isn't about vampires so much as how far parents would go for their children. In *One of Us*, the big idea is an examination of prejudice. And as with *Suffer the Children*, the novel doesn't preach a single answer but instead invites the reader to reflect.

After I find the compelling idea, I do a lot of research and generally outline the work. Now I'm really starting to see it in my head. Then: I can write! One day at a time, one chapter at a time. During the writing, there's nothing exciting to see— picture a guy sitting for hours in total silence other than the purr of his keyboard—though in my head all hell is breaking loose. When the novel is finished, I typically celebrate before the novel hangover sets in, which is sort of like that slightly lost feeling you get after a great party. After that . . . I start thinking about the next book.

Who are some of your favorite authors and how have they influenced your work?
I have few "favorite" authors in the sense that I'll read everything they write. I usually go fan on books, not authors. That being

said, authors like J. G. Ballard, James Morrow, Stephen Baxter, and Cormac McCarthy come to mind, the first three for their excellent execution of big ideas, the latter for his razor-edged prose. Otherwise, as a writer, I tend to connect with authors of books I read based on what they teach me about craft. Almost every author I've read excels in at least one thing, which I internalize while I'm reading, so I read to learn as much as to enjoy.

Where did the idea for *One of Us* come from?
I wanted to write a novel about prejudice, a very basic human trait, as it's expressed on both an individual and institutional basis. The question was what if a generation of monsters was born, but they were only monstrous in appearance? How would they be treated, and what would that say about ourselves? Adding special powers they develop at puberty would only heighten the conflict and give them the means to assert their rights. What if Spider-Man looked like a real spider? What if Superman had horns? Would we still look up to them as heroes?

For me, the concept appeared ideal for a Southern Gothic literary treatment. In Southern Gothic literature, it is typical to find a society in decay, taboo and the grotesque, class conflict, prejudice in all its forms, and wonderful language. The result was *One of Us*, which might be described as *To Kill a Mockingbird* meets *The Island of Dr. Moreau*.

What was the most challenging thing about writing this novel?
One of Us was a rare novel for me in that once I found the voice, it flowed out of me without a single speed bump. It was a real joy to write. The challenge came after, when my editor believed the novel could reach a higher level. I found his vision exciting and worked hard to achieve it.

One of Us has an amazing cast of characters. If you had to pick one, who would you say is your favorite? Who did you find the most difficult to write?

One of Us is a character-driven work, so I worked hard to ensure the reader would connect with these people. For me, I like one or more aspects of each character—Dog's hope for a fair world, Goof's humor, Jake's desire to change things, and so on. The adults were fun to write because they're so conflicted—Linda between her wants and protecting her daughter, Sheriff Burton between doing what's right and protecting the established order, and Gaines between his base needs and his faults. The challenge was to create people who are real yet larger than life, and also make the monsters sympathetic and relatable. I hope I achieved that.

Overall, though, I'd have to say Amy is currently my favorite character, while Brain was the most difficult to write. Amy is my favorite because she is so like a typical teenager while at the same time hiding the monster that's inside her. What teenager doesn't want to fit in, be perceived as perfect, and live a normal life? What teenager doesn't make mistakes as they learn the ways of the world? While many teenagers look in the mirror and see monstrous flaws, Amy's monster is on the inside, not outside. Her acceptance of what she is leads her to tell Jake, "Not one of *them*. One of *us*." This is her finally accepting there's no such thing as perfect, that normal is an illusion we all create as a society, and that there is a sense of belonging in being different.

Brain, meanwhile, was challenging to write because while he's sympathetic, he starts a horrible war in which each side seeks the annihilation of the other. He's smart enough to see things clearly, which robbed him of hope the mutagenic could ever live in peace and freedom. He sees a future in which they use their abilities to create a better world, but it's a world in which the normals serve the mutagenic. When Reggie Albod brutally beats him and then murders Dog in the sheriff's holding cells, all of this becomes concrete for him and leads to the uprising. And even though he sees the cost of what he's doing and comes to hate it, he can't stop it. Instead, he must help it succeed. This makes Brain a tragic figure. For me as the writer, he required striking just the right balance between hero and villain, similarly to the way Lucifer is portrayed in Milton's *Paradise Lost*.

Do you have a favorite scene in *One of Us*? If so, why?
There are plenty of scenes I particularly enjoyed writing, such as Sally's walk out to the Home, Amy and her friends just hanging out, Dog and his friends meeting Amy and her friends, the final chapter where Goof wraps up the novel's themes. Often, as a writer, I get excited about the big scenes that take the story in a new direction, but *One of Us* was different in that I reveled even in the minor details. Overall, though, I'd have to say my favorite scene is where Brain utters the dramatic line, "Kill the teachers." For me, this is a cathartic and defining moment, takes the story in an entirely new but inevitable direction, and clarifies the conflict between monsters and men in a way that will be settled with violence. Everything in the novel leads up to it. From here on out, there is no longer any hope for peace, though some will continue to make a stand for it.

When you're not writing, what do you like to do in your spare time?
My life is very full with my two amazing children, partner, friends, fiction writing, and day job as a journalist and educator in the lighting industry. In my spare time, I enjoy reading, learning, and binging on favorite shows. As I'm not getting any

younger, I try to exercise whenever I can and stay fit. One of my favorite things to do is talk shop over a beer with local authors and go to writing conferences. I've met a lot of incredible people with whom it's extremely enjoyable to hang out, let loose, and share our love of writing as both an art and a trade.

Without giving away any spoilers, can you tell us a bit about your next book?

My next novel, titled *Our War*, is about a second civil war in the USA. Picture Omar al Akkad's *American War* meets Steven Galloway's *The Cellist of Sarajevo*. I'm hoping the novel will be regarded as a cautionary tale as much my view of what such a conflict would look like. As with *One of Us*, I hope it will entice people to reflect.

And lastly, if you could have any superpower, what would it be?

This is a tough one! I'll tell you what superpower I'd like as an author, which is to always be understood.

if you enjoyed

ONE OF US

look out for

BLACKFISH CITY

by

Sam J. Marshall

After the climate wars, a floating city was constructed in the Arctic Circle. Once a remarkable feat of mechanical and social engineering, it is now rife with corruption and the population simmers with unrest.

Into this turmoil comes a strange new visitor — a woman accompanied by an orca and a chained polar bear. She disappears into the crowds looking for someone she lost thirty years ago, followed by whispers of a vanished people who could bond with animals. Her arrival draws together four people and sparks a chain of events that will change Blackfish City for ever.

PEOPLE WOULD SAY

People would say she came to Qaanaaq in a skiff towed by a killer whale harnessed to the front like a horse. In these stories, which grew astonishingly elaborate in the days and weeks after her arrival, the polar bear paced beside her on the flat bloody deck of the boat. Her face was clenched and angry. She wore battle armor built from thick scavenged plastic.

At her feet, in heaps, were the kind of weird weapons and machines that refugee-camp ingenuity had been producing; strange tools fashioned from the wreckage of Manhattan or Mumbai. Her fingers twitched along the walrus-ivory handle of her blade. She had come to do something horrific in Qaanaaq, and she could not wait to start.

You have heard these stories. You may even have told them. Stories are valuable here. They are what we brought when we came here; they are what cannot be taken away from us.

The truth of her arrival was almost certainly less dramatic. The skiff was your standard tri-power rig, with a sail and oars and a gas engine, and for the last few miles of her journey to the floating city it was the engine that she used. The killer whale swam beside her. The polar bear was in chains, a metal cage over its head and two smaller ones boxing in its forepaws. She wore simple clothes, the skins and furs preferred by the people who had fled to the north when the cities of the south began to burn or sink. She did not pace. Her weapon lay at her feet. She brought nothing else with her. Whatever she had come to Qaanaaq to accomplish, her face gave no hint of whether it would be bloody or beautiful or both.

FILL

———————➤

After the crying, and the throwing up, and the scrolling through his entire contacts list and realizing there wasn't a single person he could tell, and the drafting and then deleting five separate long graphic messages to *all* his contacts, and the deciding to kill himself, and the deciding not to, Fill went out for a walk.

Qaanaaq's windscreen had been shifted to the north, and as soon as Fill stepped out onto Arm One he felt the full force of the subarctic wind. His face was unprotected and the pain of it felt good. For five minutes, maybe more, he stood there. Breathing. Eyes shut, and then eyes open. Smelling the slight methane stink of the nightlamps; letting his teeth chatter in the city's relentless, dependable cold. Taking in the sights he'd been seeing all his life.

I'm going to die, he thought.

I'm going to die soon.

The cold helped distract him from how much his stomach hurt. His stomach and his throat, for that matter, where he was pretty sure he had torn something in the half hour he'd spent retching. A speaker droned from a storefront: a news broadcast, the latest American government had fallen, pundits predicting it'd be the last, the flotilla disbanded after the latest bombing, and he didn't care, because why should he, why should he care about anything?

People walked past him. Bundled up expensively. Carrying polyglass cages in which sea otters or baby red pandas paced, unhappy lucky animals saved from extinction by Qaanaaq's elite. All of whom were focused on getting somewhere, doing something, the normal self-important bustle of ultra-wealthy Arm One. Something he despised, or did on every other day. Deaf to the sea that surged directly beneath their feet and stretched on into infinity on either side of Qaanaaq's narrow metal arms. He'd been so proud of his indolent life, his ability to stop and stand on a street corner for no reason at all. Today he didn't hate them, these people passing him by. Hc didn't pity them.

Fill wondered: *How many of them have it?*

A child tapped his hip. "Orca, mister!" A pic tout, selling blurry shots of the lady with the killer whale and the polar bear. Fill bought one from the girl on obscure impulse—part pity, part boredom. Something else, too. A glimmer of buoyant wanting. Remembered joy, his childhood fascination with the stories of people emotionally melded with animals thanks to tiny machines in their blood. Collecting pedia entries and plastiprinted figures . . . and scowls, from his grandfather, who said nanobonding was a stupid, naive myth. His plastic figures gone one morning. Grandfather was sweet and kind, but Grandfather tolerated no impracticality.

On some level, the diagnosis hadn't been a surprise. Of course he had the breaks. No one in any of the grid cities could have as much sex as he had, and be as uncareful as he was, without getting it. And he'd lived in fear for so long. Spent so much time imagining his grisly fate. He was shocked, really, to have such a visceral reaction.

Tapping his jaw bug, Fill whispered, "Play *City Without a Map,* file six."

A woman's voice filled his ears, old and strange and soothing, the wobble in her Swedish precise enough to mark her as someone who'd come to Qaanaaq decades ago.

> You are new here. It is overwhelming, terrifying. Don't be afraid.
>
> Shut your eyes. I'm here.
>
> Pinch your nose shut. Its smell is not the smell of your city. You can listen, because every city sounds like chaos. You will even hear your language, if you listen long enough.
>
> There is no map here. No map is needed. No manual. Only stories. Which is why I'm here.

A different kind of terror gripped Fill now. The horror of joy, of bliss, of union with something bigger and more magnificent than he could ever hope to be.

For months he'd been obsessing over the mysterious broadcasts. An elliptical, incongruent guidebook for new arrivals, passed from person to person by the tens of thousands. He switched to the next one, a male voice, adolescent, in Slavic-accented English.

> Qaanaaq is an eight-armed asterisk. East of Greenland, north of Iceland. Built by an unruly alignment of Thai-Chinese-Swedish corporations and government entities, part of the second wave of grid city construction, learning from the spectacular failures of several early efforts. Almost a million people call it home, though many are

migrant workers who spend much of their time on boats harvesting glaciers for freshwater ice—fewer and fewer of these as the price of desalinization crystals plummets—or working Russian petroleum rigs in the far Arctic. Arm One points due south and Arm Eight to the north; Four is west and Five is east. Arms Two and Three are southwest and southeast; Arms Six and Seven are northwest and northeast. The central Hub is built upon a deep-sea geothermal vent, which provides most of the city's heat and electricity.

Submerged tanks, each one the size of an old-world city block, process the city's waste into the methane that lights it up at night. Periodic controlled ventilations of treated methane and ammonia send parabolas of bright green fire into the sky. Multicolored pipes vein the outside of every building in a dense varicose web: crimson chrome for heat, dark olive for potable water, mirror black for sewage. And then the bootleg ones, the off-color reds for hijacked heat, the green plastics for stolen water.

Whole communities had sprung up of *City* devotees. Camps, factions, subcults. Some people believed that the Author was a machine, a bot, one of the ghost malware programs that haunted the Qaanaaq net. Such software had become astonishingly sophisticated in the final years before the Sys Wars. Poet bots spun free-verse sonnets that fooled critics, made award winners weep. Scam bots wove intricate, compellingly argued appeals for cash. Not hard to imagine a lonely binary bard wandering through the forever twilight of Qaanaaq's digital dreamscape, possibly glommed on unwillingly to a voice-generation software that constantly conjured up new combinations of synthesized age and gender and language and class and ethnic and national vocal tics. Its insistence on providing a physical description of itself would not be out of character, since most had been coded to try their best to persuade people that they were real—Nigerian princes, refugee relatives, distressed friends trapped in foreign lands.

Other theorists believed in a secret collective, a group of writers for whom the broadcasts were simultaneously a recruitment tool and a soapbox. Possibly an underground forbidden political party with the nefarious endgame of uniting the unwashed hordes of the Upper Arms and slaughtering the wealthier innocents who ruled the city.

On Arms One and Two and Three, glass tunnels connect buildings twenty stories up. Archways support promenades. Massive gardens on hydraulic lifts can carry a delighted garden party up into the sky. Spherical pods on struts can descend into the sea, for underwater privacy, or extend to the sky, to look down on the crowds below.

The architecture of the other Arms is less impressive. Tight floating tenements; boats with stacked boxes. The uppermost Arms boggle the mind. Boxes heaped on boxes; illicit steel stilts holding up overcrowded crates. Slums are always a marvel; how human desperation can seem to warp the very laws of physics.

Fill subscribed to the single-author theory. *City Without a Map* was the work of one person—one human, corporeal person. He went through phases, periods when he was convinced the Author was male and times when he knew she was female— old, young, dark-skinned, light-skinned, poor, rich . . . whoever they were, they somehow managed to get hundreds of different people to record their gorgeous, elliptical instructions for how to make one's way through the tangled labyrinth of his city.

Not how to survive. Mere survival wasn't the issue for the

Author. The audience he or she wrote for, spoke to—they knew how to survive. They had been through so much, before they came to Qaanaaq. What the Author wanted was for them to find happiness, joy, bliss, community. The Author's love for their listeners was palpable, beautiful, oozing out of every word. When Fill listened, even though he knew he was not part of the Author's intended audience, he felt loved. He felt like he was part of something.

> Nations burned, and people came to Qaanaaq. Arctic melt opened the interior for resource exploitation, and people came. Some of us came willingly. Some of us did not.
>
> Qaanaaq was not a blank slate. People brought their ghosts with them. Soil and stories and stones from homelands swallowed up by the sea. Ancestral grudges. Incongruent superstitions.

Fill wiped tears from his eyes. Some were from the words, the hungry hopeful tone of voice of the last Reader, but some were still from the pain of his diagnosis. God, he was an idiot. Snow fell, wet and heavy. Projectors hidden below the grid he walked on beamed gorgeous writhing fractal shapes onto the wind-blown flurry. A child jumped, swatted at the snow, laughed at how a fish or bird imploded only to reappear as new flakes fell.

A startling, uncontrollable reaction: Fill giggled. The snow projections could still make his chest swell with childish wonder. He waved his hand through a manta ray as it soared past.

And all at once—the pain went away. His throat, his stomach. His heart. The fear and the nightmare images of twisted bodies in refugee camp hospital beds; the memory of broken-minded breaks victims wandering the streets of the Upper Arms, the songs they sang, the things they shrieked, the things they did to themselves with fingers or knives without feeling it. Every time he followed a man down a dark alley, or met one at a lavish apartment, or dropped to his knees in a filthy Arm Eight public restroom, this was the ice-shard blade that scraped at his heart. This was what he'd been afraid of.

Fill laughed softly.

When the worst thing that can possibly happen to you finally happens, you find that you are not afraid of anything.

ANKIT

————————▶

Most outsiders saw only misery, when they came to Qaanaaq's Upper Arms. They took predictable photos: the tangled nests of pipes and cables, filthy sari fabric draped over doorways and hanging from building struts, vendors selling the sad fruit of clandestine greenhouses. Immigrant women gathered to sing the songs of drowned homelands.

Ankit watched the couple in the skiff, taking pictures of a little boy. His face and arms were filthy with soot; cheap stringy gristle covered his hands. He sat at the edge of the metal grid, legs dangling over the ocean three feet below, stirring a bubbling trough that floated in the sea. Bootleg meat; one of the least harmful illegal ways to make money out on the Upper Arms. He frowned, and their cameras clicked faster.

She hated them. She hated their blindness, their thick furs, their wrongness. Her jaw bug pinged their speech—upper-class post-Budapest, from one of the mountain villages the wealthy had been able to build for themselves as their city sank—but she tapped away the option to translate. She didn't need to hear what they were saying. They knew nothing about what they saw. Their photos would capture only what confirmed their pre-conceptions.

These people were not sad. This place was not miserable. Tourists from the Sunken World looked at the people of Qaanaaq and saw only what they'd lost, never what they had. The freedom they had here, the joy they found. Gambling on beam fights, drinking and dancing and singing. Their families, their children, who came home from school each day with astonishing new knowledge, who would find remarkable careers in industries as yet unimagined.

We are the future, Ankit thought, staring the hearty dairy-fed tourists down, daring them to make eye contact, which they would not, *and you are the past.*

She inspected the outside of 7-313. House built crudely upon house; shipping container apartments stacked eight high. A flimsy exterior stairway. At least these would have windows carved into the front and back, a way to let light in and watch the ocean—as well as keep an eye on who was coming and going along the Arm itself. And she saw something else: the scribbled hieroglyphics of scalers. Where the best footholds were, what containers were rigged to ensnare roof sprinters.

It had been years since she last scaled anything. She couldn't do so now. She carried too much with her. Physically, and emotionally. To be a scaler you had to be unburdened.

The tourists took no photos of her. They looked at her and could not see where she came from, what she had been, only what she was. Safe, comfortable. No shred of desperation or rage, hence uninteresting. The little boy had run off; they turned their attention to the singing circle of women.

Ankit stopped to listen, halfway up the front stairs. Their voices were raw and imprecise, but the song they sang was so full of joy and laughter that she shivered.

"Hello," said the man who answered the fourth-floor unit door. Tamil; she knew maybe five words of it. Fyodorovna thought that Ankit's cultural comfort level would make these people feel less frightened of her—she'd been raised by a Tamil foster family—but that was stupid. Like most things Fyodorovna thought.

"My name is Ankit Bahawalanzai," she said. "You filed a constituent notice with the Arm manager's office?"

He bowed, stepped aside to let her in. A weathered, worn man. Young, but aging fast. What had he been through, back home? And what had it cost him to get his family out of there? The Tamil diaspora covered so much ground, and the Water Wars had played out so differently across South Asia. She took the seat he offered, on the floor where two children played. He went to the window, called outside. Brought her a cup of tea. She placed her screen on the floor and opened the translation software, which set itself to Swedish/Tamil.

"You said your landlord—"

"Please," he said, the slightest bit of fear in his eyes. "Wait? My wife."

"Of course."

And a moment later she swept in, flushed from happiness and the cold: one of the women from the singing circle. Beautiful, ample, her posture so perfect that Ankit trembled for anyone who ever made her mad.

"Hello," Ankit said, and repeated her opening spiel. "I work for Arm Manager Fyodorovna. You filed a constituent notice with our office?"

Every day a hundred complaints came in. Neighbors illegally splicing the geothermal pipes; strange sounds coming through the plastic walls. Requests for help navigating the maze of Registration. Landlords refusing to make repairs. Landlords making death threats. Landlords landlords landlords.

Software handled most of them. Drafted automated responses, since the vast majority were things beyond the scope of Fyodorovna's limited power (*No, we can't help you normalize your status if you came here unregistered; no, we can't get you a Hardship housing voucher*), or flagged them for human follow-up. A flunky would make a call or send a strongly worded message.

But the Bashirs had earned themselves a personal visit from Fyodorovna's chief of staff. Their building was densely populated, with a lot of American and South Asian refugees, and those were high-priority constituencies, and it was an election year. Word would spread, of her visit, of Fyodorovna's attentiveness.

She wasn't there to help. She was PR.

"Our landlord raised the rent," Mrs. Bashir said, and waited for the screen to translate. Even the poorest of arrivals, the ones who couldn't afford jaw implants or screens of their own, had a high degree of experience with technology. They'd have dealt with a lot of screens by now, throughout the process of gaining access to Qaanaaq. And anyway, her voice was sophisticated, elegant. She might have been anything, before her world caught fire. "We've only been here three months. I thought they couldn't do that."

Ankit smiled sadly and launched into her standard spiel about how Qaanaaq imposed almost no limits on what a landlord could or couldn't do. But that, rest assured, Fyodorovna's number one priority is holding irresponsible landlords accountable, and the Arm manager will make the call to the landlord herself, to ask, and that if Mrs. Bashir or any of her neighbors have any other problems, they should please message our office immediately . . .

Then she broke off, to ask, "What's this?" of a child drawing on a piece of plastislate. Taksa, according to the file. Six-year-old female. Sloppily coloring in a black oval.

"It's an orca," she said.

"You've heard the stories, then," Ankit said, and smiled. "About the lady? With the killer whale?"

Taksa nodded, eyes and smile wide. The woman was the stuff of legend already. Ample photos of her arrival, but no sign of her since. How do you vanish in a city so crowded, especially when you travel with a polar bear and a killer whale?

"What do you think she came for?"

Taksa shrugged.

"Everyone has a theory."

"She came to kill people!" said Taksa's older brother, Jagajeet.

"Shh," his mother said. "She's an immigrant just like us. She only wants a place to be safe." But she smiled like she had more dramatic theories of her own.

The children squabbled lovingly. Ankit felt a rush of longing, of envy, at their obvious bond, but swiftly pushed it away. Thinking about her brother brought her too close to thinking about her mother.

Taksa put her crayon down and shut her eyes. Opened them, looked around as though surprised by what she saw. And then she said something that made her parents gasp. The screen paused as the translation software struggled to parse the unexpected language. Finally *Russian* flashed on the screen, and its voice, usually so comforting, translated *Who are you people?* into Tamil and then Swedish.

Three seconds passed before anyone could say a thing. Taksa blinked, shook her head, began to cry.

"What the hell was that?" Ankit asked, after the mother led the girl into the bathroom.

The father hung his head. Taksa's brother solemnly took over the drawing she'd abandoned.

"Has this happened before?"

The man nodded.

Ankit's heart tightened. "Is it the breaks?"

"We think so," he said.

"Why didn't you call a doctor? Get someone to—"

"Don't be stupid," the man said, his bitterness only now crippling his self-control. "You know why not. You know what they do to those kids. What happens to those families."

"Aren't the breaks . . ." She couldn't finish the sentence, hated even having started it.

"Sexually transmitted," the father said. "They are. But that's not the only way. The resettlement camp, you can't imagine the conditions. The food. The bathrooms. Less than a foot between the beds. One night the woman beside my daughter started vomiting, spraying it everywhere, and . . ."

He trailed off, and Ankit was grateful. Her heart was thumping far too loudly. This was the sixth case she'd seen in the past month. "We'll get her the help she needs."

"You know there's nothing," he said. "We read the outlets, same as you. Think we aren't checking every day, for news? Waiting for your precious robot minds to make a decision? For three years now, when there is an announcement at all, it is always the same: *Softwares from multiple agencies, including Health, Safety, and Registration, are still gathering information, conducting tests, in order to draft new protocols for the handling and treatment of registrants suffering from this and other newly identified illnesses.* Meanwhile, people die in the streets."

"You and your family will be fine. We wouldn't—"

"You're young," the father said, his face hard. "You mean well, I am sure. You just don't understand anything about this city."

I've lived here my whole life and you've only been here six months, she stopped herself from saying.

Because I feel bad for him, she thought. But really it was because she wasn't entirely certain he was wrong.

The bathroom door opened, and out came Taksa. Smiling, tears dried, mortal illness invisible. She ran over to her brother, seized the plastislate. They laughed as they fought over it.

"May I?" Ankit asked, raising her screen in the universal sign of someone who wanted to take a picture. The mother gave a puzzled nod.

She could have taken dozens. The kids were beautiful. Their happiness made her head spin. She took only one: the little girl's face a laughing blur, her brother's hands firmly and lovingly resting on her shoulders.

KAEV

———————▸

Nothing was certain but the beam he stood on.

The gong sounded and Kaev opened his eyes. The lights came up slowly. A pretty standard beam configuration for this fight: Rows of stable columns and intermittent hanging logs. Poles big enough for someone to plant one foot upon. Three platforms, each large enough for two people to grapple on. He pressed his soles into the bare wood and breathed. A spotlight opened on his opponent, a small Chinese kid he'd been hearing about for weeks. Young but rising fast. The unseen crowd screamed, roared, stamped, blasted sound from squeeze speakers. Ten thousand Qaanaaq souls, their eyes on him. Or at least, his opponent. A hundred thousand more watching at home, in bars, standing in street corner clumps and listening on cheap radios. He could see them. He could see them all.

The city would not go away. Kaev's mind throbbed with it, with the pain of so much life surrounding him. So many things to be afraid of. So many things to want. He kept his lips pressed tight together, because otherwise he would scream.

Somewhere in the crowd, Go was watching him. She'd have

one eye on her screen, but the other one would be on him. And she'd smile, to see him step forward, to watch her script act itself out.

Kaev leaped to the next beam. His opponent stood still, waiting for Kaev to come to him. Cocky; clueless. The poor dumb thing thought he was smart enough to anticipate what would happen when. He had no idea who Go was, how much energy and money went into making sure the fight played out a certain way.

America has fallen and I don't feel so good myself.

The news had stuck with him in a way news didn't, usually. Because what was America to Kaev? Just one more place he might have come from. Every Qaanaaq orphan had a head full of origin stories, the countries they fled, the wealthy powerful people their parents had been, the immense conspiracies that had put them where they were. Kaev was thirty-three now, too old for fantasies about what might have been. He knew what was, and what was was miserable. He ran along the length of the hanging log, hands back, spine straight and low, trying to push it all out of his head.

And as he drew near to the kid, the fog lifted. The din hushed. Fighting was where the pieces came together. The kid jumped, landed on the far end of the hanging log. A roar from the crowd. Kaev couldn't hear the radio broadcaster's commentary, but he knew precisely what he would say.

This kid is utterly unafraid! He leaps directly into the path of his opponent, landing in a flawless horse stance. There's no knocking this guy into the drink . . .

Kaev always listened to his fights after they were over, a day or two later, when the buzz had faded altogether. Hearing Shiro describe his own efforts, even in the brisk, empty language of sports announcers, brought him a certain measure of peace. A flimsy, lesser cousin of the joy of fighting.

Instants before colliding with his opponent, Kaev leaped into the air and whirled his legs around. Smirking, the boy dropped to his knees and let Kaev's jump kick pass harmlessly over him— but did not turn around fast enough. In the instant Kaev landed he was already pinioning around, delivering an elbow to the boy's back. Not rooted, not completely balanced, nothing to cause real damage, but enough to make the kid wobble a little and stagger a step back.

A different kind of roar from the crowd: begrudging respect. Kaev was not their favorite, but he had gotten off a good shot and they acknowledged that. The imaginary Shiro in his head said, *I think Hao will proceed with a little more caution from here on out, folks!*

Now the younger fighter pursued him away from the center of the arena. At the outer ring of posts Kaev turned and kicked, but Hao effortlessly swerved to the side. At the precise instant that the momentum of the kick had ebbed, he leaned into Kaev's leg and broke his balance. Anywhere else and he would have been finished, but at the outer ring the posts were close enough that Kaev could stumble-step to the next one.

Yes. Yes. This!

He bellowed. He was an animal, a monster, part polar bear. Unstoppable.

In his dreams, sometimes, he *was* a polar bear. And lately he'd been having those dreams more and more. He'd spent six hours, the day before, wandering up and down the Arms in search of the woman who was said to have come to Qaanaaq with a killer whale and a polar bear, but found nothing.

He sniffed the air, his head full of pheromonic information from his opponent, and charged.

A dance. A religious ritual. Whatever it was, Kaev was free for as long as he fought. He wasn't thinking about how the spasms were getting worse, until he could barely speak a normal sentence. He wasn't worrying about how the money wasn't coming in the way it needed to, and pretty soon he'd have to move out of his Arm Seven shipping container and sleep in an Arm Eight capsule tenement or worse. He wasn't thinking about Go, and how much he hated her, and what an idiot he'd been for being so in love with her once.

He was one with his opponent and the attention of the crowd. And the whisper of cold salt water, thirty feet below.

They grappled until the gong sounded, and they separated. This was not some savage skiff-bed fight, after all. The Yi He Tuan Arena beam fights were Qaanaaq's most distinctive and beloved sport, and their champions won by agility and balance and swift punishing blows, not the frenzied grappling of street fighters. Kaev weighed more and his reflexes were better, but the kid had grace, had speed; Kaev could see why everyone liked him, why he'd been set out on this path to stardom.

Stars make money, Go had said five years ago. *People pay to see someone they recognize, someone they can root for. And you can't make a winner without a lot of losers.*

Which is how Kaev's life as a journeyman fighter began. The guy who other fighters fought when they needed to learn the ropes and build a lossless record at the same time. Not the worst career. Journeymen had a much longer shelf life than the stars, who usually fizzled out fast from one thing or another, but the stars tended to have handsome bank accounts to fall back on when they went bust. Journeymen were lucky to have a month's rent as backup.

He didn't mind the losing. He loved the fights, loved the way his opponent helped him step outside himself, and something about the fall into freezing water provided an almost orgasmic release.

What Kaev minded was the hunger, the anger, the empty feeling. What he minded, what he could never forgive Go or the crowds or the whole fucking city of Qaanaaq for, was that he hadn't had an option.

Hao was tiring, he could tell. The kid was too new, too rough. Kaev switched into stamina mode, feigning defense while modeling how to conserve energy and catch your breath while you're winded. Hao followed suit, probably without realizing what he was doing. A new trick he'd learned tonight. In moments like this, Kaev was proud of what he was. A rare and sophisticated skill, letting someone else win without the crowd knowing it. Hao's kicks connected with his thighs and side and the onlookers surged to their feet and for a few short instants Kaev was the king of Qaanaaq.

The kid got it. Kaev saw him get it. The instant when it all became clear; when he saw what Kaev was doing, and his attitude changed from cocky contempt to humbled respect. His eyes went wide, went soft. He paused—and Kaev could have kicked him in the back of the knee and followed up with a punch to the side of the head, sent him sprawling into the sea below; he saw precisely how to do it, even lifted his leg to unleash the attack— but do that and he'd cost Go millions, probably get a hit put out on him, and for what? A record of 37–3 instead of 38–2? Kaev pulled his wrist back, anchored himself; the crowd lost its mind, he could win it, their golden boy could be finished—

Laughter trembled up through Kaev. Joy threatened to split his skin wide open. He was a bird, he was bliss, he was so much more than this battered body and broken brain. In the split-second pause that gave away his advantage, he wanted to howl from happiness.